THE MYSTERIES

COLLECTION Vol: 4

OTHER ENID BLYTON COLLECTIONS

The Magic Faraway Tree Collection

The Wishing-Chair Collection

The O'Clock Tales

The Magic Folk Collection

St Clare's: The First Year

The Early Years at Malory Towers

The Chimney Corner Collection

Enid Blyton

THE MYSTERIES

COLLECTION Vol: 4

3 books in 1

EGMONT

THE MYSTERIES

Enid Blyton

EGMONT

We bring stories to life

The Mystery of the Strange Bundle First published in Great Britain in 1952
The Mystery of Holly Lane First published in Great Britain in 1953
The Mystery of Tally-Ho Cottage First published in Great Britain in 1954

This edition published 2013 by Egmont UK Limited
The Yellow Building, 1 Nicholas Road, London W11 4AN

ISBN 978 1 4052 6691 8
1 3 5 7 9 10 8 6 4 2

A CIP catalogue record for this title is available from the British Library

Printed and bound in Great Britain by the CPI Group

55060/1

EGMONT LUCKY COIN

Our story began over a century ago, when seventeen-year-old Egmont Harald Petersen found a coin in the street.

He was on his way to buy a flyswatter, a small hand-operated printing machine that he then set up in his tiny apartment.

The coin brought him such good luck that today Egmont has offices in over 30 countries around the world. And that lucky coin is still kept at the company's head offices in Denmark.

THE MYSTERY OF THE STRANGE BUNDLE

CONTENTS

1. BETS GOES SHOPPING

'Of all the miserable holidays, these just about beat the lot!' said Pip to Bets. 'Why you had to start us off on this awful flu, I can't imagine!'

Bets looked hurt. 'Well, I couldn't help it,' she said. 'Someone gave it to me before I gave it to you others. It was really bad luck that it happened at Christmas.'

Pip blew his nose violently. He was sitting up in bed, feeling decidedly better but very bad-tempered.

'*You* get it as soon as the Christmas hols begin – and you get it lighter than anyone! Then you give it to Daisy, and she gives it to Larry, and they have it all through Christmas, poor things. And then *I* get it, and poor old Fatty. What a mess-up of the Christmas hols! Hardly any left of them now!'

Pip sounded very cross indeed. Bets got up. 'All right. If you're going to be such a crosspatch,

I won't sit with you this morning. I'll go and see Fatty. I think you're very unkind, Pip, after all the games I've played with you and the books I've read you.'

She was just stalking out with her head in the air, looking very high and mighty, when Pip called to her.

'Hey, Bets – tell Fatty I'm feeling better, and ask him to get on the track of some mystery AT ONCE because I feel it's just the kind of tonic I need. And we've only got about ten days of the hols left.'

Bets grinned round at him. 'All right. I'll tell him. But Fatty can't just spin a mystery out of thin air, Pip. I think we'll have to go without one this hols.'

'Fatty can do *anything*,' said Pip, with the utmost conviction. 'I've been lying here for days, and most of the time I've been remembering all the mysteries we've ever solved with old Fatty. I've never had time to do so much thinking before. Old Fatty's a wonder.'

'I knew that without having to do a lot of thinking,' said Bets. 'All his disguises – and the way he works out the clues – and the tricks he's played on Mr Goon.'

'Oh yes!' said Pip, a broad smile on his pale face. 'It makes me feel better even to think of all those fat-headed tricks of Fatty's. For goodness sake, tell Fatty to work on some mystery or other for us – it'll do us all good. Give us some interest in life!'

'I'm going,' said Bets. 'I'll bring a mystery back for you if I can!'

'Bring some peppermints too,' said Pip. 'I've suddenly got a craving for them. No, bring a bagful of bull's-eyes, the hottest you can buy. I could do with about fifty, Bets, to go with this detective book Fatty lent me.'

'You *must* be feeling better!' said Bets. She went out of the room and put on her outdoor things. She took some money out of her moneybox. She meant to buy Fatty something too. Bets had been a very faithful visitor and friend to the rest of the Find-Outers while they had had the flu, and had spent nearly all her Christmas money on them.

She hadn't been able to help feeling guilty about giving everyone the flu and she had tried to make up for it by playing games with the invalids, reading to them, and taking them anything she thought they would like. Fatty had been very touched by the little girl's kindness. He thought the world of Bets.

Bets looked out of the garden door. Should she take her bicycle or not? It was so much quicker on a bike. She decided against it. The roads were slippery that frosty January day.

She walked down to the village and spent a good deal of money on enormous bull's-eye peppermints. Half for Pip and half for Fatty. If Pip had got to the convalescent stage of craving for sweets then presumably Fatty would soon reach it too!

She came out of the shop in time to see Mr Goon, the village policeman, sail slowly down the road on his bicycle, his nose purple with the cold air of the morning.

He saw Bets and put on his brakes too quickly. His bicycle immediately skidded on the slippery surface and Mr Goon found himself sitting down very suddenly in the middle of the road.

'Gah!' he said, glaring at Bets as if it was her fault.

'Oh, Mr Goon – are you hurt?' cried Bets. 'You sat down with such a bump!'

Mr Goon had plenty to sit down on, so he wasn't hurt, only considerably shaken. He got up and brushed down his trousers.

'These here slippery mornings'll be the death of me,' he said, looking at Bets as if she were responsible for the slipperiness. 'I just put my brakes on, see – and down I came! That's all I get for wanting to be polite and to ask after your friends. I did hear they were all down with this here flu.'

'Yes – but they're getting better,' said Bets.

Mr Goon muttered something that sounded like 'What a pity!' He straddled his bicycle again. 'Well, I must say it's been a real change for me not having that nosey-parker of a boy sticking his nose into *my* business all the time he's home for the holidays,' said Mr Goon. 'It's a funny thing how that boy sniffs out anything that's going, and gets you all into it. A good thing he's had to lie up in bed where he's out of mischief. You'll be back at school again in no time – and, for once, you won't have made nuisances of yourselves.'

'You'll get the flu yourself if you talk like that,' said Bets, stung into boldness. She was usually very scared of the policeman, especially if she met him when she was alone. 'Anyway, there's still time for something to crop up – and, if it does, we'll be on the job long before *you* are, Mr Goon!'

And, feeling rather victorious after this unexpected meeting and exchange of talk, Bets marched off with her head in the air.

'If you're seeing that big boy, tell him it's nice to know he's been kept out of mischief for once in a way!' Mr Goon shouted after her. 'I've been having a nice peaceful time, I have, without you five round my feet all the time – to say nothing of that little pest of a dog!'

Bets pretended not to hear. Mr Goon pedalled off, well satisfied. He guessed Bets would repeat everything and he knew Fatty would be mad with him – but before he could make himself a nuisance, he'd be back at school again. Toad of a boy!

Bets went to Fatty's house, let herself in at the garden door, and found Mrs Trotteville, Fatty's mother. Mrs Trotteville was fond of the little girl and smiled at her.

'Well Bets, come to see Frederick again? You really are a faithful friend. I think he must be feeling distinctly better today. I've heard the most peculiar noises coming from his room whenever I go up on the landing!'

'Oh, you don't think he's been sick again, do you?' said Bets, in alarm. 'What sort of noises?'

'Oh, voices and sounds,' said Mrs Trotteville. 'As if he's rehearsing for a play or something. You know what Frederick is like, always up to something.'

Bets nodded. She thought probably Fatty was practising various voices for his different disguises. An old man's voice – a quavering old woman's – a deep, manly voice. Fatty could imitate them all to perfection!

'I'll take you up to his room,' said Mrs Trotteville. 'He's expecting you.'

They went upstairs. Mrs Trotteville gave a sharp knock at Fatty's door.

'Who is it?' said Fatty's voice. 'I've got a visitor, Mummy!'

Mrs Trotteville looked astonished. As far as she knew, no other visitor had arrived that morning. It must have been someone the cook had ushered upstairs. She turned the handle and she and Bets went into the room.

Fatty appeared to be sunk deeply into his pillows, half-asleep. Bets could see his dark, rumpled hair but that was about all. Her heart sank. Yesterday Fatty had been sitting up, looking quite sprightly. He couldn't be feeling so well if he felt more like lying down!

She looked at his visitor. It was a plump, bespectacled woman, with an ugly, pudding-shaped black hat pulled over her forehead. A bright green scarf was wound round her neck, hiding part of her chin. Who on earth was she?

Mrs Trotteville was at a loss too. Who was this strange visitor? She advanced towards her uncertainly.

'Oh – Mrs Trotteville!' said the visitor, in a mincing kind of voice. 'You don't remember me, do you? We met at Bollingham two years ago. *Such* a nice place, isn't it?'

'Er no, I don't think I *do* remember you,' said

Mrs Trotteville, astonished. 'How did you know Frederick was ill, and who brought you up to his room? Really, er – it's kind of you – but . . .'

'Oh, your nice cook brought me up,' chattered the visitor, mopping her face with a large white handkerchief, drenched with some strong scent. 'She said you were busy so she just brought me up herself. Frederick was *so* pleased to see me. And who is this nice little girl?'

Bets was puzzled. She didn't understand this curious visitor. And why didn't Fatty sit up? Why hadn't he spoken to Bets? She looked at the mound his body made under the clothes. He must be asleep!

She poked him hard. 'Fatty! Wake up! You were awake a minute ago, because you spoke to us when we knocked at the door. Sit up and speak to me!'

Fatty took no notice. He just lay there like a log. Mrs Trotteville began to feel alarmed. She, too, went to the bed and touched Fatty.

'Frederick, are you all right? Sit up!'

Bets glanced at the visitor, who had now got up and was looking out of the window, her back to them. Her shoulders were shaking slightly. What WAS the matter? It was very peculiar and mysterious and Bets didn't like it at all.

Mrs Trotteville turned back the covers of the bed. There was no Fatty there! A dark wig had been put over a pudding basin, and bolsters had been laid in the bed. Mrs Trotteville gave a little scream.

'Fatty! Where's Fatty!'

But Bets knew where he was, of course!

2. FATTY'S TWO VISITORS

Bets swung round to the plump woman standing at the window. She ran to her and grabbed her arm. She shook it hard.

'Fatty! Fatty, you terror! You're your own visitor. Oh, *Fatty*!'

The 'visitor' collapsed into a chair. Loud explosions came from her. Yes, it was certainly Fatty all right. There was no mistaking that explosive laughter!

'*Frederick*!' said his mother, amazed and annoyed. 'Are you out of your mind? You're supposed to be in bed. What in the world are you thinking of, getting up and dressing in this ridiculous way? No, it's not funny. I'm vexed. I shall tell the doctor when he comes. Get those clothes off and get back into bed at once.'

'Oh, Mummy, give me a minute to laugh,' gasped Fatty, still collapsed in the chair. 'It was too comic to see you and Bets poking at me to make me speak, and wondering who the visitor was, and trying to be polite to her.' And Fatty went off into great laughs again.

'Well, all I can say is that you must be feeling a lot better if you can get up to such silly antics,' said Mrs Trotteville, still annoyed. 'I suppose such abnormal behaviour must mean that your temperature is normal again. Frederick, get back into bed again at once. No – not with those awful clothes on – where *did* you get them from?'

'Cookie brought them for me from an old aunt of hers,' said Fatty, pulling off the bright green scarf and the awful old hat. 'They're part of my wardrobe of disguises, Mummy. Don't pretend you don't know!'

Mrs Trotteville often had to turn a blind eye on many of Fatty's doings. There was simply no knowing what he would get up to next. She stared at the clothes in disgust.

'That *awful* scent, Frederick. I really can't even *call* it perfume! I shall have to open the window and let out the smell.'

'Yes, do,' said Fatty. 'I can't bear much more of

it myself. Gosh, I did enjoy that. Here, Bets, hang up this long black coat and skirt in my big wardrobe over there.'

He stripped off the coat and skirt, and appeared in his striped pyjamas. Bets took the coat and skirt, and was about to hang them up when Mrs Trotteville took them away from her.

'I really must tell Cook not to unload her aunt's old clothes on to him,' she said.

'Mummy, don't you dare say a word,' said Fatty, in alarm. 'Cook's a marvel. She lets me have her uncle's old things too. I've got to get proper disguises from *somewhere*. You know perfectly well I'm going to be a first class detective as soon as I'm old enough, and you have to begin practising young. Don't you say a word to Cook!'

'Frederick, I am *not* going to have the house full of old garments belonging to Cook's uncle and aunt,' said his mother firmly.

'You needn't,' almost wailed Fatty. 'I usually keep them down in my shed at the bottom of the garden – don't I, Bets? I just wanted to play this visitor trick on Bets, Mummy, that's all – so I got Cook to fetch these things from the shed for me.

Bets can take them down to the shed this very minute if you want her to.'

Fatty was now in bed. He looked beseechingly at Bets and his mother. Mrs Trotteville thought that he had suddenly gone rather pale. All this silly excitement!

'All right, Frederick. We won't say any more,' she said. 'Bets can take the things down when she goes. Put them out on the landing for now, Bets. Frederick, lie down. I'm sure your temperature must be going up again. I certainly won't let you get up for a short while this afternoon if so.'

'Mummy, can Bets stay and have lunch with me?' said Fatty, changing the subject quickly. He fully intended to get up that afternoon! 'Say she can. None of the others are coming to see me today, they're still wobbly. I'd like Bets' company – and you know she's quiet. She'd be very good for me. Wouldn't you, Bets?'

Bets beamed. To spend the day with Fatty would be marvellous. Pip was in the bad-tempered stage and too difficult to get on with amiably at the moment. It would be fun to stay with Fatty! She gazed hopefully at Mrs Trotteville, her arms full of the old clothes.

Mrs Trotteville considered. 'Well, yes, I think if Bets would like to stay, she would probably keep you from doing any further ridiculous things,' she said. 'Would you like to stay, Bets dear? And promise me that you won't let Fatty leap out of bed, or dress up, or play the fool in any way at all?'

'I promise,' said Bets happily. 'Thank you, Mrs Trotteville.'

'I'll telephone your mother and see if it's all right,' said Mrs Trotteville, and disappeared out of the room. Bets beamed again, and Fatty beamed back.

'Good old Bets,' said Fatty, snuggling down in bed. 'Gosh, I nearly burst when you and Mummy kept poking at the bolster in the bed. It wasn't a very good disguise really, but it was the best I could do on the spur of the moment. I feel better today and I was longing for a joke of some kind. I guessed you'd be coming, so I got Cookie to fetch me those things from the shed. She's a pet, is Cookie.'

'You must have been annoyed when your mother came in too!' said Bets. 'Oh, Fatty – it's nice that you're better. Have a peppermint? They're the biggest bull's-eyes I could buy. There's half for you and half for Pip.'

'I must be a lot better,' said Fatty, taking two peppermints and putting them both in his mouth at once. 'I couldn't possibly have even *sniffed* at a bull's-eye yesterday. I shouldn't be a bit surprised if I eat a lot of dinner today.'

'You look awfully pale, Fatty,' said Bets. 'Lie down for a bit. You really shouldn't have got out of bed and dressed up like that.'

'Now don't *you* start lecturing!' said Fatty. 'My legs do feel a bit funny, actually, but it was worth it. Now, spill the news. Have you got any?'

Bets faithfully gave her news. Fatty lay quiet and listened. He was feeling rather faint, but he wasn't going to tell Bets that! He hadn't realised that the effort of getting up and dressing and playing the fool would make him feel so weak. Apparently you couldn't play about with flu too much even if you *were* feeling better!

'Larry and Daisy are much better,' said

Bets. 'They're both up and about now, though they haven't been out yet. Daisy says they'll be out tomorrow if it's sunny. They're extremely bored though, and keep wishing something would happen.'

'How's Pip?' asked Fatty.

'Oh, he's better, except in his temper,' said Bets. 'Don't you go and get bad-tempered too, Fatty, when you're almost better! Oh – and I nearly forgot to tell you – I met Mr Goon this morning!'

'Ah, the great Mr Goon,' said Fatty, half-sitting up at the mention of his old enemy's name. 'And what had *he* to say?'

'Well, he said "Gah" at me, fell off his bicycle, and sat down hard in the road,' said Bets, with a giggle.

'Couldn't be better,' said Fatty, hard-heartedly. 'And what else had he got to say beside "Gah"?'

Bets told him. 'He said he'd had a nice peaceful time without that nosey-parker of a boy interfering all the time,' she said. 'He was really rather rude. He said it was a good thing you were in bed and out of mischief – and you'd be back at school again before you'd time to *do* any!'

'Ha!' said Fatty, sitting up straight now, and looking very determined. 'That's what he thinks, does he? Well, I'll be up properly tomorrow – and out the next day – and Mr Goon had better be on his guard. Things will happen as soon as I'm up!'

'What things?' asked Bets, thrilled. 'A mystery, do you mean? Oh, Fatty!'

'Yes, a mystery – even if I have to make one up myself,' said Fatty. 'If Mr Goon thinks he's *ever* going to have a nice peaceful holiday when we're home, he's wrong. Bets, we'll have some fun when I'm up. Gosh, it makes me feel better again already to think of it.'

'What sort of fun?' asked Bets, her eyes shining. 'Oh Fatty, I wish a real mystery would turn up again – but there isn't time now – we'll all be back at school before we could solve it – if one *did* turn up!'

'Never mind, we'll have some fun with old Mr Goon first,' said Fatty. 'I'll plan it. We'll all be in it. I'll think of something, don't you worry.'

Bets knew he would. There was absolutely no

one like Fatty for thinking up things. He slithered down into bed again and shut his eyes.

'Are you feeling all right?' asked Bets anxiously.

'Gosh, yes – I just got an idea, that's all,' said Fatty. 'You know how ideas come – all in a flash from your imagination – you don't even have to think of them.'

'They don't come to *me* like that,' said Bets. 'I have to think hard before I dig up an idea, and even then it's hardly ever a good one. You're a genius, Fatty!'

'Well,' said Fatty modestly, 'I wouldn't quite say *that*, you know – but I can run rings round most people, can't I? I mean, look how we've solved all those mysteries when I've been on the job, and . . .'

Fatty spent the next ten minutes unashamedly boasting, and Bets listened, unashamedly worshipping the boaster. In fact, they both had a very nice time.

'What's the time?' said Fatty suddenly. 'Surely it *must* be dinnertime, Bets. Have you got any more bull's-eyes for me? I'm starving.'

'I think I can hear dinner coming now,' said

Bets. 'Yes, it's your mother. I'll go and help her with the trays.'

Mrs Trotteville appeared, bearing a tray with two steaming platefuls of soup. Fatty eyed them in disappointment. 'Oh, Mummy! Soup again! When am I going to have a really decent meal? I'll never get better on soup!'

'You said yesterday that you couldn't possibly take even a spoonful of soup!' said his mother putting the tray down. 'Don't worry. There's roast chicken and all the etceteras if you want some.'

'That's better,' said Fatty. 'What's the pudding? Save me two helpings, Mummy.'

Mrs Trotteville laughed. 'Oh, Frederick, you do go to extremes. All right – the doctor says you can eat well now that your temperature is down. Bets, bring the tray down when you want the next course, and don't let Frederick gobble up your soup as well as his!'

3. THAT AFTERNOON

The two ate their soup in a pleasant silence. It was hot and well-flavoured. Fatty took two pieces of toast with it and crunched them up with appetite. He seemed to be hungrier even than Bets!

A distant bark came to their ears. Fatty listened and frowned. 'I do think Mummy might have let me have Buster in today,' he said. 'He'd be good for me.'

'You didn't want him in yesterday,' said Bets, spooning up the last of her soup. 'You said his bark would drive you mad.'

'Did I really?' said Fatty in surprise. 'Fancy me thinking old Buster's bark would ever drive me mad. I think he's got a very nice bark – not too yappy and not too woofy – a proper Scottie bark. I wish you'd ask Mummy if I could have him in here this afternoon, Bets. She might do it if you asked her.'

'All right. I'll ask her,' said Bets, getting up to take the tray. 'But I bet she won't let him get on the bed, Fatty. Do you really want some chicken now? I feel a bit full up already.'

'Yes. And plenty of bread sauce,' said Fatty. 'And some more toast. That soup's made me feel warm and comfortable, but it hasn't done much else. Sure you don't want me to carry the tray for you, Bets?'

'Idiot,' said Bets happily, and walked out with the tray. Mrs Trotteville was surprised to hear that Fatty really wanted chicken. She filled a plate for him and one for Bets. 'The pudding is stewed apple and rice pudding,' she said. 'He said he wanted two helpings, but I'm sure he won't want even one. There – can you manage, Bets?'

Bets arrived in the bedroom with the tray, and put it down by Fatty's bed. He eyed it with satisfaction. 'I'd better get on to that before my appetite fades away,' he said, and began to tuck in. Yes, certainly Fatty was on the mend. Nobody could eat like that if they were feeling at all ill!

He slowed down a bit before he reached the

end of the chicken and vegetables. 'What's the pudding?' he asked Bets.

'Stewed apple and rice,' said Bets. Fatty made a face.

'What a pudding to plan for someone in bed. It's bad enough to be faced with that when you're up and about. I won't have any.'

'I suppose you're pretending you would have had two enormous helpings if it had been treacle pudding?' suggested Bets, slyly. 'You're a fibber, Fatty. You can't eat another thing! Nor can I, as a matter-of-fact. I'll take this tray down now.'

'Don't forget to ask Mummy if Buster can come up this afternoon,' Fatty called to her.

Bets delivered the tray, broke the news about the lack of appetite for apples and rice, and asked about Buster.

'Well,' said Mrs Trotteville, considering the matter, 'well, I wouldn't mind if I thought Frederick would keep quiet, and not get excited with Buster tearing all over the place. Oh, and Bets, your mother said you could stay on to tea if you liked. She says Pip has got someone coming to see him this afternoon, and it would be good for you to have a change and be with Frederick for a bit. Would you like to?'

'Oh yes,' said Bets. 'But doesn't Fatty rest a bit in the afternoon? I mean – I had to sleep after my dinner when I had flu.'

'Yes, certainly he must,' said Mrs Trotteville. 'But you needn't stay with him then. You can come down here and have a book to read and then go back again when he is awake. He can bang on the floor when he has had enough sleep. And if he still wants Buster, you can take him up then.'

'Oh, good!' said Bets. 'I'll just go out into the kitchen and have a word with old Buster, Mrs Trotteville. He must be missing us all so!'

Buster gave her a frantic welcome. He tore round her on his short legs, rolled over, bounced up again, and altogether behaved as if he was about six-months-old. He barked non-stop, and the two maids sitting with their cups of tea put their hands up to their ears.

'He's going upstairs to Fatty this afternoon,' said Bets. 'Did you hear that, Buster! Going to Fatty!'

Buster thought that Bets meant he was going that very minute. He flung himself at the closed door, and barked madly. Bets laughed. 'I'll come and fetch you later on,' she said. 'In about an hour or so, Buster.'

She managed to slide out of the door before Buster could squeeze out too. She left him barking crossly. What! She had gone to see his beloved master, and not taken him, after all her promises? Wuff, wuff, wuff! Grrrrrrr!

Bets went back upstairs to tell Fatty the good news. 'I'll settle you down if you like,' she said to him. 'Then you can go to sleep, and when you wake up, bang on the floor with this stick and I'll come up with Buster. I'm allowed to stay to tea, so we've plenty of time to talk and play games.'

'Good,' said Fatty, pleased. He was now feeling sleepy and he snuggled down. 'But don't go, Bets. There's a nice comfy chair over there, look – and you can borrow one of my Sherlock Holmes stories if you like. There's a pile on that table.'

'Your mother said I was to go downstairs and read,' said Bets. 'I'd better go.'

'No, don't,' said Fatty. 'I don't like being left alone. Stay with me, Bets.'

'Don't be silly! You don't care at all about being

alone – and you'll be asleep in a few moments!' said Bets, with a laugh.

'Bets,' said Fatty suddenly, in a voice that made her look across at him in surprise. 'Bets, you *must* stay with me! Because of the Voices!'

Bets gaped at him. Voices! Whatever did Fatty mean?

'What Voices?' she said.

'I don't know,' said Fatty, still very mysterious. 'Sometimes it's a duck, I think. And other times, it's a hen. And once it was a dog whining.'

Bets was amazed. 'What – here in your bedroom?' she asked, disbelievingly. 'Fatty, you must have had a very high temperature to think you heard Voices.'

'I tell you, there *are* Voices in this bedroom when I'm all alone,' said Fatty, leaning up on one elbow. He looked very earnest. 'There's a silly old man too, who keeps asking for a cigarette. Bets, do stay with me. If you hear the Voices, we could try and find out what they are. Do stay here and sit in that chair. But don't you say a word to Mummy, will you? She'll think I've got a temperature or something again.'

'All right. I'll stay,' said Bets, puzzled and disbelieving. 'But I believe you're making it all up, Fatty, just to make me stay here with you. You shouldn't do that.'

'Bets, as sure as I lie here, there have been Voices in my room,' said Fatty. 'Will you believe me, if you hear them? See that duck on the mantelpiece? – the china one – well, I've heard it quacking. And see that dog in the picture? He barks and whines!'

'You lie down, Fatty,' said Bets, and she pushed him down. 'You're dreaming. Or just being silly. I'm going to sit in that chair and read Sherlock Holmes. Don't say another word, or we'll have your mother up here.'

Fatty lay down. Bets sat in the chair, wondering why Fatty spoke so much about Voices. She decided that he must have had such a high temperature that he had wandered a little in his mind and heard voices that were not really there. She opened her book and yawned.

Bets fell asleep, and so did Fatty. Except for a log falling in the grate, where a bright fire was burning, there was nothing to be heard. Buster was snoozing in the kitchen, keeping one eye open for the big cat. The cat had to keep a certain distance. One paw over the line and Buster flew at her!

The clock on the mantelpiece ticked on. Half past two. Three o'clock. It was raining outside, and the afternoon was dark. It would have been too dark for Bets to read if she had been awake. Half past three. Both Fatty and Bets were perfectly still, and the fire grew rather low.

Then Bets woke up with a jump. She sat up, wondering where she was. Of course, she was in the big chair in Fatty's bedroom! How low the fire was! Fatty must still be asleep, because he hadn't put on his light, and the room was really very dark.

'Quark, quark, quark!'

Bets almost jumped out of her skin. She gazed incredulously at the big china duck on the mantelpiece. Did the quacking come from there? Her heart began to beat fast. Was this one of Fatty's 'Voices'? She stared at the duck and thought she saw it move.

'Quark, quark, quark!' There it was again – a

rather deep quack, just like the noise made by the drakes on the pond. Bets couldn't believe her eyes.

'Cluck, cuk-cuk-cuk-cuk-cuk-cuk!'

Bets was glued to her chair. That was a hen clucking now – a hen in the bedroom! But how! Why? And now there was a dog whining softly!

She glanced at the picture of the dog but could hardly see it in the darkness. It whined again and gave a little yap.

And then a quavery old voice came from the wardrobe in the far corner.

'A cigarette, please, sir. Just a cigarette!'

'Oh, dear,' said Bets in fright. 'Fatty, Fatty, wake up. Your Voices are here!'

There was a click as Fatty suddenly switched on his bedside light. He sat up in bed, looking at Bets. 'Did you hear them too?' he said. 'Listen, the old man is beginning again.' He pointed over to the wardrobe. Bets looked across at once.

'A cigarette, please, sir. Just a cigarette!'

'I don't like it,' said Bets, and she rushed over to Fatty. 'I'm frightened. Fatty, what is it?'

'Quark, quark, quark!'

'Cluck, cuk-cuk-cuk-cuk-cuk!'

'Moo-oo-oo-oo!'

'Oh, Fatty, Fatty, what is it?' wept Bets, and covered her face and ears. 'Fatty, come out of this room. I'm frightened!'

'Oh, Bets, don't cry! I didn't mean to make you cry,' said Fatty, and put an arm round the scared little girl. 'I thought you'd guess what it was at once! You are a little silly, Bets, not to guess.'

'Guess what?' asked Bets, astonished. She looked up into Fatty's smiling face. 'Fatty! It's not just a trick you're doing, is it? What is it?'

'It's a bit of a secret, Bets,' said Fatty, putting his mouth to her ear. 'I'm practising to be a ventriloquist, that's all. Didn't you really guess?'

4. A LESSON ON VENTRILOQUISM

Bets could hardly believe her ears. She stared at Fatty's grinning face in amazement.

'But – but – was it you then, making that duck on the mantelpiece quack?' she said. 'And that hen cluck, and the dog bark – and that old man ask for a cigarette? It can't be you, Fatty!'

'It is though,' said Fatty. 'I've been working at it all last term. Gosh, the noises that have come from the corners of our dorm each night! And the noises in class too. Once I even got the master to open a cupboard to see if a cat was mewing there.'

'But Fatty – how do you do it?' asked Bets, staring at him. 'I've seen ventriloquists on the stage, of course – making their dolls speak – but how do you do it? Fatty, I didn't like it!'

'Now, don't you be silly,' said Fatty. 'I wouldn't have played the trick on you if I'd thought you were going to be scared. It just shows I must be really good. There's no talking duck or hen or dog or old man in this room, Bets, you *must* know that. I wanted to try and see if I could puzzle you – I didn't mean to frighten you. Gosh, I must be a better ventriloquist than I thought!'

A voice came from the wardrobe again – or at least Bets *thought* it did!

'A cigarette, please sir – just a cigarette!'

Bets looked swiftly round at Fatty and this time she laughed. 'Oh, Fatty, you're clever, but I just saw your throat moving when you said that. How do you manage to throw your voice somewhere else though? Fatty, it's marvellous! Whatever will the others say!'

Fatty sat comfortably up in bed. 'Well,' he began, 'I'll tell you a bit about it, Bets. A man came down to our school last term to entertain us. He was a ventriloquist and he had a couple of idiotic-looking dolls, whose heads could turn from side-to-side. Their eyes could open and shut, and their mouths worked up and down. You've seen a ventriloquist, haven't you? Well, he was absolutely super, this man. I honestly couldn't see either his mouth or his throat working in even the smallest movement – and yet it was his own voice that made those dolls seem to talk – and sing too!'

'Yes. I think ventriloquists are marvellous too,' said Bets. 'I haven't the faintest idea how they do it. But *you* must know, Fatty, because you can ventil – ventrilo . . .'

'Ventriloquise,' said Fatty. 'Well, I do know a *bit* now. But I've had to get it out of books, because you can't learn interesting and really useful things like ventriloquism – or conjuring – or disguising yourself – at school. Such a pity they don't have things like that in the timetable. Wouldn't I work at them!'

'Yes, so would I,' said Bets. 'Did you have to practise ventriloquism yourself then, Fatty, with nobody to help you?'

'Yes,' said Fatty. 'But it's difficult to be anywhere by yourself at school, you know, so I had to let a few of the boys into the secret. We've got about six ventriloquists at my school now.'

'But you're the best, I bet you are, Fatty,' said Bets at once.

Fatty wished he could say he was. But honesty

compelled him to admit that another boy was better than he was.

'We've got an African boy at our school,' he said. 'A Zulu prince or something. He's the best. But that's not to be wondered at, because apparently all his uncles and great-uncles and grandfathers were able to throw their voices wherever they wanted to. Anyway, when he knew I was trying to learn to throw my voice, he showed me a few tricks.'

'Tell me, Fatty,' begged Bets. 'What tricks?'

'Well,' said Fatty, banging his pillows and settling himself comfortably, 'first of all, I'll explain the name "ventriloquism". It comes from two words – "venter", which means tummy, and "loqui", which means to speak. In other words, a ventriloquist was supposed to be a man who could speak by using his tummy in some way.'

'Do you use *your* tummy then?' asked Bets.

'As a matter-of-fact, the people who thought that made a mistake. The tummy is *not* used,' said Fatty.

'Oh. What is then?' asked Bets, intensely interested.

'Well,' said Fatty, 'as far as I can see, a

ventriloquist forms his words in the ordinary way but he lets his breath escape very slowly indeed, and he closes up his glottis – his throat – as much as he can, and opens his mouth as little as possible. Oh, and he only uses the tip of his tongue.'

Bets couldn't follow this, but she didn't much mind as she had no intention of becoming a ventriloquist herself. She was quite sure she would be no good at it at all. The whole thing sounded quite impossible to do. But Fatty, as usual, had tackled the impossible and done it!

'You *are* clever, Fatty,' she said. 'Now do some more ventriloquism and let me see how you do it.'

But she couldn't see, of course, except that Fatty's throat moved a little, and once his lips moved too. 'Just a cigarette, please, just a cigarette,' came a quavering voice which didn't appear to be anywhere near Fatty at all. She instinctively looked over to the wardrobe again. Fatty was looking there too, as if somebody was really there.

'It's strange,' said Bets. 'Really strange. How do you throw your voice like that, Fatty?'

'I don't really. You just think I do, and you look at the place where you imagine the voice is coming from, and hear it there,' said Fatty. 'That's just a trick, of course. Though this Zulu boy I was telling you about can *really* throw his voice, it seems to me. Anyway, one day it sounded to us as if there was somebody calling us from outside the classroom door but when we went to see, there wasn't anyone in sight – and old Benjamin was sitting in his chair inside the room, grinning away like anything. "I fool the English boys, I fooled you," he kept saying.'

'I wish I went to your school,' said Bets. 'You always make it sound so exciting, Fatty. Fancy you being a ventriloquist now – whatever will you be next?'

'Well, you just never know when things like that will help you,' said Fatty. 'It might come in very useful with my detective work when I'm grown-up. It's a really amusing trick, anyhow.'

There came the sound of excited barking, and the thump of leaping feet on the stairs.

'Buster,' said Fatty. 'Gosh, in all this excitement about my ventriloquist act, we'd forgotten about poor old Buster. Bets, don't say a word to mother about my ventriloquist stunt.'

Before Bets could assure Fatty that she certainly wouldn't, the door opened and in came Mrs Trotteville with a tremendously excited Buster rushing in front. He leapt straight on to the bed, of course, and flung himself on Fatty. He put his paws up on the boy's shoulders and proceeded to lick him all over the face, barking loudly.

'Mercy, Buster, mercy!' begged Fatty, and disappeared completely under the bedclothes to escape the excited dog. Buster followed at once, and a curious heaving earthquake formed itself in the bed, accompanied by yells and barks.

'Frederick! Buster must come out!' cried Mrs Trotteville. 'Oh, dear, neither of them can hear me. FATTY! BUSTER! FATTY!'

Fatty appeared eventually, his hair towsled, his eyes bright, holding Buster in such a tight grip that the dog couldn't move even a leg.

'What do you do with mad dogs, Mummy?' he asked. 'Honestly, he's quite dippy.'

'Oh, Frederick – put him down outside the bed,' said Mrs Trotteville. 'That's right, Buster. If you dare to get on the bed again, I'll set the cat on you.'

'Wuff,' barked Buster rudely. 'Wuff to that!'

'Frederick, listen,' said his mother. 'It's almost teatime. You can get up, put on your dressing-gown, and stay up for two hours. You can have tea while you're up. Bets can go and get it in ten minutes' time.'

She went out of the room, and Buster immediately leapt up on to the bed again. But this time he was not so uproarious. He had given Fatty the welcome he had been saving up for him, now he was content to lie by him, licking his hand whenever it came near his black nose.

Bets got Fatty's dressing-gown and slippers, and put the armchair in front of the fire. Fatty got out of bed. At first he meant to leap out, but somehow his legs failed to obey his orders. He found that his knees were still very shaky.

'Are you going to tell the others about your ventriloquism?' asked Bets. 'Will you teach them too?'

'No, I won't teach them,' said Fatty. 'The difficulty is not so much the *learning*, Bets, it's the practising. You make all kinds of strange noises then, and people don't like it.'

'No. I can't see Mummy being very pleased if Pip tried to learn,' said Bets. 'She says he's noisy enough already. Anyway, his school report wasn't very good. She and Daddy would be sure to think it was messing about with ventriloquism that made him not work hard at his class subjects.'

'Pity,' said Fatty, beginning on the buttered toast. 'Is there any honey to go with the toast? I always think hot, buttery toast and honey make a good pair – but usually you get one without the other. No, there's no honey. Be a pet and go and ask for some, Bets. Don't be too long, or else the honey won't be needed.'

'Why not?' said Bets, surprised.

'Because there won't be any toast left to go with it,' said Fatty. 'Go on, hurry!'

'Don't dare to eat it all! I never in my life saw such lovely drippy toast – it's just so buttery!' said Bets.

She went out to get the honey. Fatty looked down at Buster, who was sitting beside him looking up adoringly, his mouth open and his tongue hanging out because of the heat of the fire. Fatty tipped up a piece of buttery toast and let two or three drops of the melted butter drip down to Buster's pink tongue. Buster was agreeably surprised. He swallowed twice and then held out his tongue again.

'Quark, quark, quark,' said Fatty, down in his throat. Buster looked at him inquiringly and wagged his tail.

'Cluck, cuk–cuk–cuk–cuk,' clucked Fatty. 'Where's that hen, Buster, where is it?'

Buster thumped his tail on the ground. But he didn't go and look for either duck or hen.

'Too sensible, aren't you?' said Fatty, with his mouth full. 'No matter where I pretend the sounds come from, you know they're made by *me*, don't you? Quark, quark, quark!'

5. MR GOON HEARS STRANGE VOICES

In three days' time, all the Find-Outers were apparently completely themselves again. Perhaps a spurt of brilliantly-fine weather had something to do with it. All of them felt that they must be out in the sunshine, however cold it was otherwise.

They went for their first walk together that holiday, enjoying the stroll, though only Bets really felt like running. 'I vote we pop into the café and have a hot cup of chocolate,' said Fatty, as they turned into the High Street. 'Come on, Buster, it's no use staring at cats that are safely sitting on walls. They won't come down for you to chase them! Funny that a clever dog like you shouldn't have learnt that elementary fact yet!'

They went into the little café and sat down at one of the tables there. In the summer, they had ice-cold milk there, and ice creams, or lemonade.

In the winter, the little shop did a roaring trade in hot milk, cocoa, and hot chocolate.

A short, plump woman came to serve them. 'Well, well,' she said, beaming at them, 'I thought you must have gone back to school. I've not seen you for so long. What would you like?'

'Hot chocolate, ginger biscuits, and currant buns please,' said Fatty. He drew a handful of change out of his pocket to pay. Fatty always had plenty of money!

'I'll pay,' said Larry. 'I've not spent half my Christmas money yet. You're always paying for us!'

Fatty let him pay. He knew that it often made Larry feel embarrassed when he so often had to allow him, Fatty, to pay for their treats. Anyway, Fatty could always pay for the second round of chocolate and biscuits! 'Flu seems to have enlarged my appetite,' he said. 'I've not stopped feeling hungry for two days.'

'How nice!' said Daisy. 'I like feeling hungry.'

'Only because you know you're going to get plenty to eat,' said Pip. 'It wouldn't be any fun being hungry if you thought there wasn't going to be even a bit of bread to chew for days!'

Nobody could think of an answer to that remark. Buster suddenly got up and went to the door. He barked loudly.

'Be quiet!' said Fatty. 'Behave yourself, Buster. Don't bark at that dear old lady.'

'He's not,' said Bets suddenly, peering through the shop window from where she sat. 'It's Mr Goon.'

'Well, I hope he keeps out of here,' said Pip, beginning on a currant bun. 'These are great – new as anything.'

Bets let her eyes wander round the shop. Up on the mantelpiece was a model of a cow, standing about two feet high. It had a head that would nod up and down if anyone set it going. She got up and went over to it.

'I like this cow,' she said. 'I'll set its head nid-nodding. Let's see if it manages to nod it the whole time we're here.'

She set the head nodding and went back to her chair, watching the cow. Buster began to bark again, and the five swung their heads round to the door.

Mr Goon was standing there, looking so plump

that the buttons on his tunic were stretched to bursting-point. 'Call this dog to you,' he commanded Fatty. 'Put him on a lead. I won't have him dancing round my ankles.'

'Why? Are you coming to have a drink of hot milk or something?' asked Fatty. He deftly put Buster on the lead, and made him sit down. Fatty was hoping against hope that Mr Goon was indeed coming to sit in the shop and have a drink. Fatty had a bright idea, and wanted to carry it out!

Mr Goon stalked in and sat down at the table next but one to the five children's. He called for a cup of cocoa and a bun.

'Cold outside for you again, isn't it, Mr Goon?' said the short plump woman, setting down a cup of cocoa and a bun in front of the red-faced policeman.

Mr Goon took no notice of her. He glanced across at the children. 'Ho, seems like I've had a nice quiet time these holidays,' he began. 'No nosey-parkering, no interfering with the law. That says something for the flu, that does. You must have felt funny not being able to stick your noses in a mystery.'

Nobody answered. Fatty spoke a few words to Larry, and Larry said a few back. Nobody looked at Mr Goon. He didn't like being ignored. He raised his voice.

'Or have you got a mystery on hand?' he began again. 'A nice juicy mystery to make a mess of?'

Fatty looked at him. 'Now how did you hear *that,* Mr Goon?' he said, in a surprised voice. 'Larry, have you been saying anything about our latest mystery?'

Larry rose immediately to Fatty's invitation to be absurd.

'Which case do you mean?' he said. 'The mystery of the red-nosed reindeer, or the one about the flying saucers? We've solved them both, haven't we?'

'Oh, yes. I didn't mean *those,*' said Fatty. 'Mr Goon probably knows all about those by now. They're stale news, aren't they, Mr Goon? No, Larry – I meant the mystery of the strange voices.'

'Gah!' said Mr Goon, biting violently into his bun. 'Strange voices – you don't know what you're talking about. Lot of silly make believe!'

The other four had pricked up their ears when they heard Fatty refer to strange voices. They all knew about his ventriloquial powers now, and he had practised a few of his tricks in front of them. Why had he mentioned strange voices to Mr Goon?

'Lot of silly make believe,' said Mr Goon again, and took a sip of hot cocoa. 'Strange voices! Gah!'

'Oh yes, that mystery's not solved yet, is it?' said Larry, speaking to Fatty in a voice loud enough for Mr Goon to hear. 'Curious case that – people hearing strange voices which aren't really there. Somebody casting a spell on them, I suppose.'

'Baby talk,' said Mr Goon, drinking his cocoa rather loudly.

'You may be right,' said Fatty seriously. 'But believe it or not, some people lately have been hearing ducks quack where there are no ducks, hens clucking, and people speaking – and yet there don't seem to be any there.'

'You'll tell me that cow on the mantelpiece will start to moo next,' said Mr Goon, swallowing the last of his currant bun. Fatty scribbled something quickly on a piece of paper and pushed it across the table to the others.

'Cow will moo,' he had written. 'But none of you is to hear it.'

Mr Goon wiped his mouth. 'Quacking ducks, clucking hens, mooing cows,' he observed sarcastically. 'Silly make believe. Bosh and rubbish!'

'It's a nice cow, isn't it?' said Bets, looking across at it. 'Its head is still going up and down.'

Mr Goon looked across at it too.

'Moo-oo, moo-oo, moo-oo,' said the cow, mooing in exact time to the nodding of its head. The mooing was so realistic, and so exactly in time with the nodding, that even the children, with the exception of Fatty, thought for one moment that the mooing noise did actually come from it.

Mr Goon stared at the cow, astounded. He glanced round at the children. Not one of them, of course, took any notice of the mooing, remembering Fatty's hastily scribbled instructions. They lifted up their cups and drank, Bets hoping to goodness that she wouldn't start to giggle.

Mr Goon looked at the nodding cow again. It

had stopped mooing – principally because Fatty had been overcome with an urge to laugh. But, as Goon looked at it, it gave such a large and unexpected moo that the policeman jumped violently. Then the mooing quietened and went on in time with the nodding of the animal's head.

Mr Goon swallowed hard. 'Moo-oo, moo-oo, moo-oo,' went the cow, nodding its head. Nobody would ever have believed that it was merely Fatty throwing the noise across to the mantelpiece!

Mr Goon felt rather sick. He didn't know what to make of it at all. He looked at the children again. They were taking absolutely no notice at all of the mooing cow. Neither was Buster, of course. Was it possible that they were not hearing what Mr Goon was hearing?

The little plump woman came bustling into the shop with some more buns for the children. The cow stopped mooing. Mr Goon cleared his throat and spoke to the shop-woman.

'Er – nice cow that of yours, my good woman – the one on the mantelpiece, I mean. Very life-like! You'd almost expect it to moo!'

'You will have your joke, sir,' said the little

woman. 'My, if I heard it moo, I'd think there was something wrong with me. I'd think I was going crazy!'

'That's just what we were saying,' said Fatty gravely. 'Strange voices are about – people are hearing them. What are they? A warning? Brrrrrr! I'm glad *I* don't hear them!'

'Well, we live in funny times, no doubt about it,' said the little shop-woman puzzled, and hurried off again. The cow began to moo once more, but so softly that Mr Goon was not absolutely sure if he was hearing it or not. Could he be imagining it? He gazed so earnestly at the nodding cow that Bets felt an irresistible giggle rising up from the very middle of her tummy. She knew from experience that they were the worst kind of giggles – the ones that heaved up and broke out helplessly.

'Talk, do talk,' she besought the others in a low voice. 'I'm going to laugh.'

All but Fatty talked in low voices, saying any nonsense that came into their heads. Fatty stopped making the cow moo. Mr Goon sat back cautiously. Thank goodness the cow was behaving normally now. Maybe his ears had just played him a trick.

'Quark, quark, quark!' Mr Goon jumped violently again, and looked all round. That was a duck quacking, no doubt about it.

QUARK! Mr Goon's eyes caught sight of a wild duck, beautifully stuffed, placed in a glass case at the end of the shop. He gazed at it, holding his breath.

'Quark, quark, QUARK!' The duck appeared to be looking at him out of its glass eye, and its half-open beak seemed to be quacking. Mr Goon leapt up, full of horror.

'That duck!' he said wildly. 'Did you hear it?'

'What duck?' asked Larry. 'Oh, Mr Goon – surely – surely you are not suggesting that the duck in the glass case is quacking!'

'Mr Goon, don't say you are hearing the strange voices!' said Fatty, earnestly and solemnly.

'Quark!' The noise seemed to come from somewhere behind Mr Goon. He gave a loud, hunted cry and ran from the shop, Buster almost tripping him up with his lead. And then the children collapsed over the table, crying tears of laughter into their empty cups. 'Mr Goon, Mr Goon, you couldn't have been funnier!'

6. SOMETHING HAPPENS AT LAST

'Oh, Fatty – HOW do you do it?' said Daisy, mopping her eyes and feeling very weak. 'The way you made that cow moo in time to its nodding was perfect. Honestly, I could have believed myself that the thing was mooing.'

'So could I,' said Bets. 'Oh, dear, don't do that sort of thing too often, Fatty – I simply won't be able to keep my giggles down if you do. Mr Goon's face! His eyes almost fell out of his head!

'He must be feeling pretty puzzled,' said Larry. 'I bet he'll wake up at night and hear noises that aren't there!'

They paid their second bill and went out. What a pity there wasn't any first class mystery to probe into! These were the first holidays in which nothing of any sort or kind had turned up. And therc were only a few days left.

'Can't we spoof old Mr Goon a bit, just to have

some kind of excitement in our last few days?' said Larry. 'That laugh did me more good than a dozen days in bed!'

'Me too,' said Pip. 'I was feeling rather low this morning, but now I'm feeling fine. That's obviously what we all need – a really good laugh every now and again.'

'And Fatty's the one to give it to us,' said Bets, squeezing his arm. 'Fatty, do let's see if we can't spoof Mr Goon a bit?'

'But how?' said Fatty. 'I mean – we can't follow him around with all kinds of noises. He'd soon begin to associate them with us. If every time he hears a cow moo or a duck quack, or hears mysterious voices going on, and sees us somewhere near, well, even *he's* wide-awake enough to put two and two together – us and the noises.'

'I suppose you're right,' said Bets with a sigh, putting away her visions of pursuing Mr Goon with strange and wonderful sounds. 'Well – perhaps something will happen to give us a bit of excitement.'

It was strange that she said that – because that

very night something did happen, though nothing very startling. They didn't know about it till the next morning.

The milkman told Larry. 'Heard about the break-in at the Cedars last night?' he said. 'It's next door but one from you. It's a small house, and a man called Mr Fellows has rented it since a week or two ago. Lived there all alone.'

'What happened?' said Larry.

'Well, apparently somebody broke in, and rifled the house from top to bottom,' said the milkman. 'We don't know if Mr Fellows was there or not – anyway, he's gone this morning. Hasn't come back yet either.'

'Who discovered this?' asked Larry, quite excited to think that all this had taken place so near to his own home. Why, he might have heard something in the night – a shout, the breaking of a window, or something. However, he had been too sound asleep.

'I found the house door open, and a window broken at the back, when I took the milk early this morning,' said the milkman. 'I peeped in at the hall door and, my, what a mess the place was in! I stepped in and telephoned the police at once.'

'Oh, did Mr Goon come?' asked Larry, disappointed. He had hoped for one moment that the Find-Outers might get in first! It was still early, only just after breakfast.

'Yes. He's there now – taking notes and looking for fingerprints and the rest of it,' said the milkman. 'He's feeling important this morning. Told me to keep my big mouth shut and not tell anyone what I found – after I'd told every single one of my customers! What does he think I am – a clam?'

'Did you notice anything at all out of the ordinary?' asked Larry.

'Nothing,' said the milkman. 'I didn't stop to look round, anyway, I telephoned the police at once. Mustn't disturb anything, you know, in cases like this.'

Larry got on his bicycle and went to tell Fatty. It might be nothing, or it might be something interesting, you never knew. Fatty would soon get the old brains to work and decide if the Find-Outers were to do anything or not!

Fatty was most interested. 'This cheers me up immensely,' he said. 'It may be a potty little robbery, but we'd better go and find out. If the house really *was* rifled from top to bottom, it looks as though someone was trying very hard to find something of great importance to him. What was it – and who was it?'

They collected Pip and Bets, fetched Daisy, and all five of them, with Buster, went up to the house that stood two doors from Larry's. It didn't look as if anyone was there. Mr Goon must have come and gone. Good.

'Now then,' said Fatty. 'Examine all the paths and beds round the house. Look for usual things – footmarks, cigarette-ends, handprints on window ledges, etc. Make notes of what you find, and we'll compare later.'

'Aren't you coming with us?' asked Bets, seeing Fatty turn away.

'No. I'm going to look in the windows and see if there's anything interesting inside,' said Fatty.

But the curtains were drawn across and he couldn't see anything. He went steadily round the little house, but not one window could he see into. The front door was closed and fastened now, and the back door was locked too.

Fatty came to the broken window at the back. It was the kitchen window. Obviously the robber, or whatever he was, had got in here. Fatty stuck his hand inside and moved the curtain. The kitchen was upside down! Drawers had been pulled from the dresser and from the table. Cupboards were open and their contents dragged out on to the floor! What could the intruder have been looking for?

Fatty suddenly heard a sound inside the kitchen. He listened. What was it? He heard it again, and then peeping in at the window once more, he made out two gleaming eyes looking at him from a cupboard.

'Miaow! Miaow!' said the owner of the eyes piteously.

'Gosh, it's a kitten,' said Fatty. 'Scared to death, I expect, and nobody to feed it or care for it, poor little thing!'

The others came round the corner of the house, notebooks in their hands. 'Here!' said Fatty, beckoning. 'There's a kitten left in the house! What shall we do?'

'Get it,' said Daisy promptly.

'How?' asked Pip. 'All the doors and windows are shut tight. We've checked that.'

'This one's broken,' said Fatty. 'If I wrap my hand in a handkerchief, I think I could put it through the broken pane and do what the thief did – undo the clasp and open the window. Then I could get in and rescue the kitten.'

'Well, go on then,' said Larry, looking all round. 'There's no one about. Mr Goon won't come back yet.'

Fatty took out a big white handkerchief. He twisted it firmly round his fingers. Then he gingerly put his hand through the hole in the broken pane and tried to reach the fastening of the window. It was a casement, opening sideways once the clasp was moved.

'Got it,' said Fatty, and jerked the clasp. It slid down stiffly and he took back his hand again. He could now easily open the window.

'Done it,' he said pleased, and hopped up to the ledge. Buster began to bark, wanting to go with Fatty.

'Keep him quiet, for goodness sake,' said Fatty.

'We don't want anyone to see me climbing in!'

They hushed Buster while Fatty climbed nimbly into the kitchen. He found the tiny kitten, which crouched back in the cupboard, spitting and scared. But it soon began purring when Fatty picked it up and petted it.

'I'll find some milk,' he called quietly to the others. 'I expect it's hungry.'

He came to the pantry and looked inside. Even that was untidy, and a broken dish lay on the tiled floor. Fancy hunting in the pantry too! Whatever had the intruder been after?

'Here you are, kitty,' said Fatty, and put down a saucer of milk for the little creature. It lapped hungrily. When it had finished, it rubbed itself against Fatty's legs, purring. He bent to pick it up, but it scurried away, and ran through the doorway into the hall.

'Puss, puss!' called Fatty. 'Come back here.'

'What's up?' said Pip's voice, looking in at the window. 'Daisy says if you hand the kitten out to her she'll take it home, as she lives so near. They've got a kitten too, and it can be with hers till somebody comes back here.'

'Right. But I'll have to find it first,' said Fatty. 'It's dashed through the kitchen door into the hall. Half a minute. I'll get it. I can hear it there somewhere.'

He went out of the kitchen door into the hall. He paused there, amazed at the untidiness. Coats, shoes, and umbrellas were all in wild confusion on the floor, flung there from the hall cupboard and from a chest of drawers.

The kitten was nowhere to be seen. Fatty went into one room after another, but the little thing was hiding, whether from fright or from play he didn't know.

Fatty took the opportunity of having a good look round. There were three rooms downstairs and three above and a bathroom. Each of them was in confusion. By the soot that lay in the fire-places, Fatty guessed that the hunter had even felt up the chimney for whatever it was that he had been looking for.

And then, as he came out from a bedroom on to the little landing, Fatty saw something in a corner, near the top of the stairs. It was bright red. He picked it up.

A child's glove, he said to himself. A very *small* glove, for a very small child. But surely there was no child here? And there's only one glove. Could Mr Fellows have been hiding a child here – kidnapped it, perhaps? – and the other fellow came to find it?

He shook his head. No, people don't look for even very small children up chimneys and in drawers. I wonder whether there are any more clothes for a child here. It doesn't look like a house where children came at all – not a single toy, not a book or a doll – and no cot.

There were no children's clothes to be seen, thrown in the muddle on the floor. All kinds of other clothes were there – men's coats, trousers, vests, shoes, hats – as well as a trouser press flung down and opened, books, cushions, papers, blankets, sheets, pillowcases . . .

'Well,' said Fatty, slipping the child's red glove into his pocket, 'I'll keep it, just in case – though in case of what I don't know! Only *one* of the pair – that's the mysterious part! Was a child here last night? – and was it dressed in a hurry, so that it dropped one glove? No, it couldn't be.'

A loud whisper penetrated to him.

'Fatty! Quick! Mr Goon's coming back. He's coming up the road. QUICK, Fatty!'

7. MR GOON IS ASTOUNDED

Almost before Fatty had time to get downstairs, there came the sound of Goon's angry voice.

'Now then, you kids! What are you doing here? Clear orf!'

Then came the sound of Buster's barking. Fatty grinned. How many, many times had this same scene been acted? – the Find-Outers snooping round – Goon finding them – ordering them off – and Buster objecting loudly! Well, Buster could certainly look after, not only himself, but all the children too.

Fatty wondered whether he could slip out of the front door. He could hear that Mr Goon was round at the back.

'Interfering with the law!' he heard, in the policeman's angry voice. 'Poking your noses in! What's it to do with you?, I'd like to know. Clear orf!'

'Well, we live just close by,' said Larry. 'It's naturally interesting to us – to Daisy and me, I mean. If burglars are in the district, I want to get some information in case they come to rob our house too, next door but one.'

'Gah!' said Goon disbelievingly. 'Tommy-rot! Just an excuse for interfering. This here job's a potty little job – no mystery in it at all. Not worth your notice, see? And take that dog away before I lose my temper with him. Nasty yappy little mongrel!'

Fatty longed to be out there with the others. Calling Buster a *mongrel*! Why, the little Scottie had a pedigree a yard long, and all his grandparents had been champions. Fatty boiled with rage. He tiptoed to the front door. He didn't want Mr Goon to catch him in the house, even though he had the perfectly good excuse to offer about rescuing the kitten.

'Where's that big boy?' demanded Mr Goon, suddenly realising that Fatty was absent. 'Still in bed with the flu, I hope. Best place for him too. Hope he gets a relapse! WILL you call this dog off?'

Larry called Buster. 'Buster, come here. I can

find some better ankles for you if you want some.'

Mr Goon snorted. That was one of the things he did remarkably well. 'Get out of this garden, all of you,' he said. 'Any more messing about here and I'll report you. Yes, and I'll go round to your parents again too – especially yours, Philip Hilton!'

Pip hastily removed himself from the garden of the little house, taking Bets with him. He didn't want Goon to make any more complaints to his parents. They had a habit of taking Mr Goon seriously! Larry and Daisy followed, Larry holding Buster by the collar. They stood outside the front gate, wondering what Fatty was going to do.

Fatty was most unfortunate. He opened the front door from inside at exactly the same moment that Mr Goon unlocked it from the outside. Mr Goon stared at Fatty as if a thunderbolt had hit him. His mouth fell open and he went a familiar purple colour. He swallowed hard.

'Good morning, Mr Goon,' said Fatty, smoothly. 'Do come in. I'll shut the door for you.'

Mr Goon stepped in, still wordless. Then he exploded into speech.

'What you doing here? HERE, in this house that's under police supervision. You want to get locked up, I suppose – being found on enclosed premises, and up to no good, I'll be bound! HO!'

Fatty stepped back out of range of Mr Goon's explosions. 'I heard a kitten mewing here,' he said still politely. 'And being a subscriber to the RSPCA – if you know what that means, Mr Goon – I naturally had to come into the house to find it.'

'Pah!' said Mr Goon, disbelievingly. 'This here house is absolutely empty! I've been through it meself with a toothcomb already!'

'This 'ere 'ouse hisn't habsolutely hempty,' said Fatty. 'Dear me, I seem to be getting muddled. Hark, Mr Goon – can't you hear the kitten mewing now?'

'Miaow!' said the kitten, and obligingly crept out from under the hall-stand. It went to Fatty and rubbed affectionately against his legs. Then it looked at Mr Goon, hissed at him and spat.

'Most intelligent behaviour,' observed Fatty. 'I hope you believe in the kitten now, Mr Goon.'

Mr Goon did. He had to. 'Take it away and take yourself off too,' he said to Fatty. 'I've work to do here. And keep out of this, see?'

'You'll be careful of the dog here, won't you, Mr Goon?' said Fatty. 'I'm not quite sure where it is – you may possibly hear it growling somewhere, and trace it by that.'

'There's no dog here,' said Mr Goon, stalking past Fatty. 'A kitten I might have missed, being so small like, but not a dog. What do you take me for?'

'It would be better not to tell you,' murmured Fatty. 'Not here, anyway.'

He was just behind the policeman, and it was as well for Mr Goon that he couldn't see the innocent expression on Fatty's face – a look that all his school teachers knew only too well.

A blood-curdling growl suddenly came from somewhere in the house. Mr Goon stopped as if he had been shot. 'What's that?' he said.

'Sounded like the dog,' said Fatty. 'What a horrible animal it must be. I think I'll go, Mr Goon, and leave you to tackle him.'

Another growl came from somewhere, and the policeman took two hurried steps backwards, treading heavily on Fatty's foot.

'Ouch!' said Fatty. 'Look out where you're going if you want to walk backwards, Mr Goon! Well – good-bye – I'll leave you now.'

'You come and help me find that dog,' said Mr Goon, changing his mind completely about wanting Fatty to clear off. 'It might want two of us to get him. Funny I didn't see him or hear him when I was here before this morning.'

Fatty grinned behind Mr Goon's broad back. He debated whether to produce another animal noise. This ventriloquism was most useful!

'All right, Mr Goon,' he said. 'If you think it's my duty to stay and help you, I will. I'm always around when duty calls, you know.'

Mr Goon was very thankful. He began to tiptoe forward into the little dining-room. Fatty followed a few paces behind. He suddenly gave a shout that made Goon nearly fall over backwards.

'Look, look – what's that? – over there! LOOK OUT!'

Mr Goon was so anxious to get out as well as to look out, that he almost fell over Fatty, trying to rush out of the room. Fatty clutched him as he went.

'It's all right! It's all right! I just caught sight of

you in that mirror over there, Mr Goon, and it was such a dreadful sight I thought it must be someone lying in wait for us. Gosh, thank goodness it was only your reflection!'

Mr Goon was very angry and very relieved. He glared at Fatty. 'Any more of this funny business,' he began, and then stopped suddenly.

From somewhere behind came the sound of heavy grunting. Mr Goon swung round at once. 'Did you hear that?' he asked Fatty, breathlessly. 'That grunting noise. What was it? It sounded out there in the hall.'

'Yes, it did,' said Fatty, clutching at Mr Goon's arm and making him jump again. 'You go first, Mr Goon. I'm scared.'

So was Mr Goon. He tiptoed into the hall and promptly fell over the kitten which made a dart at him as soon as he appeared. He retreated into the dining-room again, bumping into Fatty. The grunting noise was heard once more, this time sounding further off.

'It's a pig!' said Mr Goon, hardly able to believe his ears. 'Sounded upstairs that time. Did you think it was a pig, Frederick?'

The more frightened and puzzled Mr Goon became, the more polite he got. At this rate, thought Fatty, he'll soon be bowing to me every time he speaks! He badly wanted to laugh, but he firmly thrust down the ever-mounting guffaw that wanted to rise up and explode.

'What sort of a fellow was it who lived here, Mr Goon?' asked Fatty, innocently. 'Was he fond of animals? He seems to have kept kittens, and dogs, and pigs, anyway.'

'How was it I didn't see the pig when I was here this morning?' marvelled Goon. 'I turned everything over and looked everywhere for clues. And yet, I didn't see the dog or the pig. Shall we go upstairs to find the pig?'

'Yes. But be careful the dog doesn't rush out at you,' said Fatty. 'You go first, Mr Goon.'

Mr Goon didn't want to go first. He pushed Fatty in front of him, and then immediately wished he hadn't because a deep and ferocious growl came from somewhere behind him. Fatty was certainly practising his new talent well!

And then a new sound came to worry poor Mr Goon. A voice came from somewhere, a groaning voice that said, 'I never did it, I never! Ooooooh! I never did it! Where's my auntie?'

Goon listened, petrified. He began to feel as if he was in a nightmare. He whispered to Fatty, 'There's a man here somewhere! This beats all! We'd better get help. I'm not going to snoop round here with dogs, and pigs, and a man groaning. What's been happening since I was here this morning?'

'Look, you stay here, Mr Goon, and I'll go and get help,' said Fatty, and moved firmly into the hall. But Mr Goon clutched at him.

'No, don't leave me here alone. Can't *you* stay while I get help?'

'Remember your duty, Mr Goon,' said Fatty, solemnly. 'There is something strange here, and it's your duty to examine it. But it's not *my* duty. I'll go and get help. Good-bye!'

Goon held on to him tightly, and then the voice began again. 'I never did it, I never! Ooooooh! I never did it! Where's my auntie?'

Goon began to shake. 'What's he mean, talking about his auntie?' he whispered. 'Come on, let's go! This is a madhouse, this is.'

'Mr Goon – why not telephone for help!' said Fatty, suddenly catching sight of the telephone in the hall. 'You'd get someone here in a trice then.'

Mr Goon was so relieved at this bright idea of Fatty's that he almost embraced him. He stumbled to the telephone and dialled a number.

Fatty heard him telephoning to another constable. He tiptoed silently out of the front door, grinning as he heard Goon's agonised voice.

'Send someone up here at once. There's a fierce dog in the house – and a pig – yes, I said a pig – P-I-G. Yes, PIG, you idiot. And a groaning man who wants his auntie. AUNTIE! Yes, I did say auntie. Are you deaf, or something? Well, how do *I* know why he wants his auntie? No, I'm not daft, but I soon shall be if you don't send someone to this address at once. Yes – I do want help – YES, there IS a dog here – and a pig – and an auntie – no, not an auntie, but a man who wants one. Oh, and there's a kitten too, I forgot to mention that.'

There was a pause as Goon listened to a few remarks from the other end of the telephone. He spluttered into it again.

'Any more sauce from you, Kenton, and I'll

report you. I'm NOT having a joke with you. You come up here at once. AT ONCE, do you hear?'

Fatty heard all this and felt that he really must go somewhere and laugh. He tiptoed round to the back of the house where there was a shed he could go into and laugh in peace. He saw the broken casement window, hanging open, as he passed. He thrust his head inside, and sent a terrible growl into the house.

Mr Goon heard it. He looked round, and found that Fatty had gone. He was alone – alone in the house with a host of terrifying things! It was too much for Goon. He fled at top speed out of the front door, and didn't stop running till he came to the bottom of the road.

Fatty heard him go. And then he laughed. How he laughed! It really was the best laugh Fatty had ever had in all his life!

8. LAUGHTER IS GOOD FOR THE FLU

Fatty's laughter echoed across the next garden and came to the ears of the others. They had retreated to Larry's house, and had made their way into the back garden to wait for Fatty. Buster heard the laughter too, and pricked up his ears. He began to bark delightedly. Like everyone else, he loved Fatty's enormous laughter!

Larry climbed up onto the wall. He gave the piercing whistle that the Find-Outers sometimes used. Fatty heard it and saw Larry.

'Wait for me! I'm coming!' he called. He was soon in the garden with the others. They retired to a little out-house at the bottom of the garden.

'What happened? And why did Mr Goon rush out of the house so suddenly at top speed?' asked Daisy. 'We saw him flashing by the gate like dark blue lightning!'

Fatty began to laugh helplessly again. The

others had to laugh as they watched him. Pip gave him a punch and Buster leapt on him in excitement. Why was his master so pleased?

'Come on – tell us the joke,' said Pip.

So Fatty told them, and soon they were all helplessly sitting on the floor of the out-house, holding their sides, picturing Mr Goon's amazement at the thought of the grunting pig, the growling dog, and the groaning man.

'That auntie bit! Oh, what made you think of that?' groaned Larry, holding his aching sides. 'That's a touch of genius. Oh dear – only an idiot like Mr Goon would have taken all that in! What *will* Inspector Jenks think when Mr Goon makes out a report full of pigs, and dogs, and men that want their aunties?'

That made them all laugh again, but Fatty began to look a little more sober. He rubbed his nose thoughtfully. 'I hadn't thought of Mr Goon making out a report,' he said. 'Yes, I suppose he'll have to. The Chief Inspector will smell a rat, I should think. Especially if he knows I was with Mr Goon at the time all this happened.'

'He may not put you into the report,' said

Daisy, comfortingly. 'He'd leave you out if he possibly could. He hates admitting you are ever on the same job as he is.'

'He telephoned for help,' said Fatty. 'Let's go and see if he's met his help and if they're coming back.'

Just as they got to the front gate and hung over it, with Buster doing his best to squeeze underneath, Mr Goon came up the road with PC Kenton. PC Kenton had been most astonished to have Goon bump violently into him at the corner of the road.

'I just came to meet you,' explained Goon in haste. 'Thought you mightn't know where the house was. Come on.'

He scowled when he saw the five leaning over the gate. He especially scowled at Fatty for deserting him. Gah! Toad of a boy! However, he thought it best to say nothing whatever to any of them, in case Fatty was funny at his expense. Fatty could be rude more politely than anyone Goon had ever met.

'I bet Mr Goon's friend will be puzzled to find the house completely empty of kitten, dog, pig, and man,' said Fatty. He had brought the kitten with him to Daisy's. It had most conveniently jumped out of the window and landed at his feet while he had been standing laughing at the back of the burgled house. It was now playing with Daisy's kitten in a very friendly manner.

PC Kenton was indeed astonished to find nothing and no one in the house of the kind that Goon had described.

'Not even auntie!' he complained. 'I was looking forward to seeing auntie. You sure you weren't seeing things, Mr Goon?'

'I didn't *see* anything – except the kitten. I heard them, I keep telling you,' said poor Mr Goon, amazed to hear no sound of growl or grunt or groan, and to find nothing that could conceivably have made them.

'I can't think where auntie's gone,' said PC Kenton, maliciously.

'Don't keep on and on about auntie,' said Mr Goon, exasperated. 'Auntie, whoever she was, wasn't here. The man just kept on wanting her, that's all. I keep telling you.'

PC Kenton was inclined to make a joke of the

whole thing and this infuriated Goon to such an extent that he began to exaggerate.

'If you'd been here and heard a dog growling, just about to leap at you, and heard a pig grunting and stamping about on the floor above, and then heard a man groaning and groaning at the top of his voice, and dragging himself about the floor, well, you wouldn't have made a joke of it, I can tell you,' said Mr Goon.

'Well, all I can say is that the kitten, the pig, the dog, and the man, must have all rushed off together as soon as you left the house,' said PC Kenton, rather severely. 'You should have stayed and waited for me. Now we've lost all the animals and the man too. You'll have to make inquiries in the neighbourhood about them. See if anyone saw them rushing off together.'

Mr Goon lost some of his high colour. He didn't think people would take him very seriously if he went round asking a question like that. He changed the subject and, after a while, the two policemen fastened the open window, and went out of the front door, banging it behind them. The children saw them go.

Mr Goon crossed to the other side of the road with PC Kenton. He didn't want any awkward questions just then, and especially not from Fatty. They passed out of sight.

'A wonderful morning,' said Pip, with a sigh. 'I've forgotten all about the flu. I wonder doctors don't recommend this sort of thing for flu. I don't see how anyone can feel ill if they have mornings like this. I've never laughed so much in my life. What do we do now, Fatty?'

'I want to know if *you've* anything to report to me,' said Fatty. 'You had the job of going carefully round the house and spotting anything there was to see. Tell me what notes you made?'

'We didn't get much,' said Larry. 'We've pooled our notes together and here's a short report. I wrote it out while I was waiting for you.'

'Good work,' said Fatty, approvingly. 'Fire ahead.'

Larry read out his notes.

'We went carefully all round the house. We found out where the burglar came in. He didn't come in at the front door but over the wall at the bottom of the garden.'

'How do you know that?' said Fatty, at once.

'Well, there's a bed there, and there are very deep imprints of feet,' said Larry. 'Only a person jumping down from the wall could have made such deep prints.'

'Right,' said Fatty. 'Go on.'

'We traced the same footprints to a bush,' went on Larry. 'Here the man must have hidden, as there are many footmarks, all messed up together, as if he stood there for some time, occasionally peeping out.'

'Got a drawing of the prints?' asked Fatty.

'Of course,' said Pip, producing a sheet of paper from his pocket and unfolding it. 'But it's not much help – we think the man wore Wellingtons, about size eleven. Anyway, the marks are exactly the same as our own Wellington boots make, except that ours are smaller.'

'Right,' said Fatty again. 'Go on.'

'We found this cigarette-end,' said Larry, and passed a damp cigarette butt to Fatty. 'Can't tell much from that though. We could only find this one, and that was under some leaves. I expect Mr Goon found any others there were. We saw what must have been *his* enormous footprints everywhere too. But we know those all right. So we could tell them easily from the others.'

'Good thing Mr Goon has such colossal feet,' said Fatty. 'We always know *his* footmarks! Anything else?'

'Oh yes. We traced the footprints from the bush to the back of the house,' said Larry, reading his notes again. 'We couldn't see them on the lawn, of course, but we could trace them on another bed and also on a very soggy gravel path by the back of the house. There are quite a lot of marks, all mixed up, on the path under the broken window. He must have got over the wall, hidden under the bush and waited till he judged the time right for entering, then crept up the garden and broken the window. There's a half-brick just below the window. We think he broke it with that.'

'Yes. Probably,' said Fatty. 'That means that someone might have heard him just then. We'll find out. Any more?'

'Yes. There are other footprints, different ones, going from the front door, across the beds there in front of the house, then on a bit of the gravel path that leads to the back gate – then no more,' said Larry. 'They don't go straight from the front door to the front gate. If they had, we wouldn't have seen them probably, because there are so many other footprints there now.'

'I see – so you think someone else – probably Mr Fellows – ran out of the front door and, instead of making straight for the front gate, ran across the front beds to the back gate and disappeared out that way. That probably means he went down the road, not up,' said Fatty thoughtfully.

'Yes. That's all our notes,' said Larry, shutting his book.

'And they're really good too,' said Fatty. 'You've done better than old Mr Goon, I bet. Now, just let me think a bit and try to piece together exactly what happened last night.'

9. IS IT A MYSTERY?

'Silence while the great mind works,' said Larry. 'Quiet, Buster! Sh!'

Fatty worked out his ideas rapidly. He was soon ready with them.

'This is how I see it,' he said. 'Somebody wants something out of Mr Fellows. What, we don't know. Anyway, whatever it is, the man must, for some reason, break into the house – probably because he feels sure that Mr Fellows won't admit him if he comes to the front door. That means that he wants something that Mr Fellows won't want to give him.'

'Yes. That sounds right,' said Pip. 'But why did Mr Fellows tear out of the house like that?'

'Now wait a bit. Don't rush your fences,' said Fatty. 'The man hides till he thinks it's safe to break in – probably hoping that Mr Fellows is asleep, then he can face him suddenly – possibly with a gun – and get what he wants. So in he goes at what he thinks is the right moment.'

'I'd never have thought of all this,' said Bets. 'It's like an adventure story, the way you tell it!'

'In he goes,' went on Fatty, 'but for some reason he doesn't take Mr Fellows by surprise. Perhaps Mr Fellows has heard the breaking of the glass and has smelt a rat – anyway, hearing the man getting in at the back window, what does he do? He shoots out of the front door, leaving it wide open, and rushes out into the dark, dark night . . .'

'It wouldn't be so very dark,' said Daisy. 'There was moonlight last night. My bedroom was flooded with it.'

'You're right. So was mine. Good for you, Daisy,' said Fatty. 'Well, to go on – he fled out into the moonlit night – possibly taking with him whatever it was that the other fellow had come for. The other fellow found the bird flown but, not being certain if he had taken with him whatever it was he wanted, he proceeded to turn the house upside down to look for it. And he didn't leave any corner or drawer or cupboard – or even the chimneys – unsearched!'

'You *are* clever to work all this out,' said Bets. 'I never knew anyone who could put two and two together and make four so quickly.'

'Ah, but where Fatty scores is that he makes them come to *five,*' said Larry. 'He's always one up on Mr Goon or anyone else! Mr Goon makes two and two come to four – but old Fatty goes one better!'

'Thanks, Larry,' said Fatty, amused but also pleased. 'That's what all good detectives do. Now, the thing is, what was it that Mr Fellows rushed off with? It can't have been anything terribly bulky or heavy or he wouldn't have been able to run far with it – and someone might have spotted him and stopped him if he was carrying a suspicious parcel or big sack.'

'So they might,' said Daisy. 'Gosh, Fatty, if you work all this out much further you'll be telling us what it was the man was carrying.'

'I wish I could,' said Fatty. 'But I think I've found something that might be a help – though how, I can't possibly imagine!'

He produced the little red glove from his pocket.

They all stared at it, and Buster sniffed hard.

'It's a doll's glove,' said Daisy. 'Or a baby's. *Could* it have been a baby's?'

'I did play with the idea that Mr Fellows had kidnapped a baby or some very small child,' said Fatty. 'But I came to the conclusion he hadn't. There wasn't anything in the house to suggest that a small child had been there. Only this glove!'

Larry took the glove and turned it over. 'It's very clean,' he said. 'It couldn't have fitted a child of more than two, I should think. Where's your big doll, Daisy? – the one you had when you were three – it was nearly as big as you then!'

'She's packed away somewhere,' said Daisy. 'I'll go and get her. Wait a minute.'

While she was gone, Fatty turned to Pip. 'You showed me the drawing of the burglar's footprints,' he said. 'But what about Mr Fellows' footprints – you saw them go from the front door, across the front beds and on the path by the back gate. Did you take a drawing of them?'

'Gosh, yes – I forgot to show it to you,' said Pip, feeling in his pocket. He brought out a second folded sheet of paper and undid it carefully.

'Rather funny prints these, Fatty – smaller than the others and rather flat and indistinct.'

Fatty looked at them in silence. 'I think Mr Fellows ran out in his bedroom slippers,' he said. 'This print isn't of proper shoes or boots, with heels – it's a print of flat slippers. He may even have had on his night-things and a dressing-gown, with bedroom slippers – he went out in such a hurry. If he was in bed or just going, he wouldn't be fully dressed.'

'Yes, you're right. It *is* the print of flat bedroom slippers,' said Pip. 'Larry, go and get yours – they're flat, aren't they? We could see what kind of footmarks you make in them. There's a nice muddy bit over by the wall.'

Larry fetched his slippers and came back with Daisy, who had found the doll. It certainly was a nice big one. Fatty tried the glove on its hand.

'Yes, whatever child this glove belonged to couldn't have been much bigger than your doll, Daisy,' he said. 'But it beats me why the man dropped it, unless he *was* carrying a small child.'

He put the glove back into his pocket and looked at Larry, who was busy changing his

Wellingtons for red bedroom slippers.

They all followed him as he went to the muddy patch by the wall. 'Run over it at top speed,' said Fatty. Larry ran, first up, then down.

His mother, looking out of the window just then, was amazed to see Larry rushing up and down in the muddiest part of the garden in his bedroom slippers. She couldn't help noticing them because they were bright red!

She knocked at the window and opened it. 'Larry! What are you doing? Stop that silly game at once!'

'There! We might have known that Mummy would look out of the window at this very moment!' said Daisy. 'It's all right, Mummy – we're just trying to prove something, that's all.'

'Well, don't,' said her mother. 'And please tell the others it's almost one o'clock. I'm sure Pip and Bets ought to be going home.'

She shut the window and disappeared. Fatty looked hurriedly but carefully at the flat, smooth prints that Larry's bedroom slippers had made.

'Yes, they're very like Mr Fellows' footprints,' he said, comparing them with Pip's drawing. 'Do they *look* the same to you, Pip? You got a really good view of Mr Fellows' prints because you had to draw them.'

'Yes, exactly the same,' said Pip. 'Come on, Bets, we'll simply have to rush home! When's the next meeting, Fatty? Come to our house, will you?'

'Right,' said Fatty, folding up the paper and putting it into his pocket. 'We'll meet this afternoon at half past three – unless anyone's got to have a rest, because of what the doctor calls "the aftermath of the flu" – whatever that means. We've done some good work this morning – to say nothing of having had some great fun!'

Larry and Daisy went indoors with the doll and the red bedroom slippers. Pip and Bets shot off home. Fatty went more leisurely, his brain at work. There was more in this little happening than met the eye. Much more he thought. It wasn't just an ordinary burglary – and Fatty very much doubted if the 'burglar' had taken anything at all.

I bet Mr Fellows rushed off with whatever it was the man had come after, he thought. Where is he? Where did he put what he wanted to hide? Will he come back?

Mrs Trotteville was out for lunch, so Fatty was able to have a long and satisfying meal all by himself in front of the fire. He thought about the new problem all the time. It wasn't really a 'mystery' – not yet anyway – but it was certainly very interesting. When Jane the maid came in, she was surprised to find how much he had eaten.

'Dear me – yes, I do seem to have cleaned up the dishes rather,' said Fatty, gazing in surprise at the empty tureens and plates. 'I've been thinking and when I'm thinking I like plenty of food for thought, Jane. What's for pudding? French pancakes? Oh, good. How many? Ah, plenty of food for thought here!'

Jane laughed. Frederick was very funny and no mistake! She went out to tell the cook to make another French pancake for Fatty.

Fatty meant to work out a proper scheme for tackling this new problem immediately after lunch – but, unfortunately, he fell fast asleep in front of the fire with Buster curled up on the hearth rug beside him. He didn't wake up till the clock struck half past three.

He leapt up in horror. Goodness, he ought to be at Pip's by now. He pulled on his coat, remembering his mother's orders to put on a scarf. He decided to bicycle, with Buster in the front basket. He wouldn't be so late then.

He arrived at Pip's, ringing his bell furiously down the drive, much to Mrs Hilton's annoyance. Why must Fatty always announce his coming? Really, that boy wanted taking in hand! He was getting too big for his boots.

'Sorry we're late,' said Fatty, arriving in the playroom upstairs, with Buster dancing at his heels. 'I fell asleep. Can't think why.'

'We all did!' said Larry, with a grin. 'Another bit of the doctor's "aftermath", I suppose! Pip and Bets were still asleep when we came!'

'Well, we're wide awake now,' said Pip. 'And Mummy says you can all stay to tea if you like, Fatty. Our cook has made a big chocolate sponge, so you're lucky. Mother says we can finish it between us, if we like.'

'That's one good thing about having had flu,'

said Bets. 'Grown-ups think we want feeding up, and instead of Mummy saying, "Now don't be greedy," she keeps saying, "You *must* have more than that, dear. Take a second helping." Long may it last!'

Everyone agreed heartily. Pip produced the rest of the bull's-eyes that Bets had bought him, and they all took one. They sat round the fire, their cheeks bulging, feeling happy and comfortable.

'Now, let's talk,' said Larry. 'We had to break up the meeting in such a hurry this morning. Fatty, have you any plans? Is this a mystery, do you think, by any chance? I mean, it seems rather ordinary really, after the mysteries we've tackled before – but even a *little* one would be nice before we go back to school in four or five days' time.'

There were groans at the last few words. Nobody felt like school, but they were all fit enough to go back now.

'I think,' said Fatty slowly, 'I really do think this *may* be a mystery and, if so, we'll make the best of it. After all, a mystery, little or big, is always a mystery, and has to be solved. I vote we get down to it at once!'

10. A FEW PLANS – AND A GOOD TEA

Everyone was delighted to hear this, of course. Buster thumped his tail on the floor as if he thoroughly agreed. A mystery! He'd be in it too, all right!

'You all remember what we worked out this morning, don't you?' said Fatty. 'And you all know the few clues we have – two sets of footprints – and a small red glove – and a cigarette-end that really isn't worth anything as a clue because, except that it proves the intruder smoked, we can't tell much more from it – not even the kind it was.'

'Yes. That seems about all the clues,' said Larry.

'By the way,' said Fatty, remembering something suddenly. 'We know how the man got into the garden, hid, and then walked to the back window and got in – but does anyone know how he got away? I mean, he wasn't in the house the next day – that is, today – so he must have got away somehow. Any ideas?'

'Yes,' said Pip at once. 'We think he went out of the front door. We thought we could make out a few of his footprints in the general muddle of footmarks going up and down the front path. Anyway, there were none going back down the garden.'

'I see,' said Fatty. 'Yes, he probably did go out of the front door – and didn't bang it in case it attracted attention to him. It's a pity we can't find anyone who saw either of the men wandering about in the middle of the night – particularly Mr Fellows, who was in bedroom slippers and, presumably, dressing-gown. That's really what we ought to do next – find someone who saw one or other of them that night.'

'I don't see how we can,' objected Daisy. 'We can't possibly find anyone who was out late that night and ask them if they saw a man in slippers and dressing-gown. They'd think we were mad.'

'Another thing we ought to find out is the time the man entered the house,' said Fatty. 'That might give us some guide.'

'Guide to what?' asked Daisy.

'I don't know,' said Fatty. 'We've just got to follow up every tiny little thing. Larry, do you know the people next door to you – at the house in between yours and Mr Fellows?'

'Yes,' said Larry. 'The mother's help there has a boy. I talk to him sometimes. He's a great bird-fellow – watches them, and knows all their names and calls.'

'Is his bedroom on the side next to Mr Fellows' house?' asked Fatty.

'I don't know,' said Larry. 'Do you want me to ask him if he heard anything funny in the night – like the breaking of glass, for instance?'

'You might as well,' said Fatty. 'You see, if we can get the time the burglar went in, say at three o'clock in the morning – we could perhaps find someone who saw Mr Fellows somewhere at that time.'

'Who?' said Larry scornfully. 'I mean, how many people are wandering about at three o'clock in the morning?'

'Nobody, usually,' said Fatty mildly, 'except Mr Goon at times. But there are such things as night-watchmen – I don't know if you've ever *heard* of them, Larry – they're the men who . . .'

'All right, all right, you win!' said Larry, making a face. 'I should have thought of night-watchmen, of course. Especially as our roads are being done up now, all over the place, and there are night-watchmen to guard the tools and things left beside the road. Yes, you are right, a night-watchman might have spotted Mr Fellows in his dressing-gown. Though don't forget he might have pulled an overcoat on.'

'If it was three o'clock in the morning, he would have his pyjamas on, and they would show under an overcoat,' said Bets. 'It doesn't seem to me to matter whether he wore a dressing-gown or a coat. He'd still look a bit peculiar with pyjama trousers and bedroom slippers!'

'Well, do you propose that we go round to all the night-watchmen of the district and ask them questions about dressing-gowns and slippers?' said Larry, not at all pleased with the idea. 'Bags I don't. Night-watchmen are not awfully helpful in the daytime – if you can find them. They're sleepy and cross.'

'Well, we'll go when it's dark then,' said Fatty. 'They will presumably be wide awake then, if they have a job of watching to do. I think *I'll* go but I don't think the girls should do this, and I doubt if your mothers would let you wander round in the cold night air, Larry and Pip. The aftermath of flu would prevent such goings-on!'

'What about you then?' demanded Pip. 'Would you be allowed to?'

'I shall probably feel the need for taking Buster out for a run tonight,' said Fatty solemnly. 'My father has had to do it while I've been ill, and apparently Buster has played him up properly – run off into the bushes for ages and made Dad hunt for hours – and then he would find Buster waiting patiently for him on the front doorstep.'

Everyone laughed. 'All right, you take old Buster out for a nice long run tonight,' said Pip. 'And enter into conversation with a few night-watchmen. I can just see you sitting down on an upturned pail and warming your hands at one of those lovely holey buckets of hot cinders, and talking nineteen to the dozen!'

'And I'll have a word with the boy next door

– his name's Erb,' said Larry. 'Short for Herbert. Or for Erbert, I've never found out which. He's a nice lad, anyway. I'll give you a phone call, Fatty, if I can find out anything. I'll slip in and see him tonight – lend him a bird book, or something – and ply him with questions.'

'Right, and if as a result of your plying you find out the time of the breaking of the window, it will be a help,' said Fatty. 'I can ask the night-watchmen if they saw Mr Fellows at some definite time then. It'll make it easier for me.'

'How?' asked Bets, puzzled.

'Well, I may have an uncle who sleepwalks and who was missing at a certain time last night, and wants to know where he wandered to, for instance,' said Fatty, grinning. 'Aha! I'm going to interest quite a few watchmen in my Uncle Horatious.'

'I never knew you had an Uncle Horatious,' said Bets.

'Didn't you? He's the one that sleepwalks. I've just told you,' grinned Fatty. 'And I've got an Uncle Tobias who goes round at night looking for glow-worms – funny old fellow he is. The night-watchmen might have seen him too.'

They all laughed, and Bets gave him a punch. 'You're an idiot. You've got an imagination that's too good to be true!'

Buster got up suddenly and ran to the door, standing there with his nose glued to it.

'Buster hears tea coming,' said Pip. 'I wish I had ears like a dog. By the way, Daisy, how's the little kitten?'

'Fine,' said Daisy. 'It's a real darling. If it belonged to Mr Fellows – and I suppose it did – he must be feeling worried about it! I'd hate to desert a tiny thing like that and leave it to starve in an empty house.'

'He may come back,' said Fatty, 'and if he does, that'll make a wonderful excuse for going to see him, Daisy! I can take back the kitten, and ask him all sorts of innocent questions!'

'Good idea – *if* he comes back,' said Pip. 'Hurrah, Buster was right – it *is* the tea!'

He and Bets ran to the door and took in two large and well-loaded trays. 'Thanks,' said Pip, eyeing the trays with approval. 'Gosh, what a great chocolate sponge.'

It was a very fine tea – hot, new-made scones, sweet and buttery, strawberry jam, bread and butter, and potted salmon and shrimp paste, small ginger buns, shortbread biscuits and, of course, the large chocolate sponge, which had a thick cream filling.

'I vote we march down in a body to the kitchen after tea and give three cheers,' said Larry. 'Well, flu certainly has its good points . . . afterwards! I hope we shall all be fed just as much at school when we get there.'

'We shall be – but not in quite the same way as we are being fed up now!' grinned Pip, offering the scones round. 'I soon get fed-up at school.'

'Ha ha! Joke over,' said Larry, biting into his scone. 'Gosh, this is the most buttery scone I ever had. Buster would just love to lick my face clean after it!'

It was a lovely tea – cosy, companionable, and full of silly jokes. Buster accepted tit-bits from everyone, and was not above abstracting a biscuit from the plate when no one was looking.

They ate everything, and Pip asked everyone politely if he should go down and ask for any more. But nobody could manage another thing. Buster thumped his tail on the carpet to say that he wouldn't mind a few more biscuits but, unfortunately, nobody took any notice of him.

They played a game of *Monopoly* after tea, but had to stop before it was finished. Both Larry and Daisy had been told to get home by quarter past six, as an aunt was coming to stay.

'Will you have time to go in and see that boy next door – Erb, didn't you say his name was?' asked Fatty.

'Oh yes, I'll leave Daisy chatting brightly to Aunt Pamela,' said Larry. 'She's good at that sort of thing. Well, come on, Daisy. We must go. I'll ring you later on this evening, Fatty.'

They all went down to the kitchen and gave three cheers for their wonderful tea. The two maids were tickled and pleased. 'Go on with you,' said the cook. 'You're only doing this to get as good a tea next time you come. Oh, there's Buster. Did they give you any tea, Buster?'

Buster drooped his tail as if to say no. 'Oh, you fibber!' said Pip. 'Who stole a biscuit off the plate? You thought I wasn't looking, but I was. Good thing I was your host or I'd have had something to say to you!'

Larry, Daisy, and Fatty went to say good-bye and thank you to Mrs Hilton, who was always very strict about good manners. Then they went off together down the drive to the front gate. Fatty wheeled his bicycle.

'I hope I don't meet Mr Goon,' he said. 'I've got no light at the front. Well, so long, Larry and Daisy. Here's to the new mystery, even if it's just a tiddler – and don't forget to phone me, Larry.'

'Right,' said Larry. 'And good luck with your Uncle Horatious and your Uncle Tobias and the night-watchmen, Fatty. You'd better keep a sharp eye on those two uncles of yours in future!'

11. LARRY DOES A LITTLE WORK – AND SO DOES FATTY

Larry and Daisy arrived home just at quarter past six. Their aunt was already there. Larry chatted politely for ten minutes and then escaped, leaving Daisy to carry on the good work. He slipped up to his room and found his new book on garden birds. Erb would love to borrow that!

He went in the gate of the next door house and made his way to the back door. He rapped four times. That was the signal to Erb that he had come to see him about something.

Erb opened the door. 'Hello!' he said. 'What's up?'

'Nothing,' said Larry. 'I just wondered if you'd like to borrow my new book. It's got every single garden bird in it – all the ones we get here, of course!'

'Come in,' said Erb, eagerly. 'Mum's out. Let's have a look at the book. Coo, it's a beauty! Will you really lend it to me?'

Erb sat down at the table and opened the book. He would have been pleased if Larry had gone back home straight away and left him to it. Herbert was certainly mad on birds, Larry reflected.

He wondered how to begin his questions about the night before, when suddenly Erb gave him just the opening he needed.

'Oooh, here's a fine chapter on owls,' he said. 'And what smashing pictures. I love owls. I'm always listening out for them. There – listen – one's hooting now. Can you hear it?'

A long and beautiful quavering hoot came to Larry's ears. He sat up at once.

'Erb, did you hear any owls last night?'

Erb looked across at Larry and nodded. 'Yes, I did. They like moonlight nights, you know. One owl came so near my window that I thought he must be calling for me to come and catch mice with him. I even saw him fly past the window, though I couldn't catch the sound of his quiet wings.'

'What time did you hear him?' asked Larry. 'Did you notice?'

'Why, did you hear him too?' said Erb, surprised. 'Let's see now, I heard owls before I went to sleep – about ten that was. Then they woke me again about half past twelve – that was the time one came to my window. I got out of bed and watched for a while then.'

'Where does your bedroom face – towards our house?' asked Larry.

'No, it faces on to the next door house,' said Erb. 'The one that was burgled last night. When I looked out about half past twelve, there was still a light on downstairs in the sitting-room. Mr Fellows must have been sitting working there like he often does. Sometimes he doesn't draw his curtains, and I see him sitting at a table. But last night, the curtains were drawn. He'd got his radio on, I think. I'm sure I heard sounds coming from it.'

'I suppose you didn't hear any owls after that, did you?' asked Larry hopefully. 'There must have been a lot about, enjoying looking for mice in the moonlight.'

'Oh, there were,' said Erb. 'Something woke me later on, but I don't think it was owls. I don't really know what it was. I switched on my light and saw it was quarter past three. I went to the window and listened for owls again, and I could hear some brown owls somewhere, and some little owls too, twitting like anything.'

'Had the light gone out in the sitting-room next door?' asked Larry.

'Oh yes,' said Erb. 'But the funny thing was that I thought I saw some kind of a light down in the kitchen – the room that faces our kitchen. Not the usual electric light – torch perhaps, or a candle.'

This was all very interesting. Larry wondered if the light in the kitchen had been the torch of the man who had got in through the broken casement.

'Can't you really remember what the sound was that woke you?' he asked. 'Would it be breaking glass, for instance?'

'Well, it might have been,' said Erb, wrinkling his forehead. 'Are you thinking about the burglary next door? Well, I dare say that might have been glass breaking I heard, and it might have been the light of a torch I saw in the kitchen, I couldn't swear to it – I didn't take that much notice.'

He bent his head down to the book again and became completely absorbed in it. Larry got up. He didn't think he could get anything more out of

Erb. Erb obviously took much more interest in birds than he did in burglaries. He didn't seem at all interested in the happenings next door!

'Good-bye, Erb,' said Larry, and went back home. Erb and his owls! Larry hoped he would enjoy the bird book – he deserved the loan of it in return for all the information Larry had got out of him!

He telephoned Fatty and told him the whole conversation clearly and concisely. Fatty approved.

'You are all getting really good at reporting things,' he said. 'Thanks for such interesting details. I think there's no doubt that the burglar fellow broke the window at about quarter past three – and very soon after that Mr Fellows rushed out of the house, probably with the precious goods – whatever they were – that the other chap had come for.'

'Well, I suppose you'll now decide that your respected Uncle Horatious wandered abroad sleepwalking at round about quarter past three,' said Larry, 'and half the night-watchmen in Peterswood will hear all about him – bedroom slippers and all!'

'Quite right,' said Fatty. 'How bright you are, Larry! Anyway, thanks for all you've done. Good work. See you tomorrow and tell you anything that happens tonight!'

That night, Fatty apparently went up to bed at eight o'clock, immediately after the evening meal. His mother approved. 'You've had a long day and I'm glad you are sensible enough to go up early,' she said. 'Your father and I are going out to play bridge. Don't read too late in bed, Frederick.'

Fatty duly promised, congratulating himself on his luck. He had been afraid that he would have to undress completely and get into bed, in case his mother came up to say goodnight. Now he needn't do that.

He heard his father get into the car. He heard it go purring down the drive and into the road. Good. Now he could act.

He debated on a disguise. Should he put one on, or shouldn't he? It wasn't really necessary. On the other hand, it would be fun, and he was rather out of practice disguising himself these hols. Fatty decided he *would* do a spot of disguising. He took a torch, and he and Buster disappeared cautiously down the garden to the lock-up shed where he kept his dressing-up things.

He thought he wouldn't put on anything too noticeable. He didn't want to scare the night-watchmen, dreaming over their fires! He decided on a small toothbrush moustache, his false, prominent teeth, and no wig – just his own hair. A cap of some sort? Yes, that checked one would do well. He'd wear it back to front – it would look very fetching that way.

He chose a tweed overcoat, rather too big for him, and a blue-spotted scarf. He looked at himself in the glass. Did he look like a young man asking for information about a sleepwalking uncle? He thought he did.

He set off. He guessed he must go in the direction of the river because Mr Fellows had gone out of the back gate, which meant he was presumably going in that direction and not up the road towards the hills. Now, where was the road being mended on the way to the river?

Fatty decided regretfully to leave Buster behind. Too many people knew Buster. If they met him in company with a strange young man at night, they might think somebody was stealing him. So Buster was left behind, curled up on the rug in the shed.

Fatty went to Mr Fellows' house, and looked at it. It was in complete darkness. He stood at the back gate and looked along the road. Yes, he would go down there – and when he came to the bottom, he would see if there was any sign of a night-watchman's brazier of glowing coals.

He walked down smartly. At the end, he looked this way and that. No sign of any watchman or of the road being up. He turned to the right and made his way to the next crossroad. There he had some luck.

Red lamps burned in a row, and in the midst of them was the dark shadowy shape of a watchman's hut, with the brazier of burning coals in front of it. Fatty walked along.

The watchman heard his steps and peered out. 'Good evening,' said Fatty cheerily. 'Nice fire you've got there! Do you charge anything if I warm my hands, mate?'

'Warm 'em and welcome,' said the old fellow.

'Everybody who comes by likes a warm at my fire, so he do.'

'Do you get many people late at night?' asked Fatty, spreading his fingers over the warm glow. 'I mean, after midnight?'

'I gets the policeman, Mr Goon,' said the watchman. 'Chatty fellow he is. Handles a lot of important cases, so he tells me. And I gets a fisherman or two that likes a bit of midnight fishing. Nobody about then to disturb the fish you know.'

'I wonder if you've ever seen my Uncle Horatius,' began Fatty. 'He's a funny old fellow – walks in his sleep.'

'Do he now?' said the watchman, with interest.

'Yes, he do – er, does,' said Fatty. 'I suppose you didn't see him last night, did you, wandering about in a dressing-gown – or perhaps a coat over his pyjamas – with bedroom slippers on his feet?'

The watchman went off into a cackle of laughter just like a goose. Fatty listened to it intently, he could copy that at some time – wonderful! Cackle, cackle, cackle.

'Naw, I didn't see him,' said the old man.

'Good thing too, or mebbe I'd have thought I were asleep, and dreaming – and that's not a good thing for a night-watchman to do. But old Willie, him that's watching further along, nearer the river, he did say something about a chap in pyjamas last night. Mebbe that was your Uncle Horatius. You should ought to lock him up, Mister – he'll get himself drownded one night, sleepwalking near the river!'

'Yes. I think I *will* lock him up in the future,' said Fatty, delighted at this unexpected bit of news. 'I'll go and have a word with Willie. Hello, who's this?'

There was a ringing of a bicycle bell, and a familiar figure loomed up in the light of the nearest lamp-post. Mr Goon! Blow! What was *he* doing here?

12. A LITTLE NIGHT-PROWLING

Fatty moved off hastily, glad that he hadn't brought Buster with him. What a welcome Buster would have given the astonished Goon!

The burly policeman got off his bicycle and went over to the night-watchman. Fatty escaped into the shadows and hurried off to find Willie.

A row of red lamps again guided him. He went down a long road towards them, seeing the flash of the river at the end. The watchman's little hut was set close beside the bright brazier of burning coals.

Fatty introduced himself as before, and brought his Uncle Horatius into the conversation as soon as he could. He was afraid that Goon might turn up again! Why must he ride round the streets just when Fatty wanted them to himself!

Willie the watchman proved rather a surly fellow. He answered very shortly indeed.

'You sometimes have people asking you if they can warm themselves by your fine fire, I'm sure,' said Fatty, persevering in spite of the watchman's surliness. 'I bet my Uncle Horatius always comes to warm himself when he goes sleepwalking at nights.'

The watchman grunted. He took no interest in Fatty's uncle or in sleepwalking either.

'You might have seen him last night,' went on Fatty. 'Came out in his pyjamas and bedroom slippers. Ha, ha, ha!'

The watchman looked at Fatty. 'I seed him,' he remarked, suddenly developing quite a chatty manner. 'Leastways, I seed someone running by – pyjama legs and bedroom slippers 'e wore. Scatty fellow, I thought to myself. But he weren't old, the way he run along.'

Fatty was delighted. Ah, so Mr Fellows had run down this road. That was something! It only led to the river. Why had he gone down to the *river*?

'Was he carrying anything?' asked Fatty.

'Yes, he were. Something in his arms like, but I dunno what it was,' said the watchman. 'So he were your uncle, were he? Do he often sleepwalk?'

'On moonlight nights mostly,' said Fatty, ready to invent anything now that he had got a little information. 'You didn't see him come back, did you?'

'Naw,' said Willie, and relapsed into surliness again. Fatty was about to say goodnight when he heard the ringing of a bicycle bell again. Surely, surely that couldn't be Mr Goon once more?

But it was! Fatty escaped from the light of the burning brazier just in time. Goon sailed up to the light of the red lamps and hailed Willie.

'Are you there, my man? I want to ask you a few questions!'

Fatty hid behind a convenient bush, a really worrying suspicion forming in his mind. Was Goon cross-examining the night-watchman too – and for the same reason as Fatty was? Had he worked out the problem in the same way as the Find-Outers had? If so, Goon was growing a few brains!

'Well, Willie,' said Goon, warming himself at the brazier, first his vast front, then his rather vaster back. 'You seen anyone suspicious last night? I'm on a case again, and I'm looking out for someone.'

'You wouldn't be wanting an old uncle what sleepwalks and wears pyjamas and red slippers, would you?' said Willie.

Goon stared at him, astonished. 'Why, the old watchman away up the other road asked me that,' he said. 'I thought it was just his joke. Who's been kidding you along too?'

'A young fellow,' said Willie. 'Proper worried about his old Uncle Horatius, he was – old gent what sleepwalks at night.'

'Oh. And I suppose Uncle Horatius went for a sleepwalk last night, did he?' said Mr Goon, in such a ferocious voice that Willie was astonished.

' 'Ere! What you talking to me like that for?' he complained.

'What was this fellow like who told you this fairytale?' demanded Mr Goon.

'I didn't rightly notice him much,' said Willie. 'My eyes ain't too good now. Young, he was. Tallish. A moustache of some sort. And he was fattish too.'

Mr Goon gave an exclamation. *Fattish!* Could the owner of the sleepwalking uncle be – that boy! Was it that pest again, on the track of something as usual? Mr Goon could have shouted in rage.

The moustache was put on, of course – the sleepwalking uncle was made up. It must be – it *was* that big boy following the same clues that he, Mr Goon, had so painfully worked out himself. Where was he? Where had he gone? If Mr Goon could have got his hands on Fatty at that moment, Fatty would have had to yell for mercy!

'Now, you listen here, Willie,' said Mr Goon, suddenly making a plan. 'You listening?'

'Ay,' said Willie. 'Speak louder though. My ears ain't so good.'

Mr Goon spoke up, much to Fatty's joy. What was he going to say?

'That fellow will come back this way,' said Mr Goon. 'I want to get my hands on him, see? So when you see him coming, you holler out to him. Get him over here and keep him talking.'

'What for?' asked Willie, doubtfully. 'If he's a bad lot, I don't want to give 'im the chance of knocking me on the 'ead.'

'I'm going to hide at the other end of the road,' said Goon. 'In case he spots me. He's scared of me, dead scared. If he so much as sees the lamp on my bike, he'll run for miles. And I want to get my hands on him, see? Now, when you see him coming, you take up one of your red lamps and swing it slowly to and fro in your hands. I'll be along at once, while you're talking to him.'

'All right,' said Willie, resignedly. What with people talking about sleepwalking uncles and red slippers and bad lots and swinging lamps, Willie was fed up. He'd never get down to a nice little snooze tonight, that was certain!

Mr Goon disappeared on his bicycle. He went to the far end of the river road, got off, and hid under a tree, his bicycle beside him. Ah, he'd catch that big boy on his way back! He'd have to come back that way, because the river barred his way at the other end of the road!

Fatty debated what to do. Should he cut down to the river, make his way across somebody's back garden, and cut into the road that ran parallel with this? Or should he play a little trick on Goon?

He decided on the trick. Goon deserved one after saying that Fatty was dead scared of him! Fatty began to get to work quickly. He blackened his face with dirt. He twisted his cap the other way round, with the peak now shading his eyes. He put a white handkerchief round his neck instead of the scarf. He took off his moustache, but left in his awful teeth.

He felt about on the waste piece of ground nearby. Was there anything he could use in his trick. His hand fell upon an old sack. Good – just the thing! Fatty groped about among the rubbish left by the road-menders and came across pieces of brick and stone. He quickly slid them into the sack until it was half–full. It was very heavy.

He made his way back to the road and skirted round to the back of the watchman. Then he walked slowly by him, half-bent under the sack.

The watchman saw him, but his bleary old eyes couldn't make out who it was. He stared hard, in doubt, wishing the moon would come out from behind a cloud. He decided that whoever it was looked decidedly suspicious. It wouldn't do any harm to swing the red lamp to and fro!

He picked it up, turned himself towards Mr Goon, and swung the lamp slowly. Fatty grinned as he saw it out of the corner of his eye. He plodded on slowly, bent under the sack. If ever anyone looked a suspicious person at that moment, Fatty did!

Mr Goon saw the swinging lamp, and came quickly down the road, keeping to the shadows, his rubber-soled boots making no noise. He tried to see if Fatty was there, talking to the watchman. But to his great annoyance, when he got to the little hut there was no one there but Willie!

'Where is he? Why did you swing your lamp? He's not here!' said Goon, exasperated.

'I see a very suspicious chap shuffling down the river road,' said Willie. 'Not the chap as you wanted, but someone you'd like to get your hands on, I don't doubt. A real suspicious chap. And carrying a heavy sack too. You'd like to know what's in that sack, I reckon!'

'Ho! It certainly sounds bad,' said Goon, thinking that if he couldn't get his hands on Fatty, it would be satisfactory to get them on to someone else. 'What direction did he go in?'

'Yonder,' said Willie, nodding. And yonder went Goon, keeping to the shadows, tracking down Fatty and the suspicious sack. Fatty took a quick look back. Good! Goon was on his trail! He would lead him a nice little dance!

Down to the river plodded Fatty, and came to where the waves were silvery with moonlight. He turned down the towing-path that led to the small jetty nearby, and Goon followed stealthily, breathing so hard that Fatty could hear him.

Fatty walked slowly shuffling one foot after the other, like an old, old man. He coughed mournfully as he went, a horrible hollow cough. He suddenly stopped and put down his sack as if it was too heavy. Goon stopped too.

Fatty heaved the sack on to his shoulder again, and set off once more on his way to the jetty. He stopped suddenly again when he was almost there, and put the sack down once more, with a groan. Goon also stopped suddenly. He was very curious now. What was the old man doing with such a heavy sack? Where was he going? What was in the sack? Had he some accomplice he was meeting? Goon began to feel quite excited.

Fatty hoisted the sack on his back once again and went on his way. He came to the little wooden jetty. Moonlit water splashed against it.

Fatty went on to the jetty and sat down with his sack as if to rest.

Now was Goon's chance! He emerged from the shadows and strode heavily up to the jetty, a big figure in the moonlight.

'Now then,' he began. 'What's your name? And what have you got in that sack?'

'Bricks and stones,' said Fatty truthfully, in a sad, weary, old-man voice.

'Gah!' said Goon, in scorn. 'Nobody carries sacks of bricks and stones about, unless they're mad!'

'Mebbe I'm mad,' said Fatty, drooping his head down so that the moonlight didn't fall on his face.

'You open that sack and let me see what you've got,' said Goon, threateningly.

'No,' said Fatty, clutching the sack as if it contained rubies and diamonds.

'Come on now!' said Goon, advancing on him. 'You open that sack – and be quick about it!'

13. NEWS FROM ERB

'It don't belong to me,' said Fatty obstinately, still clutching the sack.

'Who does it belong to then?' demanded Mr Goon.

'Sh! It belongs to Mr Fellows!' whispered Fatty, on the spur of the moment, and then was horrified to realise what he had said! Mr Goon was amazed.

'Belongs to Mr Fellows!' he repeated. 'But – how did you get it? Look here, you give it to me. You are acting in a suspicious manner, and you'll be arrested in a moment!'

He grabbed at the sack, and Fatty stood up, shouting dramatically, 'No, no, don't touch it!' And then, more dramatically, he picked up the sack and flung it down into the river beside the jetty. He was very glad to get rid of it indeed. It made a most tremendous splash.

Mr Goon was bitterly disappointed. He had made up his mind that there was something very important in the sack – and now it was gone! He knelt down to look over the side of the jetty, and Fatty took to his heels at once.

Mr Goon stood up and gaped at the running figure. How could the old, shuffling fellow run like that? Mr Goon wondered if he was dreaming. He decided that he couldn't possibly catch the fellow – why, he was almost at the turning into the river-road now! What a strange thing to run like that after so much shuffling! A sentence floated into Mr Goon's mind – 'Fear lent him wings'. Well, Mr Goon hadn't got any wings. He would have to walk back at his own pace.

He knelt down again to look into the river but, of course, he could see no sign of the sack. He made up his mind to come with a boat-hook the next day and haul it up. He would find out what was in that sack if he had to go into the water himself to get it!

Willie was astonished to see yet another figure, this time racing past, instead of shuffling past. The goings-on there were in these times! It was quite certain he wouldn't get a snooze before midnight at this rate. That policeman would probably be coming back in a minute too.

Fatty fell to a walk after a bit. He guessed Mr Goon wouldn't come after him. He felt relieved to think that the policeman hadn't recognised him. But whatever had made him say the sack belonged to Mr Fellows? That was really rather idiotic, and not fair to Mr Fellows! Fatty felt distinctly uncomfortable about that.

He got home without any further adventure, feeling unexpectedly tired. Buster gave him an uproarious welcome, and Fatty discarded all his clothes down in the old shed with the little Scottie dancing round him in delight.

Then Fatty crawled tiredly up the garden path from the shed to the house. Gosh! I'm shuffling just like I pretended to, he marvelled. But shuffling's not so good when it's real!

Fatty was so tired that he was almost asleep as he climbed the stairs. He fell into bed, and immediately began to dream of red lamps following him in a threatening manner. He groaned in his sleep and Buster pricked up one ear. Then Mr Goon appeared in his dream riding on his bicycle – and fortunately the red lamps all attached themselves to him, so Fatty was at peace once more.

At breakfast the next morning, the telephone rang. The maid came in and looked at Fatty. 'It's for you, Frederick,' she said. 'Larry is on the phone.'

Fatty jumped up as if dogs were after him. There must be something up if Larry telephoned so early! He hurried to the telephone.

'That you, Fatty?' came Larry's excited voice. 'Guess what! – Mr Fellows is back! I thought you'd better know at once in case old Mr Goon doesn't know yet.'

'Gosh, yes – thanks for phoning,' said Fatty. 'But how did you know?'

'Erb told me,' said Larry. 'I was out in the garden with Daisy looking for one of the kittens that wouldn't come in, and Erb called over the wall to me. He said he was awake last night, listening to his precious owls again, when he heard the click of the gate next door.'

'Go on,' said Fatty. 'What time was this?'

'He said it was about two o'clock in the morning,' said Larry. 'He went to his window at once, wondering if it was a burglar again – but he says it was Mr Fellows. He saw him clearly in the moonlight. And he saw him again when he went into the house, because he switched the light on in the sitting-room whose window Erb can see into. And it *was* Mr Fellows all right.'

'What was he dressed in?' asked Fatty, excited by this news.

'He couldn't really see – but he *thinks* he had on a dressing-gown,' said Larry. 'He wasn't carrying anything though, so if he did rush out of the house with a parcel of some sort . . .'

'He did!' said Fatty. 'I found that out from a night-watchman last night!'

'Oh, good – well, whatever it was, he apparently didn't bring it back with him,' said Larry. 'Do you suppose he was shocked to see his house turned upside down?'

'No. He probably expected it,' said Fatty. 'Well, I'll be along at your house after breakfast. Telephone Pip and Bets, will you? We'll have to think out our next move. By the way, Mr Goon's on the same track as we are. He was very chatty with the watchmen last night too – seems to me he's been setting his brains to work. Most unusual!'

'Frederick!' called his mother. 'Your breakfast is getting cold. Do come back.'

'Good-bye, see you later, Larry,' said Fatty hastily, wondering just how much of the telephone conversation his mother had heard.

He went back into the dining-room and sat down. 'That was Larry,' he said. 'We're all going to his house this morning, if that's all right, Mummy. You don't want me for anything, do you?'

'Well, I *was* going to look through all your school clothes,' said his mother. 'But it will do another time.'

Fatty groaned. 'School! I'm usually really pleased to go back – but this flu has taken it out of me. I'd like the hols to be longer this time!'

'You look the picture of health,' said his father, putting his newspaper down. 'And judging by the number of sausages you've eaten, you feel healthy enough too. You'll go back to school on the right day, so don't try to get round your mother.'

'I'm not!' said Fatty indignantly. 'And sausages have nothing to do with how I feel. Actually, I was eating them quite absent-mindedly this morning.'

'What a waste of sausages then,' said his father, putting up his newspaper again. 'Frederick, I couldn't help overhearing part of your telephone conversation just now – I hope you are not going to get mixed up in anything to do with that absurd policeman again.'

'Not if I can help it,' said Fatty, spreading butter on his toast. 'Any news in the paper this morning, Dad?'

'Plenty. And I'm quite aware that you are hurriedly changing the subject,' said Mr Trotteville, drily.

Fatty said no more, but chewed his toast, his mind dwelling on the return of Mr Fellows. He would go and see him immediately after breakfast, taking the kitten with him – what a marvellous excuse for going! He would see what he could get out of him. He hoped that Mr Goon didn't also know Mr Fellows was back, but there was really no reason why he should have heard. Erb wouldn't have told *him*!

Good old Erb! thought Fatty, drinking his coffee. Erb had come in very useful indeed. Good thing he was so interested in night birds! He wouldn't have been nearly so useful if his interest had been in house sparrows!

Fatty took his bicycle and rode off to Larry's at top speed, with Buster in the basket. On the way, he saw Mr Goon, also on a bicycle, far in the distance. The policeman saw Fatty and waved to him frantically. He had a few questions to ask him about the night before!

Fatty knew that. He certainly wasn't going to stop! He waved back cheerily, as if he thought that Goon was simply being friendly. The policeman pedalled furiously to catch up Fatty.

Blow him, thought Fatty, and pedalled as fast as he could. He turned a corner, leapt off his bicycle, and disappeared with it into the garden of an empty house. He crouched behind the fence.

Mr Goon came by, purple and panting, and sailed up the road, marvelling that Fatty could disappear so swiftly. Fatty came out quickly, mounted his bicycle and rode off in the opposite direction. Buster was surprised at all this, but hadn't even got out of the basket!

Mr Goon's on the lookout for me, thought Fatty. I'll have some awkward questions to answer. Blow him! Does he suspect it was me last night that he followed? I wonder if he's found that sack of bricks and stones yet! He said he was going to get a boat-hook and drag it up. Well, good luck to him! It'll keep him out of the way for a bit, messing about in the river!

He arrived at Larry's out of breath. Pip, Bets, Larry, and Daisy were watching for him. Daisy was holding the kitten.

'Nobody's seen a sign of Mr Fellows,' said Larry, as soon as Fatty came up. 'We think he may be lying low for a bit. Do you think you really should go and see him? I mean, he may not be at all pleased to see you!'

'Can't help that,' said Fatty. 'I can't miss this chance. I simply must question him before Mr Goon gets at him.'

He took the kitten. 'Thanks, Daisy. Well, you funny little thing? You won't like leaving your playmate, will you, and going back to that lonely house?'

He left his bicycle at Larry's, and went up the road to the next house but one – Mr Fellows'. He looked in at the gate. Should he go to the front door or to the back? There was no sign of life in the place at all. Was Mr Fellows pretending to be still away?

I'll go round to the back, thought Fatty. I don't want Mr Goon to see me standing at the front door if he comes by.

He went quietly and cautiously round to the back. He looked in at the window there, the one that was broken. Nobody was about. Fatty debated with himself again.

It was likely that Mr Fellows would not answer any ringing or knocking if he was lying low. But *somehow* Fatty must get hold of him. How? Fatty racked his brains.

And then a splendid idea came to him. It was quite likely that Mr Fellows had been looking for the kitten, now he was back – perhaps he was worried about it. Fatty would stick his face close to the broken pane, and miaow as loudly as he could! If that didn't fetch Mr Fellows into the kitchen, nothing would!

14. AN INTERESTING CONVERSATION

'Miaow! Miaow! MIAOW!'

A most pitiful, heartrending noise penetrated into the kitchen through the broken window. The little kitten that Fatty was holding jumped when it heard his lifelike mewing. It suddenly added its own high-pitched mew.

'That's right,' whispered Fatty. 'Keep up the good work, kitty. Mew as loudly as you can!'

'Miaow!' said the kitten obligingly. 'Miaow.'

Fatty listened. He thought he heard a noise in the house. It seemed to come from upstairs.

'MIAOW-ee-ow-ee-OW!' said Fatty piercingly.

He listened again. Yes, certainly someone was moving in the house now – there were footsteps on the stairs. Then they stopped.

'Miaow,' said the kitten shrilly. It certainly was doing its best for Fatty.

A man appeared at the inner door of the

kitchen, the one that led into the hall.

That must be Mr Fellows, thought Fatty, looking at him closely. He was fully dressed, though Fatty had half-expected him to be in dressing-gown and slippers! He hadn't caught sight of the boy and the kitten yet. He was looking all round the kitchen floor as if wondering where the mewing had come from. He was a youngish fellow, with a thin face, and bright, intelligent eyes. His hair was smoothly brushed, and he didn't in the least look as if he had rushed, panic-stricken, out of his house two nights before.

'Miaow,' said the kitten again, struggling to get out of Fatty's arms. The man heard the mew and looked across to the window. He saw Fatty's head and shoulders there, and made as if to draw back at once. Then he saw that Fatty was a boy, and that he was holding the kitten.

He came forward slowly. Fatty guessed that he was annoyed at having been seen. He spoke apologetically through the broken pane.

'Sorry to disturb you, sir – but this is your kitten, isn't it? We've been looking after it through the – er – upset.'

The man smoothed back his hair. He answered cautiously. 'Yes, it's my kitten. Er – wait a minute, I'll undo the kitchen door.'

He unlocked and unbolted it. Fatty was at the door, waiting. The man stretched out his hand for the kitten, and Fatty sensed that once he had taken it, he would probably say no more than a word of thanks, and shut the door.

'I say, sir – your burglary caused quite an excitement!' said Fatty, holding on to the kitten. 'The police were here – did you know?'

Mr Fellows looked startled. 'The police!' he said. 'What for? How did they know anything about the house being empty – or, er – burgled?'

Fatty thought rapidly. Mr Fellows hadn't heard then that the milkman had reported anything – he didn't know that Mr Goon had inspected the house and found it upside down. Probably he hoped that nobody knew anything at all, either about the intruder, or about his rushing out of the house!

'I'll tell you all about it, if you like, sir,' said Fatty, stepping firmly into the kitchen. Mr Fellows now obviously wanted to know what Fatty had to say. It was news to him that the police had been into his house. He looked worried.

He shut the kitchen door and locked it. He took Fatty into the little sitting-room. Everything was now tidy and in its place. Mr Fellows had obviously been very busy since he had got back, and had cleared everything up. The kitten followed, mewing.

'Does it want any milk?' asked Mr Fellows, looking down at it. 'I'm afraid there isn't any. The milkman apparently didn't come this morning.'

'No. I expect the police told him not to as you weren't here,' said Fatty. He sat down on a chair.

'What *is* all this about the police!' said Mr Fellows irritably. 'Can't a man go away for a short while without the police coming in and snooping round! I think that is most unnecessary.'

'Well, you see, apparently burglars got in and turned the place upside down while you were away,' said Fatty, watching Mr Fellows closely. 'Didn't you find everywhere in an awful mess?'

The man hesitated. He quite obviously wasn't going to say more than he needed to.

'Yes, but I'm an untidy person,' he said. 'Er

– who did you say raised the alarm to the police?'

'The milkman,' said Fatty, stroking the purring kitten. 'He found the front door wide open when he came to leave your milk yesterday morning – walked in, saw the confusion, and telephoned the police.'

'I see,' said Mr Fellows. 'This is all news to me.'

'What time did you leave your house then?' asked Fatty suddenly. He knew quite well what time it had been, because of Erb's information, but he wanted to see what Mr Fellows had to say.

The man hesitated again. 'Oh, sometime that night,' he said. 'I – er – went to visit a friend and stayed the night with him. I came back last night to find the house a little untidy, certainly. But nothing has been stolen as far as I can see. I don't see why the police had to butt in without my permission.'

'Because of the open front door,' said Fatty, patiently. 'I suppose you did shut the front door after you when you went out, Mr Fellows?'

'Of course,' said the man, but Fatty didn't believe him. He felt sure that Mr Fellows had probably only pulled it to, not wanting the intruder in the house to hear him go. It was the intruder who had left it wide open!

Fatty debated whether or not to ask Mr Fellows what he had been dressed in when he had left the house. He decided that he wouldn't. He would only be more on his guard than ever, and would anyhow lie about it. Fatty glanced at him – he looked extremely clean and tidy and well-brushed.

Not a bit like my Uncle Horatius! thought Fatty. Now, if I want to find out if he really did wander about in a dressing-gown and bedroom slippers, I'll somehow have to slip upstairs and snoop round for them. But how?

All conversation suddenly came to an abrupt end. A big red face unexpectedly appeared at the sitting-room window, and looked in. The face owned a helmet – it was Goon!

Mr Fellows gave an exclamation. 'Who's that? Of all the brazen cheek! It's the police again! What do they think they're doing, snooping and prying on private property like this? I'll put this fellow where he belongs!'

'I certainly would, if I were you,' Fatty agreed fervently. 'A man can't call his house his own these days! Are you going to let that policeman in, sir? He's speaking to you.'

Goon had just been on his rounds and had, as a matter of routine, called in at Mr Fellows' house to see if anything had happened there. As there was no smoke from the chimneys, and everything seemed quiet, he hadn't done anything but peep in at the windows. He wasn't going to enter that house alone again if he could help it!

He could hardly believe his eyes when he saw Fatty sitting there with a man who must be Fellows. He gaped at them both. Then a familiar rage boiled up in him. That boy! That toad! There he was again, poking his nose in – and getting it there before he, Mr Goon, could get in his. How did he do it?

'Open the door, sir,' bellowed Mr Goon. 'I have a few words to say to you.'

Mr Fellows glared at the red-faced policeman. He strode to the window and opened it.

'What do you mean by peering in like this at my window?' Mr Fellows asked in a furious voice. 'Can't you see I'm sitting here talking to a friend? What's the matter with you?'

'A friend?' choked Mr Goon, glaring at Fatty. 'Is that boy your friend?'

'I shall report you for this extraordinary behaviour,' said Mr Fellows. 'My house is my own, and I am not aware that I have done anything to cause the police to pry into it.'

'But – but – there's been a burglary!' spluttered Mr Goon. 'The house was all upside down, and . . .'

'There has been no burglary,' said Mr Fellows. 'As far as I know, not a single thing has been stolen. As for the house being untidy, well, I'm an untidy person. I can turn my own house upside down if I want to, can't I?'

'The front door was wide open,' persisted Mr Goon, angry and bewildered.

'I'm forgetful,' said Mr Fellows. 'I do sometimes forget to close my doors. Now, clear off – do you hear me, CLEAR OFF!'

Fatty could have hugged himself in joy. Goon was always yelling at people to clear off, and now here was someone yelling the same thing at him. But the policeman had not finished yet.

'Well, let me tell you, you've no right to go

away and leave animals to starve in the house,' he said.

'The kitten is quite all right,' said Mr Fellows coldly, and was about to shut the window when Mr Goon put an enormous dark blue arm in to stop him.

'What about the dog?' he said. 'And the pig?'

Mr Fellows stared at Mr Goon as if he had suddenly taken leave of his senses. 'What dog and what pig?' he demanded. 'Are you crazy, constable?'

'Ho! And what about the fellow who kept crying out, and wanted his auntie?' said Mr Goon, trying to force the window open.

Mr Fellows was now quite convinced that Mr Goon was raving mad. He turned to speak to Fatty – but Fatty was not there!

No, Fatty had seen a chance to creep upstairs and examine bedroom slippers and dressing-gowns, and also pyjamas. Reluctant as he was to leave the battle-ground on which Mr Fellows and Mr Goon were squabbling so fiercely, he felt that he couldn't miss this chance.

He picked up the kitten and tiptoed out of the room. He wanted the kitten with him to provide him with an excuse for going upstairs – why should anyone think it odd if the kitten fled upstairs and needed looking for?

Up the stairs went Fatty, grinning to hear Mr Goon shouting the question about the dog and the pig. Gosh, Mr Fellows would think he was quite mad!

He saw that everywhere had been tidied up. He tiptoed into the biggest room, which he guessed was Mr Fellows' bedroom. Now – where were his slippers – and pyjamas – and dressing-gown?

15. FATTY IS PLEASED

Fatty looked round the room. No slippers to be seen! He looked under the bed. Ah, a pair of red slippers lay there, rather like Larry's, but bigger. Fatty turned them upside down and examined them.

They were muddy, very muddy! Mud had even got splashed on the tops of the slippers. It was quite obvious that Mr Fellows had been wandering about the streets in these.

Fatty slipped his hand under the eiderdown and pulled out pyjamas, striped red and white. He gave a low whistle. The bottom edges of the legs were filthy dirty – splashed with mud and clay. Fatty nodded his head. Yes, that muddy clay down by the river.

Now for the dressing-gown. It was hanging in a tall cupboard. It was dirty – but it was also messed up with hay and straw – strands stuck out here and there. Where had Mr Fellows been in his dressing-gown? Fatty thought rapidly, as he shut the cupboard door.

He didn't go to stay with a friend, he hid somewhere for the rest of that night, and all day yesterday – because he didn't want to be found in his night-clothes – questions would be asked! He hid in a barn or in a haystack or rick – and crept home in the middle of last night. I bet the watchmen were surprised to see him again, if they spotted him. Gosh, they'd think my Uncle Horatius had been out again!

The angry voices downstairs had stopped. There was the sound of a window being slammed shut. Fatty dropped down on his hands and knees and began calling.

'Puss, puss, where are you? Kitty, kitty!'

A voice came up the stairs. 'What are you doing up there? Come down at once!'

'Sorry,' said Fatty, appearing at the top of the stairs. 'The kitten's run away.'

'It's down here,' said Mr Fellows. He still looked very angry. 'You clear off now. Thanks for seeing to the kitten. I've ticked that interfering policeman off, and he's gone. I've a good mind to report him.'

'I should, sir,' said Fatty earnestly.

'I think he must be mad,' said Mr Fellows, pacing nervously up and down. 'Talking about dogs and pigs and aunties.'

Fatty wanted to laugh. He glanced round, and decided that there really wasn't any more to get out of Mr Fellows, or to hunt for in the house. He had done very nicely!

'Well, good-bye, sir – and I hope the kitten will be all right now,' said Fatty. 'Sorry to intrude and all that. Fancy you not having a burglar after all!'

'Well, I didn't,' snapped Mr Fellows. 'Clear out now. I want some peace!'

Fatty cleared out, whistling softly. A most interesting interview – and how nice to find that all his ideas had been right. Those muddy slippers! My word, if Mr Goon got into the house and did a bit of snooping, he would find a few things to interest him too!

Mr Goon was lying in wait for Fatty. He emerged from behind a tree as Fatty turned down the road to go to Larry's.

'Ho!' said Mr Goon, his face purple. 'Ho!' He seemed quite unable to say anything else for the moment.

'Ho to you,' said Fatty politely. 'Many Hoes!'

Mr Goon went a deeper purple. 'So you're his friend, are you?' he said, in a choking voice. '*That's* a bit of news, that is!'

'I'm so glad,' said Fatty politely, trying to edge past.

'Do you know what you are?' said Mr Goon, losing the rest of his temper with a rush. 'You're a pest! A toad! But I've sent in my report, see – and you'll be sorry!'

'I don't see why,' said Fatty. 'I do hope you've put in the kitten, the dog, and the pig – not forgetting Auntie.'

'There wasn't any auntie,' shouted Mr Goon. 'He just *wanted* his auntie! Gah! What with you and Kenton and that fellow up yonder, my life's not worth living.'

'No. It's a poor sort of life,' agreed Fatty, suddenly seeing Larry and Daisy out of the corner of his eye in Larry's front garden. He hoped and prayed they had got Buster with them, and would have the sense to let him out of the gate.

'I suppose you think I don't know it was you muddling those night-watchmen last night?' began Goon again, going off on a new tack, with a new grievance. 'Your Uncle Horace! Pah!'

'My Uncle *Horatius,*' corrected Fatty. 'Don't muddle up my uncles, please.'

Mr Goon advanced on him, ready to tear Fatty limb from limb. Never had he felt so angry in his life. Poor Mr Goon, he was muddled and bewildered and so exasperated that he didn't know which way to turn!

'Wuff! Wuff-wuff!'

With a delighted volley of barks, Buster suddenly shot out of Larry's front gate at sixty miles an hour. He was thrilled to see Fatty, and equally thrilled to see Mr Goon, though for rather a different reason. He leapt up at Fatty, gave him a hurried lick, and then leapt at Mr Goon.

The policeman was defeated. Fatty was bad enough – but Fatty plus Buster was too much. Mr Goon gave the biggest snort of his life, flung himself on his bicycle and wobbled down the hill, one of his feet slipping frantically on a pedal. Buster flew after him, leaping and pouncing in delight.

Fatty began to laugh. He staggered into Larry's gate. Larry held him up, laughing too. The other three were there and they made their way to the shed at the bottom of the garden. Fatty collapsed on the ground, quite weak with excitement and laughter.

They held a very interesting meeting. Everyone hung on Fatty's words as he described his peculiar interview with Mr Fellows, Goon's sudden appearance, and all that Fatty had discovered in his snooping upstairs.

'Wow! Then all your reasoning was correct,' said Bets, in admiration. 'Every single thing! He *did* rush out in pyjamas and dressing-gown and slippers – and he came back in them too – after sleeping in hiding somewhere.'

'Yes. But we still don't know what he took with him when he went – or where he has hidden it,' said Fatty. 'According to Erb, he had nothing with him when he returned. He wouldn't, anyway, I suppose – because it would be senseless to take back whatever it was that was so valuable. He might find the burglar waiting for him again!'

'Yes. He's hidden it,' said Larry. 'I wonder where? We can't very well hunt in all the haystacks and ricks round about Peterswood – there are dozens of them!'

'He's very careful in all he says,' said Fatty. 'There's something going on. I wonder what it is. Gosh, we *must* try and find out before we go back to school. An unfinished mystery. How disgraceful!'

Everyone agreed, but nobody could see for the life of them how they could get any further. Mr Fellows was not likely to help them! He had something he badly wanted to hide, that was certain. *Could* they possibly go hunting in stacks and ricks? The farmers wouldn't be at all pleased.

Fatty told the others about his escapade of the night before. They laughed delightedly.

'Oh, Fatty!' said Bets. 'I never knew anyone like you in my life. And I never shall. There's just nothing you're scared of doing.'

'I was a bit scared of old Mr Goon just now,' said Fatty. 'Honestly, he looked like an angry bull. I don't blame him. I must be pretty annoying to him. I was really glad when Buster came flying out!'

'Wuff,' said Buster, thumping his tail approvingly.

'Do you think Mr Goon has got that sack of yours out of the river yet?' said Daisy. 'Whatever will he say when he finds it is full of stones and bricks! He doesn't know it was you who dumped it there, does he?'

'No. But he'll guess it was when he finds what's in the sack!' grinned Fatty. 'You should have seen me heave it in! Old Mr Goon nearly went in after it.'

'Do you think he's gone to look for it now?' asked Bets. 'He wouldn't leave it too long, would he? Let's go for a walk down to the river and see if he's anywhere about. We can bike down.'

'Yes, let's,' said Daisy. 'You've been having all the fun, Fatty – we want some now too. I'd just love to see Mr Goon digging about with a boat-hook and bringing up a sack full of stones and bricks.'

'All right. We might as well,' said Fatty, getting up. 'Walkie – walk, Buster. Come on!'

They got on their bicycles. Pip and Bets had

theirs at Larry's, as they had bicycled there that morning. They freewheeled down the hill towards the river.

Mr Goon was not there. Fatty spotted an old boatman friend of his, painting a boat outside his shed. He put his bicycle by a tree and hailed him.

'Hello, Mr Spicer! Getting ready for spring weather? It's been pretty cold lately, hasn't it?'

'Ay, that it has,' agreed old Spicer, beaming at the five children. He knew them all. 'Why aren't you back at school yet?'

'Term hasn't begun,' said Fatty. 'Are you letting out any boats yet, Mr Spicer? I suppose we couldn't have one this morning?'

'No. I've only got the one ready that you see down there,' said Spicer, nodding his head towards a little, freshly-painted boat bobbing by the bank.

'Well, why can't we have *her*?' demanded Larry, feeling that he would like a good row more than anything else.

'That bobby rang up and asked me to have one ready for him this morning,' said Spicer. 'What's his name now – Moon?'

'Mr Goon, you mean,' said Fatty. He winked at the others. So, Mr Goon *was* going to come and jab about in the river for the sack that Fatty had thrown in. Good!

'Ay, Mr Goon. Wants a boat-hook too,' said old Spicer, painting a bright red line with a steady brown hand. 'Seems like my boat-hooks are popular this morning. He's the second one wants a boat-hook.'

Fatty pricked up his ears. 'Who's the other fellow who wants a boat-hook?' he asked, wondering if it was Mr Fellows. Maybe he wanted to fish out a sack himself!

'I never seen him afore,' said Spicer. 'Big fellow – got a scar down his cheek, and something wrong with one eye. Not a nice piece of work at all, he wasn't. He offered me ten pounds for the loan of my longest boat-hook – said he wanted specimens of the weeds growing up and down the river for some botanist fellow.'

'I see,' said Fatty. The man wasn't Fellows, that was certain. Could he be the would-be burglar, the intruder who had caused Fellows to fly out of his house with a bundle of some kind?

16. DOWN BY THE RIVER

The others were all very interested in this piece of news too. They nodded to Mr Spicer and walked off till he was out of hearing.

'Strange,' said Fatty, in a low voice. 'I don't believe that yarn about jabbing for weeds at the bottom of the river. Let's see if we can find the fellow.'

'Don't let's go too far away,' begged Bets. 'I don't want to miss Mr Goon hunting for your sack, Fatty.'

'Well, you four go and watch Mr Goon when he comes, and I'll saunter up the tow-path as soon as I've asked Mr Spicer where the other fellow went,' said Fatty. 'Perhaps it would be as well if I wasn't here when Mr Goon finds that sack and opens it – he might throw the stones and the bricks at me!'

He went back to ask Spicer in which direction

the man with the boat-hook had gone. 'I'm interested in water weeds myself,' said Fatty, quite truthfully. There were very few things that Fatty was *not* interested in!

'He went up yonder,' said the old boatman, pointing up the tow-path. 'He can't have got very far.'

Fatty went up the path, leaving the others sitting on a seat just inside Spicer's shed. From there, they could easily see when Mr Goon came down to the boat. They waited expectantly, hoping for some fun.

Fatty wandered up the tow-path, keeping his eyes open for the man that Spicer had described. He soon saw him, coming back down the path. He had a pail with him, out of which water weed was hanging. Fatty wondered for a moment if the man really was getting weed for a botanist.

Fatty stopped as the man came up to him. 'Got any snails in your weed?' he asked politely. 'I want some for my garden pond.'

'Get some yourself then,' said the man, in a surly tone. He turned his back on Fatty, and looked down into the water.

'Can I help you?' asked Fatty. 'I know a bit about water weed.'

The man turned round, scowling. 'I don't like boys who hang round,' he said. 'You're not wanted, see? Buzz off!'

Fatty didn't buzz off. He merely sauntered on till he came to a clump of thick bushes. He disappeared round them, forced his way into the centre, and parted a few branches to look through. The bushes were of evergreen box, and Fatty was very well hidden.

He saw the man look back as if to see if Fatty was still anywhere near. But there was no boy to be seen, of course. The man went slowly on his way, looking into the water as he went. He came to a stop at last, and into the water went his boat-hook. He jabbed and poked at something and finally lifted it out. Fatty grinned. An old boot! Well, if he was collecting those, there were plenty in the river!

But the old boot went back with a splash and the man went on again, taking a look round every now and again as if to see if Fatty was still about.

He jabbed again, and brought up something

that disgusted him. He threw it back quickly. Another jab and up came a mass of weeds. He put some into his pail.

'That's just for show, Mr Scarred Cheek,' murmured Fatty, peering through the bush. 'In case anyone is watching you. Are you thinking that Mr Fellows has thrown the treasure, whatever it is, into the river? Or are you just a junk-hunter, wanting to make a few pounds on anything you find? No, I think not. Junk-hunters don't pay money for the loan of a boat-hook!'

The man went slowly on down the tow-path. Fatty grew bored. What were the others doing? Had Mr Goon arrived yet?

Mr Goon had! To the delight of the four watching children, and of Buster, who had not been allowed to go with Fatty, Mr Goon had arrived at full speed on his bicycle! He had jammed on his brakes, thrown his bicycle against a tree, and yelled to Spicer.

'Got that boat ready? And I want the boat-hook too please. I'm pressed for time.'

'The boat's ready yonder, and the hook's alongside,' shouted back Spicer. Goon grunted and went to the little boat. He got in and took the oars. The boat-hook lay beside him. Off he went, and soon began to pant with the effort of his rowing.

'Come on,' said Larry, jumping up. 'Let's go and watch. I'd better carry Buster though, or he might try and leap into his enemy's boat!'

'Let's not go too near till Mr Goon gets Fatty's sack of stones and bricks,' said Bets. 'Let's just saunter up and down, and wait till we see him pull up the sack.'

'Right,' said Larry. So the four of them, with a struggling Buster in Larry's arms, sauntered up and down in the January sunshine. Mr Goon soon spotted them and exclaimed angrily under his breath, 'Those kids again! Good thing for that big boy he's not with them. I don't know what I might do to him with a boat-hook ready to hand!'

He rowed to the jetty. He had decided that it would be much easier to drag up the sack from a boat rather than from the jetty. Mr Goon feared that he might overbalance if he had to bend down and jab about from the high little jetty!

He stopped rowing when he came to the

wooden jetty and drew in his oars. He took up the boat-hook and peered down solemnly into the water. His own red face peered back at him. Mr Goon looked deeper down and tried to see the bulk of a sack somewhere. But the water was very deep just there and, try as he could, he could not see the bottom.

He looked up at the jetty. Now where had that old fellow been standing when he dropped the sack into the water? Yes, just about there! Mr Goon began to prod and jab where he thought the sack might be.

He got hold of nothing but water weeds. He pulled up hundreds of green, slimy strands and exclaimed in annoyance. Weeds, weeds, weeds – where was that sack? He'd find out what that old man had got in his sack if it took him all morning to do it!

Mr Goon got very hot jabbing here and there. He suddenly sensed somebody looking at him, and glanced up. He frowned. Those kids! Now they had come to watch him! Like mosquitoes they were, always buzzing round him. Pity he couldn't slap them all away!

Ah! What was this? His boat-hook really had got hold of something this time – something fairly solid too – and fairly heavy! This must be the old man's sack! Mr Goon puffed and panted, heaved and hauled, trying to raise the sack.

It came up with a rush and Mr Goon nearly fell overboard. The four watching children gasped, and winked at one another. Mr Goon had got the sack, hurrah! Now what would happen?

They walked right on the jetty to see. Some way off, the man with the boat-hook stood, also watching, his attention suddenly caught by Mr Goon's antics. A little way behind him stood Fatty, ready to dart into Spicer's shed if Goon's anger was too great!

Mr Goon was so excited that he didn't even notice all these spectators. He heaved the bundle into the boat. Larry looked at it intently. It didn't look to him like a sack. It looked more like a laundry bag or something like that. Was it Fatty's sack that Goon had got – or was it something else?

Goon looked at the dripping bundle. He saw that it was a bag, not a sack, but he didn't worry about that. He had only seen the bundle on Fatty's back by moonlight. Bag or sack, he was absolutely certain that this was what the old man had thrown into the river last night!

He undid the string that tied the neck. He opened it wide. He put in his hand, wondering what he was going to find – the result of several burglaries, he had no doubt.

Ah, a big stone. That would be to weight it down – and another stone – and another. Goon fished them out rapidly and tossed them into the water. Splash!

The watching children now felt sure that this was Fatty's sack – look at all the stones! But now Mr Goon was rummaging deep in the bundle. His face took on a puzzled look. He couldn't feel anything except soft, dripping clothes – or what felt like clothes.

He drew one out. He shook it – and amazement spread over his face. It was a small red coat! He put it into the bottom of the boat and delved into the bundle again.

A pair of blue trousers – long ones, but far too small for a normal boy! Goon began to snort. He pulled out various things one by one – a red belt

– a blue tie – a blue cap with a red button on top – a pair of socks – and, finally, a pair of small red shoes with laces.

Goon couldn't make them out. Why would an old man in the night carry these things about in a sack? It didn't make sense. Why had the old fellow been so determined that he, Goon, shouldn't see into the sack, or take it?

Goon looked at the array of small garments, and his face grew purple once more. That boy! That toad of a boy! *He* must have been the old man! He had spoofed Mr Goon with a sack of dolls' clothes! Yes, that's what they were, dolls' clothes! That girl, Daisy, must have been in the trick too – she must have lent them to him – stuffed them into the sack ready to trick Goon into thinking the old man had stolen something, and to make Goon follow him!

'Gah,' said Goon, in angry disgust. 'Didn't he run like a hare when he'd dumped these into the water? I thought that was funny at the time. That boy was the fellow who talked to the watchmen, and he was the old man too. He's too bad to be true, that boy. I'll not keep my hands off him this time – I'll get him, and I'll stuff these things down his horrible neck, so I will. If I lose me job, I'll do it!'

Goon shoved the things back into the bag again. He was boiling with rage, and his hands shook. He'd report that toad to the Chief. He'd make the Chief do something about him. He'd go round and complain to Mr and Mrs Trotteville. The things he'd tell them about that boy of theirs!

He took up the oars and rowed away from the jetty, muttering to himself. The four children, seeing him look so fierce, decided to go back and warn Fatty. They set off on the tow-path at top speed.

They came up to Fatty, who was grinning. He had been too far away to see what had been taken out of the bundle. All he had seen were the three stones being tossed into the water. He had thought, of course, that they were some of the stones he had put into his own sack.

'Fatty! Goon's got some other sack, not yours!' said Daisy, in an urgent voice. 'It was full of clothes – dolls' clothes, they looked like. I'm sure he thinks you put them there to spoof him. You'd better go quick before he comes! He's SIMPLY FURIOUS!'

17. A WONDERFUL SCRIMMAGE – AND A DISCOVERY

Fatty listened. He was suddenly very interested. *Clothes*! That was a funny thing for anyone to dump into the river in a sack. Goon had got the wrong sack – he would of course.

'I'll pop into old Mr Spicer's shed, I think,' said Fatty. 'I'd like to see what Mr Goon does when he lands. He won't spot me in the shed.'

He disappeared into the big, dark shed and sat down on an upturned boat. The four children turned to watch Goon rowing nearer and nearer. The scarred-faced man also watched, looking very interested in the rowing policeman. He had given back his boat-hook and now had only his pail of water weed.

Goon, still purple in the face, drew in to the bank. He threw the mooring-rope over a post and clambered out, the boat rocking dangerously under his weight. He picked up the bag into which he had stuffed the wet clothes.

He looked at the four children nearby, scowling. 'Where's that friend of yours? I want him. I've got a few things to say to him!'

'What friend?' asked Larry innocently. Goon's scowl became even more ferocious.

'*You* know who I mean – that toad of a boy!' spluttered the angry policeman.

The old boatman heard him. He was still painting his boat, and looked amused at Mr Goon.

'He's in there,' he said, pointing to the shed. 'What you going to do to him, Mr Goon?'

'In there?' said Mr Goon, delighted. Aha! Now he'd show that boy something!

He strode into the dark shed, determined to do or die this time. He'd stuff these things down that boy's neck till he yelled. He'd smother him with them! That would teach him to play tricks on him again!

Fatty was taken by surprise when Goon walked in. Larry shouted a warning just too late. Goon was on Fatty before he knew it.

And then Mr Goon had the time of his life! He caught hold of the seated Fatty, held him in an iron grip, and began to stuff the wet, dripping garments down his neck, wrenching open his collar, tearing his shirt, but not caring in the least.

Fatty could do nothing. He was half-choked, to begin with, by having things forced down the front of his neck, and Mr Goon was extremely solid and strong. He struggled and heaved, and finally fell off the boat he was sitting on, landing on the earth floor of the shed. Still Mr Goon went on relentlessly pushing everything down Fatty's neck! Trousers, coat, socks, cap, shoes, one by one, down they went. Goon was absolutely determined to punish Fatty this time!

Larry ran at Goon and so did Pip. They tried to pull the furious policeman away. Old Spicer heard the noise and came in, astonished. He stopped, gaping, when he saw the scrimmage.

The man with the water weed came too. He watched with great interest, very great interest indeed.

At last, everything was down poor Fatty's neck. He felt wet and uncomfortable. Mr Goon stood up, panting, feeling uncommonly satisfied with himself.

'You got what's been coming to you for a very long time,' he panted. 'Now just you stop poking your nose into things, Mr Nosey-Parker! Stuffing that sack with rubbishy dolls' clothes, and stuffing me up too, making me think you were a bad old man with stolen goods. Ho! Now *you've* been stuffed up good and proper!'

'Mr Goon!' said old Spicer in a shocked voice. 'You're a policeman! You can't do things like this – to a boy too!'

'Gah!' said Mr Goon, rudely. 'You go and boil your head, Spicer. That boy won't complain of what I've done, I know that! And why? Because he's been plaguing me night and day, and interfering with the law. If he complains about me, I'll complain about him – but he won't! He's got a guilty conscience, he has. He's a bad lot, and one of these days he'll come to no good.'

'Mr Goon,' said Fatty, sitting up and trying to look as dignified as he could, with dripping garments down his neck and hanging out of his collar. 'Mr Goon. I give you my word of honour I didn't spoof you with these things. I've never seen them before in my life. You owe me an apology.'

'I owe you a lot of things,' said Mr Goon, 'yes, a whole lot. But not an apology. You put those things into that sack to spoof me, made me waste half a morning for nothing, and you got what you deserved – you got them in the neck! And what's more, you can keep them! Or give them back to that girl to dress up her dolls!'

And, with a perfectly marvellous snort, Mr Goon marched out of the shed. He bumped into the man with the water weed.

'Excuse me,' began the man, 'I'd just like to know where . . .'

Mr Goon snorted at him rudely and walked past, shoving him out of the way. He was feeling fine. Oh, Mr Goon was on top of the world at that moment. He could have put the Chief Inspector in his place, too, with a few well-chosen words – if only he had been there. But he wasn't, which was perhaps just as well for the triumphant Goon.

'Oh, Fatty, Fatty, are you hurt?' said Bets, in tears. She was very scared. 'Oh, Fatty; are you all right?' She began to sob.

'I'm fine, Bets,' Fatty assured her getting up and feeling himself all over. 'Don't cry, Bets, please don't. It was a wonderful fight.'

'It wasn't, it wasn't,' sobbed Bets. 'I hated it. I hate Mr Goon. I shall tell the Chief Inspector.'

'No. Mr Goon only got back at me for all the maddening things I've done to him,' said Fatty. 'He'll feel better now. You were wonderful to come to my rescue, Bets. Now please don't cry any more. That upsets me much more than Mr Goon's attack!' He put his arm round Bets.

'Cry baby,' interposed Pip, in his nice, brotherly way. 'Shut up, Bets. Don't make a fool of yourself.'

'Let her alone, Pip,' said Fatty. 'She's really scared – and I don't wonder. Goon looked a pretty nasty bit of work when he flung himself at me. But what a peculiar thing to do – to stuff these things down my neck! Ugh! They're really wet and smelly.'

'Let's get back home and fish them out,' said Larry, seeing two or three interested children coming up on their way home from school. 'Come on, Fatty. We'll get our bikes.'

Mr Spicer grinned good-bye and patted the red-eyed Bets as she passed. The water weed man stood silently watching. The school children nudged one another and grinned. Fatty really looked very strange just then.

They got on their bicycles. Fatty had recovered now. He felt a new respect for Mr Goon. Fancy him thinking of such a thing – and doing it too! Fatty shivered as he felt some cold, wet drops running down his chest.

They rode to Fatty's house and went to his shed. They locked the door. Fatty looked round. 'Hey, where's old Buster? He never came to my rescue!'

'He went off with old Spicer's terrier,' said Larry, suddenly remembering. 'Spicer said his dog would show Buster how to catch rabbits in the fields behind the boathouse, and off they went. I never thought another thing about him! Things got so exciting that I forgot about old Buster.'

'Well, I do think he might have come to my help,' said Fatty, half-vexed. 'He'd have enjoyed it too – free nips at any portion of Mr Goon that he fancied!'

'He'll come home when he's found out that, as usual, rabbits aren't really catchable,' said Daisy. 'Oh, Fatty, you *are* wet. You'd better strip off your coat and shirt and vest and put on dry ones.'

'Larry, you go indoors and get me some,' said Fatty. 'Mummy's out, so she won't want to know what you're doing, carrying my underwear about!'

Larry disappeared. Fatty took off his coat, pulled off his shirt, and stripped off his vest. It was then easy to get rid of the damp, smelly things that Goon had put down his neck. Fatty looked at them in distaste.

'Nasty wet things! Who could have been such an idiot as to dump dolls' clothes into a sack, weight them with stones, and sink them in the river. It doesn't make sense.'

'I'll take them to the dustbin,' said Daisy, gathering them up. 'That's the best place for them.'

She lumped them together – trousers, coat, tie, shoes, socks, belt, shirt, everything – and went out to the dustbin. They heard her put on the lid and then back she came again.

Larry came in too with some clean, dry clothes. Fatty was about to put them on when he wriggled.

'I've still got something down me somewhere,' he said. 'I can feel a nasty, cold, wet patch on my tummy. Perhaps it's a wet sock. Wait a minute – I really must get it.'

He wriggled his hand down and caught hold of something. 'Got it,' he said. 'I thought I felt one last thing. It's a red sock.'

He flung it down on the floor of the shed and then began to dress himself rapidly in dry clothes. Bets bent down to pick up the little red woollen thing. It was limp and shapeless.

'It's not a sock,' she said. 'It's a glove – a little red glove.'

Fatty swung his head round quickly and incredulously. Bets had got the little glove and was pulling the fingers straight. Fatty snatched it from her.

'A little red glove. *Another* one!' he said, jubilantly. 'The pair to the one I've got in my pocket! Where is it? Look! Exactly the same!'

He pulled the first little red glove out of his trousers pocket, and put it beside the one that Mr Goon had stuffed down his back. They were an exact match!

Everyone stared at the two gloves. How very, very extraordinary!

'But, what does it mean?' asked Daisy, at last. 'You found that first glove in Mr Fellows' house.'

'And Mr Goon stuffed the second one down my neck! He's given us the biggest clue yet!' said Fatty. 'Oh, dear, dear, old Mr Goon – you've nearly solved the mystery for us by stuffing things down my neck!'

18. THAT NIGHT

There was a silence after this rather peculiar statement. Nobody could quite follow it. What did Fatty mean?

'Don't stand round me looking daft like that!' said Fatty. 'Don't you *see* what this means? It means that the bag of clothes that Mr Goon hooked up is the bundle that Mr Fellows rushed off with and threw into the river – to hide! The bundle that the other fellow was after, for some reason or other!'

'But how do you know?' asked Daisy.

'Well, because I picked up one of the red gloves in a corner of the landing in Fellows' house!' said Fatty, impatiently. 'He must have pushed everything quickly into a bag to rush off to hide it somewhere, but one of the little gloves dropped out!'

'Oh, I *see*,' said Larry. 'Yes, your red glove does

prove that this bundle was the one that Fellows rushed off with in such a hurry. But, Fatty – why are these dolls' clothes so important?'

'We'll get them and see,' said Fatty. 'Daisy, go and haul them out of the dustbin again. We'll go through them carefully. There must be *some*thing to tell us why they are apparently of such importance.'

Daisy and Larry went off to get them but just as they were going back to the shed with them, they heard the voice of Mrs Trotteville's cook.

'You children! Do you know it's nearly half past one! Your mother's been telephoning here for you, Daisy, and so has Mrs Hilton for Pip! And Frederick's lunch has been waiting for him for a long time.'

'Oh, blow, blow, blow!' groaned Larry. 'Just when we were going to do something REALLY exciting!' He hurried to the shed and told the others.

Fatty looked longingly at the bundle of wet clothes. 'Well, we must wait till this afternoon. Anyway, the clothes will be drier by then. I'll take them up to my room and dry them by the fire.'

'Promise you won't examine them till we come back?' said Bets urgently.

'I promise,' said Fatty. 'Go on, now, all of you – and I hope you don't get into a row.'

They all left at top speed, fearing that they certainly *would* get into a row.

They did. Two really angry mothers met them at their doors. 'A quarter to two! What *are* you thinking of?'

The dreadful result was that not one of the four was allowed to go down to Fatty's that afternoon, nor even to leave the house! Larry and Daisy sat disconsolately in their playroom and Pip and Bets sat in theirs. Fatty waited till three o'clock and then phoned. He wasn't even allowed to *speak* to the others.

Larry's mother was cross. 'You should really not keep Larry and Daisy so late,' she said. Fatty apologised humbly and gloomily.

Mrs Hilton said a good deal more. Fatty felt even humbler when she had finished. He could hear Bets' voice calling to her mother at the end.

'Mummy! Mummy! Ask Fatty if Buster is back, please, please ask him.'

Mrs Hilton asked him. 'Yes – tell Bets he arrived an hour ago, covered in sand and awfully hungry,' said Fatty. 'I won't let him go off with old Spicer's dog again.'

He heard Mrs Hilton's receiver click down. He turned and glared at Buster who was sitting nearby, looking very guilty.

'To think you deserted me when Mr Goon attacked me!' said Fatty. 'Shameful dog! To go rabbiting when your master is in danger! Brrrrrrr!'

Fatty went up to his room and looked longingly at all the things he had put in front of the fire. They were perfectly dry now. How he longed to examine them! But no, he had promised, and it simply didn't occur to Fatty to break such a promise. He bundled all the clothes into a drawer.

The rest of the day was extremely dull. The mystery was at a standstill till the others could come and look at the curious clothes. Buster was still feeling guilty and was not at all lively. It began to pour with rain.

The other Find-Outers were not allowed out at

all that day. They sat and moped and sulked. How maddening to be kept in just when they really had got somewhere! Bets and Pip talked about the dolls' clothes.

'Funny that they should be important enough for someone to break into Mr Fellows' house and turn the place upside down for them,' said Pip.

'I bet Mr Fellows will be going out with a boat-hook too, to try and get them back,' said Bets.

'Strange that those dolls' clothes should be for a boy, not for a girl,' said Daisy to Larry.

'How mad Mr Goon would be to know that he had made a present of such an enormous clue to Fatty,' said Larry. 'I guess nobody has ever had a clue stuffed down their neck before. Just like Mr Goon!'

They all went to bed early. Both Larry's mother and Pip's were still annoyed, and only Fatty's mother was good-tempered that day – but that was because she had been out to lunch, and hadn't been kept waiting like the others!

Fatty was tired. 'More "aftermath",' he supposed. He switched off his light early and fell into a sound sleep. His parents were up in town that evening, having driven up to a theatre and a dance afterwards. They would not be back until about one o'clock in the morning, perhaps later.

At half past ten, the whole house was in darkness except for a small light left on in the hall. The two maids were in bed and asleep. Buster slept soundly too. So did Fatty.

He was suddenly awakened by Buster barking loudly. WUFF, WUFF, WUFF! He sat up with a jerk and turned on the light. A quarter to one.

'Shut up, Buster. It's only Mummy and Dad you can hear!' said Fatty, sleepily. 'Do shut up. Surely you know the sound of their car by now!'

But Buster wouldn't stop. He leapt from the bed to the floor and barked frantically. Fatty threw a book at him.

'Shut up, I tell you! It's only Mummy coming home. You know she and Dad are out. Come here, Buster.'

Buster took not the slightest notice. Fatty thought there really might be something the matter. He jumped out of bed, pulled on his dressing-gown and opened the door. A frightened voice called to him.

'Frederick? Is that you? Why is Buster barking? Is there someone in the house?'

'I expect it's just my parents coming back,' said Fatty. 'You go to bed again. Buster's gone downstairs at top speed, so you may be sure if there's anyone down there, he'll be after them!'

Buster was still barking frantically somewhere downstairs. Fatty decided to explore. He was about to go downstairs when he caught sight of his mother's bedroom. The door was open and the landing light streamed into it. It was in utter confusion!

'Gosh!' said Fatty, switching on the light. 'Look at that. Burglars! While we were all asleep!'

He looked in his father's dressing-room and into the guestroom. Both had had their drawers and cupboards rifled and turned out. Fatty ran downstairs. Buster was standing by an open window in the sitting-room, barking madly.

'It's no good barking *now*, Buster,' said Fatty, glancing round the sitting-room, which was in as much muddle and confusion as the other rooms. 'The thief is gone – he must have been about to come into my room when you heard him and awoke. He's gone out of the same window he came in by. I wonder what he's taken. Not Mummy's jewellery, I hope.'

There came the sound of a car up the drive. It was his parents returning home. Fatty heaved a sigh of relief. Now they could take matters in hand.

Mr and Mrs Trotteville were horrified when they came indoors and saw all the confusion in so many rooms. Mrs Trotteville rapidly looked through her jewellery and valuables. They were all intact.

'It's peculiar,' she said, after about twenty minutes' search. 'I can't see that *any*thing has been taken. Even the pearl necklace I left on my dressing-table hasn't been taken. What did the thief come for?'

Fatty suddenly knew! The intruder must have been the same one who had searched Mr Fellows' house. And he had been looking for the same thing – the dolls' clothes! But why – why – why?

Fatty raced up to his room to see if they were still safe. Yes, they were there in the drawer into which he had thrown them. What a blessing he hadn't left them down in the kitchen to dry, as he had first thought of doing. He had only taken them up to his room so that awkward questions would not be asked by anyone who saw such strange things drying on the kitchen airer!

But how did the burglar know that the clothes were now in Fatty's house? Fatty soon thought that one out. The man with the water weed! He had been looking on while Mr Goon had stuffed the wet clothes down Fatty's neck. *He* had been looking for them that morning too – but it was Mr Goon who had found them – and thrown them away on Fatty!

How wild the water weed man must have been when he saw something he badly wanted being stuffed down a boy's neck! He must have asked old Spicer who Fatty was and where he lived – and then he had come to try and get the clothes back that night.

Fatty looked at the clothes in the drawer. 'There's something extraordinarily valuable about you,' he said solemnly. 'Maybe we'll find out tomorrow.'

He heard his mother talking to his father. 'Are you going to phone the police?'

'No, I'm not,' said his father's voice. 'I don't want that flat-footed policeman stamping all over my house late at night! There's nothing gone, as far as I can see. We'll let Mr Goon sleep in peace!'

'Thank goodness,' said Fatty, sliding into bed. 'I just don't feel like seeing Mr Goon again tonight.'

19. EXAMINING THE CLOTHES

To Fatty's relief, his father decided next day not to inform Mr Goon of the attempted robbery at all. Mr Trotteville had no great opinion of Mr Goon, and was not disposed to waste a morning with him.

'He'd ask asinine questions, and waste everybody's time,' said Mr Trotteville. 'Just have new fastenings put on all the windows, my dear, and another bolt on the front and back door. And perhaps Buster had better sleep downstairs.'

Buster had other views, however. He had heard suggestions like this before, but however firmly he was put into a basket in the hall and told to be on-guard, he was invariably to be found lying on Fatty's bed in the morning. As Mr Trotteville said, it was most extraordinary the way that Buster could find his way through a closed bedroom door!

Fatty telephoned the others. 'Come on down as soon as you can,' he said. 'I've news. We've had robbers in the night. No – nothing taken, as far as I can see. Old Buster drove them off. Hurry up and come down.'

They met down in the shed at the bottom of Fatty's garden. Fatty kept a good lookout for the water weed man, as he called him, when he took the clothes down to the shed. He wouldn't have been surprised to have him pounce on him from behind a tree! However, Buster trotted happily in front, and nothing untoward happened at all. Fatty was safely ensconced in the shed when the others came tapping at the door.

He shut the door and locked it. He pulled the curtains over the windows, and lit the little oil-lamp so that they were not in complete darkness.

'Why all the mystery?' asked Daisy, surprised. 'Going to do conjuring tricks, or something?'

'No. But that water weed man is somewhere around, I bet,' said Fatty. 'And I don't want him peeping in at the window while we're examining those clothes. He's dead keen on getting them. He's made two break-ins already in different houses to get them. I don't want to have to give them up at gun-point.'

'Gracious, Fatty!' said Bets, in alarm.

'It's all right, Bets. And now for the clothes,' said Fatty, taking them out of the box he had put them in. 'Use your eyes well – there's obviously something we mustn't miss! Now, the trousers first!'

He shook out the blue trousers. They were long ones, with little buttons at the top. 'No pockets,' said Fatty. 'Don't dolls' clothes ever have pockets, Bets?'

'Oh yes, sometimes,' said Bets. 'Aren't they dear little trousers? – a boy doll would look nice in those. Let me have them, Fatty.'

Bets took them. She turned them inside out. There was nothing that would tell them anything – they were just trousers with buttons. Bets passed them round to the others, and then Fatty put them down.

'Red belt for the trousers,' he said, and passed it round. 'Quite ordinary. A little brass buckle, a bit rusty – due to the river water, I suppose.'

It was duly examined. Then came the socks.

Those were turned inside out too. Bets hunted for any name marked on them, but there wasn't one.

'Dolls never have their names marked on their clothes, silly,' said Pip, when Bets remarked why she was looking so carefully.

'Mine do,' said Bets. 'I borrowed Mummy's marking tape and ink, and I've marked all my biggest doll's clothes with her name – Pamela Mary. Pass the shoes, Fatty. Gosh, aren't they small!'

'Well, they're small for a child, but big for a doll,' said Fatty. 'Very nice shoes, though – strong and well made – not like the usual dolls' shoes. These have real laces in too.'

'I suppose these clothes *couldn't* belong to some child – some tiny little child?' said Larry.

'Well, I suppose they might,' said Fatty. 'But for the life of me, I can't see why they're so important, whether they belong to a doll or a child! Not worth breaking into two houses for anyway!'

Bets undid the laces and did them up again. They really were nice little shoes! She showed one to Buster. He sniffed at it.

'Buster, who does it belong to?' said Bets.

'Go on, tell us! Surely you can tell by the smell! Whose smell is it?'

'Wuff!' said Buster, and pawed at the shoe. Bets dodged it away, and Buster sprang at it. He got it in his mouth and ran off with it triumphantly. He stuffed it into a corner and sat down on it, as if to say, 'It's mine now.'

'Bring it here, Buster,' said Bets. 'It's ours!' Buster took it into his mouth and ran round the shed to hide it somewhere. He was in a silly mood that morning and had already run off with Daisy's handkerchief and Fatty's pencil.

'Don't take any notice of him,' said Fatty. 'He's got one of his show-off fits on. Probably feels very grand because he scared off a burglar last night. All right, Buster, be an idiot if you want to. Look, here's the coat, complete with buttons and collar!'

That was examined too. Fatty ran his hands down the lining. Could there be anything hidden there that might be of value? No, he could feel nothing.

Everyone examined it solemnly. It was a well made little coat, of good material, strong and very little worn.

'The longer we look at these things, the more puzzled I feel,' said Fatty. 'Who wore them – and why should they have been stolen? At least, I suppose they *were* stolen . . .'

'By Mr Fellows, do you mean?' asked Larry. 'But how do we know he stole them?'

'Well, why should he have them and hide them as he did?' said Fatty. 'What beats me is why they are apparently of such importance. Here's the tie, look – and the cap. Nice cap. Very nice indeed. Quite a cheeky cap, in fact!'

He set it on his large head at a comical angle. Bets laughed. 'You look terrible, Fatty. Take it off.'

'Even battier than usual,' said Pip, and got a punch from Fatty. Buster, always ready for a battle, flung himself on the two boys, barking. Fatty sat up and pushed him away.

'Where's that shoe?' he said, severely. 'You bring it back here, and we'll admit you into the family circle again. And what have you done with my pencil? If you've chewed the end off, you can count it as your dinner, because you won't get any more!'

Buster retired to his corner, his tongue hanging

out. Bets thought he looked sweet. She liked him when he was 'showing off'!

'Is that all the clothes?' asked Daisy, examining the cap carefully when Fatty handed it round. 'I simply can't see anything out of the ordinary about these things at all – except that they're better made and stronger than ordinary dolls' clothes. I can't think why they are important.'

'Neither can I. But they must be,' said Fatty. He gazed at the pile of clothes rather gloomily. 'I wouldn't a bit mind Mr Goon having stuffed them down my neck if only they'd prove to be really worthwhile – help us with this rather peculiar mystery. Though I'm beginning to think we may be making a mountain out of a molehill, and that it's not a mystery at all.'

'Well, we've only got two or three days more to solve it,' said Bets. 'I don't think I could *bear* to go back to school without knowing the solution of this strange little mystery. Do you suppose we ought to take these dolls' clothes back to Mr Fellows?'

'Well, yes – I suppose we should,' said Fatty. 'I actually hadn't thought of that. We could ask him what *his* explanation is – we might find out something after all! We'll take them this afternoon. He'll be astonished to see them, I bet! He probably thinks they're still safe in the river!'

'I do WISH we'd managed to find some clue hidden in the clothes,' said Bets. 'I'm sure there must be. Let me go through them just once more, Fatty, before you put them away.'

'You think you might discover something that all five of us couldn't see?' said Pip, scornfully. 'What a hope!'

'It's always a good thing to have another check on anything if you feel you must,' said Fatty, handing the bundle of clothes to Bets. 'They're all there, Bets, except the shoe that Buster took. Hey, Buster, bring back the shoe, old fellow.'

But before Buster could do as he was told, Bets gave a loud exclamation that made everyone jump. She was examining the little red coat, and she looked up, her eyes shining.

'Look – we missed this – a little white handkerchief embroidered with daisies, and it's got a name embroidered on it too – very small!'

'Where was it?' asked Fatty, almost snatching the tiny hanky.

'There's a very small pocket here inside the coat-cuff,' said Bets, showing the others. 'So well hidden that none of us saw it. Fatty, what's the name on the hanky?'

Fatty spread out the tiny hanky so that all the Find-Outers could see the little daisies on it and the name that was embroidered all round them, making a circle of the letters.

Fatty spelt it out. 'E-U-R-Y-C-L-E-S. Eurycles! What a name.'

'Never heard it in my life,' said Larry. 'It's Greek, isn't it?'

'Yes. Greek,' said Fatty. 'Wait – wait – I've heard it before. Who was Eurycles? I'm remembering – yes, I'm remembering. EURYCLES! Of course, I remember now. What a clue!'

20. MR EURYCLES – AND A TALK WITH GOON

The others stared at Fatty in excitement. What was the clue? Who was Eurycles the Greek? And why did it matter who he was?

'Listen,' said Fatty. 'Eurycles was a Greek who lived ages ago, but he happened to be a very well-known Greek, because he had a peculiar gift – he was a ventriloquist! He was such a good one that he's never been forgotten, and he had dozens of pupils.'

'I thought ventriloquists were all modern,' said Daisy, in astonishment. 'I mean, I thought it was something that people had thought of in the last century.'

'Good gracious, no – it's a very old art,' said Fatty. 'It was well known in Greece, and all kinds of nations have practised it – the Zulus, for instance – and the Eskimos. And Eurycles the Greek was a very fine ventriloquist. I read about him when I was teaching myself to ventriloquise and to throw my voice to a distance.'

'Yes, but why should this doll's hanky have an old Greek ventriloquist's name on it?' said Daisy. 'And why is it important? I simply don't understand, Fatty. Do explain.'

'Now listen,' said Fatty, thrilled. 'When hankies are embroidered with somebody's name, that name usually belongs to the owner of the hanky, doesn't it? Right, either the one who owned that hanky and wore these clothes was called Eurycles – or his *master* was. Mr Eurycles – what could he be but a ventriloquist, and what could these clothes belong to but his talking doll?'

The others followed this with interest, and at the end Pip exclaimed, 'Of course, of course, of course – why didn't we think of it? The clothes were worn by a big doll belonging to a ventriloquist – that's why they are a bit smaller than a child's and rather big for an ordinary doll, and that's why they are very well made.'

'Yes. And I bet he is owned by someone whose stage name is Mr Eurycles, after the old Greek ventriloquist,' said Fatty, jubilantly. 'I see daylight at last!'

'Well, it's more than I do,' said Larry. 'What kind of daylight can you see? It's true that we think we know who the clothes are worn by, and probably the name of the man who owns the doll who wears the clothes . . .'

'That lived in the house that Jack built!' said Daisy, with a giggle.

'Well,' said Fatty, 'we've only got to find Mr Eurycles and ask him why the clothes are so important – why they were in Mr Fellows' custody, why they were important enough for someone to try and steal them twice, and why Mr Fellows fled out in the night to dump them in the river? Once Mr Eurycles tells us that, the mystery is solved!'

'But how do we find Mr Eurycles?' said Pip, after a pause. 'It might take ages. And we're going back to school so soon.'

There was a silence, which deepened into gloom. Only Fatty remained confident.

'I'll telephone the place that sells things for conjurers and ventriloquists,' he said. 'They'll soon tell me if there's a Mr Eurycles.'

'Or Mr Fellows might tell us,' said Daisy, suddenly.

'Yes, he might,' said Fatty. 'And he might not. If he's stolen the clothes himself from Mr Eurycles, he won't want to say very much. I'll tell you what we'll do – we'll take the clothes to him this afternoon and see his face when we show them to him – and we'll fire a few questions at him before he's got time to recover from his surprise.'

'Right,' said Larry. 'Well, let's put them away till we're ready to take them. I'm sure I heard your mother in the garden just now, Fatty, and she might want to know why we're all playing with dolls' clothes if she walks into the shed!'

The clothes were bundled anyhow into a box. Fatty shut down the lid.

'There's the hanky, look,' said Bets, holding it out to him. 'It's such a dear little hanky. I suppose I couldn't keep it in my pocket till we take the clothes to Mr Fellows, Fatty? I won't blow my nose on it.'

'Yes. You keep it,' said Fatty. 'And congratulations on finding the one thing that led us to the right solution! We're well on the way to solving the whole thing now! Very good, Bets!'

Bets blushed, and put the little hanky into her pocket. It *was* a bit of luck finding that tiny pocket in the sleeve of the little red coat!

'I vote we go and have some hot chocolate again at the café,' said Fatty. 'And some macaroons if they've made any fresh ones. I feel just like three or four macaroons.'

'Yes, all gooey and crunchy,' said Pip. 'I suddenly feel like a macaroon too. Come on. You do have some bright ideas, Fatty.'

They went out of the shed with Buster delightedly prancing round their ankles. Fatty locked the door, and they all went up the path to the garden gate.

They bicycled to the café with Buster running beside them. Fatty thought it would be good for him to have a quick run. 'Take off some of his fat,' he said. 'A fat Scottie is an offence to the eye. Do you hear that, Buster?'

'Wuff, wuff,' panted Buster. Bets giggled.

'He says that a plump master is also an

offence to the eye!' she said. Fatty stared at her in amazement.

'Bets! You've got very bright – and very cheeky all of a sudden!'

'I know. It just popped into my head,' said Bets, with another giggle. 'Sorry, Fatty. Look out, you nearly wobbled over Buster.'

'There's Mr Goon,' said Larry suddenly. 'Look – coming round the corner on his bike. Let's hope he doesn't hang round us.'

'He's probably hoping we won't hang round *him*,' said Fatty, getting off his bicycle and putting it outside the café window. 'Come on in. I smell fresh macaroons!'

They all trooped in. The little shop-woman beamed at them. They were very good customers indeed! Children always were. They ate twice as much as any grown-up who came into her shop!

'Hot chocolate for everyone, please – and macaroons,' said Fatty, sitting down at a table.

'Five macaroons?' asked the shop-woman, with a twinkle.

'Gosh, no – ten, to start with, just so we won't look too greedy,' said Fatty, with a grin.

'They're newly made,' said the little woman, warningly. 'Don't you eat too many.'

'Are you trying to put us off your magnificent macaroons?' said Fatty. 'What a hope! Ten, please – just to start with.'

Mr Goon came in. He was looking worried. 'You all right?' he said to Fatty, in an offhand voice. Fatty stared at him, amazed.

'Why this sudden concern for my health, Mr Goon?' he said. 'Why shouldn't I be all right? Are *you* in good health? Let me see your tongue. Say ninety-nine – or one hundred and sixty-two and a half, if you like.'

'Perhaps he's feeling sorry he behaved so badly yesterday,' said Bets, unexpectedly, giving Mr Goon a really fierce glare. 'Stuffing things down people's necks.'

'Shut up, young Bets,' said Fatty. 'It was a good scrum while it lasted.' He looked at Mr Goon, puzzled. It wasn't like the bad-tempered policeman to feel concerned about anything he had done to Fatty. There was something behind this. Fatty wondered what it was.

The hot chocolate and macaroons arrived.

Fatty threw another glance at Mr Goon. He was standing looking round the café, as if he had something to say and didn't know how to begin. What *could* have happened?

'Hot cocoa, sir – and a bun or macaroon?' said the little shop-woman. 'Just newly made.'

'No thanks – er – well, yes, I think I will,' said Goon, changing his mind suddenly. He sat down at the table next to the children's. He really did look worried.

He made the five children feel so uncomfortable that they fell silent. Buster was tied to the leg of the table, but even he didn't seem inclined to bait Mr Goon that morning.

Mr Goon suddenly cleared his throat with an enormous noise. 'Now he's going to talk!' whispered Pip.

'Er – you heard from Chief Inspector Jenks lately?' blurted out Goon, suddenly.

'Not a word,' said Fatty promptly. Goon at once looked vastly relieved. He edged his chair a little nearer to the children's table.

'See here,' he said to Fatty, 'I want a talk with you. Friendly-like.'

'You mean you won't fling yourself at me and stuff things down my neck?' said Fatty, attacking a macaroon. 'In a word – friendly-like.'

'It's like this,' said Goon, with his mouth full. 'You see – well – it's like this, Frederick. Er, well . . .'

'Get on, Mr Goon, and say what you want to say,' said Fatty, beginning to be impatient. 'Good gracious – you sound as if you can't say gah to a goose this morning.'

Bets gave a sudden giggle. Gah to a goose. That was just like Fatty.

Goon made a great effort and came to the point. 'It's like this,' he said. 'You remember that time we were in Mr Fellows' house together – the time you *said* you were looking for the kitten?'

'Yes,' said Fatty.

'Well, do you remember hearing a dog growl and a pig grunt, and a man groaning?' said Mr Goon, earnestly.

'The one who longed for his auntie?' said Fatty. 'I've often wondered if she ever went to comfort him. Yes, I remember. Why? What about it?'

'Well, I made out a report for the Chief

Inspector, see?' said Goon. 'Put it all in, pig and all. And the man who said he never did it and kept on about his auntie.'

'Yes. Do get to the point,' said Fatty. 'I can hardly wait!'

'I sent in the report,' said Goon, miserably. 'And the Chief don't believe a word of it. Not one word! He wasn't half snorty about it over the phone this morning. So I told him you were there too, Frederick, and heard the whole lot. I said you were a proper witness of all the facts, though I hadn't said so in the report.'

'I see,' said Fatty, at once understanding not only Goon's gloom but also his sudden anxiety to be on good terms with him! 'You want me to back you up, I suppose?'

'Yes. You see, you did hear all those noises too, didn't you?' said Goon anxiously.

'I bet you exaggerated everything in your report,' said Fatty. 'I'll back you up in any facts, but not in any exaggerations, Mr Goon. That's flat.'

Goon drummed his fingers on the table top. 'I may have let meself go a bit,' he admitted. 'I don't rightly remember. But the thing is – you were with me, Frederick, and you did hear things, didn't you?'

'All right, Mr Goon. But I don't see why you had to go and write a fairytale about the silly happenings in Mr Fellows' house,' said Fatty, crossly. He was beginning to feel distinctly uncomfortable himself. Suppose the Inspector demanded full explanations? Fatty would feel extremely small. He could only hope that nothing more would come of this.

'Thanks, Frederick,' said Goon, breathing more easily. 'We've had our scraps, like, and called each other bad names – but I knew I could depend on you to back up the truth. Thanks.'

He paid his bill and got up to go. A voice came weakly from the corner of the café. 'I never did it, I never, I never! I never did it, I . . .'

But Goon was gone – gone like a hare before the hounds. With one horrified glance at the corner, he tore out of the café. Was he being haunted? That voice, that awful voice!

21. A DREADFUL SHOCK

There was a startled silence. The voice had come so suddenly, and sounded so pathetic! Then Pip gave Fatty a vigorous punch.

'Gosh, you startled me! You might warn us when you're going to do that, Mr Eurycles!'

'I swallowed half my macaroon,' complained Larry. 'You made me jump.'

'Oh, Fatty, how *do* you do it?' said Bets. 'You sent poor Mr Goon out at sixty miles an hour! I bet he's puzzled – he didn't wait for "I want Auntie"!'

'Serves him right,' said Fatty. 'What does he want to go and write an idiotic report about pigs and dogs and groaning men for? They weren't important. I bet he spread himself too – put in bits about snarling, and the patter of pigs' feet, and the sound of a wounded man dragging himself over the floor! I know Mr Goon!'

'And now, I suppose, as he's told the Chief you

were there, you'll be asked all about it too,' said Bets. 'Whatever will you say to him? Will you tell him it was all you?'

'I don't know,' said Fatty, looking gloomy. 'Blow Mr Goon! I bet he was worried in case I said I wouldn't back up his poppy-cock story. But I'll have to.'

'Any more macaroons, Fatty?' asked Pip. 'There's one left.'

'No, thanks. This has rather spoilt my appetite,' said Fatty.

'Well, you've had four macaroons, if not five, so you can't have much appetite left to spoil,' remarked Larry. 'Finish up the macaroon, Pip?'

Surprisingly enough, no one wanted it. 'I'll go a splash and buy it for Buster,' said Pip. 'He's been so good and quiet.'

Buster was surprised and thrilled. He gulped the macaroon down at once.

'I call it a waste of a macaroon to gulp it down without a single crunch,' said Pip, looking at Buster. 'You dogs haven't learnt the art of eating yet. Wasn't he good with Mr Goon this morning, Fatty?'

'Yes. He must have known Mr Goon was in need of comfort, and wanted someone to hold his hand and say "There, there" to him,' said Fatty, still cross. 'Gone all soft-hearted, Buster? Gah!'

They got up and went off to find their bicycles. Fatty paid the bill. It was a very large one, considering it was only for hot chocolate and macaroons. Still, as Fatty said, school was looming horribly on the horizon and they might as well make hay and eat macaroons while they could!

They biked back to Fatty's, as there was still an hour before lunch. 'But we MUST leave in good time today,' said Pip. 'I really believe Mother will send us to bed on bread and water if we're late again. You're lucky not to have a fierce mother, Fatty.'

'Oh, ours isn't *fierce*, Pip,' said Bets, protesting. 'She's just keen on rules being kept. I wouldn't change our mother for anything.'

'Nor would I, idiot,' said her brother. 'But you can't deny she was pretty fierce yesterday. The thing is, we MUST leave early.'

'Let's go down to the shed again,' said Larry. 'I

left a book there. It's a detective story I thought you mightn't have read, Fatty.'

'Fatty's read every single detective story that's ever been written!' said Bets. 'He's . . . why, Fatty, what's up?'

Fatty had thrown his bicycle suddenly to the ground when they came to the shed, and had rushed up to the door with a cry. He swung round.

'Someone's been here! The lock's forced! The door's ajar – and just LOOK at the inside of the shed!'

The five stared at the shed. Fatty had swung the door open, and inside were piled all the shed's contents in an incredible muddle. All Fatty's 'disguises' had been torn from their pegs or from their chest and had been flung down. Boxes had been opened and their contents thrown out. It was a scene of utmost confusion and chaos.

'Oh, Fatty!' said Bets, trembling. 'Oh, Fatty!'

'Look at that!' said Fatty, angrily. 'That burglar fellow has been HERE while we were out – and he's messed up everything – and what's more, I'll bet he's taken those dolls' clothes!'

Fatty was right. The precious clothes were

gone. Their biggest, finest clue! The box into which Fatty had thrown them was empty. Not even a sock was left! The thief had found at last what he had looked for so persistently.

Fatty sat down on a box and groaned. This was a real shock to him. 'Why did we leave the things here?' he almost wailed. 'Why didn't we take them with us? Now we're finished – nothing to show for all our work at all!'

'It must have been the thief we heard in the garden when we thought it was just your mother,' said Larry. 'Oh, Fatty, isn't this a blow?'

'Well, we can't take the clothes and tackle Mr Fellows now,' said Pip. 'I don't see that there's anything we can do. Whatever made us leave the things here for the thief to get? And we even go out and leave the coast clear for him. We must have been mad.'

'We were worse. We were fatheads,' said Fatty, in deep dejection. 'I blame myself. How could I be such a mutt?'

It was no good talking about it. The thing was done. The thief had come and gone and had taken what he wanted away with him. Fatty heard a sound near the shed and went out to see if it was the gardener.

It was. 'Mr Hedges, have you seen any stranger about this morning?' he asked. 'Someone's been into my shed.'

'Well, I'll be blowed!' said Hedges. 'That would be that fellow with the scarred cheek, I expect. A nasty chap he looked. I turned him away once. He was trying to make me give him an order for manure. I found him in the garden! He said he was looking for me, Frederick – but I guess he was looking about for what he could steal.'

Fatty nodded and went back to the others. He was very down in the dumps. 'It was the water weed man all right,' he said. 'The gardener said he had a scarred cheek, so that proves it was the fellow we know. Blow, blow, blow! I'll never forgive myself for this.'

'Let's tidy up,' said Bets. 'We can't leave you to put everything back in its place by yourself. Come on, Daisy, I'll hand you Fatty's disguises to hang up.'

Everyone was soon busy putting the shed tidy again. It took quite a long time. As Bets was picking up a few things, she gave a sudden exclamation.

'I've just remembered – the tiny hanky with daisies on it and the name Eurycles is in my pocket,' she said. 'The thief wouldn't have found it with the other clothes.'

Everyone stared at it. 'Well,' said Fatty, fingering it, 'you'd better keep it for yourself, Bets – it's not much good to us now.'

Bets put the tiny hanky back into her pocket. She felt rather bad. It was all that was left of their wonderful collection of clues. She went on tidying up everything with the others.

'Better shove all the rest of the things into that chest,' said Fatty at last, looking at his watch. 'You ought to go. It's getting near dinnertime.'

So the last few armfuls were flung higgledy-piggledy into the chest, and the lid was shut down. Then the four got their bicycles, shouted good-byc to Fatty, and raced off.

Fatty went slowly back to the house. He was very depressed. Things had been going so well. Now all they had left of their biggest clue was the tiny hanky with 'Eurycles' embroidered on it. And a fat lot of good that was, Fatty reflected. Was there much point in trying to find out if there was a ventriloquist called Mr Eurycles? Fatty thought not. He was beginning to feel fed-up with the whole thing.

'Oh, there you are, Frederick,' said his mother, as he came slowly in. 'Dear me, you do look miserable! Cheer up! A great friend of yours telephoned this morning but you were out, so he's telephoning this afternoon.'

'Who's that?' asked Fatty, not at all interested. It was probably one of his school friends, he thought. How boring! He would see enough of them in a few days! Poor Fatty was indeed feeling depressed!

'It was Chief Inspector Jenks,' said his mother, expecting Fatty to be delighted. He thought the world of the Chief, who knew all the children very well, and had often welcomed their help in many curious mysteries.

But, far from pleasing him, the news made Fatty feel more down in the dumps than ever. Now he'd have a very difficult and awkward telephone conversation with the Chief. Chief Inspector Jenks had a high opinion of Fatty's capabilities, but a low opinion of some of his jokes. Fatty felt that things were getting worse than ever.

He ate a very poor lunch, though whether it was because he was worried, or had had too many macaroons, he didn't know. Probably both, he thought.

The telephone rang immediately after the meal ended. 'That's the Chief Inspector, Frederick,' said his mother. 'You answer it, will you?'

Fatty went. He picked up the receiver. 'Hello!' he said. 'This is . . .'

'Ah, Frederick!' interrupted a voice. 'It's you. Good. I wanted to speak to you.'

'Delighted, sir,' said Fatty, most untruthfully.

'Listen, I've had a most extraordinary report in from Goon,' said the Chief. 'He's sent in plenty of peculiar reports in his time – but this beats them all. It's so extraordinary that I didn't believe it. But when I telephoned him, he not only swore it was true but said that you would back him up. He said you were a witness to all the things in his report – though why he didn't mention you were there, when he wrote his report, I don't know.'

'Quite, sir,' said Fatty, politely.

'Apparently Goon went to inspect a house that was empty and that had been reported as burgled,' said the Chief, sounding very businesslike and brisk. 'He says that there was a kitten there, mewing – a dog which growled most ferociously, and snarled, and was ready, so he infers, to eat him up – and a pig – a *pig*, P-I-G – that grunted somewhere and stamped about overhead. Really, Frederick, I am ashamed to quote from this report!'

Fatty couldn't help grinning into the telephone. Goon had certainly let himself go!

'Go on, sir,' he said.

'And to crown everything, Goon reports that there was a wounded man in the house, who was groaning and dragging himself about somewhere, crying out "I never did it, I never. Oooooh, I never did it. Where's my auntie?" It sounds quite incredible, Frederick.'

'It does, sir,' said Fatty, trying to keep his end of the phone very business-like, and not give away anything.

There was a pause. 'Are you still there,

Frederick?' said the Chief. 'Well, I may as well tell you that as soon as Goon told me you were in the house with him, I smelt a rat! Not a dog or a pig or any other animal, Frederick, but a rat. Do you understand me?'

'Er – yes, I think I do, sir,' said Fatty.

There was another pause. Then the Chief's voice came again, a harder note in it. 'I imagine I am correct in thinking that you had something to do with the extraordinary things in this report?' he rapped out.

'Well, yes, sir,' said Fatty, wishing this one-sided conversation would end. He didn't like the sound of the Chief's stern voice at all!

'Exactly what did you have to do with it?' asked the Chief. 'Please be a little more explicit, Frederick. I'm getting tired of this yes-sir, no-sir business. You usually have plenty to say for yourself.'

'Yes, sir. Well, it's like this,' said Fatty, desperately. 'I've been practising ventriloquism, and . . .'

'Practising *what*!'

'VENTRILOQUISM,' shouted Fatty.

'Oh, ventriloquism,' repeated the Chief. 'Good

heavens! I didn't think of that. Bless us all – *ventriloquism*! What next? What an absolute menace you are, Frederick. There's no other word for it – a menace.'

'Yes, sir,' said Fatty, sensing that the Chief was not feeling *quite* so angry. 'I say, sir, there's a bit of a mystery on here – and I want to get hold of a ventriloquist myself. A man called Mr EURYCLES. How can I find out about him?'

There was a startled pause. 'Did you say Eurycles?' came the Chief's voice in amazement. 'Now why do you want to see *him*? Wait – don't say a word more over the telephone – not a word. I'm coming straight over. Keep your mouth shut till I come!'

22. AN EXCITING MEETING

There was a click as the Chief put down his receiver. Fatty put back his too, feeling rather dazed. What an abrupt ending! Why was the Chief so astonished? Did he know about their little 'mystery' then? Did he actually know anything about Mr Eurycles?

It was all very puzzling. Fatty rubbed his nose. He wasn't altogether pleased at the idea of seeing Chief Inspector Jenks that afternoon. He didn't particularly want the subject of dogs and pigs and groaning men reopened, and it might quite well be.

Mrs Trotteville was curious to know what the conversation had been about. She had heard the word 'ventriloquism', because Fatty had shouted it so loudly.

'What's this about ventriloquism, Frederick?' she asked. 'Did I hear you say you were practising it? I do wish you wouldn't. I suppose that explains all those peculiar noises that keep coming from your room when you are up there alone.'

'Yes, Mummy. But don't you get all hot and bothered about it,' said Fatty. 'I'll be back at school in a very short time. Then the house will be nice and quiet. By the way – er – the Chief Inspector is coming over here this afternoon. Do you mind if I get the other four along? They'll like to see him – especially Bets.'

'Yes, get them along if you like,' said his mother. 'But, Frederick – I hope all this doesn't mean you've been mixing yourselves up again in matters that don't concern you. I really did hope you'd not lead the others into trouble these holidays.'

Fatty was indignant. 'I *never* lead them into trouble! Mummy, how can you say such a thing! Why, even the Inspector has often told me that . . .'

'All right, Frederick,' said his mother. 'I am not going to argue with you. Telephone the others and see if they can come to tea. There is a nice new batch of cakes in today – and I brought in some macaroons from the café. You haven't had any for a long time.'

Not so very long, thought Fatty, pleased at the idea of a few more that afternoon. He went to telephone the others but, remembering the Chief's injunction to 'keep his mouth shut', he gave them no hint as to the unexpected visit, though he would dearly have liked Bets to know. She was very fond of the 'high-up policeman,' as she used to call him.

It's a pity we've got to tell the Chief that we were idiotic enough to leave the dolls' clothes unguarded, so that they were stolen, thought Fatty. That won't be a very good mark for me! I can't think how I was such a fathead. Well, the deed is done.

The Chief arrived first, in his big, black, shiny car, driven by a police-driver and, surprisingly, with him came a distinguished-looking man in plain clothes.

Fatty was at the door when the car came up the drive and stopped outside. He welcomed the Chief with pleasure. The big, burly, good-looking man grinned at Fatty.

'Well, you menace? I've a good mind to cast you off and have no more to do with you!' He turned to the tall, quiet man by his side.

'Sir, this is the boy I was telling you about. He plagues the local police, but at times he's been very useful to me. He's dependable and responsible, so you can tell him what you like. Let me introduce Frederick Trotteville.'

Fatty shook hands solemnly. He noticed that the Chief didn't tell him the tall man's name. It was obvious that he was a very big noise, Fatty thought. Probably in the Secret Service – or Scotland Yard. Anyway, a bit hush-hush. Fatty looked at him in awe.

They all went into the sitting-room, where a bright fire was burning. Mrs Trotteville had gone out to one of her bridge afternoons. Fatty was thankful. He didn't particularly want his mother to be present if his escapades with Goon were to be gone into.

They sat down. 'Now, first of all, Frederick, what do you know about Mr Eurycles?' asked the Chief, coming straight to the point as usual.

'Not much,' confessed Fatty. 'I'd better tell you

everything from the beginning, sir, then you'll see how we finally arrived at Mr Eurycles. It's a funny little story – we got mixed up in it somehow – but it's rather interesting.'

'Fire away,' said the Chief, 'we're listening. I may take a few notes as you relate your tale, but don't let that worry you. Now then?'

Fatty was just beginning his tale when he heard the loud ringing of four bicycle bells, and Buster began to bark and paw at the door.

'Oh – it's the others, sir,' said Fatty, apologetically. 'Do you mind if they come in too? I mean – they were all in it.'

'Fetch them in,' said the Chief, and Fatty went to the window, threw it up, and yelled, 'Hey, all of you! Come in here. Quick!'

The four parked their bicycles in a hurry, and rushed in at the garden door. What was up? They burst into the sitting-room, and stopped in amazement when they saw their old friend, Chief Inspector Jenks, tall and burly as ever, a wide smile on his good-humoured face.

Bets flung herself on him, and as usual he swung her high in the air and she shrieked. The others crowded round eagerly. What fun to see the Chief again – and how exciting! What did it mean?

The tall, quiet man also stood up, smiling. He seemed very much amused with all this. The Chief introduced the four newcomers to him, one by one. But again he did not say who the stranger was. The tall man was very courteous, and his shrewd, dark eyes rested in turn on each child's face. Fatty guessed that he didn't miss much!

'What have you come for? Not just to see *us*?' cried Bets.

'I came because I think you may have a tale to tell me that will help me in something else,' said the Chief. 'Frederick was just about to tell it when you arrived. Sit down, and we'll hear it.'

Everyone sat down, Bets as near the big Chief as she could possibly get. Fatty began again.

He described the breaking into Mr Fellows' house, and what the milkman had reported. He told how he and the others had gone to have a look at the house, which was so near Larry's.

'And, I suppose you managed to find an excuse

for a little breaking-in yourself, Frederick?' said the Chief.

'Well, there was a kitten left behind,' said Fatty, grinning. 'And while I was looking for it in the house, Mr Goon appeared.'

'I see – and then the dog, and the pig, and the groaning man began to haunt the house too, I suppose,' said the Chief. 'All right, we won't go into details. I've had too many already from Goon. I know all this bit, actually. It was fully reported to me at once. Tell me the bits I'm not likely to know.'

So Fatty told him of the question he had put to himself – who could have seen Mr Fellows rushing out at night? He went on to describe his talks with the night-watchmen – and regretfully he decided that he must also tell of his impersonation of the old man with the sack, and describe how he had led Mr Goon to the jetty and tipped in the sack of stones.

'Most reprehensible,' murmured the Chief.

'Yes, sir,' agreed Fatty, hurrying on. He told how the five of them had gone down to see if Mr Goon would drag out the sack next day and what he would do when he found he had been spoofed – he described the watching water weed man, which caused both the Chief and his plainclothes friend to sit up straight and look at one another.

'Give me a full description of this man, please,' said the Chief and, helped by the others, Fatty gave a very full description indeed.

'Excellent,' said the Chief. 'Most observant lot you are! I wouldn't be surprised if you told me everything the fellow had in his pockets! Wait a minute now – you say Goon arrived just then?'

'Yes, sir,' said Fatty. The Chief took a sheaf of papers from his pockets and chose one, which he read quickly to himself.

'This is Goon's report of that morning,' he said. 'But it's confused and lacks detail. I think we'd better get him along here too, now that he comes well into the tale. I may want to ask him a few questions.'

'Shall I telephone him, sir?' said Larry, at once. What a wonderful meeting! Goon would just about complete it. Poor Goon – he didn't shine on these occasions.

The Chief nodded and began to make some

notes, which he passed to the stranger. Larry telephoned, got Mr Goon at once, and gave him the Chief's message.

'What did he say?' inquired the Chief, when Larry returned.

'Well – er – not much, sir,' said Larry, embarrassed. 'Actually he just said "Lovaduck". Nothing else.'

Everyone laughed. Bets began to play with Buster, but it wasn't more than two minutes before Goon came sailing up the drive on his bicycle. He was met at the door by Fatty, who ushered him solemnly into the rather crowded sitting-room.

Goon was very nervous. He hadn't taken off his bicycle clips, nor had he stopped to brush his uniform which showed traces of his dinner. He slipped his helmet off and put it on the floor.

'Sit down, Goon,' said the Chief. 'I'm glad you came so quickly. Er – we have been hearing quite an interesting little tale from Frederick, here, and we thought you should hear it too – though no doubt you already know a good deal.'

Goon looked hurriedly and beseechingly at Fatty.

He sat down heavily, and Buster at once capered round his ankles. Fatty called him off sternly.

'Shut up, Buster. This is a serious meeting.' He turned to the Chief again. 'Shall I go on, sir? Well, that morning, Mr Goon did come down to the river, as we expected. And he took a boat and rowed to the jetty where I'd thrown in the sack of stones the night before.'

A snort came from Goon, but nobody took any notice of it. 'Mr Goon found a sack, sir – but it wasn't the sack I'd thrown in – it was another one.'

Goon stared at Fatty, his mouth open. What! That boy *hadn't* put in that sack? Then who had?

'Mr Goon opened the sack, sir, and it was full of very peculiar things. Clothes, sir – dolls' clothes – coat, trousers, belt, tie, socks – and a glove to match the one I told you I'd found in Mr Fellows' house. That made us guess the sack was the one that Mr Fellows himself had hidden in the river – so we took all the clothes home.'

'But, wait a minute, how did you get them? I thought *Goon* had them in the sack he pulled up,' said the Chief, puzzled.

'Well,' said Fatty, looking embarrassed, 'he – er – well, he *gave* them to me, sir. Gave me every single one! You look surprised – well, so was I!'

23. A STRANGE TALE

'But I don't understand,' said the Chief. 'These clothes were a most important clue. Goon, what in the world made you hand them over to Frederick?'

Mr Goon swallowed hard. His face was going a peculiar colour. That boy! That toad of a boy! Here he was in trouble again because of that boy. He couldn't think for the life of him what to answer.

But Bets answered for him. 'He didn't *give* them to him,' she said, indignantly. 'He stuffed everything down Fatty's neck – all wet and slimy too!'

'Be quiet, Bets,' said Fatty, uncomfortably. 'I'd asked for it.'

'What peculiar behaviour, Goon,' said the Chief, astounded. 'No wonder your report was hard to follow. Is it a habit of yours to stuff things down people's necks when you are annoyed?'

'No, sir,' muttered Goon, his eyes on the floor. 'How was I to know those clothes were important, sir? I wouldn't have stuffed them down his neck if I'd thought they'd got anything to do with this case. I was – well, I was downright annoyed that morning, sir.'

'I didn't mind,' said Fatty earnestly, sorry for poor Goon at that moment. 'As a matter-of-fact, I rather enjoyed it. It was very clever of Mr Goon to stuff every single thing down my neck – shoes and all!'

'Shoes? Did you say *shoes*?' said the Chief, at once. He made a quick note. 'Well, we will now leave this subject of stuffing clothes down necks, as I see it is rather painful to Goon, and get on with the next part of the tale.'

Fatty told how they had dried out the clothes – how there had been a breaking-in to his own house that night, but nothing was taken – how he had interviewed Mr Fellows, and got nothing but evasions – and, finally, how they had examined the clothes that very morning and how Bets had made her interesting discovery.

Goon was now listening intently. This was all new to him.

'We found nothing of interest at all, sir,' said Fatty. 'Until Bets here found a tiny pocket hidden in the sleeve-cuff – and in it was a handkerchief embroidered with daisies, and the name I told you – Eurycles. Bets, where's the hanky?'

Bets produced it proudly. In an intent silence, the Chief and his friend examined it. Mr Goon gaped. What was all this? What did a doll's handkerchief matter?

'What did you deduce from this handkerchief then?' asked the Chief.

'Well, first I recognised the name Eurycles,' said Fatty.

The stranger spoke directly to Fatty for the first time.

'Why did you recognise it? It is not a usual name,' he said.

'No, I know that, sir,' said Fatty. 'In fact, *I'd* never met anyone of that name in my life, though for all I know there may be plenty of Greeks called Eurycles. I recognised it because – well, because I'm a bit of a ventriloquist, as I told the Chief here.

You see, there was once a Greek called Eurycles who was a very famous ventriloquist indeed. I read about him in my book on ventriloquism.'

'Remarkable,' said the stranger, in his soft voice. 'And so you thought that the clothes must belong to a doll owned by a modern ventriloquist called Mr Eurycles?'

'Yes, that's right,' said Fatty. 'I was at a dead end as regards this mystery, and I thought perhaps if I could find out if there *really* was a ventriloquist using the old Greek name as a stage name, I could ask him a few questions. I thought *he* might be able to solve this peculiar mystery for us. That's why I asked the Chief on the telephone if he knew of anyone called Eurycles and how I could get in touch with him.'

'I see. Again I say, it's most remarkable,' said the tall man. 'Well, you'll be interested to know that there *is* a modern ventriloquist who uses Eurycles as his stage name – and that those clothes you speak of, do belong to his doll. And you'll also be interested to know that we have been searching everywhere for the clothes.'

'Why?' asked Fatty, astonished. 'Gosh, what a

lot of people are interested in those clothes!'

'I propose to tell you a little story myself now,' said the Chief's friend. 'A story which you must keep to yourselves. You are not to ask me any questions about it, you must accept my tale as it stands. It will tell you why my friend, the Chief Inspector here, was amazed when you spoke of Mr Eurycles to him.'

This was all very astonishing. Every eye was on the quiet stranger as he began his tale.

'You know the Chief Inspector and you know that I am a friend of his, in the same kind of service – we work to preserve the law and order of our country, to keep out enemies, to secure for this country the things that are right and proper.'

He paused. Everyone felt very solemn, and Bets found that she was holding her breath.

'Very well. It is our duty to discover and watch any man or woman who is working against this country and its laws. There are many of them, some in high-up places, some in lowly ones. Our duty is to watch, to sift out what we hear, and to report whenever we find anyone suspected of misdeeds against the country and its laws.'

'Spies?' whispered Bets.

'Not only spies – but any man or woman of evil intent,' said the tall man. 'Mr Eurycles was one who helped us in this. He was a clever ventriloquist who went everywhere with Bobby-Boy, his talking doll. He went to both high and low places, and gathered a great deal of information for us. Mr Fellows was his assistant.'

'Oh!' cried Daisy. 'Was he really? So that's how *he* comes in!'

'One day, one of Mr Eurycles' friends came to him with a list of names,' went on the Chief's friend. 'They were names that we wanted more than anything else! Names of people undermining every industry in our country – provoking strikes, sabotage, anything that would harm Britain – and there was also other information, very valuable indeed to us. Mr Eurycles put the information into his usual hiding-place – in the clothes that Bobby-Boy wore.'

Everyone listened intently, especially Mr Goon.

'That night, Mr Eurycles was kidnapped. The kidnappers took Bobby-Boy also, knowing that either on Mr Eurycles or on his doll, the list of names was hidden. But the ventriloquist managed to throw the doll out of the window of the car that kidnapped him.

'Following the car was one of our police cars, as it happened – not because the police suspected that Mr Eurycles was in the first car, but because they knew it to be a stolen car. When the doll was thrown out, the police in the car behind thought it was a small child and stopped their car, of course, to see.

'They lost the first car and returned to headquarters. Mr Fellows had by then reported the kidnapping of his master, the ventriloquist, so the doll, Bobby-Boy, was handed to him. Apparently he knew that Mr Eurycles had hidden something of value in the clothes, but he had no idea what. So he took the clothes into his keeping, hoping that his master would soon turn up.'

'Oh, *I* see! And then the kidnappers found out that the list wasn't on Mr Eurycles but somewhere in the doll's clothes, and have been hunting for it ever since!' cried Daisy.

'And that's why Mr Fellows ran out with the clothes in the middle of the night, when someone broke into his house – and he sank them into the river, meaning to get them again sometime,' said Pip, seeing everything now. 'And then the water weed man, who was the burglar, saw Mr Goon stuffing them down Fatty's neck, and so the next place he broke into was Fatty's. Goodness, we were in the middle of something terribly exciting, and we didn't know it!'

'Why didn't Mr Fellows look for the valuable list himself and take it?' asked Bets. 'Then he could have thrown the clothes away.'

'I imagine that he wasn't able to find it – and, anyway, he didn't know what to look for,' said the Chief. 'But *we* shall be able to find it. We have had information as to where it is. If you'll just produce the clothes, Frederick, we will show you where the invaluable list is hidden, a most dramatic ending to what you called "just a little mystery"!'

There was a dead silence. All the excitement drained out of the children as they remembered the disastrous happening of the morning.

'What's the matter?' said the Chief, surprised. 'You *have* got the clothes here, haven't you? What are you looking like that for?'

'It's awful to have to tell you, sir – but, they're gone,' said Fatty, in a low voice. 'We – we went out of the shed where we kept them, locked it behind us, and when we got back the shed was broken open – and all the clothes were gone.'

Bets burst into tears. 'What shall we do? Oh, we didn't know it was so important! Oh, Fatty, what shall we do?'

24. GOOD OLD BUSTER!

The Chief Inspector whistled through his teeth and looked at his plainclothes friend.

'This is a set-back!' he said. 'A real shock. Our scarred-faced friend again, I suppose. He's certainly determined this time!'

'That list is important to him – and to a lot of others who would like it destroyed,' said the tall man grimly. 'And, unfortunately, it is important to us too.' He turned to Fatty.

'*All* the clothes went – he took the lot?' he asked sharply.

'Yes, all except for the little hanky Bets found, which you've seen,' said Fatty. 'But if you like, we can go down to my shed and have another look in the box where we put them. But I'm pretty certain it's empty, sir.'

They trailed down to the shed, Mr Goon too, all of them feeling most depressed. To have such an exciting mystery – and then to have the right ending snatched away just as they were being so successful! It really was bad luck.

They looked into the box. It was, as Fatty said, well and truly empty. Then Bets suddenly remembered something and cried out loudly.

'The shoe that Buster took! Did we find it and hide that away too? Or did we forget it and leave it in whatever corner Buster put it?'

'We forgot it. I didn't put it in,' said Fatty. 'But would just one shoe be of any use to you, sir?'

'My word, yes – more than you'd think, if it was the right shoe!' said the Chief. 'Here, Buster boy, find that shoe!'

And, as if Buster completely understood, he ran round the shed, hunting into this corner and that – and, finally, after sniffing under an old sack, he disappeared beneath it, worried at something – and came out proudly with a doll's red shoe in his mouth!

'It's the shoe. He's found it,' said Fatty, in delight. 'Good old Buster. Clever dog, Buster.'

Buster wagged his tail proudly. The Chief

took the shoe at once and he and his friend examined it closely.

'It may be the one. Can't tell without examining it,' said the Chief. 'Anyone got a sharp penknife?'

Fatty had, of course. He always kept his pockets full of things that might conceivably come in useful some day.

The Chief took the knife and sat down on a box. He turned the shoe upside down and, with all the Find-Outers breathing heavily down his neck, he began to try and prize away the heel.

'Strongly made,' said the Chief. 'Ah – up it comes!'

The heel came away from the shoe, and the children saw a neat little hollowed-out compartment in the heel itself. In it was a thin sheet of paper tightly folded.

'It's here,' cried the Chief, as excited as the five children. His fingers delicately eased the paper from its hiding-place. He handed it, folded, to the tall man, whose eyes were now gleaming.

He unfolded the paper very carefully, and ran his eyes down a list of names and notes. They were all written in most minute writing, impossible to make out at a distance. Mr Goon, craning his neck to see if he could read anything, could only make out a blur.

'This is it,' said the tall man, a ring of triumph in his voice. 'There's a whole year's work here – invaluable, Jenks! And to think how nearly we lost it – if it hadn't been for that dog running off with the shoe as he did, and hiding it, we'd have lost it for good!'

'The thief must just have seen the bundle of clothes in the box, thought everything was there, and picked the whole lot up,' said Fatty. 'And gone off with it in delight. What a shock when he finds only one shoe!'

'Perhaps he'll come back and try and find it,' suggested Larry. 'You could catch him then.'

'Oh, we know where to pick him up now,' said the Chief. 'My word, look at this name on the list – and that – whew! This is going to make a stir!'

'It is. It's going to make several dozen people extremely uncomfortable,' said the tall man, grimly. 'What a haul! I can't believe it – and all because of these kids. Marvellous, aren't they?'

'Well, they've certainly done some good work in their time,' said the Chief, smiling. 'Very good work. They call themselves the Five Find-Outers and Dog, you know. And the things they've found out – they could really have books and books written about them!'

'But Buster's really the hero of *this* mystery!' said Bets, picking up the little Scottie and hugging him. 'Aren't you, Buster? Did you know that shoe was important, Buster? Is that why you hid it? Fatty, I'd be quite ready to believe that Buster *did* guess, you know!'

'What are you going to do now?' asked Larry, turning to the Chief.

'Well, just a few bits of work,' said the Chief. 'We must go and drop in on Fellows, to begin with, and set his mind at rest. And we must send somebody to gather in Mr Scarred-Face – or the water weed man, as you call him. He won't be wanting water weed for some time after this!'

'I do hope you'll get Mr Eurycles back some day,' said Bets. 'I hope nothing horrid's happened to him.'

'I'll let you know when he does appear again,'

said the Chief. 'I have a feeling that once we get after the people whose names are on this sheet of paper, our Mr Eurycles will find himself unexpectedly free. Quite a lot of these people will flee the country soon!'

'Er, can't we give these children a little reward for their enormous help?' said the tall man, getting up from his box and almost bumping his head against the roof.

'Oh, no, thank you,' said Fatty at once. 'That would spoil everything – we wouldn't want to solve mysteries for a reward. We do it because it's fun – and we like helping the Chief.'

'My dear fellow, there are so few people left in the world who will do things without expecting payment or reward, that I think we'll let the Find-Outers go their own good way,' said the Chief to his friend, quite seriously. That made the five feel extremely proud.

'Right,' said the tall man. 'Well, we must be going. Still, there are two things I'm going to do for these, er – what do they call themselves? – these Find-Outers and Dog. I am going to get my butcher to send his biggest and juiciest bone to this remarkably clever dog . . .'

'Wuff,' said Buster, wagging his tail most appreciatively.

'And when Mr Eurycles turns up again, I shall ask him if he would be good enough to give Frederick here a few first class lessons in ventriloquism,' said the tall man. 'He'll be delighted to do that.'

Fatty blushed with pleasure. 'Oh, sir – thank you. I don't want any reward, as you know – and I'll pay for the lessons. Gosh, wouldn't I like them! Thanks very much.'

The Chief and his friend departed. The police car revved up and disappeared down the drive. Only Mr Goon was left with the five children. They looked at one another.

Poor old Goon. He hadn't had much of a look-in this time. The Chief hadn't even said a word of farewell to him. Even Buster had done better than Goon!

'Well,' said Fatty, in a jovial tone, 'what about tea? It must surely be ready by now. Anyway, *I'm* ready for it. Mr Goon – will you join us?'

Mr Goon was so astounded at this invitation

that he could only gape. He was not a generous enemy, like Fatty, and never would be. He hardly understood this invitation, and his mouth opened and shut like a goldfish.

'Well, do answer, Mr Goon,' said Fatty. 'We'll celebrate the occasion, and I'll open the big tin of chocolate biscuits I got for Christmas. Will you, won't you, will you, won't you, Mr Goon?'

'I will,' gasped Goon, almost as if he was getting married. 'Thanks. I take it very kind of you after – er – after some of the things that have happened.'

'Well, don't you go stuffing things down my neck again!' said Fatty, leading the way in.

Goon gave a sudden grin. 'And don't you go making up dogs, and pigs, and what-not,' he said.

Bets didn't want Goon to stay to tea, but she said nothing. She liked Fatty's generous gesture, and she knew that poor Mr Goon hadn't had a very good time in this mystery – but nothing was going to persuade her to sit next to him, or even to address a word to him. She would never, ever forgive him for stuffing those things down Fatty's neck!

It was a most hilarious tea. Everyone was pleased that the little mystery had turned out to be a genuine, large-size one, and had ended so triumphantly for Buster.

Buster, of course, was amazed to find his old enemy suddenly belonging to the family circle. He gave a few fierce growls and then, as everyone made so much fuss of him, and Daisy actually addressed him as Hero Dog, he joined in the general enjoyment.

Mr Goon enjoyed himself too. Well, well – to think that toad of a boy could behave like this! After his fourth macaroon, and third piece of chocolate cake, Mr Goon was ready to be Fatty's best friend!

And then a loud grunting noise was heard under the table! 'What's that?' cried Bets, in alarm. Mr Goon looked under the table, amazed. Only Buster was there.

The others looked at Fatty's grinning face and laughed. And then, from just behind the astounded Mr Goon, came an all-too-familiar voice. 'I never did it, I never! Ooooh, I never did! Where's my auntie?'

Oh, Fatty! What are we to do with you? Tell us about your next mystery, do!

THE MYSTERY OF HOLLY LANE

CONTENTS

1. OFF TO MEET FATTY

'Bets – don't gobble your porridge like that!' said Mrs Hilton. 'There's no hurry, surely!'

'Well, there is, Mummy,' said Bets. 'I've got to go and meet Fatty's train this morning. Have you forgotten that he's coming home today?'

'But he's not arriving till the middle of the morning, is he?' said her mother. 'There's plenty of time. Please don't gobble like that.'

'I expect Bets wants to go and lay a red carpet down for Fatty, and get a band to play to welcome him,' said her brother Pip, with a grin. 'That's what you're in a hurry about, aren't you Bets? Got to go and round up the band and see that all their instruments are polished!'

'Don't be so *silly*,' said Bets crossly, and tried to kick him under the table. He dodged his legs out of the way and she kicked her father's ankle instead. He put down his paper and glared.

'Oh, Dad – I'm sorry!' said Bets. 'Please, I'm very sorry. I meant to kick Pip. You see . . .'

'Any more of this kind of behaviour at breakfast-time and you can both go out of the room,' said Mr Hilton, and raised his paper again, leaning it against the big milk jug. There was a dead silence for a minute or two, except for the sound of spoons in the porridge bowls.

'Are you both going to meet Fatty?' asked Mrs Hilton at last.

'Yes,' said Bets, glad to have the silence broken. 'But I want to go round and collect Buster first. Fatty asked me to. That's why I'm in a hurry.'

'I suppose you're going to give old Buster a bath, and then dry him, and then brush him, and then tie a red ribbon round his neck,' said Pip. 'Well, well – that will take half the morning, certainly. Are you going to wear your best dress to meet Fatty, Bets?'

'I think you're horrid this morning,' said Bets, almost in tears. 'I should have thought you'd be pleased to meet Fatty too. It's maddening that his school should have broken up after Easter, instead of before, like ours did. It means we'll go back before he does.'

Pip stopped teasing Bets. 'Yes, it's a silly idea some schools breaking up before Easter and some after. I'm coming to meet Fatty too, of course, and I'll go and collect Buster with you. I'll even help you to bath him.'

'I wasn't *going* to bath him,' said Bets. 'You know I wasn't. Pip, do you suppose Fatty will be in disguise – just to have a joke with us?'

'I hope to goodness you are not going to get mixed up in any nonsense again these holidays,' said her father, entering suddenly into the conversation again. 'I'm getting tired of having that policeman, Mr Goon, round here complaining of this and that. As soon as that boy Frederick appears on the scene, something always seems to happen.'

'Well, Fatty can't help it,' said Bets loyally. 'I mean – mysteries keep *on* happening, Dad, you can't stop them. The papers are full of them.'

'There's absolutely no need for you to be mixed up in so many,' said her father. 'That boy Frederick – or Fatty, as you so rightly call him – ought not to poke his nose into them. Leave them to the police!'

'Oh, but Fatty's *much* cleverer than our policeman, Mr Goon,' said Bets. 'Anyway, I don't expect there will be time for anything exciting these hols.'

Pip changed the subject quickly. He didn't want his father suddenly to forbid him and Bets to have anything to do with any possible new mystery, as he had done once before. He had a kind of feeling that that was what would happen if he didn't hurriedly change the subject!

'Dad, the gardener is still away,' he said. 'Is there anything you want me to do in the garden, just to help out?'

Mr Hilton looked pleased. 'Ah – I wondered if you were going to suggest giving a bit of help,' he said. 'Now, you come into my study before I go and I'll give you a list of jobs I'd like done. They'll keep you out of mischief anyway!'

Pip heaved a sigh of relief. He didn't particularly want to do any gardening, but at least he had headed his father off the subject of mysteries. It would have been dreadful if he had been forbidden to take part in any during the three weeks that were left of the holidays. He gave Bets a frown to make her understand she was not to mention Fatty again.

After breakfast, Pip disappeared into the study with his father. He came up to Bets later, as she was making her bed. He looked rather rueful.

'Look at this list! Whew! Dad must think I'm a super gardener! I'll never do all this.'

Bets looked at the list. 'Please go and do some now,' she said. 'You don't want to spend all the afternoon doing it – Fatty might want us to go to tea, or something. I wish I could help you. I'll make your bed and tidy your room, anyway. Will you be ready to start at twenty to eleven, Pip? Fatty's train gets in just before eleven, and I *must* collect Buster.'

Pip heaved a mournful sigh as he looked at his list of jobs once more. 'All right. I'll go and start now. Thanks for saying you'll do my bed and tidy up. See you later!'

At twenty to eleven, Bets went out into the garden to find Pip. He was just putting a rake away, and looked extremely hot. 'Is it time?' he called. 'Gosh, I've been working like ten gardeners rolled into one.'

'You look as if you're going to burst into flame at any minute,' said Bets, with a giggle. 'You'd better wash your hands, they're filthy. I'll go on ahead and collect Buster. Don't be long!'

She ran down the drive happily. She was tremendously glad that Fatty was coming back at last. Bets was very fond of him. She thought he must be the cleverest, most ingenious, and certainly the kindest boy in the world. The things he could do!

Those disguises of his! And the way he thinks out things – and the daring things he does!, she thought, as she turned out of the front gate and up the lane. Oh, I'm *glad* Fatty's coming back. Things are always dull without him. It's quite true what Dad said – things do begin to happen when Fatty is around!

Somebody whistled loudly when she got into the main road and she turned quickly. It was Larry, with Daisy, his sister. They waved madly and began to run.

'Are you going to meet Fatty? So are we! Where is Pip? Isn't he coming?'

Bets explained. 'I'm on my way to collect

Buster,' she said. 'Pip's just coming. Won't old Buster be pleased to see Fatty? I bet he knows it's the day he's arriving.'

'I bet he does,' agreed Larry. 'He'll be waiting for us, his tongue out, panting to go!'

But, oddly enough, Buster was not waiting. Mrs Trotteville, Fatty's mother, was picking daffodils in the garden when the three children came up. She smiled at them.

'Going to meet Fatty? It will be nice to have him back, won't it?'

'Yes, very,' said Larry. 'Where's Buster, Mrs Trotteville? We thought we'd take him along.'

'In the kitchen, I think,' said Mrs Trotteville. 'I haven't seen him for a little while. He would keep treading all over the daffodils, so I sent him in.'

Larry, Daisy and Bets went to the kitchen door and called loudly. 'Buster! Hey, BUSTER! Come along, we're going to meet Fatty!'

But no Buster appeared. There was no scamper of short, eager legs, no welcoming volley of barks. The cook came to the door.

'He's not here,' she said. 'He did come in a minute or two ago, but off he went again. He's probably gone off with the baker's boy. He likes him, goodness knows why. He's a cheeky little monkey, that boy.'

'Well, we'll have to go without Buster,' said Larry, disappointed. 'How maddening of him to go off just at this time. Fatty will be disappointed.'

They set off to the station, joined by a breathless Pip. 'Where's Buster? Don't say he's gone off just when we want him! Not at all like Buster!'

They hurried on. 'Do you suppose Fatty will play a joke on us and turn up in disguise?' said Bets. 'I do hope he doesn't. I just want to see him nice and grinning all over his face.'

'We shall be very late if we don't hurry,' said Larry, looking at his watch. 'Look – isn't that the train coming in now? – and we're not nearly there. Hurry up!'

They hurried up, and arrived at the station just as the train began to pull out again. The passengers had got out and were now walking down the platform. Two or three were waiting with their luggage for a porter.

'Look, there's old Buster!' said Pip, suddenly. 'Would you believe it! Sitting under that seat –

look – all by himself, watching.'

Sure enough, there was the little Scottie, patiently waiting there. 'How did he know that Fatty's train was due now?' said Bets, in wonder. 'However DID he know! So that's where he ran off to – the station! He was on time too, and we weren't. Clever old Buster!'

'Where's Fatty?' said Daisy, as the crowd of passengers came up to the door where the ticket collector stood. 'I can't see him yet.'

'He *may* be in disguise, just to test us and see how bright we are,' said Pip. 'Look at everyone very carefully – especially people with glasses.'

They stood silently behind the collector as everyone surged past, giving in tickets. A big, bustling woman – a pair of schoolgirls – a man with a bag – two young soldiers in khaki, each with enormous kit-bags on their shoulders – two men bundled up in thick overcoats, both wearing glasses. Was one Fatty? They were both about his build. One said something in a foreign language as he passed by.

The four children stared after him doubtfully. He *could* be Fatty. They turned to watch the rest of the passengers, but there was no one who could possibly be Fatty.

At the end came Buster, all alone. Bets patted him, thinking that he looked sad. 'So you missed him too, did you?' she said. 'Buster, was he one of those bundled-up men?'

There was now no one left on the platform except a porter. 'Come on,' said Larry, making up his mind. 'Fatty *must* have been one of those men. We'll follow them. We can't have old Fatty tricking us as easily as this!'

2. A LITTLE BIT OF HELP!

The four children went out of the station and looked up the road. Where had the men gone?

'There they are,' said Larry. 'Look – just at the corner!'

'But who's the man with Fatty?' said Pip, puzzled. 'He never said anything about coming back with somebody.'

'Look – they've shaken hands,' said Daisy. 'I expect old Fatty just fell into conversation with him to trick us a bit more. Come on, I'm sure the man who's gone off to the right is Fatty. He's got his walk somehow.'

'And he's going in the right direction,' said Pip. 'It's Fatty all right.'

They hurried after him. When they got to the corner, they paused. Now, where was he?

'There he is – talking to that woman,' said Larry. 'Hurry!'

They hurried. The man, his coat-collar turned up, wearing thick glasses over his eyes, was saying something very earnestly to a thin little woman with a shopping-basket.

The four came up behind him and listened with amusement. Oh Fatty, Fatty!

'I seek my sistair's house. You will tell me, pliss? The house, it is called Grintriss.'

'Never heard of it,' said the woman, looking most suspiciously at the bundled-up man.

'Pardon? Where is zis house?' asked the man anxiously.

'I said, "NEVER HEARD OF IT",' said the woman. 'There's no house called Grintriss that I know of. What's your sister's name?'

'Her name is Francoise Emilie Harris,' said the man, suddenly going very French.

'Never heard of her either,' said the thin little woman, looking more suspicious than ever. 'Why don't you ask at the post office?'

'Pliss? What is zis postoffis?' began the man, but the woman walked off impatiently, leaving him standing there with his bag.

Pip nudged Larry. 'This is where we come in,'

he said, in a low voice. 'We'll tell old Fatty we know where his sister lives, and that we'll take him there – and we'll lead him straight to his own house. That'll show him we've seen through him! Come on.'

'Where's his school suitcase?' said Bets, pulling Pip back as he started off after the man. 'Are you *sure* it's Fatty?'

'He's sent his luggage forward, of course,' said Pip. 'Come on – *look* at that walk – it's exactly like old Fatty's.'

They set off after the man. Daisy suddenly thought of something. Where was Buster? She looked round but he wasn't there.

'What happened to Buster?' she said. 'Surely he didn't stay behind? I was just wondering why *he* didn't know it was Fatty, and dash round his legs.'

'He would have, if he'd been with us,' said Pip. 'He didn't recognise him in that crowd at the station and he's probably patiently sitting under the seat again, waiting!'

'Oh, poor Buster!' said Bets. 'Look – Fatty has stopped another woman. What a scream he is!'

The second woman had no patience. She just shook her head and hurried off. Larry put his fingers to his mouth and let out a piercing whistle, making the others jump.

'Don't,' said Daisy. 'You know you're not allowed to do that. It's a horrible noise and makes people awfully angry.'

'It's stopped old Fatty, anyway,' said Larry, pleased. 'Look, he's turned round.'

'He's gone on again,' said Bets with a giggle. 'Let's catch him up. He's going the wrong way home now.'

They hurried after the man. 'We'll pretend we don't know it's Fatty,' said Pip. 'We'll make him think *he's* deceiving *us* – but we'll have the laugh all right, when we take him to his own house instead of to his mythical "sistair's" house.'

They caught up with the man, and he stopped, peering at them through thick glasses. He had a small black moustache. His coat-collar was turned up, and not much could be seen of his face.

'Ah! Some children! You will help me, yes?' said the man. 'I look for my sistair's house.'

'Vous cherchez la maison de votre soeur?' said

Pip, in his best French. The man beamed at him.

'Oui, oui! It is called Grintriss.'

'Grintriss! Oh, yes, we know where *that* is,' said Larry, most untruthfully, playing up to Fatty for all he was worth. 'This way, please. *Every*body knows Grintriss. A very nice house. Big one, too.'

'Beeg? No, my sistair's house is leetle,' said the man. 'Vairy, vairy leetle. Grintriss, it is called.'

'Oh, yes. Grintriss. Vairy leetle,' said Pip. 'Er – do you feel the cold, Monsieur? You are well wrapped up.'

'I have had the bad cold,' said the man, and he sniffed, and gave a hollow cough. 'I come to my sistair for a leetle holyday.'

'Holiday, you mean?' said Daisy, and the four of them began to laugh. 'That's a nasty little cough you've got. Very nasty.'

The man coughed again, and Bets began to giggle. Didn't Fatty know they were pulling his leg? How often had she heard Fatty cough like that when he was disguised as some poor old man?

They all went up the road together, the man hunched up in his bulky coat. He pulled his scarf over his chin as they met the wind at a corner.

'We are soon at Grintriss?' he asked, anxiously. 'This wind is too – too –'

'Too windy?' said Pip, obligingly. 'That's the worst of winds. They're always so windy.'

The man gave him a sudden stare and said no more. Larry guided him round the next corner and over the road to Fatty's own house. Mrs Trotteville was nowhere to be seen. Larry winked at Pip.

'We'll take him up to the front door and leave him there,' he said, falling behind to whisper. 'We'll just see what old Fatty says then!'

They marched him in firmly at the gate and right up to the front door. 'Here you are,' said Pip. 'Grintriss! I expect your sistair will answer the door herself. I'll pull the bell for you.'

He pulled the bell and banged on the knocker too. Then the four of them retreated to the front gate to see what Fatty would do. Would he swing round, take off his glasses and grin at them? Would he say 'One up to you! You win!'

The door opened, and the maid stood there. An argument seemed to arise, though the children couldn't hear all of it. The maid raised her voice.

'I said, "There's no one here of that name." And what's more, I've never heard of a house called Grintriss either.'

Bets suddenly heard quick footsteps coming up the road, and then a familiar bark. She ran through the gate, sure that it was Buster's bark.

She gave a shrill scream. 'Buster! FATTY! It's Fatty! Oh, Fatty, then that wasn't you after all! FATTY!'

She rushed down the road and flung herself into Fatty's arms. There he was, his eyes laughing, his mouth in a wide grin.

'Fatty! That wasn't you then? Oh, dear!'

'What's all this about?' asked Fatty, swinging Bets into the air and down again. 'Gosh, Bets, you're getting heavy. I soon won't be able to do that. Why weren't you at the station to meet me? Only Buster was there.'

Now all the others were round him too, astonished. Fatty! How had they missed him?

'You *are* a lot of idiots,' said Fatty, in his cheerful voice. 'I bet you met the train that comes in four minutes before mine. Buster was *much* more sensible! He knew enough to wait for the right one – and there he was, prancing round the platform, barking like mad when he saw me. I looked for you, but you were nowhere to be seen.'

'Oh, Fatty – we must have met the wrong train – and we've made an *awful* mistake,' said Daisy, troubled. 'We thought you might be in disguise, just to play a joke on us – and when we couldn't see you anywhere, we followed a man we thought was you – and, oh, Fatty, he asked us the way to some house or other – and we took him to yours!'

'*Well*!' said Fatty, and roared with laughter. 'You are a lot of mutts. Where's this poor fellow? We'd better put him right.'

The man was even now walking out of the gate, muttering and looking furious – as indeed he had every right to be. He stopped and looked at the name on the gate.

'Ha! You do not bring me to Grintriss. This is not Grintriss. You are wicket! You treat a sick man so!' He began to cough again.

The children were alarmed, and felt very sorry. However could they explain their mistake? He would never, never understand! He stalked up to them, blowing his nose with a trumpeting sound.

'Wicket! Wicket!' he repeated. 'Very bad. Wicket!'

He began to shout at them in French, waving his arms about. They listened in dismay. Suppose Mrs Trotteville came out? It would be even worse to explain their silly mistake to her than to this man.

A bell rang loudly and a bicycle stopped suddenly at the kerb. A very familiar voice hailed them.

'Now, then! What's all this?'

'Mr Goon!' groaned Larry. 'Old Clear-Orf. He *would* turn up, of course.'

Buster danced round Mr Goon in delight, barking furiously. Mr Goon kept a watchful eye on him, thankful that he had on his thickest trousers.

'Nasty little yapping dog,' he said. 'Call him off.'

Fatty called Buster, and the Scottie came most reluctantly. Oh, for a nip at that big, loud-voiced policeman! Goon spoke to the bewildered Frenchman.

'What's all this? Have these children been

annoying you? I'll report them, if so.'

The man went off into a long and angry speech, but as it was all in French, Mr Goon didn't understand a word. He debated whether he should ask Fatty to translate for him – but how was he to trust that boy's translation? Fatty looked at Goon with a gleam in his eye.

'Don't you want to know what he's saying, Mr Goon?' he said, politely. 'I can just catch a few words now and again. Er – he doesn't seem to like the look of you, I'm afraid. It sounds as if he's calling you names.'

Mr Goon felt out of his depth. These pests of children again – and this foreigner who appeared to be quite mad – and that nasty little dog longing to get at his ankles! Mr Goon felt that the best and most dignified thing to do was to bicycle away immediately.

So, with a snort that sounded like 'Gah', he pushed off from the kerb and sailed away down the road, followed by a fusillade of barks from the disappointed Buster.

'Thank goodness!' said Daisy fervently, and all the five agreed.

3. IT'S NICE TO BE TOGETHER AGAIN!

The Frenchman stared after the policeman in surprise. In France, policeman did not behave like that. They were interested and excited when a complaint was made to them, they listened, they took notes – but this policeman had said 'Gah' and gone cycling away. Extraordinary!

He began to cough. Fatty felt sorry for him, and began to talk to him in perfect French. Trust old Fatty to know the right thing to do! The others stood round, listening in admiration. Really, Fatty might be French!

'How does he learn French like that?' wondered Daisy. 'Nobody at our school could even *begin* to talk like that. Really, Fatty is a most surprising person.'

The man began to calm down. He took a little notebook out of his pocket and opened it. 'I will show you the name,' he said. 'Grintriss. Why should nobody know this Grintriss house?'

He showed Fatty something written down on a page of the notebook. The others peeped over his arm to look.

'Oh! GREEN-TREES!' said Daisy. 'Why ever didn't you say so? You kept saying Grintriss.'

'Yes. Grintriss,' repeated the man, puzzled. 'All the time I say "Grintriss, pliss, where is zis house?" '

'It's Green-Trees,' said Daisy, pronouncing it slowly and carefully.

'Grintriss,' said the man again. 'And now – where is zis house? I ask of you for the last time.'

He looked as if he were going to burst into tears. Fatty took his arm. 'Come on. I'll show you. No tricks this time, we'll take you there.'

And off they all went together, Fatty suddenly jabbering in French again. Down the road, round the corner, up the hill and into a quiet little lane. In the middle of it, was a small and pretty house, smoke curling up from its chimneys.

'Green-Trees,' said Fatty, pointing to the name on the white gate.

'Ah – Grintriss,' said the man, in delight and

raised his hat to the two girls. 'Mesdemoiselles, adieu! I go to find my sistair!'

He disappeared up the little front path. Bets gave a sigh and slipped her arm through Fatty's. 'What a shame to welcome you home with a silly muddle like this, Fatty. We meant to be on the platform ready to give you a wonderful welcome – and only Buster was there – and we'd gone off after somebody who wasn't in the *least* like you.'

'Yes, but that's the worst of Fatty when he puts on a disguise,' grumbled Pip. 'He never does look in the least like himself. Come on, Fatty – let's take you back home now. Your mother will be wondering what's become of you.'

Mrs Trotteville was quite relieved to see Fatty and the others trooping into the hall. She came out to greet them.

'Frederick! Did you miss your train? How late you are! Welcome home again.'

'Hello, Mummy! What a nice smell from the kitchen! Smells like steak and onions. Buster, what do *you* think?'

'Wuff!' said Buster, ready to agree with every word that Fatty said. He dashed round Fatty's legs, galloped behind the couch, appeared again, and then threaded his way at top speed between all the chairs.

'Jet-propelled obstacle race,' said Fatty. 'Hey, Buster, look where you're going, you'll knock me over.'

'He always behaves like that when you first come home,' said Mrs Trotteville. 'I only hope he gets over the excitement soon. I simply daren't walk a step when he goes mad like this.'

'He's a darling,' said Bets. 'I know how he feels when Fatty comes home. I feel rather the same myself.'

Fatty gave her a sudden hug. 'Well, don't *you* start racing round the furniture on all-fours,' he said. 'Tell me – any mysterious mysteries or insoluble problems cropped up this last week? What a shame you all got home before I did!'

'Nothing's turned up yet,' said Pip. 'But I bet something will now you're here. Adventures go to the adventurous, you know.'

'I do hope nothing *does* turn up,' said Mrs Trotteville. 'Or I shall have that silly Mr Goon round here again. Now, the one *I* like is your friend, Superintendent Jenks!'

They all stared at her. '*Superintendent*! You don't mean that Chief Inspector Jenks is a Superintendent now!' said Larry. 'My word, he's going up and up, isn't he?'

'We knew him first when he was an Inspector,' said Bets, remembering. 'And then he became a Chief Inspector. Now he's a Superintendent. I'm glad. He's getting very, very high-up, isn't he? I hope he'll still like to know us.'

'I expect he will,' said Mrs Trotteville smiling. 'Oh dear – I do wish Cook would keep the kitchen door shut when she is doing onions – what a smell came in here then.'

'Keep the door shut when it's steak and onions,' said Fatty, in horror. '*Shut*, did you say? Shut out a heavenly smell like that? Mummy, don't you realise that I have, as usual, been half-starved all term?'

'Your suitcase has come, Frederick. Do you want to unpack it, and get ready for lunch straightaway? We're having it early as I thought you would be hungry.'

'Mummy, I do love you when you think things

like that,' said Fatty, in a sudden burst of affection. 'I'm starving!'

'Cupboard love!' said his mother, amused at Fatty's sudden hug.

'Can all the others stay to lunch as well?' asked Fatty, hopefully.

'Yes, if you'd like to share your bit of steak and onions round,' said his mother. But not even Fatty could rise to that, and so he said good-bye to the other four very reluctantly.

'They can all come to tea this afternoon, if you like,' said Mrs Trotteville. 'I'll get in plenty of cakes. Frederick, do control Buster. He's gone mad again. It really makes me giddy to watch him.'

'Buster! Behave yourself!' said Fatty, and the mad little Scottie turned himself miraculously into a quiet and peaceful little lamb, lying down on Fatty's feet and licking his shoes.

'Come back at three,' said Fatty, and took the others to the front gate. 'We'll have a good old talk and you can tell me all the news. So long!'

'I suppose, Frederick, you don't know anything about a bulky-looking foreigner who came to the front door this morning, and told Jane that this house was Grintriss, and wanted to force his way in and see some sister of his – do you?' said Mrs Trotteville, when Fatty came back. 'He kept talking about some "wicket children" when Jane told him this wasn't the house. You hadn't anything to do with him, I suppose? You haven't been up to your tricks again already, I hope.'

'Of course not,' said Fatty, looking quite hurt. 'Poor fellow – I found him at the front gate, and we all took him to the place he wanted to go to. Green-Trees, down Holly Lane. Oh, Mummy, there's that heavenly smell again. Do you mind if I go and smell it even nearer? I haven't seen Cook or Jane yet.'

'Very well,' said Mrs Trotteville. 'Oh, Frederick – it's very nice to have you back – but I do wish I always knew what you were up to! Please don't get mixed up in anything alarming these holidays. Pip's mother was saying to me only yesterday that everything has been so *peaceful* this last week.'

There was no answer. Fatty was already in the kitchen sampling half-fried strips of onion, while Cook and Jane giggled at him, and promised to provide him with new gingerbread, hot scones and home-made raspberry jam when the others came to tea that afternoon. They loved Fatty.

'A caution, that's what he is,' Cook told her friends. 'Honestly, you just never know what's going to happen when Frederick is about.'

Fatty enjoyed his lunch thoroughly, and told his mother all about his last term. He appeared, as always, to have done extremely well.

'Though there *may* be something on my report about the – er – the advisability of sticking to my own voice,' he said, making his mother look up in surprise. 'It's all right, Mummy. It just means that my ventriloquism has been rather successful this term.'

One of Fatty's talents was the ability to throw his voice, and he was now a very fine ventriloquist indeed – but unfortunately, the teachers at school did not approve of this as much as the boys did. Fatty's class had spent one whole morning searching for an apparently-injured man somewhere up in the school attic. The groans had been tremendous and had caused a great sensation.

When it had been discovered that it was merely

a ventriloquial stunt of Fatty's, there had been another sensation – but not a very happy one for Fatty. In fact, he hadn't felt it wise to do any more ventriloquism that term which was, he thought, a great pity. He would get out of practice!

At three o'clock exactly, there was the tramp of feet going down the garden to Fatty's shed. Fatty saw Larry, Daisy, Pip and Bets passing by under his window and hurriedly stopped his unpacking.

He shot downstairs with Buster, and went to join the others in his big shed at the bottom of the garden.

This was playroom, store-room, changing-room – anything that Fatty wanted. He had a key for it, and kept it well and truly locked. There were too many disguises and odd clothes there that he didn't want grown-ups to see. His mother would certainly have been astonished to see some of the old things he had picked up at jumble sales – dreadful old hats, ragged shawls, voluminous skirts, corduroy trousers, down-at-heel boots!

'Hello!' said Fatty, appearing just as the others were looking in at the shed window to see if he was there. 'I'll unlock the door. I slipped down just after dinner to light the oil-stove. It should be nice and warm now.'

They all went in. It certainly was nice and warm. The sun slid in at one window and lit up the inside of the shed. It looked dusty and untidy.

'I'll clean it up for you,' promised Daisy, looking round. 'It's nice to meet like this again, isn't it? – all the Five Find-Outers together!'

'With nothing to find out!' said Pip. 'I like it best when we've got something exciting on hand. And remember, Fatty, we go back to school a whole week before you do, so there isn't a great deal of time to get going on something.'

'We can always practice a bit,' suggested Larry. 'You know – go out in disguises – or do a spot of shadowing – or watching.'

'Yes. We could do that,' said Fatty. 'I want to practise my ventriloquism too – I've got out of practice this last term.'

'Oh, yes, *do* practice that!' begged Bets. 'Let's make some plans.'

'Right,' said Fatty, obligingly. 'We will!'

4. A FEW LITTLE PLANS

Many ridiculous plans were discussed that afternoon over a really super tea. Cook had kept her word, and there were lashings of hot scones and raspberry jam, new and very sticky gingerbread with raisins in, and a big round chocolate cake with a special filling made by Cook.

Buster had dog biscuits spread with potted meat, and approved of this very highly.

'It's three-treats-in-one for him,' explained Fatty. 'First he gets a fine sniff at the biscuits and potted meat. Then he gets a fine lick at them. Then he gets a wonderful crunch from them. Three-meals-in-one, so to speak.'

'Wuff,' said Buster, thumping his tail hard.

'And what is more,' said Fatty, cutting himself a huge slice of the chocolate cake, 'what is more, we can have every bit of this cake to ourselves. Potted-meat-biscuits take the *whole* of Buster's attention. He hasn't even *seen* this cake yet.'

'And when he does, it won't be there,' said Pip. 'Not if I can help it, anyway.'

They got back to their plans again. Fatty was in an uproarious mood, and made them all laugh till they choked.

'What about taking a clotheshorse with us, Larry, and going into the main street and pretending to be workmen chipping up the road?' suggested Fatty. 'Just you and I, Larry. Pip's not big enough yet to pass as a workman. We could put the clotheshorse round us, like workmen do, hang a red flag on it, and chip up the road!'

'Don't be an idiot,' said Larry. 'We'd get into an awful row.'

'I bet old Mr Goon would let us sit there all morning chipping up the road,' said Fatty. 'He'd never dream of asking us what we were doing.'

'Fatty, I'm going to dare you to do something,' said Daisy, with a sudden giggle. 'Look – I'm trying to sell these tickets for our church sale. I dare you to try and sell one to Mr Goon.'

'Easy!' said Fatty. 'Very easy! Give me one. I'll sell it tomorrow. That shall be my little task.'

'What shall *I* do?' asked Larry.

'Er – let me see – yes, what about you putting on overalls, taking a pail and a leather, and going to clean somebody's windows?' said Fatty.

'Oh, no!' said Larry, in alarm. 'Nothing like that!'

'Yes, do, do!' begged Daisy and Bets.

'Only you'll have to choose a house that is all on one floor – a bungalow, for instance,' said Pip. 'You won't need a ladder then, and there wouldn't be as many windows to clean! Larry as window-cleaner! That's good!'

'Do I have to *ask* if I can clean the windows?' said Larry, looking desperate. 'I mean, I can't just go to a house and start cleaning, can I? They might have their own regular window-cleaner.'

'Yes, that's true. You must ask first,' said Fatty, solemnly. 'And if you get any payment, you can buy one of Daisy's sale tickets.'

'Oh,' said Larry. 'That's a bit hard.' It occurred to him that these sudden plans were rather a mistake!

'What shall *I* do?' said Pip, with a giggle. They all looked at him. 'You can shadow Mr Goon sometime tomorrow,' said Fatty firmly. 'Shadow him so that he doesn't know you're following him – do it really properly.'

'All right,' said Pip. 'I can do that, I think. What about the girls?'

'We'll think of something for them to do when we've done our tasks,' said Fatty. 'Now, anyone want this last bit of gingerbread – or shall I cut it into five?'

It was duly cut into five. 'Anyone seen Superintendent Jenks these hols?' asked Fatty, handing round the gingerbread. 'Really good that he's promoted again, isn't it?'

'Super!' said Bets.

'Yes – super – intendent,' said Pip, and everyone punched him. 'No, none of us has seen him – we're not likely to see him either, unless we have something in the mystery line to solve.'

'I wish he'd hand us over a few of his cases,' said Fatty, stacking the plates together. 'I'm sure we could help. I mean, we've had a good bit of experience now, haven't we?'

'The only thing is, Mr Goon always knows about the cases too, and he does get in our way when we're both working on the same mystery,' said Daisy. 'I wish we could work on some more clues – and suspects – and all the rest. It *is* such fun!'

They got out some cards and began to play a game. It was nice to be all together again. Things weren't the same somehow without Fatty. He said and did such ridiculous things, and nobody ever knew what he would do next.

Pip looked at his watch after a time and sighed. 'I must go,' he said. 'Come on, Bets. We shall only get into a row if we're late. Why does time always go so fast when you don't want it to?'

'Don't forget, Pip and Larry, you've got jobs to do tomorrow,' said Fatty, slipping the cards back into their case. 'Report here tomorrow after tea – and I'll have the money for Mr Goon's ticket ready for you, Daisy!'

She laughed. 'It will be more difficult than you think!' she said. 'Come on, Larry.'

As Fatty cleared up the shed when the others had gone, he wondered how he could get Mr Goon to buy the ticket. He ran his eye over the clothes hanging up at one side of the shed. He must certainly disguise himself, for Goon would never, never buy a ticket from him if he went as himself!

I'll go as an old woman, and pretend to read his hand! thought Fatty. He believes in that sort of nonsense. It should be fun!

Pip was also planning his own task. When should he shadow Mr Goon? Of course, it would be easiest to do it in the dark; but he didn't know what time Mr Goon went out at night, and he couldn't very well hang about outside his house for hours. No, it would have to be in the morning, when Goon went out on his bicycle. Pip would take his and follow him. He would pretend that Goon was a suspect – a burglar or a thief – and track him wherever he went!

So, next morning, Pip got his bicycle and set out to the street where the policeman lived. There was his house, with POLICE above it in big letters. Pip got off his bicycle, propped it against a big tree, and then quietly let all the air out of one tyre.

Now he could mess about with the wheel, pretending to pump up his tyre, and nobody would bother about why he was there, even if he had to wait for half an hour or more.

He did have to wait a good time, and got rather tired of pumping up his tyre and letting the air out again. But at last Mr Goon appeared; wheeling his bicycle out, his trousers neatly clipped in at the ankles.

Pip was surprised to see a skinny little boy of about eleven following Goon to the door. Goon shouted a few words to him, mounted his bicycle ponderously and rode off up the street. Pip slid onto his saddle and rode off too.

Goon didn't seem to have the slightest idea that he was being followed. He sailed along, waving to this person and that in a very condescending manner. He got off at the front gate of a house, propped his bicycle up against the fence, and went to the front door. Pip waited beside a hedge.

Out came Goon again, and rode down the road and into the main street. He got off at the post office and went inside. Pip got tired of waiting for him and thought longingly of ice creams. He was just near a shop that sold them. He suddenly decided to nip in and get one.

But while he nipped in and got one, Mr Goon came out and sailed away again on his bicycle. Pip only *just* managed to spot him, crammed his ice cream down his throat so that he almost froze himself, and raced after Goon.

On the way, he passed Mrs Trotteville, Fatty's mother. She had Buster with her, and as soon as he saw Pip, and heard his voice calling out 'Good morning,' he left Mrs Trotteville and raced after Pip.

'No, Buster. Not this morning. Go back, there's a good dog!' shouted Pip. But Buster laboured after him, panting. Fatty had gone out without him – so he would go with Pip. But Buster couldn't keep up with Pip on his bicycle and was soon left behind. He followed at a distance, still panting.

Mr Goon had gone down a lane that led nowhere except to a farm. Pip just managed to see him disappearing round the corner. He guessed what he had gone to the farm for. The farmer had been complaining bitterly that his sheep had been worried by dogs. Goon must have gone to get details of the dogs. Oh, well – Pip could sit under a hedge and wait for Goon to come out again. It was a bit dull shadowing him, really. He wondered how Larry was getting on with his window-cleaning.

Pip got off his bicycle, hid it in a ditch and then crept through a gap into the field. Sheep were there, with some fat woolly lambs about three months old. They were skipping about in a ridiculous fashion.

Pip sat with his back against a hawthorn tree and watched them. Suddenly he heard the scampering of feet and loud panting breath – and in another second, Buster had flung himself on him through the gap in the hedge! He licked Pip's face and yelped for joy. 'Found you!' he seemed to say. 'Found you!'

'Oh, Buster!' said Pip. 'Stop licking me!' He pushed Buster away, and the dog ran out into the field in a wide circle, barking. Some nearby lambs started away in alarm and ran to their mother-sheep.

And then a loud and familiar voice came through the hedge. 'Ho! So it's that toad of a boy's dog that chases Farmer Meadows's sheep, is it? I might have guessed it. I'll catch that dog and have him shot. I've just this minute been to the farm to get particulars of sheep-chasing dogs – and here I've got one caught in the act!'

Mr Goon came crashing through the hedge, and Pip at once sprang to his feet. 'Buster wasn't chasing the sheep!' he cried, indignantly. 'He came to find *me*. He's only arrived this very minute.'

'I'll catch that dog and take him off with me,' said Mr Goon, simply delighted to think that he could find such a good reason for catching Buster.

But it wasn't so easy to catch the Scottie. In fact, it was far easier for Buster to catch Mr Goon, as the policeman soon realised when Buster kept running at him and then backing away. In the end, he had to shout to Pip to call him off. Pip called him – and Goon just had time to mount his bicycle and pedal away at top speed!

'I wonder where Fatty is,' groaned Pip. 'I must find him and tell him about this. Blow you, Buster – what did you want to follow me for? NOW you're in for trouble!'

5. FATTY ENJOYS HIMSELF

Pip got on his bicycle and rode off. Buster ran beside him, keeping a good look out for Mr Goon. He would have very much liked another pounce at his ankles – but Goon was out of sight, on his way home. Visions of a nice hot cup of coffee, well-sugared, and a slice of home-made cake floated in his mind.

Pip rode to Fatty's house, but he wasn't there. 'Blow!' said Pip. 'I suppose he's gone off to sell his ticket to Mr Goon. I wish I'd seen him. I bet he looks exactly like some old woman shopping in the town!'

Fatty had had a most enjoyable time in his shed choosing a disguise to wear when he went to sell the ticket to Mr Goon. He had chosen a rather long black skirt, a black jumper, a shapeless dark red coat and a hat he had bought at the last jumble sale.

It was black straw, and had a few dark red roses in the front. Fatty put on a wig of dark hair, and made up his face, putting in a few artful wrinkles here and there.

He looked at himself in the mirror and grinned. Then he frowned – and immediately the face of a cross old woman looked back at him out of the mirror!

I wish the others could see me, thought Fatty. They'd hoot with laughter. Now, where's my handbag?

The handbag was a very old one of his mother's. In it was a powder compact, a handkerchief and a few hair-pins, all of which Fatty kept there for use when he disguised himself as a woman. He delighted in taking out the powder case and dabbing powder on his nose, as he had so often seen women do! His mother would have been most astonished to see him.

He unlocked the door of his shed, and opened it a little, listening. Was anyone about? Or could he slip safely out and into the road?

He could hear nothing, so he slipped out of the shed, locked the door and made his way up the side path through the shrubbery.

As he went through the bushes, a voice hailed him. 'Hey, you! What you doing there?'

It was the gardener, looking with interest at the shabby old woman.

Fatty immediately went all foreign. He flapped about with his hands, moved his shoulders up and down and said, 'Ackle-eeta-oomi-poggy-wo?'

'Can't you speak English?' said the gardener. 'See, there's the kitchen door if you want anything.'

'Tipply-opply-erica-coo,' said Fatty in a most grateful voice, and slid out of the gardener's sight. He grinned to himself. His disguise must be pretty good if the gardener didn't see through it!

He decided that it would be quite a good idea to go on being rather foreign. It was so easy to talk gibberish! Fatty could go on and on for a very long time, apparently speaking in a foreign language, shrugging his shoulders like his French teacher at school, and waggling his hands about.

He made his way down the road. Nobody took the least notice of him, which was very good. Fatty decided that he looked rather like one of the faded old women who sometimes sat on committees with his mother.

He came to the road where Goon lived and went up to his house. Was Goon in? Fatty knocked at the door.

It opened, and a skinny little boy stood there, the same skinny little fellow who had followed Goon to the door when Pip had been waiting for him.

The boy looked at him with sharp eyes. 'Mr Goon's out,' he said. 'There's only my Mum in. She's cleaning. If you want to leave a message, I'll call her.'

'Ah – zat would be kind,' said Fatty, giving the boy a sudden beaming smile. 'I vill come in.'

He pushed past the boy and went into Goon's office. He sat down, spreading out his skirts and patting the back of his hair with his hand.

'I'll fetch me Mum,' said the boy, who didn't quite know what to make of this visitor. Was she a friend of Mr Goon?

' 'Ere, Mum – there's a funny old foreign lady come to see Mr Goon,' Fatty heard the boy say. 'She's set herself down in the office.'

'All right. I'll see what she wants,' said Mum's

voice. Mum then appeared at the office door, wiping her hands on an apron of sacking.

Fatty gave her a gracious smile and nodded his head. 'I come to see dear Mr Goon,' he announced. 'He is expecting me, yes?'

'I don't rightly know,' said Mum. 'He's out just now. Will you wait? I'm just cleaning for him – I come every morning. I have to bring Bert with me because it's holidays, but he's useful.'

Fatty beamed at the skinny little woman, who really looked very like Bert. 'Ikkle-dokka-runi-pie,' he said, in a very earnest voice.

'Pardon?' said Mum, startled. 'You're from abroad, aren't you? I had a foreigner once who lodged with me. She was very clever – read my hand like a book!'

'Ah, so!' said Fatty. 'I too read the hand. Like a book.'

'Do you really?' said Mum, and came a little further into the room. Fatty racked his brains to remember who she was. He knew he had seen her before. Then he remembered. Of course – she was a friend of Jane, the maid, and sometimes came to help Cook when they had a party – he had heard them talking about her – what was her name now? Ah, yes – Mickle.

Mum wiped her hands again on her apron and held one out to Fatty. 'What's my hand tell you?' she asked, eagerly.

Fatty took it in his and frowned over it. 'Ah – your name it is Mickle! Mrs Mickle. You live at – at – Shepherd's Crescent . . .'

'Coo!' said Mum, most impressed. 'Is that all written in my hand? Go on.'

'You have five sisters,' said Fatty, remembering the gossip he had heard. 'And er – er – you have brothers – how many? It is difficult to see in your hand.'

'I've got six,' said Mum helpfully. 'Perhaps they're hidden under that bit of dirt there. I'd have washed me hands if I'd known you were coming.'

'I see illnesses here,' went on Fatty, 'and children – and cups and cups of tea – and . . .'

'That's right!' broke in Mum, quite excited. 'I've bin ill many a time – and I've got five children – Bert there is the youngest – and the cups of tea I've had – well, I must have had thousands in me life!'

'Millions,' said Fatty, still bent over her hand.

'Fancy you even seeing them cups of tea there,' said Mum. She raised her voice. 'Bert! This lady's a real wonder at reading hands. You come and listen.'

Bert was already listening just outside the door. He came right in when his mother called. He looked at Fatty disbelievingly.

'Where do you see them cups of tea?' he asked. 'How do you know they're not cups of coffee?'

Fatty decided that he didn't much like Bert. He thought it would be very nice indeed to read Bert's hand and see a great many scoldings there. But Bert didn't ask to have his hand read. He kept them both firmly behind his back as if afraid that Fatty would start reading them at once. Young Bert already had quite a lot of things in his life that he didn't want anyone to know about!

Someone rode up to the front gate and got off a bicycle. 'Coo, here's Mr Goon back already and I haven't got the kettle on for his coffee!' said Mum, and disappeared at once. Mr Goon opened the front door and came heavily into the hall. Mum called out to him.

'Mr Goon, sir! There's a lady wanting to see you. I've put her in the office.'

Mr Goon went into the kitchen. 'Who is she?' Fatty heard him say. 'What's she come for?'

'I didn't make so bold as to ask her *that,*' said Mum, putting a kettle on the stove. 'She's from abroad by the sound of her – funny-looking, you know, and speaks strangely.'

'She read Mum's hand,' said Bert, slyly.

'You hold your tongue, young Bert,' said Mum, sharply. 'She read it like a book, sir – knew me name and everything. One of these clever ones. You ready for your cup of coffee, sir?'

'Yes. I could do with one,' said Goon. 'I've been attacked by a dog this morning.'

'You don't say!' said Mum. 'Did he bite you?'

Mr Goon liked sympathy. He enlarged quite a bit on Buster's lighthearted game with him.

'It's a wonder my trousers aren't torn to bits,' he said. 'The dog came at me time and again. If I wasn't pretty nippy, I'd have been bitten more than I was. Good thing I had my thickest trousers on.'

'Well, there now! What a thing to happen to

you Mr Goon!' said Mum. Bert stared down at Mr Goon's trousers to see if they were torn. They didn't appear to be.

'You going to report the dog?' asked Bert.

'I caught it chasing sheep,' said Goon, taking off his helmet. 'Very serious crime, that, for a dog. I tried to catch it but I couldn't. I'd give anything to have that dog here under lock and key. I'd teach it a few things!'

'What would you give me if I got it for you?' asked Bert. Goon stared at him. Mum was taking no notice; she was busy at the cupboard with a cake-tin. Goon nodded his head towards the hall, and Bert followed him there.

Fatty had heard every word. He wondered whose dog this was that Goon was talking about. He knew that the farmer had been worried by sheep-chasing dogs. It never occurred to him that Goon was actually talking about Buster.

A whispered conversation followed. Fatty only caught a few words, but he guessed the rest. Goon was arranging with young Bert to catch the dog and bring it to him. A sum of money was mentioned. Fatty frowned. How wrong of Goon to do a thing like that! He wished he knew whose dog it was – he would certainly warn the owner!

Goon appeared in the office, looking rather pleased with himself, and young Bert went back to the kitchen.

Fatty didn't get up. He held out a gracious hand and bowed in a very ladylike way. Goon was rather impressed with this behaviour, though not with Fatty's clothes.

'What can I do for you, Madam?' said Goon.

'I am a friend of Mrs Trotteville,' said Fatty, truthfully. 'A vairy GREAT friend.'

'Ah,' said Goon, impressed. He was in awe of Mrs Trotteville. 'You staying with her, then?'

'I shall be wiz her for three wiks,' said Fatty, sticking to the truth. 'I sell tickets for the beeg sale. You will buy one, yes?'

'Er – well – er – can I offer you a cup of coffee?' said Goon, seeing Mum coming in with a tray. 'I hear you can read hands. I suppose you'll be doing that at the sale?'

'You would like me to read your beeg, beeg hand now – and you will buy a ticket?' offered Fatty.

Mr Goon couldn't resist having his hand read. Mum fetched another cup of coffee – and Mr Goon held out a large hand, palm upwards, to Fatty. How Fatty wished that Larry and the others could see him!

6. A FEW REPORTS

That evening, after tea, the Five Find-Outers met in Fatty's shed as arranged. Fatty was there first, grinning whenever he remembered how he had read Goon's hand. In his pocket was the money that Goon had given him for Daisy's ticket. Easy!

The others all arrived together. Fatty welcomed them. He had orangeade and biscuits, which everyone was pleased to see, in spite of the fact that they had all had a very good tea not half an hour before.

'Now, are we all ready? We'll have our various reports,' said Fatty. 'You first, Pip – you seem to be bursting with news.'

'I am,' said Pip, and poured out the story of how he had shadowed Goon, seen him go to the farmhouse, and waited for him in the field. He told how Buster had also shadowed *him*, and burst on him as he sat watching the sheep and the lambs.

'Then old Buster got excited and some lambs were afraid and scampered away, making the sheep run,' said Pip. 'Up came old Mr Goon and said that Buster ought to be shot for worrying sheep!'

'Good gracious!' said Daisy. 'Surely he didn't mean that? Buster has never, never chased a sheep, has he, Fatty?'

'Never,' said Fatty, who was listening intently. 'Go on, Pip.'

'There's nothing much more to tell except that Mr Goon was idiot enough to try and catch Buster,' said Pip. 'And Buster had a fine old game with him, of course, trying to nip his ankles. It would have served Mr Goon right if he *had* nipped them! The only reason that Mr Goon said that Buster was chasing sheep was just so that he could report him – but, oh, Fatty, Buster *couldn't* be shot just on Mr Goon's report, could he?'

'Don't worry. I'll see that he isn't,' said Fatty, grimly. 'We'd get on to Chief Inspector – I mean, Superintendent – Jenks at once! It's funny, though, when I went to see Mr Goon this morning, he came in talking all about some dog or other that he wanted brought in for sheep-chasing – I bet it was Buster, though he didn't say the name.'

'But, why did he tell you?' said Pip, surprised. 'He might have guessed you'd hear about it from me.'

'Oh, he didn't know *I* was sitting there in his office,' said Fatty. 'I was disguised, of course. I'll have to think about this story of yours, Pip. I have an idea that Mr Goon has made some arrangement with a nasty, skinny little kid to catch Buster. Son of a woman who was cleaning the house for Mr Goon.'

'I saw him at the door,' said Pip, remembering. 'Gosh, he'd never have the nerve to catch Buster, surely?'

'I don't know. We'll have to watch out,' said Fatty. 'Listen and I'll tell you how I sold the ticket to Mr Goon.'

Daisy gave a shriek of delight. 'Oh, did you really manage to? Oh, Fatty, you *are* clever! You must have been really well disguised.'

'Well, I was,' said Fatty, trying to be modest. 'As a matter-of-fact, I don't believe even Bets here would have guessed it was me. I went as a friend of my mother, a foreign one, rather down-at-heel – you know, old-lady-gone-to-seed-a-bit! Staying with dear Mrs Trotteville for three weeks.

Everyone roared. 'Oh, Fatty!' said Bets. 'It's so true too – you are a friend of your mother – and you *are* here for three weeks. Marvellous!'

'I sold the ticket by reading Mr Goon's hand,' went on Fatty, enjoying himself. 'He stuck his great fat paw on my knee, and I exclaimed over it, and said how extraordinary it was – and so it was, with its enormous fingers and great fat palm. I could hardly see the lines on it for fat.'

'What did you tell him?' asked Daisy.

'Oh, I told him his name was Theophilus, and that he had plenty of nephews – one very clever one called Ern,' said Fatty. Everyone laughed. Mr Goon disliked Ern intensely. 'I told him he would handle a lot of money,' went on Fatty.

'Yes! His wages every week!' grinned Pip.

'But the best bit was where I looked hard at his hand – like this,' said Fatty, clutching Daisy's hand suddenly and making her jump. He peered closely at it, then held it away, then peered at it again.

'Ha! Zis is a vairy pee-culiar thing I see!' said Fatty, sounding like the Frenchwoman again. 'I see – a boy – a beeg boy.'

There were roars of laughter at this. 'Oh, Fatty!' said Bets. 'You pretended you saw yourself in Mr Goon's hand! What did he say?'

'He seemed very startled,' said Fatty, in his own voice. 'He said, "What! That toad! Tell me more".'

'So you told him more?' said Larry, grinning.

'Oh, yes. I said, "BEWAAAAARE of zis big boy. There is some mystery here. Ze big boy and the mystery are togezzer!" ' Fatty paused and twinkled round at the others.

'That made Mr Goon sit up, I can tell you. He said, "What! A mystery! Go on – tell me about it. What mystery is it?" '

'What did you say?' said Bets, with a sudden giggle.

'I said, "I do not know zis mystery. It will come. But BEWAAAAARE of zis beeg boy!" '

'Oh, Fatty! I do wish I'd been there,' said Bets, and the others all agreed fervently. Oh, to have sat and watched Fatty reading Mr Goon's hand!

'Is that all?' asked Daisy. 'Tell us it all over again.'

'No. Not now,' said Fatty, reluctantly. 'We ought to hear Larry's story. Time's getting on. Anyway, the result of all this amazing hand-reading was that Mr Goon handed over the money for Daisy's ticket like an absolute lamb. He even said that if I was going to be at the sale, he'd be along for another hand-reading to see if the mystery was any nearer. He simply BEAMED at me!'

'Oh, dear – what a wonderful morning you had,' said Larry, as Fatty handed over the money to the delighted Daisy. 'Now I'll tell *my* story.'

'Yes, tell yours,' said Daisy. 'You should have seen him dressed up as a window-cleaner, Fatty! He borrowed an old pair of dirty blue dungarees, put on a frightful old cloth cap that has hung in the shed for ages, and made himself filthy – hands, face, and neck! Honestly, I'd never employ him as a window-cleaner. He looked more like a sweep.'

Fatty grinned. 'Good work,' he said to Larry. 'Go on, tell us what you did.'

'Well,' said Larry, 'I dressed up, just as Daisy's

told you. And I took an old pail and a leather, and off I went.'

'Where did you go?' asked Fatty.

'Well, I remembered I'd better not choose a house that needed a ladder for upstairs windows,' said Larry. 'So I tried to think of a bungalow somewhere, with the windows all on one floor. And I remembered seeing one next to that house called Green-Trees – do you remember, the one that that gentleman went to – the man we mistook to be Fatty.'

'Oh, yes, I remember the bungalow too,' said Fatty. 'Good for you! In Holly Lane, wasn't it? A little place with an untidy garden, standing a bit back from the road.'

'That's right. What a memory you've got, Fatty! You never miss anything,' said Larry. 'Well, I took my pail and my leather and walked up the path to the bungalow. I knocked at the door.'

'Was anyone in?' asked Bets.

'I didn't think so at first, because nobody answered,' said Larry. 'So I knocked again, very loudly. And a voice said "Come in." I opened the door and yelled inside, "Window-cleaner! Is it all right to do the windows now?' And somebody shouted "yes!" '

'Who was it? Did you see?' asked Fatty.

'No, I didn't,' said Larry. 'Anyway, I got some water from a tap outside, and started on the back windows – two of them. There wasn't anyone in the room there; it was a bedroom with a single bed, a chair, and a table – rather poor. As I was doing those windows, I heard the front door slam and somebody went up the path to the road. I didn't see him – or her, it might have been.'

'Was the house left empty then?' asked Fatty.

'I thought so, at first. But when I came round to the front to do the two front windows, I saw there was someone inside that room,' said Larry. 'And this is the strange part of my story.'

Everyone sat up at once.

'Strange – how do you mean?' asked Fatty.

'Well, at first I thought there wasn't anyone in the room,' said Larry, 'and I thought I'd hurry up and clean the windows and go, glad to have finished the job – actually, when I was doing it, I thought it was a bit silly! And then I suddenly saw someone on the floor.'

'On the *floor*! Hurt, do you mean?' asked Pip.

'No. He didn't seem to be hurt,' said Larry. 'He seemed to be feeling the chairs – he felt first one, and then another, muttering to himself all the time.'

'But what for?' asked Fatty. 'And who was he, anyway?'

'I don't know. He looked a very *old* man,' said Larry. 'He had a kind of nightcap on his head, and he wore pyjamas and a dressing-gown. He kept feeling one chair after another – underneath them – and then he came to a chair that seemed to satisfy him. He nodded and gave a kind of chuckle.'

'Extraordinary! What did he do next?' asked Fatty, most interested.

'He crawled over the floor to a kind of wheelchair, and somehow got into it,' said Larry. 'His nightcap slipped off, and he was quite bald, poor old fellow. He sat in front of some kind of stove, and then he dropped off to sleep as I watched him.'

'Didn't he see you looking in?' asked Bets.

'No. I think he's almost blind,' said Larry. 'He had to *feel* for the chairs – as if he couldn't really see them. Funny, wasn't it?'

'Yes. Very funny,' said Pip. 'I wonder what he was feeling all over the chairs for. Do you suppose he had got something hidden in one of them? Money, perhaps?'

'Possibly. He might be afraid of robbers and have hidden his little hoard somewhere odd that he considered safe,' said Fatty. 'Well, it's a peculiar story, Larry, and it's a good thing you weren't a real window-cleaner – a dishonest one might easily have guessed what the old man was doing! Making sure his savings were still safe!'

'I stripped off my dungarees in the bushes, cleaned myself up a bit with the leather, and went home,' said Larry. 'I'd really rather work on a *real* mystery than do all this pretend shadowing and disguising and window-cleaning. It doesn't really *lead* to anything!'

But Larry was wrong. Quite wrong. It led to quite a lot of things. It led, in fact, to a really first class mystery!

7. WHERE IS BUSTER?

For the next day or two, Fatty kept a sharp eye on Buster, wondering if the skinny little boy would really try to kidnap him. But there seemed to be no sign of Bert.

And then one evening, Buster disappeared! Fatty had gone out on his bicycle with the others to the cinema, and had left Buster safely in the kitchen with the cook, who was very fond of him. When he came back, he sat down and finished a book he was reading, and it wasn't until he had finished it that he realised that Buster had not come scampering to be with him as usual.

He went to the door and shouted, 'Buster! Where are you?'

It was half past ten. Cook and Jane had gone to bed. His mother and father were out playing bridge and the house was very quiet.

'BUSTER! Where are you?' yelled Fatty again.

A voice came from upstairs. 'Oh, Frederick, is that you shouting? You did give me a start! Isn't Buster with you? He wanted to go out at half past nine, and we thought he heard you coming in to put your bicycle away, so we let him out. Didn't you see him?'

'No, Jane! I haven't seen him since I've been in,' said Fatty. 'Where on earth can he be? I'll open the front door and yell.'

He stood at the front door and shouted, 'Buster, BUSTER!'

But no Buster came. Fatty was puzzled. Where could he have gone? Well, perhaps he would come in when his mother and father came back.

But Buster didn't. It was a very worried Fatty who greeted his parents when they came in at twelve o'clock.

'Frederick! Why aren't you in bed?' began his mother. 'It's midnight!'

'Have you seen Buster?' said Fatty. 'You haven't? Gosh, then, where can he be?'

'He's probably gone to visit one of his friends and forgotten the time, like you do sometimes!' said his father. 'Get to bed now. Buster will be back in the morning, barking outside at six o'clock and waking us all.'

There was nothing for it but to go to bed. Fatty undressed and got between the sheets. But he couldn't help remembering the whispered conversation he had heard in Goon's little hall – and Bert's mean little face. Had Bert somehow got hold of Buster?

Buster didn't come barking at the front door in the morning. He hadn't even appeared by breakfast-time! Fatty was by now quite certain that, somehow or other, the skinny little boy had managed to get hold of the little Scottie. He went out into the garden to investigate. Perhaps he could find something to explain Buster's disappearance.

He did find something. He found a small bit of liver attached to a short piece of string. Fatty pounced on it, frowning fiercely.

'That's it! That little beast, Bert, must have come along with some liver, tied it on a bit of string, and drawn it along for Buster to follow him. And old Buster leapt at it and got the liver and chewed the string in half. Then he must have followed Bert – and probably more liver – till Bert managed to slip a lead on him and take him off.'

He threw the bit of liver away and went indoors angrily. The telephone rang as he walked into the hall. His father was there and picked up the receiver.

'Hello! Yes, this is Mr Trotteville speaking. Who's that? Mr Goon? What's that? Do speak up, please, I can only hear a mumble.'

There was a short silence. Fatty stood nearby, listening. Mr Goon! Now what was this?

'I can't believe it!' said Mr Trotteville into the telephone. 'Buster has never chased a thing in his life – except your ankles. All right, come and see me. I don't believe it!'

He put the receiver down and faced Fatty. 'That fellow Goon says your dog Buster was caught red-handed last night, chasing sheep.'

'It couldn't have been Buster,' said Fatty. 'It must be some other dog.'

'He says he's got Buster in his shed now,' said Mr Trotteville. 'He'll be shot, you know, if this is true. Where was he last night?'

'Someone came and enticed him away,' said Fatty. 'Someone who's told a lie about Buster!

Who says they saw him chasing sheep?'

'A boy called Bert Mickle,' said his father. 'Goon says this boy was out walking in the fields last night, and actually saw Buster worrying the sheep. He managed to catch him, and slipped a rope under his collar. He took him to Mr Goon's, but the policeman was out, so the boy locked the dog in the shed there – and he's there still. Now what are we to do?'

'It's an absolute untruth,' said Fatty, looking rather white. 'It's a plan laid between them. I'll pay Mr Goon back for this. When's he coming, Dad?'

'In half an hour's time,' said Mr Trotteville. 'I'll have to see him. I can't bear the sight of him.'

Fatty disappeared. He knew quite well that Buster had not been chasing sheep. He also knew that the horrid little Bert had told a lot of lies, and he was sure that Goon knew it. And Buster might be shot because of all that!

Fatty raced down to his shed. He put on a red wig, inserted some false plastic teeth in front of his own, and dressed himself in an old suit, with a butcher boy's blue-and-white apron in front. Then he jumped on his bicycle and rode off down to Goon's house. He stood whistling on the pavement opposite, apparently reading a comic with great interest – but all the time he was watching for Goon to come out.

Goon came at last and wheeled his bicycle out of the front gate. He looked exceedingly pleased with himself, and hummed a little tune as he rode off.

The butcher boy opposite scowled and folded up his comic. Leaving his bicycle beside the kerb, he crossed the road and went round to the back of Goon's house.

He glanced at the shed in the garden. A subdued but angry barking came from it. Then a scraping at the door. Fatty bit his lip. That was Buster all right!

He knocked at the back door. Mrs Mickle came, wiping her hands on her apron as usual.

'You're wanted up at home, Mrs Mickle,' said Fatty. 'Message to say you're to go at once.'

'Oh, dear! oh, dear! I hope my mother's not been taken ill again,' said Mrs Mickle. 'Bert! I'm wanted up at home. You'd better keep on here till

I come back. Mr Goon's out.'

'Bert had better go with you,' said Fatty, firmly. He wanted them both out of the way as quickly as possible.

'No, I'm staying here,' said Bert, thinking of the tarts and buns he could take out of the larder with both Mr Goon and his mother out of the house.

That was that. Bert was not going to move, Fatty could see. All right, he would make him!

Mrs Mickle took off her apron and fled up the street. Bert stood at the front door and watched her go. Fatty nipped in at the back door and hid himself in a cupboard outside the kitchen.

Bert came back, having shut the hall door. He whistled. Ha, now for the larder! Fatty heard him go into the kitchen and open the larder door. It creaked. Fatty peeped out of the cupboard.

A hollow voice suddenly spoke behind Bert. 'Beware! Your sins will find you out. BEWARE!'

Bert turned round in a hurry. There was nobody in the kitchen at all. He stood there, trembling, a small jam tart in one hand.

'Who took that dog away last night?' said another voice, which seemed to come from behind the kitchen door. 'Who took him away?'

'Don't, don't!' cried poor Bert, and the jam tart fell from his hand. 'I took him, I took him! Who is it talking to me?'

A loud growling came from another corner and Bert yelled. He looked all round for the dog but couldn't see one. Then a loud mee-owing began. 'MEEE-ow! MEEE-ow!'

But no cat was to be seen. Bert began to howl and tears poured down his cheeks. 'Mum!' he cried. 'Mum!'

But Mum was far away up the street. Fatty began again. 'Who told a lie? Who took that dog away?'

'I'll tell the truth, I will, I will!' sobbed Bert. 'I'm a bad boy, I am.'

'BEWARE!' said the deep hollow voice again. It was too much for Bert. He fled into the hall and out of the front door, leaving it open as he went. Fatty heard the scampering of his feet, and grinned. So much for Bert. Served him right – trying to get an innocent dog shot!

Fatty went to the garden shed. He had with him a bunch of keys that he had seen hanging from a hook on the kitchen dresser. One of them unlocked the shed.

Buster flew at him, barking in delight. He careered round Fatty, and Fatty picked him up and squeezed him till the little Scottie had no breath left in his body. He licked Fatty's face vigorously.

Then Fatty suddenly caught sight of something – Mr Goon's enormous black cat sitting high up on a wall, watching Buster, out of sleepy insolent eyes. He knew he was too high up for any dog to catch. An idea came to Fatty.

'Just half a minute, Buster, old fellow,' he said, and put the Scottie inside the house, shutting the kitchen door on him.

Then he went to the great tomcat. He stroked it and murmured flattering things into its pricked-up ear. It purred loudly. Most animals loved Fatty!

It allowed him to lift it off the wall and fondle it. He walked with it to the shed and took it inside. He set it down on a sack that had evidently been placed there for Buster, and stroked it.

Then he went swiftly to the door, shut it, locked it, and took the keys back to the kitchen. Buster had been frantically scraping at the door, trying to get to Fatty. Fatty picked him up, and went out of Goon's house, across the road to his bicycle. He put Buster in the basket, and rode off whistling shrilly like an errand boy, thinking happy thoughts!

All right, Mr Goon! You can take my father down to see Buster in the shed – threaten to have him shot! You'll find nothing there but your own black tomcat! Fatty grinned at his thoughts, and Buster yapped happily in the basket. Why had he been shut up like that? He didn't know. But nothing mattered now. He was with Fatty, and Buster's world was cheerful and happy once more.

Fatty shot in at his side gate and cycled down to his shed. He tore off his errand boy things. Then he shut Buster up in the shed, with many apologies, and went back to the house. Was Mr Goon still there? Well, he could say what he liked! Buster was safe!

8. MR GOON GETS A SHOCK

Mr Goon had been at Fatty's house for about five minutes, and was thoroughly enjoying himself. He knew that neither Mr nor Mrs Trotteville liked him, and it was pleasant to Mr Goon to bring them such bad news about Buster.

Fatty sauntered into the room, and Mr Goon looked at him triumphantly. 'Morning, Mr Goon,' said Fatty. 'Lovely April day, isn't it? Got any mystery in the offing yet?'

'I've come about that there dog of yours,' said Mr Goon, almost joyfully. 'Been caught chasing sheep again.'

'Rubbish,' said Fatty, briskly. 'Never chased one in his life!'

'I've got evidence,' said Goon, going slightly purple. 'And I've got the dog too, see? Locked up in my shed.'

'I don't believe it,' said Fatty. 'I'll have to see the

dog first, before I believe it's old Buster. He's not the dog in your shed, I'll be bound.'

Mr Trotteville looked at Fatty in surprise. Fatty winked at him. His father heaved a sigh of relief. He had no idea what Fatty was up to; but he began to feel that somehow, somewhere, Goon was not going to get away with this tale about Buster.

Goon went very purple indeed. He turned to Mr Trotteville. 'If you'll be so good, sir, as to come along with me and identify the dog, it would be a great help,' he said. 'Frederick had better come too. After all, it's his dog.'

'I'll come all right,' said Fatty. 'You coming too, Dad?'

'Yes. I'll get the car out,' said his father, still puzzled over Fatty's attitude. 'You can come with me, Frederick. You cycle off, Mr Goon, and we'll be there as soon as you are.'

Mr Trotteville went to get the car. Goon disappeared on his bicycle, purple but still triumphant. Fatty went to the telephone.

'Oh, is that Mrs Hilton? Good morning. Please may I speak to Pip? Won't keep him a minute.'

Pip was fetched. Fatty spoke to him urgently.

'Pip? Listen. No time for explanations. I want you to do something for me.'

'Right,' said Pip's voice, sounding excited. 'Hey, is this a mystery starting up?'

'No. Nothing like that. Listen now. I want you to come up here quickly, unlock my shed, get old Buster out of it, and bring him down to Mr Goon's house. Put him on a lead. Don't come into Mr Goon's – just wait outside till I come out. Tell you everything then!'

Click. Fatty put down the receiver. He rubbed his hands and grinned. Aha, Mr Goon, you are going to be very, very surprised!

He got into the car beside his father, who glanced at him sideways. 'I gather, Frederick,' he said, 'that you are quite happy about this Buster affair now? But you possibly do not want to tell me why?'

'How right you are, Dad,' said Fatty, cheerfully. 'I'll just tell you this: Mr Goon played a very dirty trick, but it's not going to come off!'

'There was silence after that. Mr Trotteville drove straight to Goon's house, and the two of them got out. Goon himself had just arrived, and was astonished to find the house completely empty. No Mrs Mickle, no Bert!

Mr Trotteville and Fatty went in at the front door, and at the very same moment Mrs Mickle and Bert arrived at the back. Bert's eyes were red, and he looked frightened. Mrs Mickle was in a rage.

She spoke to Mr Goon. 'I'm sorry to have left the house so sudden-like, Mr Goon – but that dratted boy of the butcher's come along and told me I was wanted at home, so I left Bert here in charge, and rushed home – and I wasn't wanted after all. Just wait till I get that butcher's boy!'

Bert gave a sudden sniff. Mrs Mickle looked at him in disgust. 'And Bert, who I left here just to stay till you were back, sir, he come racing home, howling like I don't know what. Scared of being left in your place alone, and telling such tales as I never heard the like of in my life!'

'Mr Trotteville, this is the boy who caught Buster chasing sheep last night,' said Goon.

'I never!' said Bert suddenly, and burst into tears. 'I never, I never!'

'Bert! How can you tell stories like that?' said his mother. 'Why, you stood there and told Mr

Goon all about it this morning. I heard you!'

'I never, I never, I never,' said Bert, and sniffled again.

'He's a bit nervous, I expect,' said Goon, surprised and most displeased. 'You caught the dog yourself, didn't you, Bert?'

'I never,' said Bert, who seemed quite incapable of saying anything else.

Goon gave up. 'Well, the dog's in the shed, and it's the very dog Bert brought in and put there himself.'

'I never!' said Bert, making Mr Goon long to box his ears. The big policeman strode out through the kitchen and into the garden, taking with him the keys of the shed. He inserted one into the lock, and flung the door open, expecting Buster to rush out and declare himself.

But no dog arrived. Instead, Mr Goon's extremely large black cat strolled out haughtily, sat down outside the shed, and began to wash himself.

Goon's eyes nearly fell out of his head. Fatty gave a roar of laughter and Bert howled in fright. Bert *had* put Buster into the shed; and to see the black cat come out instead of the dog was quite terrifying to poor Bert.

'I never, I never, I never!' he sobbed, and hid his face in his mother's apron.

Goon's mouth opened and shut like a goldfish's, and he couldn't say a word. The cat went on washing itself, and Bert went on howling.

'Well, Mr Goon, if it's a cat that was shut into this shed, and not Buster, I really don't think it's worth while our wasting our time with you any more,' said Mr Trotteville, sounding quite disgusted. 'Did you say that you yourself saw the dog that was put into the shed?'

Goon hadn't seen Buster. He had been out when Bert arrived with the dog and he had just taken Bert's word for it. Now he didn't know whether Bert had shut up a dog or the cat. He glared at the boy as if he could bite him.

Bert howled afresh. He put his hand in his pocket and took out a coin. He held it out to Goon. 'Here you are. I've been wicked. Here's the money you gave me, Mr Goon. I'll never go after dogs again for you.'

'Well, I think we've heard enough,' said Mr

Trotteville, coldly. 'Goon, you deserve to be reported for all this. I've a good mind to do so. Come on, Frederick.'

'But – but I don't understand it,' said Goon, his eyes popping out of his head. 'Why, I *heard* that dog barking in the shed, I tell you! Listen! Isn't that him barking now?'

It was! Pip was walking up and down outside, with Buster on the lead, and Buster had recognised Mr Trotteville's car parked nearby. He was barking his head off in delight.

They all went to the front door – and poor Goon nearly fainted when he saw Buster, Buster himself, pulling on Pip's lead and barking frantically.

'Hello, Pip,' said Fatty, in a very ordinary voice. 'Thanks for taking Buster for a walk. Slip him off the lead, will you?'

'No. No, don't,' said Goon, finding his voice suddenly. 'Wait till I'm indoors.'

He shot into the house and slammed the door. Fatty grinned at his father. 'I *should* like to know how the cat took the place of the dog,' murmured Mr Trotteville, getting into the car with Fatty and Buster. Pip got in too, puzzled, but grinning all over his face.

'Tell you when we get home' said Fatty. 'My word, I wouldn't like to be young Bert right now!'

Young Bert was indeed having a bad time. Mrs Mickle was crying, Bert was howling, and Goon felt rather like howling himself. He felt a fool, an idiot – to bring that high-and-mighty Mr Trotteville down to show him a dog locked up in his shed – and then his own black cat walked out! Gah!

Bert told a peculiar tale of voices in every corner, when he had been left alone in the house. Goon looked round uneasily. Voices? What did Bert mean? He suddenly remembered Fatty's ability to throw his voice, just like any ventriloquist. *Could* Fatty have been here? No, impossible!

The more poor Goon thought about it, the more impossible everything seemed. He looked at Bert with so much dislike that the skinny little boy decided he'd slip off home. What with his Mum cross with him, and Mr Goon looking as if he'd like to eat him up, and those voices he had heard, life wasn't worth living! So Bert slipped off home.

'I think Pip and I will get out of the car, and have an ice cream, Dad,' said Fatty to his father, as they drove down the main street. 'I somehow feel like one. You can have one too, Buster.'

'Right,' said his father and stopped. 'I'm glad Buster's all right, Frederick. I'll hear all about it later.'

Fatty and Pip got out with Buster. 'I say, do tell me what's been happening!' said Pip.

'Come in here and I'll tell you,' said Fatty. 'Goon tried to play a very dirty trick – and it didn't come off. Come along.'

And over three ice creams, Fatty told the horrified Pip the dreadful story of how Buster had nearly been shot for doing something he hadn't done! Pip almost choked over his ice cream!

'Look, there's Larry and Daisy and Bets,' said Pip, suddenly. 'Let's have them in and tell them too.'

But it turned out that the other three had already had ice creams, and were now on their way to fetch something. 'Larry left the leather behind in the garden of that bungalow whose windows he cleaned the other day,' explained Daisy. 'And

Mummy's been hunting for it everywhere. So we thought we'd better go and find it in the bushes. It's sure to be there still.'

'We'll all come – and then you can come back home with me and I'll tell you a most peculiar tale,' said Fatty. '*Most* peculiar, isn't it, Buster?'

'Not a mystery, is it?' asked Bets, hopefully, as they all went along together. Fatty shook his head.

'There's not even the smell of one,' he said. 'Look – isn't this the place, Larry – that little bungalow there?'

'Yes,' said Larry, and went into the garden. He came back quite quickly, looking rather scared.

'I say, there's somebody shouting like anything in that bungalow. It sounds as if they're yelling "Police! Police! Police!" '

'*Really?* Come on, we'll see what's up,' said Fatty, and they all trooped in at the gate. Fatty went to the door. It was shut. From within came a curious croaking shout.

'Police! Police! Fetch the police!'

'Whatever can be the matter?' said Fatty. 'I'd better go in and see!'

9. THE OLD MAN IN THE BUNGALOW

The five children and Buster went up the path. The front door was shut. Fatty went to look in at one of the windows, and the others followed.

Green curtains were drawn back to let the light into the room. In the middle of the room sat an old man in a small armchair. He was beating on the arms and shouting, 'Police! Police! Fetch the police!'

'It's the old man I saw when I cleaned the windows,' said Larry. 'What's the matter with him? Why does he want the police?'

They all looked at the old fellow. He had on a dressing-gown over pyjamas, and a nightcap that had slipped to one side of his bald head. He had a small beard on his chin and a scarf tied loosely round his neck.

By the stove stood a wheelchair with a rug half-falling off it, and on a shelf nearby was a small portable radio, within reach of the old man's hand. The children could hear it playing loudly.

'Something's upset the old fellow,' said Fatty. 'Let's try the door and see if it's unlocked.'

They went back to the door, and Fatty turned the handle. The door opened at once.

They all went in, Buster too. The old man neither heard nor saw them. He still sat in the chair, beating its arms, and wailing for the police.

Fatty touched him on the arm, and the old fellow jumped. He stopped shouting and blinked up at Fatty with watery eyes. He put out his hand and felt along Fatty's coat.

'Who is it? Is it the police? Who are you?'

'I'm someone who heard you shouting and came to see what was the matter,' said Fatty speaking loudly. 'Can we help you? What has happened?'

It was clear that the old man could hardly see. He peered round at the others and drew his dressing-gown round him. He began to shiver.

'Look, you get back to the fire,' said Fatty. 'I'll take one arm – Larry, you take the other. The old fellow has had a shock of some kind – he's trembling. Turn off that radio, Bets!'

The old man made no objection to being helped to his own chair. He sat down in it with a sigh, and let Daisy arrange his cushions and rug. He peered at them again.

'Who are you all? Fetch the police, I say,' he said, and his voice quavered as he spoke.

'Do tell us what's the matter,' said Daisy. But he couldn't hear her, and she repeated the question loudly.

'Matter? Matter enough. My money's gone!' he said, and his voice rose to a howl. 'All my money! Now what's to happen to me?'

'How do you know it's gone?' said Fatty, loudly. 'Didn't you keep it in the bank, or the post office?'

'Banks? I don't trust banks!' wailed the old fellow. 'I hid it where nobody could find it. Now it's gone.'

'Where did you hide it?' asked Larry.

'What? What's that?' said the old man, cupping his hand over his ear. 'Speak up.'

'I said, "WHERE DID YOU HIDE IT?" ' repeated Larry. A sly look came over the old fellow's face. He shook his head.

'I shan't tell you. No, that's my secret. It was hidden where nobody could find it. But now it's gone.'

'Tell us where you hid it, and we'll have a good look for it ourselves,' said Daisy, loudly. But the old man shook his head more vigorously than ever.

'You get the police!' he said. 'I want the police! Two hundred pounds, that's what's gone – all my savings. The police will get it back for me. You get the police.'

Fatty didn't in the least want to go and find Mr Goon. Goon would turn them all out and not let them help at all. He would be bossy and domineering and a perfect nuisance.

'When did you miss the money?' he asked the old man.

'Just now,' he said. 'About ten minutes ago. I looked for it, and it was gone! Oh, I'm a poor old man and people have robbed me! Get the police.'

'We will,' said Fatty, comfortingly. 'Just tell us when you *last* saw the money. Do you remember?'

'Course I remember,' said the old fellow, pulling his nightcap straight. 'But I didn't *see* it. I'm nearly blind. I *felt* it. It was there all right.'

'When was that?' asked Fatty, patiently.

'Last night,' said the old man. 'About midnight, I reckon. I was in bed, and I couldn't sleep, and I sat up and worried about my money. You see, I'm all alone here since my daughter's gone away. Well, I got out of bed and I came in here. And I felt for my money. It was there all right.'

'I see,' said Fatty. 'So somebody must have taken it between then and now. Has anyone been to see you this morning?'

'Yes. Yes, of course,' he said. 'But I'm muddled now. I misremember who came – except my granddaughter, of course – she comes every day and cleans round. She's a good girl. And the grocer came. But I misremember. You get the police. They'll find my money for me!'

A big tear fell from one eye and rolled down his cheek. Bets felt very sorry for him. Poor old man – all alone, and worried about his money. Where could it be? Had it really been stolen – or had he just forgotten where he had put it? If only he would tell them!

'We'll have to tell Mr Goon,' said Fatty to the others. 'It's a pity. We might have been able to clear this up ourselves if we'd had a chance.'

The five children suddenly heard footsteps coming up the path. Who was it? There was a loud knock at the door, then the handle turned, and a man walked in. He stared in surprise at the children. Buster barked loudly.

'Hello!' said the man. He was young and smartly-dressed. 'Who are you? Are you visiting my great-uncle? Hello, Uncle! How are you?'

'Oh, Wilfrid – is it you?' said the old man, putting out a hand as if to find out where Wilfrid was. 'Wilfrid, my money's gone!'

'What! Gone? What do you mean?' asked Wilfrid. 'Didn't I tell you somebody would rob you if you didn't let me put it into the bank for you?'

'It's gone, it's gone,' said his uncle, rocking himself to and fro.

'Where did you keep it?' asked Wilfrid, looking all round. 'I bet it's not gone, Uncle! You've forgotten where you hid it! Maybe up the chimney – or under a floorboard?'

'I'm not telling anyone,' said the old man. 'I want the police! I'm tired. I want my money and I want the police!'

'We'll go and telephone the police, if you like,' Fatty offered. 'I see there are telephone wires leading next door. I expect they'd let me use the phone.'

'What are *you* doing here, anyway?' said Wilfrid, suddenly.

'Nothing. We just heard the old man calling,' said Fatty, thinking it better not to say that Larry had gone to find the leather he had left behind in the bushes, and had heard the old man shouting as he passed the bungalow. 'Anyway, we'll go and telephone now. The police will be up in a few minutes, I'm sure.'

'Good-bye,' said Bets to the old man, but he didn't hear her. He was moaning softly to himself. 'My money! Now what shall I do? All gone, all gone!'

The five of them went out with Buster. They went down the path and walked beside the fence till they came to Green-Trees. They went up the path to the blue front door. Fatty rang the bell.

A pleasant-faced woman answered it. She looked very French, and Fatty decided that she must be the sister whose house the bundled-up man had tried so hard to find.

'Excuse me,' said Fatty, politely. 'Do you think I might use your telephone? The old man in the bungalow next door has been robbed, and we want to tell the police.'

The woman looked startled. 'A robbery? Next door? Oh, the poor old man! Yes, come in and use my telephone! It is in this room here.'

She spoke English extremely well, but had a slight accent which was rather pleasant. She was very like her brother, dark and plump.

She took them into a room off the hall. A couch stood by the window, and a man lay on it coughing. He turned as they came in.

'Henri, these children want to use the telephone,' said the woman. 'You do not mind?'

'Enter, I pray you,' said the man, and then stared. 'Ah!' he said, 'zeese children I have seen before – n'est-ce-pas?'

'Yes,' said Fatty. 'We guided you to Green-Trees, you remember?'

'Yes, Grintriss,' said the man with a smile. He looked quite different now, without his bulky overcoat, scarf and pulled-down hat – younger and pleasanter. He coughed. 'You will pardon me if I lie here? I am not so well.'

'Of course,' said Fatty. 'I hope you don't mind our coming in here like this, but the old fellow next door has been robbed of his money – or so he says – and we want to tell the police.'

Fatty picked up the receiver of the telephone. 'Police Station,' he said.

A loud, sharp voice answered. 'PC Goon here. Who's calling?'

'Er – Frederick Trotteville,' said Fatty. 'I just wanted to tell you that . . .'

There was a loud snort from the other end and a crash. Goon had put down his receiver in a temper! Fatty was astonished.

'Gosh! I got Mr Goon, and as soon as I began to speak to him, he crashed back the receiver!' said Fatty. 'I suppose he's still furious about Buster. Well, I'll try again.'

He got the police station once more, and again Goon's voice answered.

'Look here, Mr Goon,' said Fatty. 'Will you go to the bungalow called Hollies, in Holly Lane. There's been a robbery there.'

'Any more of your nonsense and I'll report you to Headquarters,' snapped Goon. 'I'm not going out on any wild goosechase, and have you come back here and shut my cat up in the shed again. Ho, yes, I . . .'

'MR GOON! LISTEN!' shouted Fatty. 'This isn't a joke, it's . . .'

Crash! Goon had put down his receiver again. Fatty put down his and stared in comical dismay at the others. 'Mr Goon's mad! He thinks I'm spoofing him. What shall we do?'

'Ring up Superintendent Jenks,' suggested Daisy. 'It's the only thing to do, Fatty!'

'I will!' said Fatty. 'It'll serve Mr Goon right!'

10. GOON TAKES CHARGE

Fatty rang through to Police Headquarters in the next town, and asked for Superintendent Jenks.

'He's out,' said a voice. 'Who wants him?'

'Er – this is Frederick Trotteville,' said Fatty, wishing the Superintendent was in. 'I just wanted to say that a robbery has been committed at a bungalow called Hollies, in Holly Lane, Peterswood, and the old man who's been robbed asked me to tell the police.'

'You want to ring up *Peterswood* Police then,' said the voice.

'I have,' said Fatty. 'I – er – I can't seem to get hold of them. Perhaps you could ring through to tell them?'

'Right,' said the voice. 'Robbery – Hollies – Holly Lane – Peterswood. And your name is . . .?'

'Frederick Trotteville,' said Fatty.

'Ah, yes, I know! Friend of the Super, aren't

you?' said the voice, in a more friendly tone. 'Right, sir – leave it to me.'

And so, once more, the telephone rang at Goon's house, and once more he answered it, snatching it up angrily, sure that it was Fatty again.

'Hello, hello! Who's that?' he barked.

A surprised voice answered, 'This is Headquarters. Is that PC Goon? A boy called Frederick Trotteville has just . . .'

'Pah!' said Goon, unable to help himself.

'What did you say?' said the voice, still more surprised.

'Nothing. Just coughed,' said Goon. 'What about this here boy?'

'He reports a robbery at the bungalow called Hollies, Holly Lane, in your area,' said the voice.

Goon's mouth fell open. So Fatty hadn't been trying to spoof him! There really had been a robbery. What a pest of a boy! Playing tricks on him and Bert – and the cat – and getting away with Buster – and now finding a robbery! What a toad of a boy!

'Are you there?' said the voice, impatiently.

'Have you got what I said?'

'Er – yes – yes,' said Goon, scribbling down a few notes. 'Thanks. All right. I'll go right along.'

'You'd better!' said the voice, puzzled and annoyed. There was a click. Goon stared at the telephone and clicked back his receiver too. Now he'd get a rap on the knuckles for making Fatty ring Headquarters. Why hadn't he listened to him when he telephoned?

He got out his bicycle and yelled to Mrs Mickle, 'Be back in half an hour, I expect. Have my dinner ready! This is an urgent job.'

The five children had not left Green-Trees by the time Goon cycled up. They were talking to the Frenchman, whose name turned out to be Henri Crozier. They told him all about the old fellow next door.

'I can see the front gate and front path of the bungalow from my couch,' said Henri. 'I got my sister to put the couch here because it's a pleasant view, and I can see people who come and go down the road.'

They all looked out of the window. 'You must have seen us going in then,' said Fatty. 'Did you?'

'Oh, yes,' said Henri, 'First I saw zis boy – what does he call himself – Larry? He went in and up the path – and then he came running back to you, and you all went up the path and in at the front door.'

Larry went red. He hoped to goodness that Henri wasn't going to ask him why he had first gone in at the gate. It wouldn't be at all easy to explain how it was that he had left a window-leather in the bushes!

Fortunately, his sister came bustling in just then. Her name was Mrs Harris and her husband, who was away, was English. She carried a box of French chocolates, very rich and creamy.

'Oh, thanks,' said Daisy, and took one. They all helped themselves, and then there came a sudden exclamation from Henri.

'See, the police have arrived!'

Sure enough, Mr Goon was wheeling his bicycle up the front path next door. The door opened as he came and the young man, Wilfrid, appeared. He said something to Goon and they both disappeared into the bungalow.

'Well, now, perhaps the old man will be happy,'

said Fatty. 'My word – what a super chocolate! We don't get chocolates like that here, Mrs Harris.'

'We'd better go,' said Pip, looking at his watch. 'Do you know it's almost one o'clock? Good gracious! Mother said we must be back by five to. Hurry up, Bets.'

The five said good-bye to Henri and his sister. 'You will come again?' said the sister. 'Henri is so bored. He has been very ill and now he comes to me to – how do you call it? – to convalesce. Come and see him again.'

'Thank you. We will,' said Fatty, hoping fervently that Mr Goon would not also take it into his head to go and see Henri and his sister, and ask them if they had noticed visitors at the bungalow that morning! It might be very awkward to explain Larry's visit there an hour or so before. Blow that window-leather! And yet, if Larry hadn't gone to find it, he wouldn't have heard the old man shouting.

'Gosh, I never got Mummy's window-leather after all!' said Larry. 'What an idiot I am. I'll slip in and get it now.'

'No, you won't,' said Fatty, firmly. 'You'll leave

it there. We don't want Mr Goon to come rushing out and asking you what you're doing. You can get it when Mr Goon's not there.'

They all went home. Fatty was thinking hard. Why wouldn't the old man say where he had hidden his money? It was silly of him, because he might have made a mistake when he hunted for it – it might quite well still be in the bungalow in some place he had forgotten.

Larry said that the old fellow was crawling about, feeling under the furniture, the day he went to clean the windows, thought Fatty. Why feel so *much* of the furniture? Did he sometimes put the money in one place and sometimes in another? Or perhaps he divided it up – it might be in notes – and put it in several places. That's quite likely. Well, it's not a *real* mystery, only an ordinary robbery. Mr Goon will soon find the robber. He's only got to get a list of the people who visited the bungalow this morning, and weed them out.

That afternoon, Goon arrived at Fatty's house. He asked for Fatty – and Jane showed him into the study.

'That policeman wants you, Frederick,' said

Jane, when she found Fatty. 'I hope Buster hasn't got into trouble again!'

'Wuff,' said Buster, and danced round Jane. Fatty debated whether to take the little Scottie into the study with him or not. He thought he would. It might keep Goon in his place!

So in marched Fatty, with Buster at his heels. Goon was standing at the window, frowning. He was feeling angry about a lot of things. He was angrier still when he felt Buster sniffing at his heels.

'Come here, Buster,' said Fatty. 'Oh, won't you sit down, Mr Goon? Anything I can do for you?'

Goon swung round, eyeing Buster balefully. That dog! Had that tiresome Bert locked him up in the shed the night before, or hadn't he? He couldn't get a word out of Bert now.

Goon sat down heavily and took out his bulky notebook. 'I've come about the robbery,' he said.

'Well, I'm not guilty,' said Fatty, smoothly. 'I do assure you I . . .'

'I know you're not guilty,' said Goon, looking as if he wished Fatty were. 'What I want to know is, how did you come to be around there just when the old man was yelling blue murder?'

'He wasn't,' corrected Fatty. 'He was yelling for the police.'

'Pah!' said Goon. 'You know what I mean. Seems a funny thing to me the way you kids are always about when anything happens. Snooping round. Prying. Interfering with the law.'

'If that's all you've come to tell me, you might as well say good-bye,' said Fatty, getting up. 'I mean, I can easily bike over to the Superintendent this afternoon and tell *him* everything. I don't want to interfere with the law. I want to help it. We couldn't help being there just at that moment. Well, good morning, Mr Goon.'

Goon looked extremely startled. 'Now, you sit down,' he said, trying to speak pleasantly. 'I'm only just saying what a remarkable thing it is that you always seem to be around when things happen. Nothing wrong in saying that, is there?'

'You mentioned something about snooping. And prying,' said Fatty.

'Ah, well, I'm a bit upset-like,' said Mr Goon, taking out an enormous handkerchief and wiping his forehead with it. 'Let's forget it. I don't want to interview you, but the law's the law. It's the last thing I wanted to do today – see you again. But I've got to ask you a few questions seeing as you and the others were the first on the spot, so to speak.'

'Ask away,' said Fatty, 'but don't be too verbose – I've got plenty to do.'

Goon wondered what 'verbose' meant – something rude, he'd be bound! He determined to look it up in the dictionary when he got back. Verbose!

He began to ask Fatty a few routine questions.

What time had Fatty and the others been there? Anyone about? Anything disarranged in the living-room? What had the old man said?

Fatty answered shortly and truthfully, thankful that Goon had no suspicion that they had actually gone to the bungalow garden to fetch something. Goon imagined that they had been out for a walk, and had heard the old man's yells as they passed.

'That's all,' said Goon, at last. Fatty thought that he had asked the questions very well. He had left nothing out that might be useful.

Goon looked at Fatty. 'Er – I suppose you've got your own ideas about this already?' he said.

'Oh, yes,' said Fatty. 'I've no doubt it will be quite easy to find the robber. Didn't the old man give you a list of the people who had been to visit him this morning?'

'Well, he seemed so muddled,' said Goon. 'He might have been remembering *yesterday's* visitors. He's old and forgetful. I wouldn't be surprised if that money isn't still there somewhere. Er – hm – what do you think about it all?'

Fatty wasn't going to give Goon any help at all. He remembered how Goon had given Bert money to catch Buster. He got up suddenly, not wanting to look at the policeman any more.

'Good morning,' he said to Goon, and showed him out very firmly. Let Goon find out what he could – Fatty didn't mean to help him!

11. TEA AT PIP'S

The Five met that day in Pip's playroom at half past three. Mrs Hilton had said they might all go to tea, and had sent Pip and Bets out to buy cakes from the baker's.

They had staggered in with baskets full, and had arranged all the goodies themselves on big dishes. They were set on the table, ready for tea.

'Why do you put them under our noses like this?' groaned Daisy. '*Look* at those macaroons – all gooey and luscious. What a terrible temptation.'

'And look at that gingerbread cake – and that fruit cake,' said Larry. 'We never seem to have such nice teas as you do, Pip.'

'Oh, it's only when people come to tea that Mummy goes a splash like this,' said Pip. 'Buster, you've got your favourite tit-bit – dog-biscuits spread with potted meat. Sniff!'

Buster sniffed, shot out a pink tongue – and the

biscuit disappeared with one crunch!

'Oh, Buster! Manners, manners!' said Fatty. 'You don't see your master doing things like that, do you?'

Everyone laughed. Pip got out some cards and shuffled them. Fatty told them of Goon's visit to him that afternoon.

'How you could bear to be polite to him when you knew he had planned to have Buster shot, I *don't* know!' said Pip.

'Well, I *wasn't* awfully polite actually,' admitted Fatty. 'Also, I was a bit afraid he'd ask why we were there. I wish to goodness you'd taken away that window-leather, Larry. I wouldn't put it past old Mr Goon to snoop round the garden and find it.'

'Blow!' said Larry. 'Mummy keeps on asking about it. I really must get it soon. I would have bought a new one, but when Daisy and I looked in the shop this afternoon, the big ones were very expensive.'

'I'll get it from the bungalow garden for you,' said Fatty. 'You mustn't go bursting in at the garden gate in full daylight, and come out waving a window-leather! I'll go tonight and get it, when it's dark.'

'I shouldn't have gone in daylight anyhow,' said Larry, a little offended. 'I'm not *quite* an idiot. But I'd be glad if you got it for me, actually, because it's difficult for me to slip out at night. It's easy for you – you can always say you're taking Buster for a walk.'

'I usually do take him for a run last thing at night,' said Fatty. 'I'll go tonight, and I'll bring the leather here to you tomorrow.'

'Are we going to go and see that old man again?' asked Daisy. 'Are we going to treat this as a mystery – a rather small one, I know – and try to find out who the robber is, or are we going to let Mr Goon get on with it, and not bother about it at all ourselves?'

'Well, I don't actually think there's much mystery,' said Fatty. 'Either the money is still there, hidden, and the old fellow has forgotten where, or someone's taken it who knew it was hidden. If so, it can only be one of his relatives, I should think. Quite a straightforward case. Anyway, I somehow don't want to have anything more to do with Mr

Goon, after this Buster business. I just can't bear the sight of him.'

'Right. Then we won't count this as a mystery,' said Daisy. 'We'll just go on hoping. What I *was* going to say was that the person who would *really* know who visited the old man this morning would be that Frenchman – Mr Henri. He lies on that couch and watches everyone who passes – and he has a really good view of the bungalow's front door.'

'Yes. You're right,' said Fatty. 'He would be the first one we'd ask for a bit of information. But I think we'll leave this to Mr Goon. To tell you the truth, I'm a bit afraid of somebody asking about a window-cleaner! Somebody may have spotted Larry – and we'd look rather foolish if it came out about his cleaning the windows.'

'I always thought it was rather a silly thing to ask me to do,' said Larry. 'I said so at the time.'

'Well, maybe it was a bit mad,' said Fatty. 'We'll forget it. Come on, whose deal is it? We'll just have time for a game before tea.'

They had a hilarious game, and an even more hilarious tea. During the game, Buster discovered that by sitting on a chair, he could reach his plate of potted-meat biscuits, and he devoured every one of them without being noticed. He then quietly jumped down and went and lay by Bets.

'Isn't he good and quiet today?' said Bets, patting him. 'He's usually too silly for words when we play cards and don't take any notice of him. Last time he smacked all my cards out of my hand, I remember. Didn't you, Buster?'

'Wuff,' said Buster, in a quiet voice. He was beginning to feel very guilty.

Larry tickled him. Buster didn't jump up and caper round as he usually did. He just let Larry tickle him. Larry looked at him closely.

'Why don't you wag your tail?' he said. 'Don't you think Buster's gone rather quiet? Buster, old fellow, what's up?'

Buster's tail remained quite still, without a wag. Bets looked at him in alarm. 'He can't be feeling well! Buster! Good dog! Stand up, Buster, and wag your tail!'

Buster stood up, looking the picture of misery, head down and tail down. What a fuss the children made of him! He was patted and petted, stroked and fondled.

'Should we take him to the vet?' said Bets. 'Fatty, do you think anything's wrong?'

'We'll try him with one of his favourite potted-meat biscuits,' said Fatty, getting up. He saw the empty plate at once.

'BUSTER! You greedy pig! How dare you show such bad manners when I take you out to tea! I'm ashamed of you. Go to the corner!'

'Oh, what's he done?' cried Bets, as poor Buster walked to the nearest corner, and sat there, face to the wall.

'Eaten every single one of his biscuits while we weren't looking,' said Fatty. 'I never heard a single crunch, did you? Bad dog, Buster! No, Bets, you're not to go to him. Look at the plate next to his biscuits, too. It looks as if Buster has been taking a few licks at that macaroon!'

'Well, I'd rather he was naughty than ill,' said Bets, making up her mind to slip Buster a bit of macaroon at teatime. 'Oh Buster! What a thing to do!'

Buster made a moaning sound, and hung his head still more. 'Take no notice of him,' said Fatty, 'another word from us and he'll burst into tears.'

'It wouldn't matter. He'd lick them all up,' said Bets. 'That's the best about being a dog – if you upset a dish, you can always lick up the mess.'

'Now don't even mention Buster's name,' said Fatty, firmly. 'He's in disgrace. Come on, it's my turn to play.'

Buster had to remain in the corner while the five children had their own tea. Bets spilt some runny strawberry jam on the clean tablecloth.

'Get something to wipe it,' said Pip. 'You really are a messer, Bets.'

'I'm a dog. I'm going to lick it up,' said Bets, and she did, which made them all laugh. Tea became more and more hilarious until Pip laughed so much that he fell off his chair and pulled a plate of cake slices on top of him.

The door opened and Mrs Hilton looked in. 'What was that crash?' she said. 'Is anybody hurt? Oh, *Pip*! What *are* you doing on the floor with cakes all over you? Please get up. Remember you are the host.'

'Be hostly, Pip,' said Bets, and Pip began to laugh again. Buster came out of his corner hopefully when he saw the pieces of cake on the floor.

'No, Buster, the floor is perfectly clean and we can eat the slices ourselves, thank you,' said Pip. 'Has Mummy gone? Oh, dear, I really must be hostly. Shall we let Buster come out of his corner? I'm sure he must be very sorry now.'

So, much to Buster's joy, he was allowed to join the others again, and was so pleased to be in favour that he went round licking everyone in all the bare places he could find.

'Really, we need a towel!' said Daisy. 'That's the third time you've licked my knees, Buster – they're dripping with lick!'

The evening went too quickly. Fatty exclaimed when he looked at the playroom clock. 'Whew! Almost seven o'clock. You have your supper at seven, don't you, Pip?'

'Gosh, yes. And we've got to go and wash and get tidy,' said Pip, scrambling up. 'Sorry to rush you off; but you know what our household's like – everything on the dot. See yourselves out, will you?'

Fatty, Larry, Daisy and Buster went downstairs quietly and out of the garden door. It was getting dark. 'It's a pity we haven't a mystery on hand,' said Larry, turning on his bicycle lamp. 'I feel like one, somehow. It's nice when we've got our teeth into a good, juicy mystery!'

'Well, one may turn up at any time,' said Fatty. 'Your lamp all right, Daisy? Good-bye, then. We'll see each other sometime tomorrow.'

They all cycled off, parting at the corner. Fatty yawned. He had slept very little the night before because he had been so worried about Buster. He felt very sleepy now.

I'll go to bed early, he thought. I'll take a book and read. I'll soon be asleep.

So, much to his parents' surprise – for Fatty was usually rather a late bird – he went up to bed about a quarter to nine, with Buster at his heels.

He had a bath, and was soon settled into bed. He opened his book and read a page or two – and then, before he had even turned out his light, he was fast asleep! Half past nine struck. Ten o'clock. Half past ten. Eleven. Everyone in the house was now in bed, and Fatty's light was the only one left on.

Buster lay quiet for some time. Then he stirred. Why hadn't Fatty taken him out for a run?

He leapt on the bed and woke Fatty up with a jump.

'Gosh, it's you, you little wretch!' said Fatty, sitting up suddenly. 'I thought you were a burglar or something. What's the time? – almost half past eleven! Now don't say you want a walk at this hour, because you won't get one. I'm going to turn out the light, see?'

It was just as he switched off his lamp that Fatty remembered something. Blow, blow, blow! I never went to get that horrible window-leather. BLOW!

He thought about it. Well, he *must* go and get it. He had promised Larry – and, anyway, it was important. He swung his feet out of the bed and dressed hurriedly. 'We'll be back soon,' he said to Buster. 'We'll only be a few minutes!'

But he wasn't back soon. Fatty had a most peculiar midnight adventure!

12. STRANGE HAPPENINGS

Fatty went cautiously down the stairs with Buster. Buster always knew when he had to be quiet. He almost held his breath as he padded downstairs at Fatty's heels!

'Out of the garden door, Buster,' whispered Fatty, and Buster led the way down the side passage. Fatty unlocked and unbolted the door quietly, and closed it again. He locked it behind him.

Then he and Buster made their way to the back gate and slipped out into the road.

Buster liked this. It was exciting to be all alone with Fatty late at night. Smells seemed much stronger than in the daytime. Shadows were more exciting. Buster jumped up and gave Fatty's hand a small lick.

'We're going to that bungalow called Hollies,' Fatty told him. 'Got to collect something for Larry.

If I can't find it, *you'll* have to sniff about for it, Buster.'

'Wuff,' said Buster, happily, and ran on ahead. Up this way – down that – round a corner – and by a lamp-post. The street lights went off at twelve. Soon it would be midnight, and then there would not be even a lamp to break the darkness.

It was a very cloudy night, and the clouds were low and thick. Fatty felt a spot of rain. He put his hand in his pocket to make sure he had his torch. Between the lamp-posts the way was very dark. Yes, his torch was there – good.

I'll need it when I creep into the bungalow garden, thought Fatty. I'll never find Larry's leather without a light.

He came to the turning into Holly Lane. The street lamps suddenly went out – twelve o'clock! Fatty got out his torch. He simply couldn't see a step in front of him without it on this dark night.

He came to the front gate of the little bungalow. It was all in darkness. Fatty stood and listened. Not a sound could be heard. He could go and search in safety.

He opened the front gate, shut it softly, and

went up the path with Buster. He turned off to the side of the bungalow and went into the little thicket of bushes there. He switched on his torch and began to hunt around.

He couldn't see the window-leather anywhere. Blow Larry! He came up against a fence – the fence that separated the bungalow garden from the one belonging to Mr Henri's sister. He stood and considered the matter.

Could the wind possibly have blown the leather over the fence? he wondered. No. Leathers are such heavy things when wet, as Larry's was. On the other hand, the wind might have dried it, and it would then become dry and light. The wind *might* take it then – there has been quite a breeze.

Fatty climbed over the fence, torch in hand. He hunted all about the garden there. It was very much tidier than the garden of Hollies. He began to get into a panic. Where was this tiresome leather? Surely Goon hadn't found it?

He heard a noise and switched off his torch. It was the sound of a car engine coming up the road. Fatty thought he would wait for the car to pass, and then have one more look.

But the car didn't pass. It seemed to stop quite near by. Fatty frowned. Why didn't the car go through some gateway, and on into its own garage, so late at night?

Then he remembered that there was a doctor's house opposite. Possibly the doctor had come home for something, and gone into his house for it. He would come back in a few minutes and drive off again to a patient.

So Fatty crouched under a bush and waited, with Buster by his side. The car's engine had been turned off. Fatty could hear no footsteps at all. But he suddenly thought he could hear a bump or two – and surely that was somebody panting?

He was puzzled. It all sounded rather nearer than the doctor's house. Surely the car wasn't outside *Hollies*? If so, what was going on?

Fatty crept back to the fence that separated the two gardens. He climbed over it cautiously, lifting Buster up too, and putting him down in the bungalow garden.

'Ssh, Buster!' he whispered. 'Quiet now!'

Buster froze still. He gave a tiny growl as if to

say 'Funny goings-on somewhere!' then was quite quiet. Fatty crept between the bushes, and stopped suddenly.

He could see a torch bobbing along about two feet above the front path. Somebody was there, carrying it – somebody who was panting hard! Somebody who wore rubber-soled shoes, too, for not a footstep could be heard!

Fatty suddenly heard a whisper. So there were *two* people then? Who were they? And what in the world were they doing? Surely they weren't kidnapping the old man?

Fatty frowned. He had better find out about that poor old fellow. He slept in the back room of the bungalow. That was where Larry had seen his bed.

If I slip round to the back, and shine my torch in at the window, I could perhaps see if the old man is there or not, he thought. So he crept round the bushes once more and came to the back of the little bungalow.

The window was open. Fatty was just about to shine his torch through the opening when he heard a noise.

Someone was snoring! Snoring very loudly indeed! The old man was safe then. Fatty stood and listened for a while, and then made his way back into the bushes. He really *must* see what was up!

He heard the sound of the front door closing very quietly. He heard a tiny little cough, but he caught no sound of footsteps going down to the gate. He stood and listened, his ears straining for the slightest noise.

He heard another door being shut – the door of the car perhaps. Yes, that was it. Then the car engine started up suddenly, and began to throb. Almost at once, the car moved off down the road. Fatty leapt to the front fence and shone his torch on it. He saw only a dark shadow as the car drove away. His torch could not even pick out the number.

What a peculiar business, thought Fatty. What did those fellows come to fetch – or perhaps they *brought* something? I'll go and peep in at the front windows.

But thick curtains of some green material stretched across the front windows, with not a crack between them to shine his light through. Fatty went to the front door and tried it.

No, that was now locked. It was all most mysterious. What were the midnight visitors doing in the bungalow?

Fatty went to the back and took another look through the window. This time he shone his torch on the old man. Yes, there he was on his bed, fast asleep, his nightcap all crooked. Beside him was a plain chair, and a small table. There didn't seem to be anything else in the room at all.

Fatty switched off his torch, and went round to the front. He was puzzled to know what to do for the best. He didn't like to wake the old man; he would be sure to be in a terrible fright if Fatty awoke him suddenly – and how was Fatty to explain to him about the midnight visitors? The old man would be so terrified that he wouldn't go to sleep again!

It will have to wait till morning, said Fatty to himself. I'm not going to ring up Mr Goon. For one thing he wouldn't believe me – for another thing there may be a simple explanation – and for a third thing, I can't see that it will matter waiting till morning.

So he went off with Buster at his heels, puzzled and half-doubtful about leaving the old man all by himself, with midnight visitors coming and going!

He let himself in at the garden door, and he and Buster went upstairs very quietly. They disturbed nobody. Buster curled up at once in his basket and went to sleep.

Fatty lay awake thinking over everything for a few minutes, and then fell off to sleep as suddenly as Buster. He didn't awake till full daylight. Fatty leapt out of bed in a hurry!

'Gosh, I must have been sleepy!' he said. He stirred Buster with a bare foot. 'Wake up, sleepyhead! You're as bad as I am!'

He didn't remember about his midnight adventure for a minute or two, he was so much engrossed in dressing as quickly as he could. Then he suddenly remembered and stopped. 'Whew! Was it a dream, or real? Buster, do you remember our midnight walk too? If you do, it was real.'

Buster did remember. He gave a small wuff, and leapt on Fatty's warm bed.

'Get down,' said Fatty. 'Well, I'm glad you remember our walk last night too. Funny business, wasn't it, Buster? Shall we pop round to that bungalow immediately after breakfast, just to see what's happened – if anything?'

So, after breakfast, Fatty got his bicycle and set off slowly with Buster running beside him, panting. 'This will do you good, Tubby One,' said Fatty, severely. 'Why is it that you always get so chubby when I'm away at school? Can't you possibly go for walks by yourself?'

Buster was too much out of breath even to bark. Fatty turned into Holly Lane, and rode up to the bungalow. The door was shut, but the green curtains were now pulled back from the windows. Fatty peeped in to see if things were all right.

He got a terrible shock! Mr Goon was there – a most important Mr Goon – and with him was Mr Henri from next door! The old man was nowhere to be seen.

But what startled Fatty most was that there was not a stick of furniture in the front room! It was completely empty – not even a carpet on the floor!

He stood gaping in at the window. Mr Goon

swung round and saw him. He stepped to the window and flung it open, scowling.

'You here again! What have you come for? Nobody knows about this yet!'

'What's happened?' said Fatty.

Mr Henri began to explain. 'About seven o'clock zis morning,' he said, but Mr Goon interrupted him. He didn't want Fatty to know more than could be helped. Interfering toad!

Fatty wasn't going to be put off however. He had to know about this. He spoke rapidly to Mr Henri in French, asking him to reply in French and tell him everything.

So, to the accompaniment of Mr Goon's scowls and snorts, Mr Henri explained everything in French. He had awakened at seven o'clock that morning and had heard somebody yelling. His bedroom faced towards the bungalow. At first, he hadn't taken much notice and fell asleep again.

'Then,' he said, in his rapid French, 'then I awoke later and the noise was still there – shouting, shouting, always. So I dressed and came to the bungalow to see what was the matter.'

'Go on,' said Fatty.

'It was the old man shouting,' said Mr Henri, still in French. 'The door was locked so I got him to unlock it – and when I came inside, I saw that this room was quite empty – except for the curtains, which had been drawn across the windows so that nobody might see into the empty room. The old man had awakened this morning, and staggered out to this room – and when he found everything gone, he yelled the place down!'

'It's a mystery!' said Fatty amazed, and Goon swung round sharply. 'Mr Goon – we're in the middle of a mystery again! Got any clues?'

13. SUSPECTS – AND CLUES!

Mr Goon didn't feel that he could possibly stand any cheek from Fatty at that moment. He was completely mystified, he had no clues at all, and he simply couldn't *imagine* when, how, or why, all the front room furniture had been removed.

'You clear orf,' he said to Fatty. 'This has got nothing to do with you. It's a job for the police.'

'I must just go and see how the poor old man is,' said Fatty, and brushed past Goon to go to the back bedroom. Goon scowled. He looked round the room helplessly. Except for the stove, which kept alight all night, the fender, one lamp, and the green curtains, there was nothing left in the room. What was the point of taking all the furniture away? It wasn't worth much anyway!

Fatty was talking to the old man, who was almost weeping with shock. 'My money first – then my furniture!' he moaned. 'All my money

– then my furniture! What's to become of me?'

'Didn't you hear anybody?' asked Fatty.

'No, no! Not a thing did I hear,' he said. Fatty stopped questioning him. It was plain that he was too upset to say anything sensible.

Mr Goon made a few notes in his black book. 'I must know the granddaughter's address,' he said. 'She'll have to come along here and take this old fellow to her home. He can't stay here alone, with no furniture. Hey! What's your granddaughter's address?'

'It be 5, Marlins Grove, Marlow,' said the old man. 'But you won't get me there, that you won't. It's full of pesky old women, always grumbling and nagging. I'm not going there.'

'But you can't stay here all alone with no furniture!' shouted Mr Goon, half because the old man was deaf, and half because he was angry.

'Don't yell at him like that,' said Fatty, seeing the poor old fellow cower back. Mr Henri touched Goon on the shoulder.

'My sistair, she is vairy kind,' he said in his broken English. 'She has a small bedroom. Zis old man can stay there till his granddaughter arrives.'

'Well, that would help a bit,' said Goon, putting his notebook away. 'Will you lock up after you? I must go back to my house and telephone all this to my Chief. It's a funny business – can't make it out – first the money, then the furniture!'

He turned to Fatty. 'And you'd better go home,' he said. 'There's no call for you to meddle in this. Always snooping round. What made you come up here this morning I just can't think. Wherever I find trouble, I find you!'

It took quite a time to explain to the trembling old man that the people next door would help him. But when he understood, he seemed to think he would like to go there. Mr Henri went to tell his 'sistair' everything, and sent a gardener to help Fatty to take the old fellow to his house. Between them they carried him there, and kind Mrs Harris soon got him into a warm bed.

'I'll just keep him warm here, till his family come,' she said. 'I don't mind driving him over to Marlow if it will help. What an extraordinary thing to happen – taking away his furniture in the middle of the night. I never heard even the smallest noise!'

Fatty went back to the bungalow. He had a good look round. He was just as puzzled as Mr Goon. There was no doubt that the old man had hidden his money somewhere in his furniture – perhaps in several places – but the money had gone.

So WHY take the furniture! wondered Fatty. We'll have to get busy on this – there should be at least a few clues – and everyone who visited the old man yesterday morning up to the time he discovered that his money was gone, is on the list of suspects.

Fatty examined the bedroom. The bed was a plain iron one with an ordinary wire spring. Nobody could ever hide money in that. The mattress was thin and poor. Money might have been hidden in that – but, no, it would have to be sewn up again each time the old man took it out. He was too blind to do that. Anyway, it was clear that nobody had unsewn and then re-sewn the mattress. All the threads were dirty, and had obviously been untouched for years.

The pillow was thin and hard. Fatty took off the slip and looked at it. No, nobody had ripped the pillow up and re-sewn it.

He looked at the floorboards. There were no

marks anywhere to show that any had been taken up. All were nailed down fast. The chimney-place was no good for hiding anything either. The stove fitted too closely.

'Well, it beats me. WHY did somebody take the risk of coming at midnight and carrying out all the furniture, when the money had obviously been stolen?' said Fatty. 'Unless – unless – they were sure it was still there, somewhere in the furniture! They didn't like to risk coming and making a really good search, so they took *all* the furniture, meaning to search it at leisure.'

He thought about that. 'No, that seems silly. But then everything seems a bit silly. Buster, don't you think this is rather a *silly* mystery?'

'Wuff-wuff,' said Buster, quite agreeing. He wasn't very interested in this little house. Not even the smell of a mouse! He pawed at Fatty's leg.

'All right. I'm coming,' said Fatty. 'I'll just lock the door. I'd better leave the key with Mr Henri.'

He locked the door, and then went to have one more look for Larry's leather in the daylight. No, it was gone. He hoped that Larry wouldn't get into trouble over it.

Fatty made his way to the house next door, after fixing a bit of paper to the front door of Hollies. On it he had written 'KEY NEXT DOOR' just in case the granddaughter should come back.

Mrs Harris answered the door and told him to come in. 'We are having a cup of coffee,' she said. 'You must join us. My brother would like a word with you too.'

Fatty also wanted a word with Mr Henri. He thought it would be distinctly useful to have a list of all the people that Mr Henri had seen going to the Hollies the morning before. One of those people must have been the thief who took the money.

Mr Henri was ready to tell all he knew. He was just as much interested in the matter as Fatty was. He had already made a neat list, and he showed it to Fatty.

Fatty ran his eyes down it. There were six people on the list.

1 Lady with papers or magazines.
2 Window-cleaner.
3 Grocer's boy.
4 Man in car, number ERT 100. Carried bag.

5 Man, well-dressed, young, stayed for only a minute.
6 Young woman, stayed a long time.

Fatty read the list again. 'Quite a long list,' he said. 'It will be a bit of a business checking all these. I wonder if the old man could help a bit with some of them.'

'He said his granddaughter came to do some cleaning,' said Mr Henri, 'so that must be the "young woman". And he says he thinks his nephew came – but he's so muddled. He doesn't seem to remember any of the others. I can give you more details, of course. For instance, the woman with the magazines or papers wore a red coat and had a hat with red roses on it.'

'Yes, all the details would be a help,' said Fatty. 'What about the grocer's boy?'

'He came on a bicycle with the name of "WEL-BURN" on the front of the basket,' said Mr Henri, who seemed a remarkably observant fellow. 'A red-haired boy.'

'Did you notice if the window-cleaner had a name on his pail or bicycle?' asked Fatty, wondering if the cleaner had noticed how remarkably clean the windows of Hollies had been! After all, Larry had cleaned them only a day or two before!

No. Mr Henri hadn't seen the window-cleaner's name. But he thought it must be the same that his sister had. They could ask her.

'Well, we can go through all these, and see if any of them are *likely* to have taken the money,' said Fatty. 'But I think we can cross out the grocer's boy, for instance.'

'Ah, no,' said Mr Henri. 'He was in Hollies for quite a long time. It might well be he.'

'Oh! Yes, you're right. We must go into every one of these names,' said Fatty. 'Well, I'll get the others to help. They'll have to do some real detective work, I can see!'

He drank his coffee and talked a little longer. Mr Henri was now back on the couch, coughing rather a lot. 'It is the excitement,' said his sister. 'He is really much better. Come and see him whenever you like, and ask him what you like. It is a puzzle he would like to solve!'

Fatty said good-bye and went. He was just

walking home when he suddenly remembered that he had come on his bicycle. Where had he left it? Oh, yes, by Hollies. He went back to get it and wheeled it to the road.

A thought flashed into his head. The car that had taken away the furniture last night! It must have stood just here, in the road outside Hollies' front gate. But now he was sure that it couldn't have been a car. It must have been a small van of some kind – perhaps a small removal van.

He looked down on the road. It was not a good road, and was muddy and soft just there. The marks of wheels were plainly to be seen.

'Ah!' said Fatty, pleased. 'I'm a really bad detective lately! I nearly forgot to check up for wheel marks! And here they are, under my nose.'

The tyre-marks were big and wide – too wide for an ordinary car, Fatty decided. Much more like those of a small removal van. He got out his notebook and sketched the pattern left in the mud by the tyres. Then he measured them across and entered the figures down in his notebook. The tyre patterns were so plain that Fatty thought the tyres must be quite new. That might be a help.

Nearby was a lamp-post, and a mark on it caught Fatty's eye. It was a straight brown mark, almost a cut in the white lamp-post. Fatty looked at it.

That van might quite well have run too close to it, he thought. Anyway, it's worth noting down. 'Van may be painted a chocolate-brown, and may have a scratch on wing about two feet from ground.' Well, we're getting on – I hope!

He shut his book, put it into his pocket, and rode off with Buster in the front basket. He wanted to call a meeting of the Five Find-Outers that afternoon. This *was* a mystery, after all. And it needed getting down to, because there were quite a lot of suspects.

What a bit of luck that I went to look for Larry's window-leather last night! he said to himself, as he cycled home. If I hadn't gone and heard all that noise last night and hadn't gone again to explore this morning, old Mr Goon would have had the field to himself. He wouldn't have told us a thing. Now, as it happens, I know more than he does!

'Wuff,' said Buster, agreeing thoroughly. 'Wuff-wuff-wuff!'

14. FATTY TELLS QUITE A STORY

At three o'clock that afternoon, Larry, Daisy, Pip and Bets came along to Fatty's shed. He was already there, and on the bench at one side were two or three sheets of neatly-written notes. Fatty was just reading them over.

'Come in!' he called, and the four trooped in. They looked excited. Fatty had already telephoned them to say that there really *was* a mystery now, and they wanted to know all about it.

'All sorts of rumours are flying round, Fatty,' said Larry. 'Is it true that somebody took away all the furniture in the middle of the night from Hollies Cottage – and the old man was found lying on the floor because the thieves even took his bed?'

Fatty laughed. 'How do people get hold of these things? It's true that the furniture went – but the old man slept peacefully all through the robbery, on his own bed. They didn't touch that. They did the job so quietly that he never heard a thing, snored all through it.'

'How do you know that,' said Pip, a little scornfully. 'You weren't there!'

'Well, it so happens that I was,' said Fatty, surprising the others very much. They stared at him.

'You were *there* – last night – when the furniture was all taken away?' said Larry at last. 'Well, why didn't you stop them then?'

'Because I had no idea what was being taken,' said Fatty. 'It was pitch dark, and they did the whole thing so quietly. But look, let me tell you everything in its right order – quite a lot has happened actually – and we've got to get right down to this, and really find out what's going on.'

'Yes, but just let me interrupt for a minute,' said Larry. 'Did you find my window-leather? Mummy was on and on about it this morning.'

'No, I didn't,' said Fatty. 'I'm sorry about that, but honestly it wasn't anywhere to be found. All I hope is that Mr Goon didn't find it.'

'Well, he'd think it belonged to the woman who cleans Hollies Cottage,' said Daisy. 'We'll just have to buy Mummy another one, Larry.'

'Blow!' said Larry. 'That really was a silly idea of yours, Fatty – making me go and clean those windows.'

'Yes, but remember that it was all because of that that we're in on this mystery,' said Fatty. 'It really began with you seeing that old man crawling about jabbing at all his furniture – and then us going back to collect your leather and hearing him yelling for the police.'

'That's true,' said Larry. 'Well, all right, I'll say that a very silly idea happened to turn out well – but that's as far as I'll go.'

Fatty changed the subject. He picked up his notes. 'Now, listen,' he said. 'I've written out a short summary of what's happened so far – just to get our minds clear, so to speak – and I'll read it. Then we'll discuss any clues, and all the suspects, and make plans. Ready?'

'Yes! This sounds good!' said Pip, settling himself comfortably on a box.

'Well, get ready to use your brains,' said Fatty. 'Buster, sit still and listen too. It disturbs me if you keep snuffling for mice in that corner. Sit, Buster.'

Buster sat, his ears pricked as if he were quite

ready to listen. Fatty went quickly through his notes.

'The mystery begins when Larry goes to Hollies to clean the windows. He saw the old man there, crawling about, poking at his furniture. We know now that he was looking to make sure that his savings were safely where he had hidden them – either the whole two hundred pounds in some particular chair or sofa, or divided up and put into different places. Possibly in some carefully-prepared, hidden pocket under a chair or chairs.'

'Oh, that reminds me!' said Daisy, suddenly. 'Excuse my interrupting, Fatty, but our cleaner told me she knew the old man when he was younger – and he was an upholsterer, so he'd know very well how to make some kind of hidden pockets in furniture, wouldn't he?'

'What's an upholsterer?' asked Bets.

'Bets! You're a baby!' said Pip, at once. 'It's someone who makes chair covers and curtains, and stuffs couches and chairs and things – isn't it, Fatty?'

'Yes,' said Fatty. 'That's an interesting bit of information of yours, Daisy. Very interesting. The old man probably made himself quite a lot of hiding-places here and there in the upholstery of his chairs or sofas. I'll just add a note about it.'

Daisy looked pleased. 'It's a sort of a clue, isn't it?' she said. 'A very small one, I know.'

'It all helps to fill in the mystery,' said Fatty. 'I always think of our mysteries as jigsaws. We've got a great many bits and pieces – but not until we fit them together properly do we see the whole picture. Now, then, I'll go on.'

'We're listening,' said Bets, happily.

'Well, we come next to when we all of us went with Larry to find the leather he had left behind,' said Fatty. 'And we heard the old man yelling for the police. He is certain that his money was in its usual place – or places – about midnight the night before, but in the morning it is gone. He doesn't discover that it's gone, however, until six people, at least, have been to Hollies Cottage for some reason or other.'

'And all those six are suspects then, till we prove them otherwise,' said Larry. 'Good! Who are they, Fatty?'

'All in good time,' said Fatty. 'Don't keep

interrupting. Buster, sit! There is NO mouse in that corner!'

Buster sat, looking as if he knew better than Fatty where mice were concerned. Fatty went on.

'We decided at this point that it was only a question of straightforward robbery, and that Mr Goon would be able to deal with it,' he said. 'But last night I went to get Larry's leather, and as I told you, I arrived just about the time the car, or lorry, or van, came to remove the furniture out of that front room.'

'Extraordinary!' said Larry, unable to stop himself from interrupting.

Fatty went on to describe what he had heard. 'Actually I *saw* nothing,' he said. 'And I didn't even know till this morning that the midnight visitors were taking away all the furniture. I didn't know that they might have a van or a lorry – I thought it was a car. I imagined they might be kidnapping the old man, but I both saw and heard him, fast asleep, on his bed in the back room.'

'What did you *think* was happening?' asked Pip.

'I simply couldn't imagine!' said Fatty. 'All I

heard were a few thuds and bumps and pants and a whisper – and it was all over quite quickly really. Well, I thought I'd better go back to Hollies early this morning, just to see if I could find out anything, and when I got there, I had quite a shock.'

'Why?' asked Bets, hugging her knees. 'This is awfully exciting, Fatty!'

'Well, I found Mr Goon there, and the old fellow, of course, and Mr Henri, that Frenchman you all thought was me in disguise. He is staying with his sister next door, as you know, and he heard the old man yelling for help again early this morning. So he went to see what the matter was and then called the police.'

'Oh, so Mr Goon was in on this pretty quickly!' said Larry, disappointed.

'Yes. But I wasn't much later in arriving,' said Fatty, 'and wasn't I amazed to find no furniture in that front room. Of course, I knew at once what had happened, because I'd actually heard the men removing it last night – though I didn't tell Mr Goon that, of course!'

'What happened next?' asked Bets.

'Nothing much. Mr Goon went off, leaving Mr Henri and me with the old man – and Mr Henri's sister said she'd give him a room till one of his relations came along. So he's there now. I had a good look round Hollies, but couldn't see anything to help me. Then I went back to Mr Henri, and got a proper list of the people he had seen going to the bungalow yesterday morning. They're the suspects, of course.'

'Let's have a good look,' said Larry; but Fatty hadn't quite finished.

'I've only got one clue,' he said, 'but it *might* be an important one.' He told them about the well-marked prints of the tyres in the mud outside Hollies, and showed them the pattern in his notebook.

'I *think* it must have been a small removal van,' he said, 'because the distance between the front and back wheels was rather more than there would be in even a big car. Oh – and the car or van may be a chocolate-brown. There was a new brown mark on a nearby lamp-post, as if the van's wings had scraped it.'

'Well, it seems as if we have got to tackle the

suspects,' said Larry, 'and look out for a chocolate-brown van which probably has new tyres of a certain pattern. We'd better all copy out that pattern, Fatty. It would be maddening to see a chocolate-brown removal van with new tyres – and not be able to check the pattern!'

'Yes. Well, will you make four tracings of the diagram in my notebook?' said Fatty. 'I'll go on with the list of suspects and we can discuss them. You can trace the markings while you're listening.'

Fatty turned to his list of six suspects. He read them out. 'One – Lady with papers or magazines, dressed in red coat, and black hat with roses. Two – Window-cleaner. Three – grocer's boy, from Welburn the grocer's, red-haired, and was in the bungalow quite a time. Four – man with bag, came in car with number ERT 100. Five – well-dressed young man, who stayed for only a minute. And six – a young woman who stayed a long time.'

'Quite a list,' said Larry. 'A window-cleaner, too! I wonder if he noticed how clean the windows were!'

'That's what *I* wondered,' said Fatty, with a

laugh. 'I'm going to have a word with the old man about these suspects; he may be able to give me a few more clues about them. Then we must tackle each one.'

'I never much like that,' said Bets. 'I'm no good at it.'

'Yes, you are,' said Fatty. 'Anyway, doesn't your mother have Welburn's for her grocer? You could hang about for the grocer's boy, and have a word with him when he brings your groceries. You and Pip could do that.'

'Oh, yes!' said Bets, glad that Pip was to help her. 'What about the lady with the magazines? Would she be the vicar's sister? It sounds rather as if it was somebody delivering the Parish magazine.'

'Yes. I can easily find that out,' said Fatty. 'Mother knows her. I'll go and see if she was delivering at Hollies that morning. If so, she's not a suspect, of course. But we can't afford to rule anyone out till we've proved they're all right.'

'And we can look out for car ERT 100,' said Pip. 'I wonder who the young man is – and that young woman who stayed such a long time.'

'Probably the old man's granddaughter,' said

Fatty, shutting up his notebook. 'She comes to clean for him. Pip, you and Bets get on with the grocer boy suspect. Larry, you finish these tracings, will you, and let us each have one. I'll go and find out a bit more about these six people if I can. Daisy, will you wander about with Buster, and see if you can spot that car – ERT 100, remember?'

'Right!' said everyone and got up. This was exciting. A mystery they could really work on! Now who, of all those six, was the thief?

15. FATTY GETS GOING

Fatty went straight off to Mr Henri. His sister, Mrs Harris, was quite pleased to see him. Fatty had excellent manners, and the Frenchwoman liked a boy who knew how to behave.

Soon he was sitting beside Mr Henri's couch. 'Well, have you come to ask me more questions?' said the man, in French. 'We will speak in French, will we not? It is so much easier for me – and you, you talk French like a native! You are a most accomplished boy!'

Fatty coughed modestly, and restrained himself from agreeing whole-heartedly with Mr Henri. 'I just wanted to ask you a few things about our six suspects,' he began.

'Ha! Mr Goon also asked me many questions,' said Mr Henri. 'He is a stupid fellow; but he asks good questions. They are well-trained in this, your police.'

'Oh,' said Fatty, disappointed to hear that Goon had had the bright idea of questioning Mr Henri too. 'Blow Mr Goon! Well, it can't be helped. Mr Henri, who, of all these six people on our list, went into the bungalow – right inside, I mean?'

'All of them,' said Mr Henri. 'The door could not have been locked. Everyone turned the handle and walked in.'

'What! The window-cleaner too?' said Fatty.

'Yes, he too,' said Mr Henri. 'By the way, my sister says that he is the same one she has. He came to do her windows first, and then went to Hollies.'

'Does she think he's honest?' asked Fatty.

'Perfectly,' said Mr Henri. 'And a good cleaner. But you should see him and question him, Frederick.'

'Oh, I will,' said Fatty. 'Decidedly. You told me too about the lady with the papers or magazines. I think she may have been the vicar's sister, delivering Parish magazines.'

'So? I do not know what they are,' said Mr Henri. 'But yes, the lady may have been of that type – she too went in, but she did not stay long.'

'What about the well-dressed young man you

said went in for a short time?' asked Fatty.

'Well, he came again, when you were there,' said Mr Henri. 'You saw him – quite well-dressed. Did he not say who he was?'

'Gosh, that was the old man's great-nephew!' said Fatty. 'He called him uncle, I remember. So he came during the morning, *too*, did he – before we got there – and afterwards as well? Very interesting! I'll find out where he lives and do a spot of interviewing.'

'The young woman must have been the grand-daughter who cleans and cooks for the old fellow,' said Mr Henri. 'There was also the man who came in a car – that is all, is it not? Well, which do you suspect the most?'

'I don't know,' said Fatty. 'I really don't. The one I suspect *least* is the lady with magazines – but even so I'll have to check up. The worst of it is Mr Goon has probably checked up too. That makes it more difficult for me. I mean, a policeman has the right to interview people. I haven't!'

Mrs Harris came in. 'You will stay to tea, won't you?' she said. 'We are just going to have it.'

Fatty shook his head most regretfully. 'I'm

awfully sorry. Nothing I'd like better. But I must go and do a spot of interviewing before Mr Goon gets too far ahead of me.'

He shook hands politely, thanked Mr Henri, and let himself out. It was about a quarter to five. He was quite near the vicarage. Should he chance his luck and go and see if the vicar's sister was in?

Fatty decided that he would. So he cycled away quickly and was soon riding up the vicarage drive. He saw somebody just by the house, kneeling on a mat, weeding. The vicar's sister! What a bit of luck!

Fatty got off his bicycle and said, 'Good afternoon.' The vicar's sister looked up. She was a small, kindly-faced woman, who knew Fatty's mother well.

'Ah, Frederick!' she said. 'Do you want to see the vicar?'

'Well, no, I really wanted to see *you,*' said Fatty. 'I won't keep you a minute. It's about that poor old man whose money has been stolen. I and my friends happened to be the first ones to help him when he discovered his loss. And . . .'

'Yes, I was *so* sorry to hear about that,' said the vicar's sister. 'I had been to see him myself only that morning, left him the Parish magazine, you know – his granddaughter reads it to him – and he was sitting in his chair, quite happy, listening to the radio. It was going so loudly that I could hardly hear myself speak!'

'Did you see anything suspicious at all?' asked Fatty. 'We couldn't see anything out of the way when we arrived there.'

'No. Everything seemed just as usual,' said the kindly-faced woman. 'I just left the magazine, had a few friendly words and went. Such a pity to hide money in one's house – a real temptation to thieves.'

'Yes,' said Fatty. 'Well, thanks very much. I didn't think you could help me really – but you never know.'

'How did you know I called there yesterday?' asked the vicar's sister, looking suddenly puzzled.

'Oh, I just heard that you did,' said Fatty, turning his bicycle round. 'Thank you very much. My kind regards to the vicar and his wife!'

One off the list of suspects, said Fatty to himself as he rode away. I felt sure that 'woman with magazines' sounded like the vicar's sister. Anyway, it's quite, quite obvious she had nothing to do with the money. She didn't say if Mr Goon had gone to see her – I suppose he hasn't, or she would have told me. Well, I should have thought he would have shot along to interview her, even though he knew she wasn't really a suspect.'

But Goon had not thought of the vicar's sister. The description of the woman with the magazines had rung a different bell in Mr Goon's mind. Aha! A red coat – and a black hat with roses! Didn't that sound like the woman who had sold him that ticket and read his hand? The woman who had actually seen that boy Frederick in his hand – and a mystery also!

There's more in this hand-reading business than anyone would guess, said Mr Goon to himself. Much more. I don't reckon that woman who read my hand has got anything to do with the theft of the money, but I'm pretty certain she's the woman with the papers who visited Hollies yesterday morning, so I'll go and interview her – and maybe she'll read my hand a bit more. Maybe she could tell me more about this mystery she saw in my hand.

Poor Goon! He had no idea that his visitor, the woman in the red coat, who had sold him the sale ticket, had been Fatty in disguise! He cycled hopefully up to Fatty's house, and rang the bell. The woman had told him she was staying for three weeks with Fatty's mother, so she should still be there.

Fatty had just arrived back himself, and was washing his hands in the bathroom. He saw Mr Goon cycling up the drive and was puzzled. *Now* what did Mr Goon want? He dried his hands and slipped downstairs, going into the lounge, where his mother was sewing.

Jane came into the room almost at once. 'Mr Goon, the policeman, would like a word with you, Madam,' she said.

Mrs Trotteville frowned. She was not fond of Mr Goon. 'Show him in here,' she said. 'Don't go, Frederick. It may be something to do with you.'

Mr Goon came in, his helmet in his hand. He was always on his best behaviour with Mrs Trotteville. 'Er – good evening, Madam,' he said. 'I wondered if I could have a word with the lady who is staying with you.'

Mrs Trotteville looked surprised. 'There is no one staying with me at present,' she said. 'Why do you think there is?'

'But – but there must be!' said Mr Goon, startled. 'Why – this lady – she came to see me the other morning and sold me a ticket for a sale of work. She said she was a friend of yours and was staying with you for three weeks. I wanted to see her to ask her a few questions. I have reason to believe that she was one of the people who went to Hollies – where the robbery was, you know – on the morning that the old man discovered that his money was gone.'

Fatty turned round and poked the fire vigorously. How marvellous! How super! Goon really and truly thought that one of the suspects was the woman in the red coat who had visited him and read his hand – Fatty himself in disguise!

'Really, Mr Goon, I can't think why in the world this woman said she was staying with me,' said Mrs Trotteville, very much on her dignity. 'I have never heard of her in my life!'

'But – but she sold me this ticket for a sale!' said poor Mr Goon, in anguish. 'Is it a dud, then?' He pushed the ticket at Mrs Trotteville.

'No. It is not a dud,' she said. 'I also have those tickets for sale.'

'She read my hand too,' wailed Goon. 'And the things she said were true.' He stopped suddenly. No, it wouldn't do to tell Mrs Trotteville what the woman had said about a big boy.

Fatty was having a violent coughing fit, his handkerchief to his face. His mother looked at him, annoyed. 'Frederick, go and get a drink of water. Mr Goon, I'm sorry not to be able to help you; but I do assure you that I have no friend who goes about reading people's hands. Someone has – er – deceived you. Still, you've got the ticket. You can always go to the sale. There will be plenty of good things for you to buy.'

Mr Goon made a peculiar noise – half snort and half groan. He got up, said good evening, and stumbled to the door. That woman in the red coat! Who could she have been? Telling him fairytales like that – making him stump up for a silly sale of work ticket! What a waste of money. All the same, she did warn him against that boy, and she did know that a mystery was near.

Strange. Most peculiar.

Fatty appeared in the hall. 'Oh, are you going, Mr Goon?' he said. 'Do let me see you out. Very strange that that woman should have said she was staying here, isn't it? By the way, how are you getting on with this new mystery? For mystery it is! You no doubt have plenty of clues?'

Goon looked at him with a surly face. 'Yes, I have,' he said. 'And one or two of them you won't like – Mister Clever! I told you you'd poke your nose into things once too often!'

'What exactly do you mean by that?' said Fatty.

'Wait and see,' said Goon, rudely. Fatty opened the door and Goon marched out. Fatty called after him politely.

'Oh – er, Mr Goon! Did that woman who read your hand warn you against a big boy, by any chance? She did, did she? Well, take her advice. Beware of him!'

And Fatty gently shut the door on a most bewildered Mr Goon. Now – HOW did Fatty know what that woman had read in his hand? Goon puzzled over that for a very long time indeed!

16. MOSTLY ABOUT WINDOW-CLEANERS

It was too late to do anything else that evening. Fatty decided that he would go and see the window-cleaner first thing the next morning, then he would go to Pip's at ten o'clock for the next meeting of the Five. By that time, the others might have something to report, too.

'After the meeting, I'll see if I can find that young man – the great-nephew,' said Fatty. 'And have a word with the granddaughter too. By then, we might be able to see daylight a little. My word, fancy Mr Goon going right off the track, and coming up here to trace a woman who doesn't exist – the woman who read his hand. Poor old Mr Goon. He's got hold of a bit of jigsaw that doesn't fit!'

Fatty decided that he would dress up in old clothes the next day, find the window-cleaner, and pretend that he wanted some advice about going in for window-cleaning himself. He might get the man to talk more freely if he thought he was not being interviewed.

I'd better go early, or he'll be off to work, thought Fatty, and arranged with Cook to have breakfast an earlier hour than usual. He was up in good time and came down just as Jane brought a tray of breakfast for him into the dining-room. She looked in surprise at Fatty.

'My word! Are you going in for chimney-sweeping or something?' she said. 'Where *did* you get those dirty old clothes? Don't you let your father see you!'

'I won't,' said Fatty, and began on his breakfast. He propped his notebook in front of him as he ate, considering all the facts of the robbery and the removal of the furniture. Pity they couldn't find out where the furniture was – it would help matters a good deal!

He had the address of the window-cleaner. Mr Henri's sister had given it to him. '62, North Street, Peterswood. The other end of the town. Well, I'll be off.'

Fatty didn't cycle. His bicycle was too expensive-looking to be owned by a young man who wanted a job at window-cleaning. He set off at a good pace, with Buster at his heels.

It took him about twenty minutes to get to the address. Number 62 was a smart little house. Evidently window-cleaning was quite a well-paid occupation. Fatty walked round to the back door.

A man sat there, cleaning some boots. He looked up at Fatty and Fatty grinned.

'Hello, mate! What do you want?' said the man, liking the look of this cheerful-faced boy.

'Just wanted to ask you if you could give me a few hints about your job,' said Fatty. 'I might like to take it up – if anyone would teach me!'

He spoke in a rough kind of voice, so that the man would not suspect him to be any other than he seemed.

The window-cleaner looked him up and down.

'You seem a likely sort of lad,' he said. 'I might do with a mate meself. When are you free?'

'Oh, not for some time,' said Fatty hastily, marvelling at the ease with which you could get a job. He then began to ask the window-cleaner a few questions: how much did a ladder cost? Could one be bought second-hand?

Were leathers expensive?

'Look here, if you want a job at window-cleaning, you come and be my mate,' said the man, at last. 'You and I would get on fine. Don't you worry about ladders and leathers – I'll supply those if you like to come in with me. You go home and think about it, and let me know.'

'Right,' said Fatty. 'That's kind of you. I say, did you hear about that robbery at Hollies?'

'I should think I did!' said the man, taking up another boot to clean. 'Why, I was cleaning the windows that very morning! Funny thing was, though I hadn't cleaned them for a month, they were as clean as could be! I told the old man that when I went in for my money. His granddaughter was there, ironing the curtains, and she seemed surprised to see me – said another window-cleaner had been along a day or two before, and hadn't asked for any money at all.'

Fatty listened to this with great interest, hoping that Goon wouldn't get suspicious if he heard about the other window-cleaner!

'Have the police asked you if you saw anything when you cleaned the windows that morning

– anything unusual, I mean?' asked Fatty.

'No. I haven't seen the police,' said the man. 'I've got nothing to fear. I've been a window-cleaner for years and everyone knows me. Anyway, I couldn't have taken the money – the granddaughter was there all the time, ironing away!'

'Yes. That certainly rules you out,' said Fatty, thinking that the window-cleaner was another suspect to cross off. 'Well, I must go. Thanks very much for your help. If I decide to be your mate, I'll come right along and tell you.'

The window-cleaner waved a shoe-brush at Fatty, and the boy went round to the front, untied Buster from the fence and walked back home. He was thinking hard.

Why hadn't Goon interviewed the window-cleaner? He had had time. Didn't he know who the man was? Well, he was one up on Goon over that. Another suspect gone!

Fatty arrived at Pip's just after ten o'clock. The other four were sitting waiting for him in Pip's playroom. Fatty was surprised to see such long faces.

'What's up?' he said. 'Bets, you look as if you're

going to burst into tears!'

'Fatty, something awful's happened,' said Daisy. 'Simply AWFUL! Mr Goon found that window-leather Larry used, and it had our name on it – Daykin! Mummy always marks all her household cloths.'

'Good gracious!' said Fatty. 'If only I'd known that! I'd never have let that leather lie there so long.'

'Well, we're in an awful fix now,' said Larry, 'and really I can't help saying again, Fatty, that it was a most idiotic idea of yours to tell me to go and clean windows. You see Mr Goon saw the name "Daykin" on the leather, and he knows that my name is Larry Daykin, and he immediately leapt to the conclusion that one or other of us five had played the fool, and was the window-cleaner on the morning of the robbery!'

'Whew!' said Fatty, and sat down suddenly. 'This is a blow!' He sat and stared at the serious faces of the others.

'Did he come up to your house with the leather?' asked Fatty.

'Of course he did,' said Larry. 'And what's more,

he took the leather away again, saying something about its being a "piece of evidence" – whatever that may be. So Mummy hasn't got it back yet!'

'And he had us in, Larry and me, and asked us outright if we had cleaned the windows of Hollies two mornings ago,' said Daisy. 'But, fortunately, we were able to say we hadn't because, as you know, it was a day or two *before* that that Larry cleaned them – not the morning of the robbery. But we felt AWFUL! We *had* to say it was Mummys leather, of course, but we didn't dare say that Larry had cleaned the windows with it two days before the robbery – we just kept on saying that we didn't clean the windows on the *robbery* morning.'

'And *he* kept on saying "Then how did this leather get into those bushes?" said Larry. 'He's most awfully suspicious about it. It's dreadful. I don't know what will happen when Dad comes home and hears about it. I bet he'll get out of Daisy or me that I was idiot enough to clean the windows two or three days before that robbery! He'll think I'm stark staring mad!'

'I'll go and see Mr Goon,' said Fatty, getting up. 'I can put things right, I think.'

'How?' asked Larry.

'Well, it so happens that I've been to see the actual window-cleaner who *did* clean the windows on the robbery morning,' said Fatty. 'Man called Glass – good name for a window-cleaner!'

Nobody could raise even a smile.

'Well, anyway, this fellow says he *did* clean the windows that morning, and when he'd finished he went into the bungalow, and the granddaughter was there – ironing curtains or something, he said – and she paid him his money.'

'Oh, what a relief!' said Larry, looking more cheerful. 'If Mr Goon knows *that*, maybe he won't keep on trying to make me say I was there cleaning windows that morning too. Honestly, Fatty, I began to feel that he thought I'd stolen the money!'

'I'm sorry about this, Larry,' said Fatty. 'I'll go and see Mr Goon now.'

He went off with Buster, leaving four slightly more cheerful children in Pip's playroom. Daisy got up.

'Come on, let's go out. I feel quite depressed. Let's have some ice creams – always a good cure for things that make us feel miserable!'

Fatty went straight to Mr Goon's. He saw the policeman's bicycle outside and was thankful. Mrs Mickle answered the door.

'Mr Goon in?' asked Fatty. She nodded and showed him into the office. The skinny little Bert stood slyly in the hall. Fatty gave him a look.

'Hello, Skinny! BEWAAAAAAARE!'

The 'beware' seemed to come from behind Bert, and reminded him of those awful voices he had heard a day or two ago. He looked behind him, gave a yelp and disappeared.

No one was in the office – but draped over a chair seat, was Larry's window-leather! Fatty's eyes gleamed. He spoke softly to Buster.

'Buster! Look, what's that? Fight it, then, fight it!'

And Buster leapt on the leather in delight, caught it in his teeth and dragged it round the room, shaking it and worrying it exactly as if it were a rat.

'Take it outside, Buster,' said Fatty, and Buster obediently ran into the front garden with it, growling most ferociously.

Mr Goon walked into the room thirty seconds later, looking quite jubilant. Ha! He had got Larry and Daisy into a fine old fix. Larry was the window-cleaner, was he? Then he was one of the suspects on the morning of the robbery. What would his father have to say to *that*?

But Fatty soon made him look a little less jubilant. 'Oh, Mr Goon,' he began, 'I thought it might interest you to know that I have this morning interviewed the window-cleaner who cleaned the windows of Hollies on the morning of the robbery – a man called Glass, living at 62 North Street, Peterswood.'

'What?' said Goon, startled.

'He told me he cleaned the windows, then went into the bungalow for his money. The grand-daughter of the old man was there, ironing, and she paid him. He couldn't have stolen anything under the very eyes of the young woman, so I should think we needn't consider the window-cleaner any further. What do you feel about it Mr Goon?'

Mr Goon felt furious. He cast his eyes round for the window-leather – he would face Fatty with that and see what he would say! But where WAS the leather? He couldn't see it anywhere.

'Are you looking for something, Mr Goon?' asked Fatty, politely.

'That leather,' said Mr Goon, beginning to be agitated. 'Where's it gone?'

'Oh, dear, I do hope Buster hasn't got it,' said Fatty. 'He's out there growling like anything, Mr Goon. Would you like to see what he's got?'

Mr Goon looked out of the window. Buster had torn the leather to pieces! Nobody would ever have known that it had once been a most respectable window-leather.

'That dog!' said Mr Goon, in a tone of such fury that even Fatty was surprised.

'I'll go and scold him,' said Fatty, and went out. 'By the way, you didn't thank me for coming to give you information about Mr Glass the window-cleaner, Mr Goon!'

Mr Goon said the only thing he felt able to say – 'Gah!'

17. A TALK IN THE ICE CREAM SHOP

Fatty went straight back to Pip's house, but the others were not there. 'I should *think* they've gone to have ice creams,' said Mrs Hilton. 'I believe I heard somebody mention the word!'

'Right. Thank you,' said Fatty, wishing he had his bicycle. All this rushing about on foot would make him quite tired! 'I'll go and find them, Mrs Hilton.'

He went off with Buster, who still proudly carried a small bit of the window-leather in his mouth. Fatty stopped at a shop in the main street, and bought a magnificent leather. It cost him a lot of money. He stuffed it into his pocket, and went on to the café.

The other four were there, eating ice creams. They were very pleased indeed to see Fatty's cheerful face.

'Is it all right?' asked Bets eagerly, and Fatty

nodded. He ordered a round of ice creams for everyone, and two for himself, as he was one behind the others.

'I went to see Mr Goon,' he said, 'and I told him how I'd gone to see the real window-cleaner this morning. He was most annoyed.'

'I bet he was!' said Larry. 'He was just too pleased for anything to think he'd got *me* pinned down as one of the suspects. But what about the leather? He's still got that. He'll come and flourish it at Daddy tonight, and make an awful scene.'

'Buster, come here,' said Fatty, and Buster came. From his mouth hung the last bit of the window-leather. He wagged his tail.

'Well, well, well, if Buster hasn't taken it upon himself to remove that leather from Mr Goon's office, fight it, and chew it to bits!' said Fatty, solemnly. 'Is that the very last bit, Buster?'

'Wuff,' said Buster, and dropped it. Larry picked it up. 'Yes,' he said, 'look! There's a bit of the name-marking on this corner – Dayk! Oh, Buster, you're the cleverest, cheekiest, best dog in all the world!'

'And he deserves a double ice cream!' said

Daisy, thankfully. 'Oh, Fatty, I don't know *how* you do these things, but there's simply nobody like you for putting things right – going straight for them . . .'

'Taking the bull by the horns, tackling the fury of the storm, putting the enemy to flight, and all the rest of it,' said Fatty, grinning. 'No, but honestly, I was really upset. Mr Goon had something on us there; and you and Daisy could have got into a fearful row, Larry, all through my fault.'

'But now Mr Goon can't do anything, can he?' said Bets, happily. 'He knows who the real window-cleaner was – you've told him – and he hasn't got the leather any more.'

'And Mummy's the only one who has suffered,' said Larry. 'She's lost her window-leather for good now!'

'Oh, I forgot,' said Fatty, and pulled the brand-new leather from his pocket. He tossed it across to Larry. 'A present for your mother,' he said.

'Oh, *thanks*,' said Larry, delighted. 'Mummy will be so thrilled that she won't say another word about Mr Goon's accusations.'

'Tell her he made a mistake,' said Fatty. 'And a

bad mistake it was for him!'

'Fatty! Pip and I saw the grocer's boy when he came with the groceries last night,' said Bets, remembering.

'Good for you!' said Fatty. 'What happened?'

'Well, Pip and I kept biking up and down the drive, waiting for him,' said Bets. 'And he came at last, on his bicycle. Pip had let down his tyre so that it was a bit flat and he yelled out to the boy to ask if he'd lend him his pump.'

'Good idea,' said Fatty. 'So, of course, you just fell into conversation. What did the boy say?'

'Not much,' said Bets. 'Your turn now, Pip, you tell.'

'I asked him if he ever went to Hollies, where the robbery had been,' said Pip, 'and he was simply thrilled to tell us all he knew. But it wasn't much.'

'Tell me,' said Fatty. 'Just in *case* there's something.'

'Well, he went to the front door as usual,' said Pip. 'He knocked, and shouted "Grocer". Someone called "Bring the things in," and in he went.'

'Who was there?' asked Fatty.

'The old man was there, with the radio on full

strength,' said Pip, 'and a young woman, the old man's granddaughter. He said she called the old fellow "Grandad". She was very busy sewing something green. She told him to take all the things out of the basket and put them in the little larder. So he did.'

'And that was all,' said Bets. 'He just stayed and listened to the radio for a bit and then went.'

'Yes. Mr Henri said the boy was in the bungalow for quite a time,' said Fatty. 'That explains it. Well, *he* couldn't have taken the money either. The granddaughter was there all the time.'

'Perhaps *she* took it,' said Larry. 'She had plenty of chance!'

'Yes. But why take it that morning when so many people seemed to be in and out?' said Fatty. 'Anyway, we'll know better when we see her. She *sounds* a good sort, I must say, going up and looking after old Grandad like that. Still, you never know!'

Fatty took out his notebook, and opened it at his page of suspects. 'We can cross quite a few off,' he said. He drew his pencil through 'grocer boy'. Then he crossed out 'window-cleaner'. He also crossed out 'Lady with magazines'.

'Oh, have you found out about her too?' asked Pip, interested.

'Yes,' said Fatty, and told them. He also related how Goon had gone wrong, and had imagined that the lady with the papers, 'in red coat, black hat with roses' must have been the funny old thing who had sold him Daisy's ticket for the sale, and had read his hand – and how Goon had gone to Fatty's house to ask his mother if he might interview her!

Everyone roared. 'Oh! You had told him that you were staying with Mrs Trotteville for three weeks, so he thought the woman must still be there!' giggled Bets. 'Whatever did your mother say?'

'Oh, she soon put Mr Goon in his place,' said Fatty. 'Poor old Mr Goon, he's getting a bit muddled over all this! No, Buster, you can NOT have another ice cream. That was a double one, in case you didn't notice!'

'Good old Buster – eating up that leather!' said Larry, patting him. 'I must say, it was a very fine way of getting rid of – of – *what* is it I want to say, Fatty?'

'A fine way of getting rid of a bit of incriminating evidence,' said Fatty, promptly. 'No, I'm not going to explain that, Bets. Use your brains.'

'Who have we got left on the list of suspects now?' asked Daisy, craning over Fatty's arm to see. 'Oh, man in car, with bag – ERT 100. Fatty, I looked all over the place but I couldn't see any ERTs and I didn't see 100 either. Shall we stroll round again and look? I feel it must be a local person.'

'Right. And then I think I'll go and interview the smartly-dressed great-nephew, and find out what he wanted Great-Uncle for that morning,' said Fatty. 'He apparently went in for a very short while, and then came out and, if you remember, he turned up again when we were there listening to Granpa's laments about his money having been stolen.'

'Yes. The granddaughter had left by that time,' said Pip. 'Where does this fellow live?'

'Mr Henri told me,' said Fatty, turning over the pages of his notebook. 'Here we are – the old man told him the address, because Mr Henri wanted to get in touch with his relatives – Number 82 Spike Street, Marlow. Apparently, both he and the granddaughter live at Marlow – though at different addresses.'

'When will you go and see them? Today?' asked Daisy. 'Shall we come too?'

Fatty considered this. 'Yes. On the whole, I think it would be a good idea,' he said. Mr Goon has probably interviewed them both by this time, and if they see me coming along full of questions, too, they may resent it. But if we all blow along, full of innocent curiosity, so to speak, we might do better.'

'I can't go before lunch,' said Daisy. 'Nor can Larry. We've got an aunt coming. We could meet you about three though, outside your house, on bicycles. We'll have tea at that nice little café in Marlow High Street.'

'Yes. That's settled then,' said Fatty, putting his notebook away. 'Come on out, and we'll look for ERT 100.'

They paid the bill and went out, Buster still with his tiny bit of leather. He growled at every dog he met.

'Don't be an idiot, Buster,' said Fatty. 'You don't really suppose any other dog wants your smelly bit of leather, do you?'

They looked at every single car they saw, or that passed them. Not an ERT anywhere! They went to the car park and examined every car there, which made the attendant extremely suspicious of them.

'What are you looking for?' he called.

'An ERT,' said Fatty.

'What's that?' asked the attendant. 'Never heard of it. There aren't no erts here, so you can go away.'

'You're right,' said Fatty, sadly. 'There isn't a single ERT to be seen.'

'There's Mr Goon,' said Bets suddenly, as they walked out of the car park. 'Perhaps he's looking for ERTs too.'

'No. He has other ways of finding out who owns any car,' said Fatty. 'The police can always trace any car by its number – and Mr Henri is sure to have given Mr Goon the number. Old Mr Goon will be one up on us over the man with the bag and car ERT 100.'

Buster ran out into the road, barking, when he saw Mr Goon riding by. Goon kicked out at him, and nearly fell off. 'That pesky dog!' he shouted, and rode on at full speed.

'Buster! You've dropped your bit of incriminating evidence,' said Fatty disapprovingly, pointing to the rag of leather that had fallen from Buster's mouth when he barked at Goon. Buster picked it up meekly.

They all went to Larry's house first. In the drive stood a car. 'Hello! Who's this?' said Larry. 'Not our Aunt Elsie already, surely? No, it isn't her car.'

A man came down the front steps of the house carrying a neat brown case. 'It's the doctor!' said Daisy. 'Hello, Dr Holroyd! How's Cook?'

'Much better,' said the doctor, smiling round at the five children. 'Well, there doesn't look to be anything wrong with *you*!' He got into his car, started the engine, and put it in gear. He went off down the drive.

Bets gave a loud yell, and pointed. 'ERT! ERT 100! Look, do look! ERT 100!'

So it was. 'Gosh, to think we all stood here with it staring us in the face,' said Fatty, 'after hunting for it all the morning! Man with a bag too – why EVER didn't any of us think of a doctor?'

'We're not nearly as bright as we imagine,' said

Daisy. 'Good old Bets! She spotted it.'

'Shall you go and interview him?' asked Pip.

'No. I'm sure he couldn't help us at all,' said Fatty. 'He couldn't *possibly* have stolen the money – everyone knows Dr Holroyd! I expect he just went to have a look at the old man, and then shot away again in his car. All the same, we ought to feel very ashamed of ourselves not to have spotted the number, when it was right in front of our noses!'

'There's Aunt Elsie! Quick, Larry, come and wash!' said Daisy suddenly, as a small car crept in at one of the gates. 'Good-bye, you others!'

They fled, and the other four walked sedately down the drive. 'See you at three outside your house!' called Bets. 'Good-bye, Fatty. Good-bye, Buster! Hang on to your bit of – of – discriminating evidence!'

18. A CHAT WITH WILFRID – AND A SURPRISE

Everyone was outside Fatty's gate at three o'clock, Buster included. 'I'll have to put him into my bicycle basket,' said Fatty. 'Marlow's too far for him to go on his four short legs. Up with you, Buster!'

Buster liked the bicycle basket. He sat there happily, bumping up and down when Fatty went over ruts. He looked down on other dogs with scorn as he passed them.

It was about three miles to Marlow, and a very pleasant ride on that fine April day. They asked for Spike Street when they got there. It was a pretty street leading down to the river. Number 82 was the last house, and its lawn sloped down to the water.

The five got off their bicycles. 'Put them by this wall,' said Fatty. 'Then we'll snoop round a bit to see if we can find the great-nephew – Wilfrid King is his name. We've all seen him, so we know what he is like.'

They sauntered alongside the wall that ran round the little front garden of Number 82. They came to a path that led to the river. They went down it, looking across to the lawn that led down to the water.

They could see no one. They came to the water's edge and stood there. Then Fatty gave Daisy a nudge. A boat lay bobbing not far off, and in it a young man lay reading, a rather surly-looking fellow, in smartly creased grey-flannel trousers and a yellow jersey.

'There's Wilfrid,' said Fatty, in a low voice. 'Let's call out to him and pretend to be very surprised to see him. Then we'll fall into conversation. Remember, we've just ridden over here to see the river – it's such a lovely day!'

Wilfrid, however, saw them before they could hail him. He sat up and stared. 'Aren't you the kids who heard my great-uncle shouting for help the other morning?' he said.

'Oh, yes! Why, you're Wilfrid, aren't you?' shouted back Fatty, appearing to be most surprised.

'Fancy seeing you here! We've just ridden over, it's such a fantastic day.'

'Did you meet that fat-headed policeman?' asked Wilfrid. 'He's been over here today asking umpteen questions. Anyone would think I'd robbed the poor old fellow myself!'

'Oh, has Mr Goon been over?' said Fatty. 'Do come and tell us. *We* think he's a bit of a fat-head too. But, really, fancy thinking *you* would rob your great-uncle. Poor old man! – I wonder who did.'

'Ah!' said Wilfrid, and looked knowing.

'What do you mean – AH!' said Larry.

'Oh, nothing. That policeman wouldn't see a thing even if it was right under his nose,' said Wilfrid. 'I told him that it was I who kept on and on at my uncle, begging him to put the money into a bank. It's most dangerous to keep it in the house. Anyway, it appears that a lot of people visited Hollies that morning – there are quite a few persons who *might* have stolen the money!'

'Yes, that's true,' said Fatty. 'It's funny how many people went in and out all the time. Still, the old man's granddaughter was there most of the time, cleaning or something. She can probably clear most of the ones who came.'

'Yes. She can clear me, for instance,' said Wilfrid. 'She was there when I went in. Marian's my cousin, and she and I don't get on, so I didn't stay long. She actually wanted me to help her with the work! Me! She said if I was going to stay long, I could jolly well put up the curtains for her, so I just walked out.'

'Well, anyway, she can clear you, as you say,' said Fatty. 'It's a funny thing – she can clear most of the people who went in and out, except perhaps the doctor and he doesn't really need to be cleared.'

'Oh, is that so?' said Wilfrid. 'Have you got a list of the suspected persons? I'm there too, I suppose.'

'You can be crossed off if Marian, the granddaughter, can clear you,' said Fatty, handing him the list.

'My word!' said Wilfrid, looking at it. 'Six of us, and all crossed off except for Marian and myself.'

'Yes. And you say that Marian can clear you, so you'll be crossed off too soon,' said Fatty. 'Perhaps Marian has already seen Mr Goon, and he's crossed you off.'

'She's out for the day,' said Wilfrid. 'I told him that, so I don't expect he's seen her yet. I say, all of us will be crossed off – except one.'

'Except one,' said Fatty, watching Wilfrid as he bent his head thoughtfully over the list. 'Did you know where the old man hid his money, by any chance?'

An angry look came over Wilfrid's face. 'No, I didn't. He would never tell me. I thought that if only he would, I would take it and put it into the bank, but now it's too late. Somebody else has got it.'

'And you think you know who?' said Fatty quietly.

Wilfrid hesitated. 'Not for certain. I'd better not say any more. You're only kids, but you might go and say something silly.'

'Yes. We might,' said Pip, who had begun to dislike Wilfrid. It was quite apparent to them all that Wilfrid thought his cousin Marian had taken the money – but they couldn't help thinking that *he* would have had it, too, if he could!

'We must go,' said Fatty, looking at his watch.

'Well, I hope that Marian clears you, Wilfrid – it's rather important that she should!'

They went back to their bicycles and rode off to the little café they liked. Not a word was said till they got there.

They were early, so there was no one else in the room. They began to talk in low voices.

'It can't have been Wilfrid who took the money. If he and his cousin dislike each other, she certainly wouldn't have sheltered him if he *had* taken the money right in front of her eyes.'

'So he can't be the thief,' said Pip. 'Well, then, who is?'

'It looks like Marian,' said Fatty. 'We'll go and see her after tea. What beats me is why somebody took all that *furniture* away the next night. I keep going round and round that, but I just can't see where that bit of the jigsaw fits into the picture.'

'I can't either,' said Daisy. 'The furniture was cheap stuff – worth very little. *Could* the thief have imagined that the money was still there? No, I give up. It's a puzzle!'

They had a good tea and then went to call at Marian's house, hoping that she would be in.

'Here we are,' said Fatty. 'Number 5, Marlins Street. Why, it's a little hotel!'

So it was – a small boarding-house, beautifully kept. The children rang the bell, and a neat, middle-aged woman came to the door.

'Is Miss Marian King in?' asked Fatty. 'If so, may we see her?'

'I don't think she's in yet,' said the woman. 'I'll go and find out. Come into the drawing-room, will you?'

They all trooped in. And old lady was there reading. She smiled at the children and nodded.

'Do you want to see someone?' she asked.

'Yes,' said Fatty. 'We'd like to see Marian King, if she's in.'

'Ah, Marian!' said the old lady. 'She's a sweet girl! Good to her mother, good to her old grandad – and good to tiresome old ladies like me. She's a dear.'

'We know she used to go and do all kinds of things for her grandfather,' said Fatty, glad to have some information about Marian.

'Oh, yes! That girl was always thinking of him!' said the old lady. 'Taking him up titbits she had cooked. Doing his washing and ironing. As particular as could be, she was. She told me she was going to take down, wash, and iron his curtains last time she went – quite a job – and kind of her too, because the old man wouldn't be able to see them!'

'Yes, she did do the curtains,' said Daisy, remembering what had been seen by the grocer's boy. 'She must have been very fond of her grandfather.'

'Oh, she was!' said the old lady. 'She thought the world of him and couldn't bear him to live alone. And now I hear that the poor old man has been robbed of his money – dear, dear, Marian will be so upset!'

Fatty wondered why the woman who had opened the door had not come back. Had she forgotten they were waiting? He decided to go and find out. He slipped out of the room and into the passage. He heard voices at the end and walked down the carpeted hallway.

Someone was crying. 'I don't know *what* to say about Marian. First, that policeman comes to see her and I say she's out – now these children.

Where *is* she? She's been gone for two days now! People will say she took the money! It isn't like Marian to do this. Oh dear, oh dear, I do so hope she's not come to any harm!'

Another voice comforted her. 'Well, you do as you think best. Marian's a good girl, that I will say, and as for stealing money from her old Grandad – and she so fond of him, too – why, that's nonsense. I do think you should let the police know tomorrow that she's missing. I do indeed.'

'But they'll think she's run off with the money; it'll be in all the papers,' said the first voice, sobbing. 'My girl Marian, my only daughter, as good as gold!'

Fatty went back quietly to the drawing-room. He was worried – and very puzzled. This was something he hadn't expected. Where had Marian gone? *Could* she have taken the money? Everyone seemed to speak well of her – and yet – and yet – why had she gone away?

Fatty entered the drawing-room and spoke quietly to the others. 'I don't think we'll wait.' He turned to the old lady and spoke politely.

'If the maid comes back, will you please say

we're sorry we couldn't wait? Thank you!'

The old lady nodded, thinking what well-behaved children these were. The five went out, and collected Buster from the post to which he had been tied. He was delighted to see them.

'Don't say anything now,' said Fatty, in a low voice. 'I've got some news.'

They mounted their bicycles, and waited until they were beyond Marlow in a deserted country road. Fatty jumped off his bicycle. The others did the same. They went to a gate, leaned their bicycles there and gathered round Fatty, puzzled at his serious face.

'Marian has disappeared,' he said. 'I overheard her mother say so. They're terribly upset – half-afraid she's gone off with the money, and worried about what the papers will say if they get to hear of her disappearance! What do you think of that?'

'Gosh!' said Larry. 'It really does look as if she's the thief. After all, she's the one most likely to have wormed herself into the old man's confidence and got his secrets out of him – where the money was kept, for instance.'

'Yes. There doesn't seem any other reason why

she's gone,' said Fatty. 'Well, until she comes back, we can't get much further in this mystery. We don't know two important things – where or why Marian has gone, and where or why the furniture has gone. This is one of the most puzzling mysteries we've tackled.'

'Yes. And I'm sure that NOBODY could solve it, even if they knew all we know,' said Pip. 'Well, let's get back. There's not much more we can do now.'

So they rode back to Peterswood, disappointed and puzzled. Well, perhaps the simplest explanation was the right one: Marian had taken the money and gone off with it!

And yet – what about that stolen furniture! Could that have been Marian too? They gave it up!

'It's too mysterious a mystery!' said Bets. 'Mr Goon CERTAINLY won't solve it!'

19. AN EXTRAORDINARY FIND

Fatty was unusually quiet that evening. The five of them, with Buster, were down in Fatty's shed. Bets slipped her hand through his arm.

'What's the matter, Fatty? Are you worried?'

'I'm puzzled more than worried,' said Fatty. 'I really am. I CAN'T believe that the granddaughter, Marian, would rob an old man she had been looking after so lovingly. And, yet, I feel certain that Wilfrid hasn't got the money, and what's more, doesn't know where it is.'

'Then is there somebody else – a seventh person – that we don't know about?' asked Larry.

'I did wonder if there could be,' said Fatty. 'Someone who perhaps went round the *back* of the bungalow that morning of the robbery, and got in without being seen. Mr Henri could see everyone going in at the front, but not at the back.'

'Yes. That's true,' said Daisy. 'Also, I suppose it *is*

possible that he wasn't looking out of his window every minute of the time.'

'That's so,' said Fatty. 'But I think the old man would have mentioned anyone else. Mr Henri had a good talk with him, and is pretty certain there was no one else.'

'Let's have a game,' said Pip, who was getting just a bit tired of all this talky-talk.

'No. You have one, and let me think,' said Fatty. 'I'm at my wits end – and yet I feel as if there's some clue that would give me the key to the whole mystery!'

'Well, anyway, the money's gone,' said Pip. 'So has Marian. It's a bit fishy.'

'Perhaps it's still at Hollies,' suggested Bets. 'In a place where nobody has looked.'

'I hunted everywhere,' said Fatty. 'It's such a *small* place – there really is nowhere to hide anything, once you rule out the chimney and the floorboards. There's no furniture now to speak of – just the old man's bed, a chair, and a little table in that back room. And a lamp, a stove . . .'

'That old fender,' put in Daisy.

'And the curtains,' said Bets. 'They had to leave

those, I suppose, in case old Mr Goon came by at night and shone his torch in at the window. He'd have discovered the bare room then, of course.'

'Oh, come on, do let's have a game,' said Pip. 'I know when I'm beaten. There's something peculiar about all this, something we don't know about.'

Fatty grinned suddenly. 'All right!' he said. 'I'm inclined to think you're right. There are some bits of this jigsaw that we haven't got – it isn't that we can't fit them into the picture. We just haven't got them. Hand over the cards, Pip. You never shuffle properly.'

When the others went, Fatty walked part of the way with them, Buster at his heels. It was a lovely evening, and looked like being a glorious day tomorrow.

They went round a corner in a bunch, and bumped into a burly form. 'Hey!' said a familiar voice. 'Can't you look where you're going?'

'Oh, good evening, Mr Goon,' said Fatty. Out for a little stroll? Solved the mystery yet?'

'Oh, yes!' said Goon. 'No mystery in it at all – if you're talking about the Hollies affair, that is. Plain as the nose on your face. It's that girl, Marian.'

Fatty was thunderstruck. 'What do you mean? Surely she didn't take the money?'

'You wait and see the papers tomorrow morning,' said Mr Goon, enjoying himself. 'Thought yourself so clever, didn't you? Well, you're not.'

'Has the money been found?' asked Fatty.

'You wait and see,' said Mr Goon again. 'And look here – I bin thinking – do you know anything about that lady that read my hand?'

Mr Goon looked extremely threatening and Bets promptly went behind Larry.

'Let me see now, which lady do you mean?' asked Fatty, as if plenty of people read Goon's hand.

Goon gave one of his snorts. 'You're a pest!' he said. 'But this time I'm on top, see? You watch the papers tomorrow morning!'

He went on down the road, looking very pleased with himself. Fatty gave a hollow groan.

'I do believe that policeman knows something we don't. Blow him! I'll never forgive myself if we've let him get the better of us. It rather looks as if Marian is the black sheep.'

'I thought she was,' said Pip. 'Going off like that. Perhaps they've found her, money and all.'

'We'll have to wait for the morning papers,' said Fatty. 'Well, good-bye. It's sad to think this mystery is coming to an end, while we're still in the middle of it, so to speak.'

Bets squeezed Fatty's arm. 'Perhaps something else will happen,' she comforted him. 'You never know!'

'It's not very likely,' said Fatty, and gave her a hug. 'Good-bye – see you tomorrow, all of you.'

Fatty was down early the next morning to see the papers. There was nothing on the front page, but inside was a whole column. It was headed:

MISSING GIRL
AND
MISSING MONEY

It then went on to describe Hollies, the old man, the missing money, the sudden disappearance of the furniture, and now the disappearance of

Marian! It didn't say that Marian had taken the money – but anyone reading the news about the Hollies affair would immediately gather that Marian had taken both money and furniture!

Now I suppose the hunt is on, Fatty thought. Everyone will be looking out for Marian. I suppose her mother told the police the girl was missing – or, more probably, Mr Goon wormed it out of her and reported it. Gosh, I wish I could have been a bit cleverer over this mystery! I do feel that I've missed something, some clue, that might have been the key to the whole affair.

Fatty put down the paper and thought. I'll go round to Hollies once more, he decided. For the last time. Just to see if any bright idea comes to me. I'll go by myself without any of the others. I'll just take Buster with me.

He fetched his bicycle and rode off. He soon came to Holly Lane and went into Green Trees to get the key. Mr Henri still had it.

'The old man has gone to Marlow,' he said. 'They came to fetch him last night.'

'Oh, and so I suppose when he asked for Marian and was told she was missing, he made a fuss!' said Fatty.

'I'll tell you something he told me,' said Mr Henri. 'He said that Marian knew where his money was. He had actually told her, and made her promise she would never, never tell anyone.'

Fatty groaned. 'So it looks as if she was the only one who knew – and I must say, things look bad for her now. Well, if she took it, she deserves what's coming to her! May I have the key, Mr Henri? I know I'm beaten, but I just want to have a last look round.'

Mr Henri gave it to him, and Fatty went off next door. He let himself in. The curtains were drawn across the windows, and the room was dark. He switched on the light, but it was very dim. He drew the curtains away from the windows and the sun streamed in.

Fatty remembered how Marian had washed and ironed the curtains on the morning of the robbery. Surely she wouldn't have done that if she had been going to steal the money and clear out! thought Fatty. It doesn't make sense. In fact, nothing makes sense!

He stood there, looking at the fresh, green

curtains. He had his hand on the side-hem that ran from the top of the window almost down to the floor. It felt stiff and he rubbed it between finger and thumb.

'Funny,' said Fatty, and felt the hem a bit higher up. Then he felt it round the bottom of the curtains. He held it to his ear and rubbed and squeezed. A faint crackle came to him.

Fatty suddenly grew excited – tremendously excited. He was filled with sudden exultation.

'I've found the money! I believe I've FOUND THE MONEY! Gosh, what a bit of luck!'

He took out his pocket-knife and ripped up the bottom hem of the curtain, cutting the stitches. The hem was now loose enough for him to insert finger and thumb.

He felt about, and came across something papery. He pulled it out gently and stared at it, whistling softly. It was a five pound note, rather dirty – a five pound note!

So that's where she hid the money – to keep it from Wilfrid, who had begun to suspect that it was somewhere in the furniture! He must have come and threatened her that he would search for it after she had gone that morning! And so she ripped open the hems of the curtains she was ironing, and sewed the money into them. What an idea!

The curtain hems were packed with the five pound notes. Fatty could feel them all the way round. He debated what to do about it. Should he take the money out? No, he might get into trouble. It would be perfectly safe to leave it there – nobody had guessed so far, and not a soul was likely to guess now.

'Anyway, no one will come here,' said Fatty. 'And what's more, I'll make certain they don't!'

He went out of the bungalow and locked the door. He put the key into his pocket. I shan't take it back to Hollies. I'll just tell Mr Henri I'll keep it – and ask him to keep an eye on anyone who comes up to the front door. Wilfrid's got a key, that's certain, but I don't think he'll come again – and Marian certainly won't.

Fatty was so excited that he found it difficult to keep his news to himself. Finding the money had suddenly shed light on all kinds of things.

Marian hadn't taken it. She had hidden it in the

curtains to make sure that Wilfrid didn't find it if he hunted for hiding-places in the furniture. She hadn't even told the old man where she had put it, in case Wilfrid wormed it out of him – and the old fellow, looking for it after Marian had gone that morning, had thought it was stolen.

Why had Marian disappeared? Not because she had taken the money. She hadn't! Had Wilfrid anything to do with her disappearance? It was almost certainly Wilfrid who had come with some kind of van or lorry that night and removed all the furniture. Why? Probably because Marian vowed that she hadn't got it, but that it was still hidden at Hollies.

The pieces are fitting again, said Fatty to himself jubilantly. If only I could find Marian – or the furniture. Would the furniture still be in the van? It would obviously be dangerous for Wilfrid and his helper to unload it anywhere. His people would be very suspicious to see furniture suddenly appearing in the house or in the yard. He probably had to leave it in the van.

Another thought struck him. Perhaps Wilfrid's family are in the house removal business! Maybe they have big vans, and it might be in one of those. Gosh, I'll have to find out quickly!

Fatty could hardly get home fast enough. Quick, quick! He might defeat Goon yet, and solve the whole thing before Marian was arrested!

20. NIGHT ADVENTURE

Fatty rushed to the telephone directories in the hall as soon as he got home. He wanted to look up King's of Marlow. Were they furniture removers? They must be! He was certain they would be. Quick – he must find King's in the directory.

There were a good many Kings – A. King, Alec King, Bertram King, Claude King, Mrs D. King . . . all the way down the list of Kings went Fatty's eager finger. At last, he came to the end of them.

He was bitterly disappointed. Not one of the Kings was a furniture remover. There was a butcher and a baker; but the Kings apparently did not go in for house removals. Fatty stared at the list in despair.

I'll go down it again, very, very carefully, he thought. Now then – A. King, Alec King, Bertram King, Butcher, Claude King, Dentist, Mrs D. King, Edward King, the King Stables, Henry King . . .

wait now – stables! STABLES! That's it! That's it! Stables mean horses – and horses mean horse boxes – horse boxes mean vans capable of removing furniture! I've got it, I've got it!

Fatty threw the directory on the floor and did a most complicated jig up and down the hall with Buster flying after him, barking. He knew that Fatty was excited, so he was excited too.

Mrs Trotteville suddenly came out from the lounge into the hall. 'Frederick! What on earth are you thinking of? I have a meeting in the lounge, and you choose just this minute to act like a wild animal.'

'Oh, Mummy! I'm so sorry,' said Fatty, and in his excitement and jubilance, he went up and hugged her. 'But I've just made a great discovery, and I was celebrating it. *So* sorry, Mummy.'

'Well, go and celebrate down in your shed,' said his mother. 'And, by the way, please don't forget that your grandfather will be here by the eleven o'clock train. I want you to meet him.'

Fatty stared at his mother in the utmost dismay. 'Gosh, I'd forgotten every word about it! Oh, Mummy – I *can't* meet Grandad! I'm so sorry.'

'But you must, Frederick,' said his mother, shocked. 'I have this Committee meeting – and, besides, you always do meet your grandfather. He is only coming for the day and would think it very rude of you if you go off somewhere. You *knew* he was coming.'

Fatty groaned. 'Yes, but I tell you I forgot every word about it. I promise you I did, Mummy. It isn't that I don't *want* to meet him or be with him – I do; but it just happens that I've got something very, very important to do, and it can't wait.'

'Well, either it must wait, or you must get Larry or Pip to do it for you,' said Mrs Trotteville, in an icy voice. She went back to her meeting and shut the door.

Fatty stared at Buster, who had put his tail down at Mrs Trotteville's annoyed voice. 'That's done it!' said Fatty. 'JUST when I'm really on to something. Edward King, the King Stables, Marlow – another bit of the jigsaw that was missing, and now I can't fit it into the picture because Grandad's coming. Why, oh why, did he have to come today?'

Fatty was very fond of his grandfather, but it really was most unfortunate that he should have to meet him and entertain him on this day of all days.

'The old man's furniture will be in a horse box,' he told Buster. 'It might be discovered at any moment – but *I* want to find it, Buster. What a shock for old Mr Goon if I produce both the money *and* the furniture!'

He debated whether to telephone Larry or Pip and tell them his ideas. 'No,' he decided. 'If I get them to go over to Marlow and snoop about for a horse box with furniture inside, they may make some kind of silly move and spoil everything. I'll have to put it off till tonight.'

So Fatty went to meet his grandfather, and entertained him well the whole day.

'Any more mysteries?' asked the twinkling-eyed old man. 'In the middle of one, I suppose? Well, mind you don't let that policeman – what's his name? – Goop – Goon – get the better of you!'

'I won't,' grinned Fatty. 'I'll tell you all about it next time you come, Grandad.'

He saw his grandfather off at six o'clock that evening, and then dashed round to Pip's. Fortunately, Larry and Daisy were there too. Bets was delighted to see Fatty.

'Oh, Fatty! You do look excited. Has anything happened?' she asked.

'Plenty,' said Fatty and poured out everything – the finding of the notes in the hem of the curtains – his idea about removal vans which now might be horse boxes, or so he hoped – and his determination to go to Marlow that night and hunt for a horse box full of furniture!

'I'll come with you,' said Larry at once.

'You and Pip can both come,' said Fatty. 'We'll go and see the film called *Ivanhoe* at the cinema first – and then, when it's quite dark, we'll go hunting for horse boxes!'

'Can't Daisy and I come?' asked Bets.

'No,' said Fatty. 'Sorry, Bets, old thing. You can't come to the cinema with us either, because you two girls can't wait about afterwards for us. We may be ages.'

'All right,' said Bets. 'Oh, my goodness! – isn't it exciting? Fatty, you really are very, very clever. Fancy thinking of the curtain hems!'

'I didn't really,' said Fatty, honestly. 'I just happened to be holding a hem, and it felt – well, rather stiff. But it does clear Marian, doesn't it? She didn't take the money – she merely hid it from Wilfrid!'

'Why did she disappear then, I wonder?' said Daisy.

'I don't know. That's a bit of the jigsaw I just simply can't fit in anywhere,' said Fatty. 'Still, we're getting on!'

The three boys cycled off to Marlow, after an early supper. Buster, unfortunately, was not allowed to go with them, as cinemas do not welcome dogs. He howled dismally when Fatty left.

Ivanhoe was exciting and the three boys enjoyed it. Along with the excitement of the film, was an added feeling of delicious suspense – the thought of the 'snooping' they meant to do afterwards! They didn't even wait to see the short second film, but came out into the clear night at the end of *Ivanhoe*.

'I've found out where the stables are,' said Fatty. 'I rang up and inquired. King's thought I wanted to hire a horse – but I don't! The stables aren't by the river; they are away up on the hill.'

They turned their lamps on and cycled quietly along a country road. Soon Fatty turned to the right, up a steep hill. 'This is the way,' he said. 'Good, here comes the moon! We won't be in the pitch-dark tonight.'

They had to get off their cycles because the hill was so steep. A private road branched off to the left and the boys walked up it. They left their cycles in the shelter of a hedge.

Buildings loomed up nearby. A horse coughed. 'These must be the stables,' said Fatty, in a low voice. 'Keep quiet and walk in the shadows.'

Nobody appeared to be about. The stable-doors were all shut. A horse stamped occasionally, and one whinnied a little.

'Where do they keep the horse boxes?' whispered Fatty. 'I can't see any here.'

'Look, there's another path up there, quite a wide one,' said Pip. 'Perhaps they're along there.'

They went up the broad path. The moon suddenly shone out brilliantly and lighted every rut in front of them. Fatty stopped suddenly.

'Look, see those tyre-marks? Aren't they the same pattern as the one in my notebook, the one you copied Larry? You ought to know – you made four copies!'

'Yes, they *are* the same pattern,' said Larry and got out his copy. He shone a torch on it, though the moonlight was almost brilliant enough for him to read by. 'Yes, it's the same. Goody! We're on the right track. Wilfrid must have taken a horse box to remove all the furniture, and brought it away up here.'

The path went on for quite a way and, at last, came out into a field. No horses were there just then, but the boys could see half-a-dozen in a field a good way down.

'Look – horse boxes, and lorries, and carts!' said Pip, pointing. Sure enough, neatly arranged in a big corner of the field, was a fine collection of horse boxes. The boys went over to them.

'Look inside each one,' said Fatty. There were four, and none of them were locked. The boys shone their torches inside; but to their great disappointment, each horse box was empty, save for a few bits of straw. Fatty was puzzled.

'Let's look at the tyres,' he said. 'Find a horse box with newish tyres, the pattern clearly marked.'

But none of the horse boxes had four new tyres, and the patterns on them were not a bit the same as the one Fatty had seen outside Hollies.

The boys looked at one another. 'Now what?' said Pip. 'Dead end, again!'

'Better look round a bit,' said Fatty. 'It is possible that Wilfrid hid away the horse box with the furniture.'

So they hunted round. They walked across the big field – and at the other side was a copse. Fatty saw a bridle-path leading into the bushes. He followed it, and suddenly came to a muddy piece where, plainly to be seen, were tyre-marks, and each of the three saw at once that they were the ones they were seeking!

Out came Fatty's notebook. 'Yes! These are the ones! Come on, we're on the trail now!'

They followed the bridle-path, and then, neatly pushed into a clearing, they saw a small horse box!

'Brown!' said Fatty. 'And look – here's a scratch on the back wing where it scraped that lamp-post. *Now* we're on the track!'

The boys tried the door. It was locked. 'I thought

it would be,' said Fatty. 'Here, give me a shove-up, and I'll look in at the window. Half a mo, I've dropped my torch!'

He picked it up and flashed it on. Then Pip and Larry hoisted him up to look into the window of the horse box. He saw that it was badly broken. He flashed his torch inside.

'Yes, the furniture is here!' he called softly. 'All of it! Hello – wait – what's this!'

Before he could say any more to the others, a loud scream came from inside the horse box. It so startled Pip and Larry that they let go of Fatty. He fell to the ground with a bump.

The scream rang out again. Then came an anguished voice. 'Help! Oh, help! Help me!'

'Who is it?' whispered Pip, scared. 'We've frightened somebody. Let's go.'

'No,' said Fatty. 'I know who it is. It's Marian! Gosh, she has been locked up with the furniture!'

21. MARIAN

Fatty rapped on the locked door. 'Hey! Don't be scared. Can we help you?'

There was a silence, and then a trembling voice came from the horse box. 'Who are you?'

'Just three boys,' said Fatty. 'Are you Marian?'

'Yes. Oh yes, but how do you know?' said the voice. 'I've been locked up here for ages. Wilfrid locked me in – the beast!'

'Whew!' said Fatty. 'How long have you been there?'

'It seems as if I've been here for days,' said Marian. 'I don't know. Can you let me out?'

'I think I can force the door,' said Fatty. 'What a pity the window's so tiny, Marian – you could have got out of it.'

'I smashed it, hoping someone would hear the noise,' said poor Marian. 'And I yelled till I couldn't yell any more. That beast of a Wilfrid got a horse and dragged the box into some safe place, where nobody could hear me.'

'I'll soon have you out,' said Fatty, and took out a leather case of finely-made tools, small but very strong. He chose one and began to work at the door with it.

Something snapped. Fatty tried the handle and the door opened! A white-faced girl stood there, smiling through her tears.

'Oh, thank you!' she said. 'I've been so miserable. What made you come here tonight?'

'It's a long tale,' said Fatty. 'Would you like us to take you back to your mother? She's frantic about you. And what about food? I hope you've had something to eat and drink while you've been kept prisoner.'

'Yes. Wilfrid put plenty of stuff in the box,' said Marian. 'Not that I could eat much. He's a beast.'

'I agree,' said Fatty. 'I suppose he kept on worrying you to tell him where your grandfather kept his money?'

'How do you know about all this?' said the girl, in wonder. 'Yes, Wilfrid got into debt, and he asked my Grandad – his great-uncle – to give him some money and Grandad wouldn't. Wilfrid was very angry. He knew Grandad kept his money hidden somewhere, and he asked me where it was.'

'And did you know?' said Fatty.

'Yes, I did,' said Marian. 'Grandad told me a little while ago; but often enough, I've seen the old man grope about under this chair and that, when he thought I wasn't there, to feel if his money was safe. But I never told a soul.'

'You remember that morning you washed the curtains?' said Fatty, 'Did Wilfrid ask you again for the money then – to tell him where it was?'

'Yes, and I told him I knew, but that I wouldn't ever tell a mean thing like him!' said Marian. 'He said he only wanted to borrow some and he'd put it back later; but I knew him better! He would never repay it!'

'Go on,' said Fatty.

'Well, that morning he said, "All right, Marian. When you've gone, I shall come back and hunt everywhere – and I'll find it, you see if I don't!" And I was dreadfully afraid that he would.'

'So you were very, very clever and sewed the notes into the hem of the curtains!' said Fatty.

Marian gave a little scream. 'Oh! *How* do you know all this? Surely Wilfrid hasn't found them? Oh, I've worried and worried since I've been shut up here. I wanted to tell Grandpa not to be upset if he couldn't find his money – I'd kept it safe for him – but I didn't get a chance.'

'It's all right. The notes are still inside the hems,' said Fatty. 'It was a brilliant hiding-place. Tell me, what made Wilfrid come and take away the furniture?'

'Well, that afternoon, Wilfrid came to see me at my home,' said Marian. 'He said he'd been to Hollies and Grandad was moaning and crying because his money had gone – and Wilfrid accused me of taking it. He said he'd get the police if I didn't share it with him!'

'Well, well, what a pleasant person our Wilfrid is!' said Fatty.

'I swore I hadn't got the money. I said it was still at Hollies, in the living-room, in a place he'd never find,' said Marian. 'And I told him I'd get it myself the next day and take it to a bank, where Wilfrid couldn't possibly get his hands on it.'

'I see. So he took a horse box in the middle of

the night, and went and quietly collected every bit of furniture from the living-room,' said Fatty. 'He meant to go through every stick of it at his leisure and find that money before you took it to the bank.'

'Yes, but he couldn't find it because it was in the curtains, and he didn't think of taking those down,' said Marian. 'And, oh dear, when he went through the furniture and ripped it to pieces, he still couldn't find the money, of course, so he got me up here by a trick, pushed me into the van, and locked the door.'

'But why?' said Fatty, puzzled.

'Oh, he was quite mad, quite beside himself,' said Marian, trembling as she remembered. 'He said I could either find the money myself in the furniture or, if I was lying, I could tell him where I'd hidden the money in my own home! And here I've been ever since, shouting and yelling, but nobody heard me. And each day, Wilfrid comes to ask me if I've got the money, or will tell him where it is. He's mad!'

'He must be,' said Fatty. 'Cheer up, Marian, 'everything's all right. We'll take you back home, and tomorrow we'll deal with dear Wilfrid. Will you come up to Hollies at half past ten? We'll be there, and you can take the money out of the curtains yourself.'

'Oh, yes, I *must* do that,' said Marian. 'How do you know all these things? It's strange to find you three boys here, in the middle of the night, telling me all kinds of things!'

'You walk along with us to where we've left our bikes,' said Fatty, taking Marian's arm. 'I'll tell you how we know – as much as I can, anyhow. Larry, take the number of this horse box, will you?'

The boys took Marian back to where they had left their bicycles, passing the quiet stables as they went. Fatty told Marian a good deal of his tale, and she listened in amazement.

'Poor Grandad!' she said. 'He must have been so upset. Never mind, he'll be all right when he gets his precious money back. How marvellous you three boys are – finding out everything like that. You're better than the police!'

Fatty took Marian back to her own home. 'It's not so late as you think,' he told her. 'It's not eleven o'clock yet. Look, there's still a light in that side-window. Shall I ring the bell for you?'

'No. I'll slip in at the side door and surprise my mother,' said Marian. She gave Fatty a sudden hug. 'I think you're a marvel! I'll be up at Hollies at half past ten tomorrow morning without fail, with some scissors to undo the hems!'

She disappeared. Fatty waited till he heard the side door open and shut softly. Then he and the others went to get their bicycles from the front hedge.

'Good work, wasn't it?' he said, with much satisfaction.

'My word, yes!' said Larry. 'Gosh, I was so scared when I heard Marian screaming in the van that I let go of you, Fatty; you came down an awful bump.'

'That's all right,' said Fatty, in great good humour. 'My word, what an evening! Who would have thought that Wilfrid would shut Marian up like that! He must be in great need of money to do such a thing. I have an idea that that smartly-dressed young man is going to get into considerable trouble.'

'Serve him right,' said Pip. 'He deserves it.

I think Marian is a really nice girl. I *thought* she couldn't have stolen that money!'

They were now cycling quickly home. Pip began to feel uncomfortable. 'Hey!' he said. *'I'm* going to get into trouble too, being out late like this.'

'I would, as well, if my parents didn't happen to be out,' said Larry. 'You're lucky, Fatty, your parents never seem to mind.'

'I'm older than you are,' said Fatty, 'and wiser! If you get into trouble tonight, Pip, just say that something unexpected happened that you can't yet tell about, but that everything will be explained tomorrow morning.'

'Right,' said Pip. 'What are you going to do now, Fatty? I bet I know! You're going to ring up Superintendent Jenks!'

'Quite right. Go to the top of the class!' said Fatty. 'Well, we part here. See you tomorrow morning, half past ten, at Hollies. Bring the girls too.'

Fatty put away his bicycle when he got home and let himself in at the side door. His parents were playing bridge in the lounge. Good, he wouldn't disturb them. He would telephone Superintendent Jenks from his mother's bedroom – where there was an extension – not from the hall. He could say what he liked there.

He tiptoed into his mother's room and shut the door. He went to the telephone and dialled the police headquarters number. A voice answered almost immediately.

'Police station here.'

'Is Superintendent Jenks in?' asked Fatty. 'If not, I'll ring his private number. It's important.'

'He's not here. I'll give you his private number,' said the voice.

'Thank you,' said Fatty and rang off. He telephoned the private number. He heard the Superintendent's voice almost at once.

'Yes. What is it?'

'Frederick Trotteville here,' said Fatty. 'First of all, my hearty congratulations, sir, on your promotion!'

'Thanks, Frederick,' said the Superintendent, 'but I don't imagine that you're ringing me up at almost midnight just to tell me that.'

'No, sir,' said Fatty. 'The fact is, we've done a bit of work on that Hollies affair.'

'Hollies affair? Oh, yes, the old man whose

money was stolen, whose furniture disappeared, and then the granddaughter vanished – am I right?' said the Superintendent.

'Quite right, sir,' said Fatty. 'Er . . .'

'Wait now,' came the Super's voice, 'let me hazard a guess, Frederick. You've found the money, you've located the furniture, and you've got the girl! Am I right?'

'Well, yes sir,' said Fatty, with a laugh. 'How did you know?'

'Oh, I had a report in two days ago from Goon, in the course of which he complained that Frederick Trotteville was greatly hampering the course of justice,' chuckled the Superintendent. 'I imagined that meant you were getting on with the case a lot better than he was. Actually, he said that it was pretty certain the girl had gone off with the money, and should be arrested as soon as found.'

'Did he? Well, he's not quite right,' said Fatty. 'Would you care to come along to Hollies, the bungalow where all this happened, at half past ten tomorrow morning, sir, and I'll have the whole affair neatly tied up for you?'

'Right, I'll be there,' said the Super. 'I was

coming over anyhow to see what was happening. I didn't like the disappearance of the girl – from all accounts, she's a good girl. I hope you will produce her, Frederick.'

'I hope to sir,' said Fatty, trying to sound modest. 'And – er – will Mr Goon be there?'

'Of course!' I'll have a message sent to him,' said the Super. 'Well, well, I don't know why we don't leave all our local affairs to you, Frederick. How's little Bets? Is she in on this too?'

'Oh, yes. We all are,' said Fatty. 'Right, sir. We'll all be up at Hollies at half past ten. Goodnight!'

Fatty put down the telephone, and rubbed his hands gleefully. Good, good, good! He was about to do a delighted jig round the room when he stopped. No – his mother's bedroom was just over the lounge – it would cause quite a lot of trouble for Fatty if someone came up to hunt for the elephant stamping round the room above!

I'll go and find old Buster, he thought. I can hear him scraping at my bedroom door now. I'm coming, Buster. Good news, old thing! Get ready to bark your head off, Buster. Hurrah!

22. QUITE A PANTOMIME!

Quite a lot of people walked up Holly Lane the next morning. Fatty, Larry, Daisy, Pip and Bets went first, talking excitedly. Bets and Daisy had been tremendously thrilled the night before when Pip and Larry had crept in to tell them the news of the Marlow adventure.

Fatty went up the front path, took the key from his pocket, and unlocked the door. Mr Henri, at the window next door, saw them, and left his couch. In a minute or two, he was walking up the path.

'Good morning!' he said. 'You did not leave me the key, Frederick, and that young man – what is his name? – ah yes, Wilfrid – he was annoyed to find I did not have it. He said he had forgotten his own key, and wished to enter Hollies to see that all was right.'

'Oh, he did, did he?' said Fatty. 'Thought he'd

have one more hunt round, I suppose. Good thing he didn't.'

'He is coming back again soon,' said Mr Henri.

'Good! Couldn't be better,' said Fatty. 'The more the merrier. Would you like to stay, Mr Henri? There is going to be a bit of a do here soon – you might enjoy it. After all, you've been in this affair almost from the beginning.'

'I stay with pleasure,' said Mr Henri, beaming. 'Ah, who comes now?'

'It's Marian!' said Fatty. He darted to the door to meet her. She looked much better now. She smiled round at the others. Then she saw the empty room.

'Oh, how bare it looks without the furniture!' she said. Her eyes went to the curtains. She put out a hand and felt one of the hems. Fatty smiled at her.

'Really good hems, aren't they?' he said. 'Marian, I wonder if you'd be sweet enough to go and sit in the back bedroom till we call you. I want to produce you as a sort of . . . well, sort of a surprise.'

'Yes. I'll go,' said Marian. 'But let me leave the

door open. I want to hear everything.'

'You're setting the scene as if a play was going to be acted!' said Bets, giggling.

'Well, a play *is* about to be acted,' said Fatty. 'Now, who's this?'

It was Mr Goon. He looked a bit puzzled as he rode up to the gate. He got off his bicycle, wheeled it up to the front door, and put it against the wall.

Fatty opened the door for him. 'Welcome!' he said. Mr Goon scowled.

'What you doing here?' he said. 'You'd better clear orf. The Superintendent's coming. He wants particularly to talk to me about this here case. I've got all my notes with me, so just you clear of. And keep that dog away from my ankles, or I'll report him to the Super.'

'Sit, Buster', said Fatty. 'My word, Mr Goon, what a sheaf of notes you've got! Wonderful work! Have you solved the mystery?'

'No mystery about it,' said Goon, scornfully. 'That girl went off with the money – *and* the furniture. I'll soon have my hands on her. I've had information about where she is.'

'Really?' said Fatty. 'Anywhere in this district?'

Goon snorted. 'No! Miles away! Anyway, I'm not saying any more. You're not going to pick my brains. Me and the Superintendent are going to have a good talk, and you'd better clear out before he comes. Get along now!'

'Here he is,' said Fatty, as a sleek, black police car drew up at the gate, and the Superintendent got out with a plain clothes man behind him. Bets tore out to meet him. He swung her up into the air.

'If it isn't young Bets! Well, well, how nice to see you again! Well, Daisy, how are you? Larry, Pip, Frederick, you all look very merry and bright.'

'I told them you were coming, sir, but they wouldn't buzz off,' said Goon, hoping that the Superintendent would take the hint and send the five away. But he didn't. He asked who Mr Henri was, and Fatty explained.

Goon rustled his sheaf of notes and coughed. The Superintendent turned and looked at him sharply.

'Got something to say, Goon?' he inquired.

'Well, sir, yes, of course, sir,' said Goon, looking hurt. 'I supposed you wanted to see me about this Hollies case, sir. If you could just send these kids away . . .'

'Oh, no. They may have something to say that would help us, Goon,' said his chief. 'They may even know a few things that we don't know!'

Goon looked most disbelieving. 'There's really not much to this case, sir,' he said. 'Just a bad girl who robs her old grandfather of his money, gets away with his furniture too, and does a disappearing act.'

'But I thought she was a girl of very good character, Goon, said the Super. 'Girls like that don't suddenly do wicked things. How do we know she stole the money anyway?'

'She didn't,' said Fatty, to Goon's surprise. 'Nobody stole it.'

'You're potty,' said Goon, quite forgetting himself. 'Where's this money then, if nobody stole it?'

'The girl hid it,' said Fatty. 'She was afraid her cousin Wilfrid would get it, if she didn't put it somewhere safe.'

'Pah!' said Goon. 'What a tale! I'll believe that if you show me where she hid the money!'

'Right,' said Fatty, and stepped to the curtains. He put his finger and thumb into the hem whose stitches he had snipped the day before, and pulled out a five pound note. He displayed it to Goon, Mr Henri and Superintendent Jenks. They all stared in surprise, and Goon gaped, his mouth open in amazement.

'See – a five pound note!' said Fatty, and took another from the hem, rather as if he were doing a conjuring trick. 'The hems of the curtains are full of these notes – a first class hiding-place. You remember that Marian, the girl, was washing and ironing curtains, don't you, on the morning of the supposed robbery, Mr Goon? Well, Wilfrid came and threatened to look for the money when she had gone, if she didn't give it to him then and there . . .

'And she was scared he'd find it, so she took it from its hiding-place – wherever that was – and undid the curtain hems to make a new hiding-place!' said the Superintendent. 'Sewed them all up again too. A most ingenious girl, this Marian.'

Mr Goon swallowed two or three times. He could find nothing at all to say. Mr Henri laughed in delight.

'Very neat,' he said. 'And now you will tell us where the lost furniture is, yes?'

'Pah!' said Goon, unable to stop himself.

'What did you say, Goon?' asked his chief. 'Can *you* tell us where the furniture is?'

'No. And nobody can!' said Goon. 'Nobody saw it go, nobody knows who took it, nobody knows where it is. I've had it searched for everywhere!'

'Frederick, can you throw any light on this subject?' asked the Superintendent.

'Yes,' said Fatty. 'Wilfrid and another man came at midnight and carried it out piece-by-piece.'

'Gah!' said Goon. 'Anybody would think you were there!'

'Well, as it happened, I was,' said Fatty. 'It was taken away in a horse box – got the number, Larry? Yes, OKX 143 – and it is now in that same horse box, rather the worse for wear, in a copse near the stables belonging to King's, in Marlow. I can take you there any time you like, Mr Goon.'

'You've got the money, you've got the furniture, but you haven't got the girl!' said Goon. 'And I've had information where she is!'

'That's clever of you, Mr Goon,' said Fatty. 'You tell me where *you* think she is – and I'll tell you where *I* think she is!'

'I have information here that she's gone across to Ireland,' said Mr Goon.

'And I have information that she's in the next room,' said Fatty, with a grin. 'Marian! Are you there!'

And, to Mr Goon's undying amazement, Marian walked shyly into the room! Mr Henri gave an exclamation. He had wondered who Marian was. The Superintendent glanced at his amazed plain clothes officer and winked.

'Quite a pantomime!' he said, and the plain clothes man grinned and nodded. He moved forward and asked Marian a few questions. Where had she been since she disappeared? Why had she gone away? He wrote down her answers rapidly, while Goon listened in the utmost astonishment.

'I understand, then, that these three boys found you locked up in the horse box last night?' he said. 'And that your cousin Wilfrid was responsible for detaining you there?'

'Here, wait a minute!' said Goon, unable to

believe his ears. 'You say these kids found her in that horse box. How did *they* know about it? Why wasn't *I* told?'

'Frederick telephoned me last night,' said his chief. 'Quite rightly, too. It is possible that you might not have believed him, Goon.'

Goon collapsed. His face went slowly purple and he turned and looked out of the window. That boy! That toad of a boy!

'And now all we want to complete the merry little company is our friend, Wilfrid,' said the Superintendent. 'I imagine that even *you* can't supply him, Frederick?'

Fatty was about to say sorrowfully that no, he was afraid he couldn't, when he heard the front gate click. He looked out of the window and saw – Wilfrid!

Yes, Wilfrid had chosen that moment to come back and hunt round once again for the money. He saw that the door was now open and hurried to go inside. He stepped over the threshold – and stopped abruptly. The plain clothes man moved casually beside him.

'Oh!' said Wilfrid. 'What's all this? Something

happened?' Then he saw his cousin, and went very white.

'Marian! What are you doing here?'

'You thought I was still in the horse box, didn't you?' said Marian. 'Well, I'm not. I'm here. I've come to get the money of Grandad's I hid away – see, in the hem of the curtains! You won't get it, Wilfrid! You won't have it to pay your bills!'

Wilfrid stared at the notes that Marian was pulling out of the curtain hem. He ran his hand over his forehead. Then he made a sudden backward dart for the door.

But the plain clothes man was there, and a hand with fingers of steel gripped Wilfrid's arm and held him fast.

'Don't go yet, Wilfrid,' said the Superintendent. 'There are quite a lot of questions we want to ask you.'

His voice was suddenly very different from the merry, kindly voice that the children were used to. Bets shivered a little. The Super was their friend, their very good friend, but to people like Wilfrid he was an implacable enemy, stern and unyielding. Wilfrid stood before him, as white as a sheet, trembling from head to foot.

'Johns – you and Goon stay here and let him tell you about the midnight move,' said the Superintendent. 'Where he parked the van and everything. Then, take him along to the police station. I'll be there in an hour.'

'Right, sir,' said Johns, the plain clothes man. Goon muttered something, but nobody could catch what he said. Still, as nobody listened, it didn't matter! Poor Goon, he looked very downcast as the five children and Marian went away with the Superintendent.

Mr Henri went with them and said good-bye at the gate. 'I have such a story to tell to my sistair,' he said. 'Please to come and see us soon! Au revoir!'

'Where are we going?' asked Bets, hanging on to the burly Superintendent's arm.

'Well, isn't there some place here that sells ice creams and macaroons?' said the big man. 'I had an early breakfast – and I don't often see you. I'd like to give you all a treat this morning – Marian too! She looks as if she wants feeding up a bit! Been starved in that horse box, I expect, Marian!'

'I couldn't eat very much,' she said. 'But I'm

quite all right now, thank you. So is my mother. She was *so* thankful to see me. I'd still be a prisoner if it wasn't for these three boys!'

'Ah, here is the place I mean,' said the Superintendent, stopping outside the spotlessly clean café. 'Yes. Best macaroons I ever had in my life came from here. In we go!'

And in they went, Buster too, much to the surprise of the little shop owner, who didn't expect quite so many customers all at once – seven – and a dog, who was as good as a customer any day, because he was just as fond of macaroons and ice creams as the children were!

'Er – twenty-one macaroons please. Oh, I beg your pardon, Buster – twenty-four, I mean,' said the Superintendent. 'And a first round of eight ice creams – and orangeade for everyone but the dog.'

'Yes, sir,' said the woman, and hurried away. She brought the orangeade at once. 'The other things are just coming,' she said.

The Superintendent lifted his glass. 'Let us drink to the day when Frederick Trotteville becomes my right-hand man!' he said. Fatty blushed with pride, and they all drank heartily.

Then Fatty lifted his glass. 'To my future chief, Superintendent Jenks!' he said, and everyone again drank heartily. Now, only the Superintendent had any orangeade left.

'Ah, can't waste it!' he said. 'To the Five Find-Outers – and Dog. Many Happy Mysteries!'

Yes, we all wish them that. Many more mysteries – and may each one be more mysterious than the last!

THE MYSTERY OF TALLY-HO COTTAGE

CONTENTS

1. AT PETERSWOOD STATION

One afternoon, four children and a dog walked into the little railway station at Peterswood. The dog ran about happily, his tail wagging all the time.

'Better put Buster on the lead,' said Pip. 'We're early, and two or three trains may come through. Here, Buster – come to heel, old boy!'

The little Scottie trotted up, his tail wagging nineteen to the dozen. He gave a few short barks.

'Yes, I know you're longing to see Fatty,' said Pip, bending over him to clip on his lead. 'So are we all! Hey, keep still!'

'Hang on to him – here comes a train!' said Larry. 'It's going right through.'

Buster stood his ground bravely until the train gave a piercing whistle as it tore through the station – then he tried to scuttle under a wooden seat and dragged Pip after him. He sat down with his back to the train and trembled. That awful whistle!

'It made *me* jump!' said Bets. 'Cheer up, Buster – Fatty will soon be here. We've loved having you while Fatty's been away, and you've been very, very good!'

'Even Mummy likes you!' said Pip, patting him. 'Though she didn't want us to keep you at all while Fatty was in Switzerland!'

'I can't think *why* Fatty had to go off to Switzerland for a whole fortnight, and be away all Christmas time,' complained Bets.

'Well, he had to go with his parents,' said Daisy. 'I expect he had a really good time in all that snow.'

'Yes,' said Larry, with a laugh. 'What's the time? Gosh, we're early! What shall we do?'

'It's cold on the platform. Let's go into the waiting-room,' said Daisy. 'Come on, Buster.'

Buster sat firm. Pip pulled on the lead. 'Come on, idiot. We're only going into the waiting-room. Fatty's train isn't due yet.'

Buster refused to move. Fatty was coming on one of the trains that clattered into the station, and would alight on this platform – and, therefore, Buster wished to wait there and nowhere else.

'Tie him up to the seat,' said Larry. 'He'll be miserable if we make him go into the waiting-room. Buster, you're an idiot. *I* wouldn't sit down on that icy-cold stone platform for anything.'

They tied Buster to the seat and left him there. They went into the waiting-room, which had a very minute fire, but was at least sheltered from the cold wind that blew through the station.

'There's one thing,' said Daisy, sitting down on a hard wooden bench. 'Fatty won't be in disguise, so he can't trick us this time! He'll be arriving with his father and mother, and will have to be himself.'

'I'm glad,' said Bets. 'I want to see him just as he really is, big and jolly and grinning all over his face! We haven't seen him for months! Three months at school – and then he rushes off to Switzerland!'

'I bet I know what he'll say as soon as he sees us,' said Pip, grinning. 'He'll say, "Well, got any mystery on hand?" '

'And we haven't,' said Larry. 'Peterswood has been as good as gold. Mr Goon can't have had anything to do at all!'

Mr Goon, the village policeman, had indeed had a peaceful fortnight. Not even a dog had chased a sheep, and nothing as exciting as even a small burglary had happened. Mr Goon had had plenty of time for snoozing in his big armchair!

A taxi drove up to the station, followed by a second one. A man leaned out of the window of the first one and beckoned to the one and only porter.

'Hey, porter! Come and take these cases. Look likely, we've not got much time!'

The voice was loud and clear. The porter ran up at once, and took two small cases. A man got out of the taxi and helped out a woman. Both were middle-aged, well-dressed and cheerful-looking. The woman carried a tiny white poodle.

'Darling Poppet!' she said. 'Don't get a cold in this icy wind!' She tucked the little thing under her fur coat and only its quaint little pointed nose looked out. The four children, watching from the window of the waiting-room, thought it was very cute!

Four or five people got out of the second taxi, all rather hilarious. They had evidently come to see off the first two.

'Hurry up, Bill – you've not got much time to get the tickets!' said the woman with the dog.

'Plenty of time,' said Bill, and strode into the station. 'Hello, is that a train in the distance? My word, we'll have to hurry after all!'

The woman rushed on to the platform with the little dog. 'Oh, it isn't our train after all!' she said. 'It's going the other way. Oh, Poppet, what a shock I got!'

The newcomers made such a stir and commotion that the four children came out of the waiting-room to watch. Everyone was very hilarious.

'Well, be sure to have a good time!' said a red-haired man and he thumped the man called Bill on his back, so that he had a coughing fit.

'Ring us when you get there. We'll miss you and your parties!' said a woman.

The woman with the dog sat down on the seat

to which Buster was tied, and set the little poodle down on the platform. At once, Buster began to sniff at her woolly fur, and the little poodle yelped in sudden fright. Buster ran round to the front of the seat, twisting his lead across the woman's legs. She screamed and snatched Poppet up at once, afraid that Buster was going to snap at the poodle.

To make matters worse, another train thundered into the station at that moment and Poppet nearly went mad with fright. She leapt out of her mistress's arms and tore off at top speed. Buster tried to race after her, forgetting all about his lead, and nearly strangled himself! He got caught up in the woman's legs, and she fell over, squealing loudly.

'Oh! Catch Poppet, someone! Oh, what's this dog doing? Get away, you brute!'

There was a terrific commotion. All four children tried to catch Poppet, and then Pip went to rescue poor Buster who was being well and truly scolded by the scared woman. She was very angry indeed.

'Whose dog is this? What do you want to tie

him up under a seat for? Where's a policeman? Where's my dog?'

'Now, now, Gloria, don't get upset,' said the man called Bill. Nobody took any notice of the train that had just come in, not even the four children. They were so concerned about Buster, and poor frightened Poppet!

So they didn't even notice Fatty stepping from the train with his father and mother – an extremely sunburnt Fatty, looking the picture of health. He soon saw the others, and was rather astonished to find them so engrossed that they weren't even looking out for him!

'You get a taxi, Mummy,' said Fatty. 'I'll walk back with the others. I see they're here.'

Fatty walked over to where Pip was trying to apologise to the angry woman and her husband. He now had his hand firmly on Buster's collar, and Buster was trying his hardest to squirm away. He began to bark loudly – and then suddenly wrenched himself from Pip's hand.

'Well!' said a familiar voice. 'At least *some*body recognises me! Hello, Buster!'

All the four swung round at once. Bets ran

at Fatty, almost knocking him over. 'Fatty! You're here!'

'It looks like it!' said Fatty, and then there was a general clapping of backs and friendly punches. Buster nearly barked the station down, he was so excited. He pawed so hard at Fatty's legs that Fatty had to lift him up and carry him!

'Whose dog is that?' demanded the man called Bill. 'I never saw such a badly-behaved one in my life. Knocked my wife over, and made her coat all dusty! Ah – there's a policeman – come over here, my good man. I want to report this dog. It's been out of control, attacked my wife's poodle, and caused my wife to fall down!'

To the children's horror, there was Mr Goon! He had come to buy a paper at the station, had heard the commotion, and walked on to the platform to see what it was. He still had his bicycle clips on his legs, and his bulging eyes gleamed with pleasure.

'Sir! This dog made a savage attack, you say! Just let me take down a note. Ah, this dog's been a pest for a long time – a very long time!'

Mr Goon took out his notebook and licked his

pencil. What a bit of luck to have a real complaint about that horrible dog!

The train pulled out of the station, but nobody noticed. Everyone was looking at the little group of children surrounded by grown-ups. Buster leapt out of Fatty's arms as soon as he saw Mr Goon and danced joyfully round his ankles. Mr Goon flapped at him with his notebook.

'Call this dog off! Here, you, call this dog off. I'll report him all right. I'll . . .'

Suddenly the woman gave a squeal of joy. 'Oh, here's Poppet back again – with Larkin. I thought you weren't going to come in time to take Poppet back home with you, Larkin!'

Larkin was a strange-looking fellow, who stooped as he walked, and dragged one leg behind him in a limp. He looked fat and shapeless in an old and voluminous overcoat, and had a scarf round the bottom part of his face and an old cap over his eyes. He carried Poppet in his arms.

'Who's this?' demanded Goon, looking with surprise at the odd fellow who suddenly appeared with Poppet.

'Oh, it's only Larkin, who lives in the cottage in

the grounds of Tally-Ho, the house we rent,' said the woman. 'He was told to come to the station in time to collect Poppet and take her back again with him. He's going to look after her, but I *did* want to have my darling Poppet till the very last minute, didn't I, Poppet?'

She took Poppet into her arms and fondled her. She spoke to Larkin again. 'You'll look after her well, won't you? And remember all I told you to do. I'll soon be back to see to her. Take her now, before our train comes in and scares her.'

Larkin shuffled off, limping as he went. He hadn't said a word. Poppet had been handed back to him as if she were a doll, and was now snuggled into his coat again.

Mr Goon was growing impatient. He still had his notebook in his hand. The children were wondering whether they could make a dash and go, but Mr Goon had his eye on them.

'Now, Madam,' said Mr Goon, 'about this dog here. Can I have your name and address, please, and . . .'

'Oh! Here's our train!' squealed the woman, and immediately everyone elbowed poor Mr

Goon aside and began to kiss and shake hands and shout good-bye. The man and woman climbed into a carriage and off went the train, with everyone waving madly.

'Gah!' said Mr Goon, in disgust, and shut his notebook. He looked round for Buster and the others – but they were gone!

2. IT'S FUN TO BE TOGETHER AGAIN!

The five children and Buster were halfway down the road, running at top speed!

'Good thing that train came in when it did!' panted Pip.

'Horrid old Mr Goon! He *would* turn up just then!' said Bets. 'It wasn't Buster's fault. He wasn't doing any harm.'

'Let's hide somewhere till Mr Goon's gone by,' said Daisy. 'He's got his bike, I expect, and he'll have a few nasty things to say to us if he sees us.'

'Oh yes, let's hide,' said Bets, who really was very scared of the big policeman.

'Right. Here's an empty watchman's hut!' said Fatty, spotting it standing beside a place where the road was being repaired. 'Hop in. It will just about take us all. The back is towards where Mr Goon will come from. He'll sail right by!'

They crowded into the little hut – only just in

time! Mr Goon turned the corner on his bicycle and came sailing down the road at top speed, on the look out for the Five – and especially for that pest of a dog!

They all watched him sail past, his feet going rapidly up and down on the pedals. They caught sight of his grim face as he went by. Fatty grinned.

'There he goes. Well, we'd better keep out of his way for a day or two,' he said. 'I expect he'll be after us about old Buster. What *did* happen? Tell me. I was really surprised to find you all on the platform with your backs to me, not caring whether I arrived or not!'

'Oh, Fatty – everything happened so quickly!' said Bets, as they walked home with him. She told him all about tying Buster up to the seat, and how the man and woman had arrived with their friends, and how Poppet had got mixed up with Buster.

'It was such a to-do!' said Pip. 'I'm really sorry about it, Fatty – just as your train arrived too!'

'That's all right!' said Fatty. 'I was only pulling your leg about it. Has Buster been good with you and Bets while I've been away?'

'He's been angelic!' said Bets. 'I *shall* miss him. Mummy wouldn't let him sleep in my room or Pip's, as he does in yours, Fatty – but he was *most* obedient, and only came scratching at my door once in the middle of the night.'

'You're a very well-brought-up dog, aren't you, Buster?' said Fatty, and the little Scottie danced in delight round his ankles. 'Blow Mr Goon! It was bad luck that he came up at that minute. I bet he'll be after us for details of "Savage Behaviour of Dog out of Control". I expect that's what he wrote down in his notebook. We'll have to think what to say to him.'

'Here we are,' said Pip, stopping by Fatty's gate. 'When shall we see you again, Fatty? You'll have to go in and unpack now, I suppose?'

'Yes,' said Fatty. 'Come round tomorrow to the shed at the bottom of my garden. And if you see Mr Goon, just say that as *I* own Buster, I'm the one for him to see. Well, so long! All news tomorrow!'

He went through the gate and round to the garden door of his house. Bets sighed. 'Oh, I do wish we could all have had tea together or something. I'm just longing for a good talk with Fatty. Isn't he *brown*?'

Much to Bets' relief, Mr Goon didn't appear at her home that day. When she and Pip set out the next morning to go to Fatty's shed, they both kept a good look out for the policeman, but he didn't appear either on foot or on his bicycle.

Larry and Daisy were already down in the shed with Fatty. It was warm and cosy, for the oil-lamp was lit and burning well. Fatty was just the same old Fatty, handing out bars of chocolate, and opening bottles of ginger beer and lemonade. He grinned at Pip and Bets.

'Come on in. Seen old Mr Goon?'

'No. Has anybody seen him?' asked Bets.

Nobody had. Buster went over to Bets and lay down beside her. 'He feels as if he belongs to you as well as to me now,' said Fatty, smiling at Bets. He was very fond of little Bets, and she thought the world of Fatty.

'You *are* brown, Fatty!' said Bets, looking at his sunburnt face. 'If you wanted to disguise yourself as a foreigner, you'd easily pass for one.'

'Good idea!' said Fatty. 'I might try it on old

Mr Goon! I'm longing to get back to some real detective work again, and try out a few disguises. I don't get much chance at school – I only dressed up once last term.'

'What as?' asked Daisy, with a giggle. 'Go on, tell us. I know you want to!'

'It wasn't anything much,' said Fatty airily. 'Our French teacher fell ill and the Head had to send for a new one – and he – er – arrived early, and made a bit of a fool of himself.'

'Oh, did *you* pretend to be him?' said Pip. 'What did you do, Fatty? You really are mad!'

'Well, I togged myself up, put on a moustache and those false teeth of mine,' said Fatty, 'and a wig of curly black hair, and a smile you could see a mile off because of the teeth . . .'

The others laughed. They knew Fatty's frightful false front teeth!

'Did you ask for the Head?' asked Bets.

'Gosh no, I'm not as stupid as all that!' said Fatty. 'I knew I'd find three or four of the teachers watching the football that afternoon, so I made my way to them and talked to them very *earnestly* about the school. 'And ze dear boys – zey await my coming, is it not? And ze – how you call him? – ze Head – he awaits me also? Zis is ze football, is it not? Boom-boom – how zat boy kicked ze ball!'

Fatty acted a Frenchman to the life, and the others roared at him. 'I don't think they liked me very much,' said Fatty. 'They all muttered something about classes and wandered off one by one. My teeth put them off, I suppose. They were really surprised when the *real* French master turned up!'

'What was he like? Anything like you pretended to be?' asked Larry.

'Not a bit. He was little and rather bald, and had a beard and teeth you'd hardly notice!' said Fatty. 'It all caused quite a commotion. A scare went round that the first man must have been someone who wanted to get in and rob the Head's safe – and the poor new man couldn't *think* why people were so surprised to see him.'

'I don't know how you dare to do such things,' said Pip. 'I'd *never* dare, and if I did I'd be found out at once. I can't think why you're hardly ever spotted, Fatty. There must be something about you – you do carry things off so well!'

Fatty looked pleased. 'Oh well, I've got to practise a bit if I'm going to be a real detective some day. Have some more ginger beer? Now, have you found any mystery? A mystery would be just about the best news I could hear.'

'There's not been a sniff of one,' said Larry, drinking his ginger beer. 'Mr Goon must have been thoroughly bored this Christmas – I don't believe anything's happened at all.'

'Sad,' said Fatty. 'After two weeks of doing nothing but fall about in snow, I did hope I could exercise my brains as soon as I got home.'

'Tell us about Switzerland,' said Bets. 'Did you really fall down much?'

It appeared that, far from falling down even once, Fatty had done extremely well in all forms of winter sport, and had carried off quite a few prizes. He tried to talk about them modestly but, being Fatty, this was very difficult.

'Still the same old Fatty,' said Larry, after about twenty minutes of listening to Fatty's exploits. 'The Wonder Boy! Can't put a foot wrong, even on skis!'

'Didn't stand on his head once!' said Pip,

grinning. 'My cousin Ronald said he was more often upside-down than the right way up, when *he* went to the winter sports. But not our Fatty!'

'Don't tease him!' said Daisy. 'You'll stop his traveller's tales. He's got plenty more, haven't you, Fatty?'

'Well, *I* want to hear them, even if nobody else does!' said Bets, who never minded Fatty's boasting.

Fatty sighed heavily. 'Ah well, I don't want to bore you!' he said. 'You tell me *your* news. How many Christmas cards did you have? Was your turkey done to a turn? Did the fairy doll look nice at the top of your Christmas tree?'

'Shut up, Fatty,' said Pip, and gave him a punch. That was the signal for a general scrimmage in which Buster joined in delight. They were all shrieking so loudly that nobody heard a knock at the shed door. Buster was almost barking his head off, and he didn't hear it either.

The shed door opened, and Fatty's mother, Mrs Trotteville, looked in. 'Frederick!' she called, in amazement. 'FREDERICK! Whatever is going on here? You'll have the oil-stove over. FREDERICK!'

Buster heard her first, and stopped barking. He

stood and stared at her, and then gave a yelp as if to say, 'Stop this fooling, everybody! Beware!'

Pip suddenly caught sight of Mrs Trotteville and extricated himself from the heap of bodies on the floor. Fatty was underneath, having been well and truly pummelled.

'Fatty!' said Pip, in Fatty's ear. 'Look out – danger!'

With a great heave, Fatty sat up and looked round. He saw the open door and his mother standing in astonishment there. He smoothed back his hair and grinned.

'Oh, Mummy! I didn't hear you, I can't think why!' said Fatty, politely. 'Do come in. Have a chocolate – or some lemonade? I think there's a drop left.'

'Don't be foolish, Frederick,' said his mother. 'Really, to see you behaving like this – you must all have gone mad! You'll certainly have that oil-stove over, and then the whole place will go up in flames.'

'I've got a bucket of water ready over there, Mummy,' said Fatty. 'Honestly, you don't need to worry. We were only – well, actually, we were so *pleased* to be together again that we – er – we . . .'

'I can't wait while you think up some silly explanation,' said Mrs Trotteville impatiently. 'I just came to say that that policeman, Mr Goon, is on the telephone and wants to speak to you. I do hope, Frederick, that you haven't upset him *already*. You only came back yesterday.'

Goon on the telephone! The Five looked at one another in dismay. That meant he was going to get after old Buster after all. Blow!

'All right. I'll go and speak to him,' said Fatty, getting up and brushing the dust off various parts of himself. 'Blow Mr Goon! It's all right, Mummy – don't look at me like that, there's a dear. I HAVEN'T DONE ANYTHING WRONG, truly I haven't.'

And off he went up the garden path and into the house, Mrs Trotteville behind him, and Buster scampering along too.

The others looked at one another. Now what horrid things had Goon to say?

3. POPPET THE POODLE

Mr Goon was getting impatient. Why didn't that toad of a boy come to the telephone? He began to bellow into it at his end.

'Hello! HELLO! Are you there? HELLO!'

When Fatty picked up the receiver, he was almost deafened by Mr Goon's yells. He shouted back.

'HELLO, HELLO, GOOD MORNING, HELLO, HELLO, HEL . . .'

This time it was Goon that was almost deafened. 'Ho – you've come at last, have you?' he said. 'What you yelling at me like that for?'

'Nothing. I just thought we were having a kind of shouting match,' said Fatty, in a most polite voice.

Goon began to boil. Fatty always had a very bad effect on him. He spluttered into the telephone.

'Now then, you look here, and don't you . . .'

'Can't hear you properly,' said Fatty, in a most concerned voice. 'Mr Goon, can you speak a little closer to the mouthpiece?'

'*No*!' roared the angry policeman, 'and just you look here, I . . .'

'Look where? Down the telephone, do you mean?' said Fatty inquiringly.

Poor Mr Goon nearly flung down the telephone. He roared again. 'I want you to come down here to my house tomorrow morning at ten o'clock sharp,' he shouted. 'About that complaint, see? That dog's out of control, and well you know it.'

'There wasn't time for you to get a proper complaint,' said Fatty.

'Ho, I got enough to go on,' said Goon.

'No, you didn't,' said Fatty, exasperated.

'What's that you say?' bellowed Goon.

'Nothing of any importance,' said Fatty. 'Right – I'll be along tomorrow – with my witnesses – including Buster.'

'No, don't you bring that there pest of a dog!' cried Mr Goon. But it was too late – Fatty had put down the receiver with a bang. Blow Goon!

He went to tell the others, and they listened gloomily.

'We'll all come with you,' said Bets loyally. 'And of course we'll take Buster. He's the defendant, isn't he? – is that what you call it? – and he ought to speak up for himself!'

'He'll speak all right!' said Pip. 'What a nuisance Mr Goon is! We haven't got a *great* deal of the holiday left, and we don't want it messed up by Mr Goon.'

'Let's go for a walk,' said Fatty. 'The sun's out now, and I want to get the taste of Mr Goon out of my mouth!'

They all laughed. 'You say such silly things!' said Daisy. 'Come on, let's go down to the river. There are some baby swans there, and the parents bring them to be fed. We'll take some bread.'

They put on their coats and went up the garden path to the kitchen door to ask for bread. The cook put it into a basket for them and they set off for the river.

They fed the swans and then wandered up the river path, enjoying the pale January sun. The swans swam with them for some way, the little cygnets following behind. They came to a small gate that led on to the river path, and Bets looked over it idly.

Then she pulled at Fatty's arm. 'Look – isn't that exactly like the dear little poodle we saw yesterday at the station – the one whose mistress made all the fuss about Buster?'

They all looked over the gate. 'No, I don't think it's the poodle,' said Pip adding, in his usual brotherly way, 'you *always* jump to conclusions, Bets. Now I come to look more closely, it's not a *bit* like the poodle we saw. It's too big.'

An argument began. 'It's not too big, it's about the right size,' said Daisy.

'You girls have no idea of size,' said Larry loftily.

'I'll soon prove it, anyway,' said Bets suddenly, and she began to call loudly. 'Poppet! Poppet, are you Poppet? Here, Poppet!'

And the poodle straightway ran over to the gate, its stiff little tail wagging like a pendulum!

'There you are!' said Bets triumphantly. 'What did I tell you? Poppet, you're a darling! Fatty, isn't she sweet? She trots about as if she learns ballet dancing!'

'So she does,' said Fatty, seeing exactly what Bets meant. 'At any moment now, Poppet will rise on her toes and pirouette! Poppet, why did you cause all that upset with Buster?'

Poppet put her little pointed nose through the gate and sniffed at Buster, who sniffed back. He licked the tip of Poppet's nose, and Bets laughed.

'He likes her! I wonder if she's lonely without her mistress? I didn't much like the look of that man who took her back home, did you?'

'Well, I didn't like what I could *see* of him, which wasn't much,' said Fatty. 'I wonder where they live – in that cottage there, I suppose.'

A small, not very well-kept cottage stood at the side of the garden. Much further away rose a big house, probably the one that Poppet's master and mistress had left the day before. No smoke rose from its chimney, so presumably it was now empty. But smoke rose up from the chimneys of the little cottage steadily and thickly, and the five children immediately pictured the muffled-up man sitting hunched over a roaring fire.

Poppet wanted Buster to play with her. She pranced away from the gate, came back, and pranced away again, looking over her shoulder as if to say, 'Do come! I'd like a game with you!'

Buster scraped at the gate and whined. 'No, no, Buster,' said Fatty. 'You're already in enough trouble with Mr Goon without getting into any more! We'd better go.'

They were just turning away when a voice came from the cottage. 'Poppet! 'Ere, Poppet. Where are you? You come along in!'

Poppet immediately disappeared into a bush to hide, and lay there quietly. The children watched in amusement.

'Where's that dog gone?' said the voice, and footsteps came down a path – limping, shuffling steps – and into view came the same man they had seen the day before, dressed in much the same way, except that now he had no scarf round his neck.

The children saw that he had a dirty-looking, unkempt beard and moustache, shaggy eyebrows and bits of grey-black hair sticking out from under his cap. He wore glasses with thick lenses, and seemed to be short-sighted as he peered here and there for the hidden dog.

'I bet you could dress up EXACTLY like that awful man,' whispered Bets in Fatty's ear. He turned and nodded, amused.

'Just what *I* was thinking!' he said. 'He'd be very easy to copy, shuffle and all! Look at Poppet – she's not going to give herself away – she's lying as still as a mouse.'

'Poppet! Poppet! Where *is* that wretched dog!' said the man in an exasperated voice. 'Wait till I get you, I'll show you I mean what I ses! Slipping out like that!'

Another voice came on the clear wintry air. 'Bob Larkin! Didn't I tell you to help me with them potatoes? You come in and do them!'

The man scowled. 'I'm just coming!' he said. 'I'm after this dratted dog! It's got out.'

'Oh, I hope to goodness that gate's shut!' cried the second voice. 'We'll get into trouble all right if anything happens to that precious dog!'

A woman now came into sight, very thin, wearing a draggled skirt and a dull red shawl wrapped tightly round her. Her hair was so extraordinary that the children gaped to see it. It was obviously a wig, mouse-colour and much too curly – and much too crooked!

'That's a wig,' muttered Daisy to Bets. 'Poor thing, I expect she's bald.'

The woman was not a very attractive sight for, besides the wig, she wore dark glasses. She coughed now and again, and pulled a thick green scarf round her throat and chin. Then she sniffed loudly.

'Bob Larkin! You come on in. I'm not going to make my cold worse coming out here and yelling for you. You come on in!'

The man suddenly saw the little dog hiding in the bushes. He pounced on her and gripped her. She whined in sudden fear. The man shook her angrily.

'Here, hold on,' said Fatty, at once. 'She's only a little thing.'

The man swung round and peered short-sightedly at the watching children. He hadn't noticed them before. Buster gave a sudden growl.

The man looked hard at the little Scottie, then at the children again. 'Why, you're the kids whose dog caused all that rumpus yesterday!' he said. 'Mr Goon's been round to see me about that. That dog of yours is going to get into trouble, see? Now you get off that gate and go away – and don't you start telling me what I'm to do! I'm in charge here, and I'll complain to that bobby if you make any trouble!'

This wasn't pleasant hearing. Bets felt frightened, and took hold of Buster's collar. Buster's nose was still sticking through the bars of the gate, and he growled when Bob Larkin took hold of Poppet's collar very roughly and dragged her up the garden.

'Yes, you'd like to go to Poppet's help as much as we would, Buster, old fellow,' said Fatty, frowning after the man. 'But you've got into enough trouble for the time being. I'm sorry that man recognised us.'

'I suppose he and Mr Goon have cooked up a whole lot of complaints between them,' said Larry. 'Well, at least you know that Mr Goon's been to see this Bob Larkin, and you won't be surprised when he tells you tomorrow!'

'What an unpleasant pair,' said Fatty, as they walked on.

Buster growled and ran back to the gate,

pawing at it. 'Good old Buster!' said Pip. 'Sorry we can't let you do a bit of rescue work!'

They went back feeling rather subdued. An interview with Goon tomorrow – and an upset over a dear little dog like Poppet. Things didn't look too good! Even Fatty couldn't think of any jokes, and they parted with hardly a smile.

'Tomorrow at Mr Goon's, at ten o'clock,' said Fatty, when they said good-bye.

'Right,' said the others, and went off looking extremely gloomy!

4. A SLIGHT VICTORY

Fatty's mother had already inquired why Mr Goon had wanted him on the telephone. When he told her, she looked vexed.

'How unfortunate! Who is this woman that Buster tripped up?'

'I don't know,' said Fatty. 'She and her husband appeared to be going off on some trip or other, and four or five of their friends came to see them off. They were pretty noisy. I think they live at that house called Tally-Ho down by the river – next to the Daniels. I don't know what their name is.'

'Oh, *those* people!' said his mother.

'You sound as if you know them, but don't want to!' said Fatty, amused.

'I know which people you mean, but I certainly don't have anything to do with them,' said Mrs Trotteville. 'They have behaved very badly since they took Mrs Peters' house while she went to America – giving silly parties, going out in boats at all hours of the night – and, so I hear, not paying their bills! Let me see, what is their name? Oh yes – Lorenzo, I think!'

'Well, it was they who complained to Mr Goon about Buster,' said Fatty.

'I see,' said his mother. 'I heard they were rather fourth-rate film actors, both the man *and* the woman – but haven't had any film work to do for some time. Anyway, if they have gone away, Mr Goon can't make much of a complaint. He's just being unpleasant, I expect.'

'Well, I'm going now, Mummy,' said Fatty. 'I hope I come home all in one piece – and I hope Buster leaves Mr Goon all in one piece too!'

'You do exaggerate, Frederick!' said Mrs Trotteville. 'Just be firm with that tiresome policeman, and don't take too much notice of what he says!'

'I won't,' said Fatty, feeling suddenly quite cheerful. 'Good-bye, Mummy – I'll tell you what happens as soon as I get back.'

He set off on his bicycle, Buster in the basket.

The others were already waiting for him outside Goon's house. Bets looked rather pale and Fatty squeezed her arm.

'Cheer up! We're going to have some fun. I've got a lot saved up to say to Mr Goon!'

They went to Goon's front door and knocked on it. Rat-a-tatta-tat-tat-TAT!

There came the sound of slippered feet and the door opened. It was the woman who came to clean the house for Mr Goon. She stared at them in surprise.

'We've come to see Mr Goon,' said Fatty. 'He told us to be here at ten o'clock.'

'Did he now?' said the woman, looking as if she didn't quite know what to do. 'Well, he didn't say anything to me about that. He went out in a hurry about half an hour ago – maybe he'll be back soon.'

'We'll come in and wait then,' said Fatty firmly. 'He said ten o'clock, and it's exactly ten now.'

A clock in Goon's office began to strike just as if it had heard what Fatty said. The woman motioned them into the hall.

'I'd better not put you into Mr Goon's

office,' she said. 'He's got private things in there – important things. I don't have to move so much as a sheet of paper if I dust in there.'

'We'll wait in the parlour then,' said Fatty, and they all marched into a musty, fusty little room.

'I'll be out in the garden hanging up the washing,' said the woman, 'but I'll hear Mr Goon when he comes and tell him you're here.'

'Right,' said Fatty, and the woman disappeared. They looked round the room. There was a large photograph on the mantelpiece of Goon's mother and father and family. The five children went to look at it in delight.

'Pa Goon looks as big as Goon is now,' said Larry. 'And, oh *look* – this boy with eyes sticking out of his head must be Mr Goon!'

They all chuckled at the sight of Goon as a boy. 'He's very like Ern,' said Bets and, indeed, he was! Ern was one of Goon's nephews, who had once been to stay with him and had a most unpleasant time!

'I wonder what Ern's doing,' said Bets, remembering the admiration he had had for Fatty. 'He came to see you just before Christmas, Fatty, to give you a Christmas present he'd made you – and he almost burst into tears when he heard you were in Switzerland.'

'Poor Ern,' said Fatty. 'I've no doubt he'll turn up again with whatever it is. Hello – is that Mr Goon?'

It was and, judging by the heavy tramp of feet in the hall, there were two others with him. Fatty debated what to do. Should he go and announce himself? But if Goon had visitors, he wouldn't be too pleased to be interrupted.

'We'd better wait a bit,' he said to the others. 'Perhaps that woman will hear him and go and tell him we are waiting.'

'She's busy talking to the woman next door,' said Bets, looking out of the window. 'How they can understand what the other is saying, I really don't know – they're both talking at once!'

Voices came from the office next to the room the children were sitting in. First they were fairly quiet, and then they became loud. The children heard various words, and at first took no notice.

Then a word came that made Fatty sit up. 'Lorenzo!' Now, where had he just recently heard that name? It certainly rang a bell!

'They've *got* to be traced!' said a voice that was not Goon's. 'These Lorenzos are the ones we want, I'm sure. Get hold of anyone who knows anything about them. Get hold of their best friends here and ask questions, and . . .'

The voice fell and the next words could not be heard. Fatty listened in wonder. He remembered now where he had heard the name Lorenzo – his mother had said it was the name of the people who owned Poppet, the little poodle.

Funny! thought Fatty, it sounds as if they've run into trouble. I hope they have – if so, old Goon won't bother about Buster!

There was the sound of movement in the little office, and then footsteps. The visitors must be going!

'Well, good-bye, Goon,' said a voice. 'You'll have to get going on this – it's a big thing. Pity we've just missed those rascals! Find out what you can from the Larkins, they may be able to tell you something. If we can't get our hands on the Lorenzos, we might at least be able to get hold of that picture. So long!'

There was the tramp of feet to the front gate. Fatty sat still, feeling startled. Why, what was this going on? Something had unexpectedly cropped up, that was certain. A sudden feeling of excitement surged up in him – it might be a mystery! Something was up! Something had to be found out! He'd tackle Goon about it and get the Five Find-Outers on the job at once!

Bets was surprised to see Fatty's face suddenly go red with excitement. She thought he was feeling nervous at having to meet Goon and she slipped her hand through his arm. Fatty never even noticed it! He was thinking so very hard. What *could* the Lorenzos have done? What was this 'picture'? He must find out, he must!

Goon came back from the front gate humming a tuneless song. He was evidently feeling pleased with life. He didn't go back into the office but walked straight into the parlour, not knowing that anyone was in it.

He stopped dead when he saw the five children there, Buster safely on Fatty's knee. Buster barked at once and tried to leap off, but Fatty held on to his collar.

'What's all this?' thundered Mr Goon. 'What are you here for?'

Fatty stood up. 'Well, you said ten o'clock, and it's now twenty past,' he said. 'Perhaps you're too busy with the Lorenzo case to see us now?'

Mr Goon looked extremely startled. 'The – the Lorenzo case?' he said. 'What do you know about *that*?'

'Not much,' said Fatty honestly. 'We couldn't help overhearing a few things just now, that's all.'

Mr Goon lost his temper. 'Oho! Listening with your ear to the keyhole, I suppose? Eavesdropping on the law! There's a penalty for that kind of thing, Mr Snoopy, let me tell you that! How *dare* you listen to private matters?'

'I didn't. I couldn't help hearing,' said Fatty. 'We all heard a few things. Short of stopping up our ears we couldn't help but hear. As for listening at the keyhole, that's nonsense. Your door was wide open and you know it.'

'Now, none of your cheek,' said Goon, beginning to go purple. 'I remember now, I told you to come about this here pest of a dog of course. Yes, a serious complaint has been made, very serious.'

He took out his notebook and looked through it, while the Five gazed at him. Larry, Daisy, Pip and Bets hadn't the remotest idea what Fatty had been talking about, of course, because they didn't know who, or what, these mysterious 'Lorenzos' were.

'I know that the Lorenzos made a kind of complaint yesterday,' said Fatty, 'and I know that you've been to see the Larkins, who are in charge of Poppet . . . and . . .'

'How do you know that?' almost shouted Mr Goon. 'Snooping round – interfering – I can't get rid of you. You're a toad of a boy. I always said so! Now about this here dog of yours . . .'

'If the Lorenzos have gone off and nobody knows where, any complaint they made is not likely to be of any use to you,' said Fatty scornfully. 'Hadn't you better forget about Buster, and concentrate on finding the Lorenzos – or the picture, whatever it is, Mr Goon?'

Mr Goon knew when he was beaten. He shut his notebook and began to bluster. 'Well, if there's anybody else makes a single complaint about that dog – a *single* complaint, I say – he'll soon learn what happens to dogs that are out of control. Time he did too! If ever there was a more aggravating dog – yes, and a more aggravating set of children – I'd like to hear of them.'

'I'll be sure to let you know if ever we do hear of any,' said Fatty, in his most courteous voice, the one that always drove poor Goon to fury. 'Well, I take it you don't need us any more – unless you'd like to tell us a bit about this new case, so that we might help you?'

'GAH!' said Mr Goon furiously, and drove the Five out before him, Buster barking madly. They all went out of the front gate and Mr Goon bellowed over it, almost shaking his fist at them.

'And if you try interfering with the law, and messing about in this case, and telling me clues that aren't clues, I'll come and tell your parents!' he shouted.

'Mr Goon, Mr Goon, you'll be had up for a breach of the peace,' said Fatty solemnly. 'You're making everyone look out of their windows.'

Mr Goon retreated hurriedly into his house, muttering fiercely. The children got on their bicycles and rode off.

'A slight victory to us, I think,' said Fatty happily. 'Buster, you can breathe again!'

5. NOT SO GOOD!

The chief topic of conversation that day was the five children's interview with Goon. Larry, Pip, Daisy and Bets could hardly wait till they got to Fatty's shed to ask him what he meant about the Lorenzos.

'Who are they? How did you know about them?' demanded Larry.

'I didn't. But my mother happened to mention this morning that the people who owned Poppet were called the Lorenzos,' said Fatty. 'So when I heard the name spoken by that other policeman – or perhaps he was a sergeant by his manner to Mr Goon – well, it just rang a bell, and I knew they were all talking about the people who made a complaint about Buster!'

'But what have they done – the Lorenzos, I mean?' asked Bets.

'I don't know any more than you do,' said

Fatty. 'Except that they seem to have gone away just when the police wanted them for something. And there's something about a picture too. My mother told me that they didn't pay their bills, so perhaps the trouble is about *that*!'

'Is it going to be a mystery?' asked Pip.

'I hope so,' said Fatty cheerfully. 'And if it is, old Buster here led us to it – didn't you, Buster? You've got a nose for mysteries now, haven't you?'

'Wuff,' said Buster, thumping his tail on the floor of the shed. Fatty gave him a biscuit.

'Well, there you are – a small reward for leading us to a probable mystery,' he said. 'The trouble is, we don't know enough about it to set about solving it. I mean, we don't *really* know what the mystery *is*!'

'Ring up Superintendent Jenks and ask him,' suggested Larry.

Fatty shook his head. 'No. I don't somehow think he'd like it – and I'd have to tell him I overheard talk about it in Mr Goon's house – and Mr Goon would get into trouble for discussing things like that without first finding out if anyone was about. After all, for all he knew, that woman in the kitchen might have overheard every word!'

'Well, I don't see how we're to find out *any*thing,' said Larry. 'Mr Goon certainly won't let us in on it.'

They discussed the matter over and over again. Should they go and interview the old fellow called Bob Larkin and see if they could get anything out of him? No, because he was already annoyed with them and, anyway, Goon had got to interview him – and, anyway again, they didn't know what to ask the old fellow!

'We're being silly,' said Fatty, at the end of the long discussion. 'We're trying to run before we can walk. Let's forget it now – and sleep on it tonight. Things may be clearer tomorrow morning.'

Fatty spoke the truth! Things were indeed much clearer the next morning! The Five Find-Outers knew as much about the mystery as Goon did!

It was in all the papers, splashed across the headlines.

Priceless old picture stolen from famous gallery. Thieves just escape the net of the police, leaving their dog behind. Police looking everywhere for the Lorenzos.

Mrs Trotteville was down to breakfast first, and saw the paper. She gave an exclamation. 'Why – the thieves are those Lorenzos! The ones that live next door to the Daniels. No wonder all Peterswood disliked them!'

Fatty came in at that moment, and his mother told him the news. 'The thieves were the people you told me about yesterday, Fatty – the Lorenzos. I told you how badly they behaved, and what wild parties they gave. They upset their neighbours, the Daniels, very much. See, they're in the news this morning – the police are after them. My goodness me – our Mr Goon will be puffed up with importance over this. It's right under his nose!'

Fatty slid into his seat and took the paper, his eyes gleaming. Aha! If it was all in the papers, it didn't matter about Mr Goon not telling him anything. The Five Find-Outers could make their own plans, and get going themselves. What a thrill!

Fatty read and read! He forgot all about his breakfast, and never even saw his father come into the room.

'Good morning, Frederick,' said his father, and neatly took the paper from Fatty's hands. 'What about eating your bacon and egg? By the look of it, it's almost congealed on the plate!'

'So it is!' said Fatty, surprised. 'Well, it isn't often I don't get on with a meal. My word, Mummy, this is a bit of excitement for dull old Peterswood, isn't it?'

'I hope it doesn't mean you're going to get mixed up with that aggravating policeman again,' said his father, pouring milk over his porridge. 'Actually, I should imagine that your friend, Superintendent Jenks, will send a good man down here to deal with anything that arises. I can't imagine that Moon – Coon – what's his name now? – Goon – could tackle a big thing like this. That picture was priceless – worth at least five hundred thousand pounds!'

'I won't get mixed up with Mr Goon,' said Fatty. 'It's much more likely he'll get mixed up with *me*! Anyway, I think I'll ring up

Superintendent Jenks and ask if I can do anything to help.'

'Well, he seems to think a lot of you, goodness knows why,' said Mr Trotteville, 'and it does seem as if you have a few brains sometimes, Frederick. Now, for pity's sake, eat up that horrible-looking mess on your plate.'

Fatty swallowed his breakfast, thinking hard. The telephone went just as he had finished it, and he rushed to answer it, quite sure it must be the Superintendent ringing up to ask his help!

But it wasn't. It was Larry, very excited.

'Hey! Did you see the news in the paper? It *is* a mystery after all! Right under our noses. When are we going to get on to it?'

'I'm going to ring the Super,' said Fatty. 'We'll get on to it all right. I'll telephone you later. Ring Pip and Bets for me, will you?'

'Right, Chief!' said Larry, with a chuckle, and hung up. Peterswood was in the news! And he and the rest of the Find-Outers would soon be right in the middle of something!

Fatty sat down and thought for a while. What should he tell the Superintendent? That he had seen the two Lorenzos on the station yesterday? – but then, many people had. Should he ask if he could go and see the Larkins? He might be able to get something out of them that Mr Goon couldn't. Anyway he was certain that he could do *some*thing.

He went to the telephone and dialled the number. It was engaged. He tried again in ten minutes. It was still engaged. The police phone lines were humming today in that district!

At last he got through and asked for the Superintendent. 'It's Frederick Trotteville here,' said Fatty. 'He knows me.'

His name was passed through to the Chief's office – and Fatty heard the Superintendent's voice, sharp and impatient.

'Yes, Frederick? What is it?'

'Sir, it's about the Lorenzos,' said Fatty. 'As it's right where I live, can I do anything?'

'I fear not,' said the Chief. 'The Lorenzos are not there – and I doubt if the missing picture is either. If they could be found, they would be found together!'

'Oh,' said Fatty, in disappointment. 'Then

– isn't there *any*thing I can do, sir?'

'Nothing, except keep your eyes and ears open as usual,' said the Chief. 'I'm sending a man down to go over the house with a toothcomb, just in *case* the picture's there – but I've no real hope of it.'

'Will Mr Goon be working on the case, sir?' asked Fatty, rather forlornly.

'Yes, but there isn't much case at Peterswood to work on,' said the Superintendent. 'I wish Goon had kept his eye on the Lorenzos more – they've a shocking reputation, as everyone now knows!'

'I suppose I couldn't go and talk to the Larkins, sir, could I?' asked Fatty, feeling that this mystery was slipping out of his hands altogether!

'No. Certainly not,' said the Chief at once. 'My man is doing that, with Goon. No sense in your butting in there – you'll do more harm than good. I don't mean that you mustn't pass the time of day with them if you meet them, but you must remember that this case has really left Peterswood now – and gone goodness knows where! I don't for one moment think that the Larkins can possibly know anything that will be of the slightest help to us.'

'I expect you're right, sir,' said Fatty, feeling very down in the dumps indeed. 'Well, I won't keep you, sir. Good luck!'

He put down the receiver and looked gloomily at Buster, who was sitting nearby, with cocked ears.

'No go, Buster,' he said dolefully. 'It's all come to nothing. The mystery has fled from Peterswood and disappeared. Now I must telephone the others.'

The other four were most disappointed. 'Oh, Fatty!' said Daisy, 'there must be *some*thing we can do! There really must. Come along up here to us, and we'll get Pip and Bets too, and talk about it. You *do* sound miserable!'

So they all met at Larry's at half past eleven and sat down to a mid-morning snack of hot buns from the oven and cups of cocoa. They felt more cheerful after a couple of buns each.

'The Chief really did seem to think we can't do a thing this time,' said Fatty. 'Apparently, the two main things are – *one*, to find the Lorenzos, who are probably out of the country by now – and *two*, to find the picture. And the Chief thinks that where one is, the other will be there also.'

'Well, we can't possibly go gallivanting all over the country looking for them ourselves,' said Daisy. 'So we must just be content to do nothing.'

'I think we might keep a watch on the house, perhaps?' said Larry. 'Just in *case* the Lorenzos come back to it.'

'They won't,' said Fatty.

'But what about their little dog?' said Bets. 'Mrs Lorenzo really did seem attached to it – she might send for it, mightn't she? If it suddenly disappears, we'd know that the Lorenzos had sent a messenger of some sort for it.'

'That certainly is a point,' said Fatty. 'Yes, perhaps on the whole, we won't give this up straightaway. But the thing is – how on earth are we to keep a watch on the Larkins to *see* if any messenger is ever sent? I mean, the house is some way from where we live, and we can't spend all our days – or nights – there!'

'Hopeless,' said Pip, who didn't particularly want to spend any part of a cold day or night watching people like the Larkins. 'We can't do it. If we knew somebody who lived next door, it would be easy – but we don't, so . . .'

'Hello!' said a voice, suddenly interrupting, and a tousled head peeped round the door. 'I've been to your house, Fatty, and your mother sent me here. I've brought the Christmas present I made you!'

'ERN!' cried everyone. And sure enough it *was* Ern, plump as ever and red in the face. Good old Ern!

6. THE SAME OLD ERN!

Ern came right into the room beaming, and holding rather a large parcel.

'Still the same old Ern!' said Fatty, and solemnly shook hands with him. Ern thereupon felt that he must shake hands with everyone, even Buster. Buster was very pleased indeed to see Ern, and leapt on him as if he were a long-lost friend.

'This is an unexpected pleasure,' said Fatty. 'How are your twin brothers, Sid and Perce? We haven't seen them since we all solved the mystery of the vanished prince – do you remember?'

'Coo, yes,' said Ern. 'That wasn't half a do! I enjoyed that, I did. Perce is all right, as far as I know. I don't seem to notice him much. Sid's all right too.'

Sid had been a great toffee-sucker, unable to speak at all at one time because of the toffee glueing up his mouth! Bets remembered and giggled.

'Does he still suck toffee?' she asked.

'Well, he rationed himself up to Christmas, because he wanted to save money to buy presents,' said Ern. 'But then everyone went and gave him tins of toffee, of course, and he's off again. Can't get a word out of him now.'

'Except "Ar", I suppose?' said Pip. 'He used to say "Ar" quite a lot, I remember.'

'Yes. Well, he still says it,' said Ern. 'He isn't much of a talker, old Sid.'

'Sit down and have a bun,' said Daisy. 'What's in that parcel?'

'Coo, I was almost forgetting,' said Ern, beaming round again. 'It's something I made for you, Fatty. We did carpentry at school last term, and I said to myself, "Ah, Ern – this is where we do something for Fatty!" And I made *this*!'

He pulled off the paper and showed Fatty a small table, plain and simple. He had polished it till it shone.

Everyone exclaimed in surprise. 'Why, *Ern*!' said Bets, amazed, 'did you really make it all yourself?'

'Never let anyone touch it but meself!' said Ern proudly.

Fatty examined it from every side. 'It's a masterpiece,' he said. 'A beautiful piece of work. Thanks, Ern. I like it very much.'

Ern was bright red with delight. 'No kidding?' he said. 'You *do* like it?'

'I tell you, it's a masterpiece,' said Fatty. 'First rate! We'll have it in my shed at home so that we can all see it and use it as much as possible.'

Ern was quite overcome. He swallowed once or twice, rubbed his sleeve over the table-top to make quite sure it was perfect, and then beamed at everyone again.

'Nice to see you all again,' he announced, sitting down. 'Anything on? Any mysteries going? I heard about them people called Lorenzos. Proper set-up, that was! I bet my Uncle Goon's excited!'

'Have you seen him yet?' asked Daisy.

'Oooh no!' said Ern, in horror. 'I'd run a mile if I saw him. I'm scared stiff of him – he'd scold me as soon as look at me! I kept a good look out for him this morning, I can tell you.'

They discussed the Lorenzo case, and how maddening it was that the most important things concerned – the Lorenzos themselves and the picture – had both gone.

'So, you see, there's nothing much we can do, Ern,' said Fatty. 'I can't see anything we can get hold of – no clues or suspects, like we usually do.'

'Yes, it's bad luck,' said Ern sympathetically. 'I was hoping I might be able to help a bit, if you really wanted me. I'm coming to stay in Peterswood. My Mum's got to go to hospital for a bit – she's got a bad leg, poor Mum – so us kids are going to relations and friends for a week.'

'Good gracious, you're not staying with Mr Goon again, are you?' said Bets.

'You bet I'm not!' said Ern. 'When my Mum suggested it, I fell off my chair in fright, I did.'

'What did your Mum say then?' asked Pip. The Five were always interested in the doings of Ern's large family.

'She said, "All right, Ducks, I'll think of someone else," ' said Ern. 'And she did.'

'Who was it she thought of?' asked Bets. 'Anyone we know?'

'I don't reckon so,' said Ern. 'It's my father's cousin – a Mrs Woosh.'

'What a wonderful name!' said Daisy.

They all tried it over. 'Woosh! Mrs Woosh. Whooooosh!'

'Sounds as if her husband ought to make rockets,' said Larry, and everyone laughed.

'Where does your Auntie Woosh live?' asked Bets.

'She's in the cottage belonging to a Mrs Daniels, who lives at High Chimneys,' said Ern. 'Her husband is the gardener, and she helps in the house. She's got twins – girls they are, about the same age as Sid and Perce.'

Ern stopped when he saw the sudden, intense interest on Fatty's face, at the mention of the Daniels. He looked at Fatty in surprise.

'What's up?' he said. 'You look all sort of worked up, Fatty.'

'I am,' said Fatty. 'I'm all of a dither, as our cook says when she falls over Buster. The Daniels! Did I *really* hear you say the Daniels, Ern?'

'Yes,' said Ern, puzzled. 'What's wrong with that?'

'Nothing,' said Fatty. 'It's perfect. It's too good to be true! Don't you know that the Daniels live next to the house that the Lorenzos rented, Ern? And we wanted to keep a watch on it, but it's a good way from our own homes – and . . .'

'COO!' said Ern, light dawning on him suddenly. 'You mean – I say, do you mean I can come into this because I'll be able to pop my head over the hedge and watch any goings-on at the house next door?'

'You've got it, Ern!' said Fatty, and clapped him on the back. 'We were almost on the point of giving up the mystery when you came in – now we'll be on it full-speed! WHAT a bit of luck that you'll be staying with the Wooshes!'

Ern was so overcome that he was speechless for a moment. He stared round with bright eyes, and opened and shut his mouth like a goldfish.

He suddenly found his voice. 'I'll do my bit,' he said, in a suddenly solemn voice, just as if he were going off to war. 'You just give me my orders, Fatty – and I'll obey!'

Thereupon a most animated conversation began. The newspapers were fetched from downstairs, and everyone pored over the reports of the Lorenzo case. The Five Find-Outers meant to get every single bit of information they could find.

'It even says here that they left Poppet the poodle behind,' said Bets. 'And here's a picture of her in Mrs Lorenzo's arms. And listen, it says: "Gloria Lorenzo is passionately attached to her little poodle, whom she has had for seven years. It is the first time she has ever left the little dog behind – and therefore it seems that the Lorenzos meant to flee the country".'

'Ern could keep an eye on those awful Larkins, too,' said Daisy, 'and see that they don't ill-treat dear little Poppet.'

'I'll keep an eye on them,' promised Ern. 'You just give me my orders!'

'He could keep an eye on Tally-Ho, the house, as well,' said Larry. 'Just in *case* the picture has been left behind, hidden there somewhere after all. If he sees any suspicious strangers about, he'd have to report to us at once.'

'Yes, I will,' said the excited Ern. 'I'll have my bike, see – and I'll keep it all pumped up and ready to fly off to Fatty's if I've anything to report.'

They talked and talked. It was all most exciting. Ern's face grew redder and redder and his hair became more and more tousled. He had never had such a thrilling morning in his life!

'I expect old Mr Goon will be round there quite a bit,' said Fatty. 'He'll keep an eye on the Larkins, and on the house too. So look out for him.'

'Lovaduck!' said Ern, suddenly doleful. 'I forgot about my uncle. I'd better keep out of his sight. He'll go mad if he sees me snooping around.'

'He certainly will,' agreed Fatty. 'Don't let him know you're staying at the Wooshes if you can help it. Don't let him see you at all, in fact!'

'Oh, I won't,' said Ern fervently. 'I'm scared of my uncle, I really am, sure as my name's Ern Goon.'

Buster gave a sudden growl when he heard the name of Goon. 'There!' said Ern, 'he thinks the same as me. Good old Buster. I know how you feel about snapping at his ankles. I'd like to do it too.'

Buster thumped his tail on the floor, and looked at Ern with approval.

'Hey,' said Pip, 'how old are these twins of your

aunt's? About Sid and Perce's age, did you say? You could have a game of ball with them, perhaps, and let the ball go into Tally-Ho gardens – and slip over and look for it – or . . .'

'Coo yes, I'll be able to think of plenty of excuses for slipping into next door,' said Ern. 'I'll pry into every corner – you never know where that picture might be hid, do you!'

'Well, it probably wouldn't be in the rubbish-heap or in the coal cellar,' said Fatty gravely. 'I wouldn't bother about the picture, Ern – just keep your eyes and ears open and report anything unusual to us – strangers about, or noises in the night, or lights.'

'Yes, and report to us if the Larkins are cruel to little Poppet!' said Bets. 'If they are, I'll get the RSPCA to report them. I will. I really will!'

'Good old Bets,' said Fatty. 'Don't worry, the dog is a valuable one and the Larkins won't dare to starve it or hurt it badly.'

'Just *look* at the time!' said Pip, in horror. 'We'll be late for our dinner again – and Mummy will blame *you*, Fatty, as well as us! Come on, Bets, for goodness sake!'

Larry and Daisy came to the front gate to see them off. They all rode away on their bicycles, Ern too.

'So long!' he said, with his usual beaming smile. 'I'm off to the Wooshes now. They're expecting me for dinner. I've got all my things in my bike-basket!'

'So long!' said Fatty, amused at the tiny bundle in Ern's basket. Ern obviously didn't think he needed much luggage for a week's stay at the Wooshes! 'And thanks very much for the splendid table, Ern.'

Ern rode off, pleased at the sight of Fatty riding away on his bicycle with the table under one arm. He'd be able to tell those twins something, when he got to his aunt's!

7. ERN HAS AN IDEA

Ern arrived late at his aunt's, having quite forgotten that his uncle, the Daniels' gardener, knocked off work at half past twelve and went in for his dinner.

Mrs Woosh was not too pleased with him. 'Oh, here you are at last, Ern!' she said. 'Well, we've almost finished dinner – and thinking you weren't coming, Liz and Glad have eaten your share of the stew.'

'Oh!' said Ern dismayed, for he was very hungry indeed. 'Sorry I'm late, Aunt. I've been with my friends and forgot the time.'

'What friends?' asked his aunt, in surprise.

'Well, there's Frederick Trotteville, and the Hiltons and . . .' began Ern proudly.

Liz and Glad tittered. 'Oooh, isn't he *grand*!' said Liz. 'Those aren't his friends, are they, Mum?'

'You hold your tongue, Liz,' said Mrs Woosh.

Liz nudged Glad and they both went off into giggles that made Ern long to slap them.

'If you were my sisters,' he began, glaring at them, but Mrs Woosh stopped him.

'Now, Ern, don't start throwing your weight about as soon as you come. There's some cheese over there that your uncle left, and some bread. Help yourself. We've got plenty of pudding left.'

Ern sighed in relief and began on the bread and cheese. The twins sat and stared steadily at Ern for a few minutes, nudging each other every time he put a huge bit of bread and cheese into his mouth. He decided that they required a firm hand. They needed a brother, that's what they needed – someone like Ern himself, Ern decided. *He* would keep them in their place all right!

At last, Glad and Liz slipped away from the table and went out into the garden to play. Mrs Woosh heaved a sigh of relief.

'I'll be glad when the holidays are over,' she said. 'Always under my feet, those twins are. I don't know how your Ma manages with Sid and Perce, Ern – but twins are a handful, my word they are! If one isn't in mischief, the other is.'

'Mum's always saying the same about Sid and Perce,' said Ern. 'I'll take the twins off your hands for you a bit, Auntie – play ball with them, and such-like.'

'That's right, Ern,' said Mrs Woosh. 'I expect you know about the happenings next door, don't you? The Lorenzos, I mean, who were in the papers today. My word, I could tell you of some goings-on there, I could!'

Ern felt excited. He might hear something important – something he could report back to Fatty. He wondered if he ought to write anything down in his notebook. Yes, perhaps he'd better – his aunt might let a few clues drop! That would be fine.

So Ern pulled a notebook out of his pocket, licked his pencil, and glued his eyes on his aunt.

'You tell me everything!' he said. 'And don't leave NOTHING out, Auntie!'

His aunt was pleasantly surprised to find Ern so interested in her chatter. Neither her husband nor the twins ever listened to her for more than a few seconds, and she was a born talker. She leaned her elbows on the table and began.

'Well, the Lorenzos came about six months back. They took the house, furnished, from the Peters' who are in America. They brought their own staff with them, and . . .'

'What about the Larkins?' said Ern, remembering what the Five had said about them. He'd better ask for news of them too!

'Oh, the Larkins – they've been in that cottage for donkeys' years,' said Mrs Woosh. 'Don't interrupt me, Ern. I don't have time for them Larkins – dirty, untidy couple they are, shuffling and sniffling about. I just pass the time of day and that's all. He's supposed to look after the boilers, and go up to the house for the boots to clean and things like that.'

'They've got the little poodle, Poppet, haven't they?' said Ern, trying to scribble fast enough to keep up with Mrs Woosh's chatter.

'Yes, and why the Lorenzos left it with them, goodness knows!' said Mrs Woosh. 'We once had a cat, and it wandered into their garden – and would you believe it, they stoned the poor creature, and almost broke one of its legs.'

Ern was horrified, and wrote down 'legs' and

underlined it. On and on went his aunt, telling him about the extraordinary parties that the Lorenzos gave; 'midnight bathing in the river and hide-and-seek in the garden afterwards,' she said. 'And once they all dressed up as animals, and I wasn't half-startled to meet a giraffe and a bear going along the lane that night!'

Ern was soon so fascinated that he forgot to write in his notebook. He began to wish that he too lived next door to people like the Lorenzos – there would always be plenty of excitement!

'The house is shut up now,' said Mrs Woosh, 'no lights, no smoke from the chimneys. I passed the time of day with Mr Larkin yesterday, and he said that even he and his wife can't get in. Not even to air the house. He says the police have got the keys.'

Ern decided this might be important, so he wrote down, 'Shut house. Keys.' His aunt frowned.

'Why do you keep scribbling in that notebook of yours, Ern, when I'm talking to you? That's rude. Anyone would think you were your uncle, PC Goon – he's always got a notebook he's scribbling in. My word, I've just thought of an idea!'

'What?' said Ern, his pencil poised over his notebook at once. 'Quick, Aunt!'

'I'll ask Mr Goon in to tea while you're here – I'll tell him it's just so he can see his nephew. But really it'll be because I want to hear what he's got to say on this Lorenzo business!' Mrs Woosh looked delighted at her idea. 'He's a wonderful man, your Uncle Theophilus Goon – always on to something. Yes, I'll ask him to tea.'

Ern stared at her in the utmost horror. He could think of nothing worse than having his uncle to tea, and being made to sit opposite his big, angry face. Why, he didn't even want his uncle to *know* he was in Peterswood.

'Please, Auntie, don't ask him,' begged Ern. 'He – well, he isn't very fond of me. I'm very scared of him.'

'Oh, go on with you!' said Mrs Woosh. 'He's not a bad fellow. I always say it's useful to have a policeman in the family.'

Ern didn't think so. He could have done without Mr Goon in his own family, that was certain! He put away his notebook gloomily. What a pity it had reminded Mrs Woosh of his uncle!

'Well, I'd better wash up, I suppose,' said Mrs Woosh. 'You go on out and play with Glad and Liz, Ern. You'll get on with them fine!'

Ern wasn't so sure that he would. He put on his coat and went out. He was immediately pelted with bits of earth, and greeted with squeals of laughter. He looked round to see where the twins were. Up in that tree!

Ern was about to shout at them, when he stopped. The tree was a tall one. It stood by the hedge, and overlooked the Larkins' cottage and garden. It would, in fact, be a perfectly splendid spying-place!

Ern decided not to be angry about the clod-throwing. He called up the tree, 'Hey, you kids! Like me to show you how to build a house in a tree?'

There was a moment's silence. Then Glad looked down cautiously. 'Yes. But don't you try punishing us when you come up. We'll push you down, if you do.'

Ern immediately felt like punishing them. But he must keep guard on his temper. The twins might come in very useful!

The tree was some kind of evergreen fir, very tall and broad. Its branches were admirable for climbing. Ern went up to where the twins sat. They grinned at him.

'Did we hit you with the clods of earth? We waited and waited for you. Did Mum talk to you all that time?'

As the twins never really expected any answers to their questions, they didn't at all mind when Ern ignored them, and began to make a peephole through the thick branches, so that he might look down on the Larkins' cottage over the hedge.

'What are you doing? Are you going to make a house up here? Can we live in it? Will it have a chimney?'

Ern found that he could see right down into the Larkins' garden – in fact, the cottage was so near that he could smell the smoke from the chimney. He took out his knife and began to cut away some of the greenery, so that he could have a kind of window through the branches to peep from. The twins watched him with interest.

'What are you doing? Is that a spyhole? Can we spy on the Larkins? We don't like them.

Let's throw a stone down their chimney!'

The last idea appealed to Ern very much. He had never tried throwing stones down a chimney, but it certainly looked quite easy from where he sat. Then he reluctantly dismissed the idea from his mind. No, he might be lucky enough to get one stone down the chimney, but there would be a dozen stones that missed – and they would rattle on the tiles and bring out the Larkins in fury. That would never do!

'Now you listen to me,' said Ern, taking command firmly. 'We'll play that the Larkins are our enemies, see? And we'll play that we've got to keep a watch on them and all they do. So we'll build a little house up here, and I'll keep watch.'

'Us too!' said the twins, both together. Ern nodded.

'All of us – when I'm not up here, you two can take a turn – and you'll have to report to me, see, because I'm your chief. This is our hidey-hole!'

The twins were thrilled. They gazed at Ern in admiration. He was clearly much, much cleverer than he looked.

'I'll go down and see if there's any bits of

wood and stuff to bring up here,' said Ern, and disappeared rapidly. He stood at the bottom and called up cautiously, 'Now, keep watch while I'm gone, you two!'

He met his uncle as he walked back to the cottage. Uncle Woosh was a tall, silent man who only came into the house for meals and for very little else. Ern was rather afraid of him, but decided that his uncle was the man to ask about planks and nails.

'Yes. Get what you want out of my shed,' said his uncle. 'Plenty there.' He took himself off, and Ern ran to the shed, pleased.

Now to build a little place up in that tree – what a fine spyhole! What would Fatty say to *that*!

8. ERN KEEPS WATCH

Two days went by. Fatty and the others pored over the papers each day, but there was no more news of the Lorenzos, except that the police seemed more or less certain that they were hiding somewhere in the country, waiting to fly out as soon as things had quietened down a little.

'I should have thought that it would be very difficult to hide *any*where, with everyone on the look out for you,' said Daisy. 'I mean, the Lorenzos would be very easy to recognise – their photographs have been in every single paper!'

'You forget that they have been actors,' said Fatty. 'It would be easy for them to disguise themselves so that nobody would know them.'

'Yes. I forgot that,' said Daisy. 'After all – if anyone was after *you*, Fatty, you'd be able to disguise yourself so that nobody in the world would recognise you!'

'Like you do sometimes now,' said Bets. 'Oh, Fatty, things are a bit dull at present – can't you disguise yourself? You know, dress up as something. You do look so very, very brown with all that dazzling Swiss sun – you'd pass anywhere for a foreigner. Go on, just for a bit of fun!'

'I'll think about it,' said Fatty, making up his mind that he would certainly do a bit of disguising, as Bets suggested, and have a little fun. 'By the way, I wonder how Ern is getting on. We haven't seen anything of him for two days.'

Ern had been getting on well. He now had the twins almost eating out of his hands – in fact, they were quite embarrassing in their hero-worship, and followed Ern about whenever they could.

He had made the house in the tree. Ern was very good with his hands, and thoroughly enjoyed taking charge of the proceedings, ordering the twins about, and showing off his clever carpentry.

Even his Uncle Woosh had taken an interest, and had helped Ern considerably. His aunt thought it was a lot of silly nonsense.

'Messing about up trees!' she said. 'Getting filthy dirty. Just look at the state the twins are in, after being up there all the morning!'

Their father looked at them and made one of his rare remarks. 'Can't see a mite of difference in them,' he said. 'They're always dirty.'

He walked out, followed by a string of exasperated remarks from his wife. Ern followed him.

'Women!' said Mr Woosh, with a backward jerk of his head towards the cottage. 'Women!'

Ern nodded understandingly. Once his uncle had discovered that Ern, like himself, was interested in carpentry, he had been very friendly. Ern was quite enjoying his stay, especially now that the twins were so completely under his thumb.

The house in the tree was finished. It was quite an elaborate affair, and made of good strong planks securely fastened down. There were three walls and a very peculiar roof, that had to fit under some rather awkward branches. The missing wall, of course, was the 'spyhole' that looked through the branches down onto the Larkins.

The twins' mother gave them some cups and plates, and allowed them to have snacks up in the tree. The twins were too thrilled for words, and were ready to do anything in the world that Ern told them.

Ern felt as excited as his two cousins. He had never imagined that it would be so easy to build a house up a tree. Of course, his uncle had helped a lot. Ern had to admit that.

He and the twins sat up there continually – but Ern preferred it when he was quite alone. There was something very thrilling indeed about sitting up in the thickly-leafed evergreen, in his own little tree house, peering quietly through the opening he had cut in the greenery.

The Larkins had no idea that they were being spied on by three children. To the twins of course, it was merely a game – but to Ern, it was serious. He was helping Fatty. He might be able to gather a few clues for him. He might see something suspicious – he might even help to solve the Lorenzo mystery! Though Ern had to admit to himself that that wasn't *very* likely!

He peered down at the Larkins' cottage

whenever he could, watching for any sign of movement. He had supplied himself with a tin of bull's-eye peppermints, enormous things that bulged out his cheek, but lasted for a very long time. He also had a comic that he read at intervals, and he really thoroughly enjoyed himself, sucking away at his bull's-eyes, hidden in the little tree house he had built.

Old Man Larkin doesn't do much! Ern thought. Just goes out and picks some sprouts – and does some shopping – and lets the dog out and yells for it to come back. Poor little dog, it looks down in the dumps all right, and I'm not surprised!

Certainly Mr Larkin didn't appear to do very much work. As for Mrs Larkin, she hardly appeared at all. Apparently she had a bad cold, and Ern could often hear her coughing. Once when she ventured out for a minute or two to hang up some washing, Ern could hear her sniffing all the time. Sniff, sniff! Cough! Sniff, sniff!

She groaned as she bent down to pick up her washing basket. Ern watched her, thinking she was a very ugly woman with her extraordinary wig of hair, and her very white face and red nose.

Poppet came out with her, her stiff little tail down. She kept well out of Mrs Larkin's reach. The woman spoke to her in a hoarse voice, 'Don't you dare run off, or I'll punish you, nuisance that you are!'

Poppet slunk into the house, and Mrs Larkin followed, sniffing. Ern scribbled down a few notes about her in his notebook. He had torn out the notes he had made when his aunt had chattered to him, because when he examined them afterwards, such words as 'Donkeys' years', 'legs', and 'midnight bathing' didn't make any sense to him.

But sitting in peace up the tree, he could write quite sensibly. 'She sniffs and coughs,' he had written down. 'She wears a wig. Her voice is hoarse and croaky. Poppet is afraid of her. She groans when she picks things up.'

After two days had gone by, Ern decided that it would be a good idea to go and see Fatty and the others again, so off he went, notebook in pocket.

He found all the Five, with Buster, down in Fatty's shed, playing a game of cards. They were very pleased to see him.

Buster welcomed him at the top of his bark. Ern felt pleased to see that the table he had made for Fatty was standing in the middle of the shed, with a plate of chocolate biscuits on its polished top. He stood and grinned.

'Come in, Ern. Make yourself at home,' said Fatty, gathering up the cards. 'We've just finished our game. What's your news?'

'Well, I haven't much,' said Ern. 'Except that I've got a house up in a tree that looks right down on the Larkins' cottage, and into the grounds of Tally-Ho. I sit there and watch like anything.'

'Is it *really* a house in a tree?' said Bets, thrilled. 'Oh, I *would* like to see it! Ern, you *are* clever!'

Ern blushed. He drew out his notebook and gave it to Fatty. 'I've made a few notes,' he said. 'Not that they're worth anything – but you never know!'

Fatty glanced through them rapidly, and handed back the notebook. 'Very good,' he said. 'You're doing well, Ern. Yes, those might come in useful sometime – if only we could get going!'

Ern was pleased. 'You got anything interesting to tell me?' he asked.

'Nothing,' said Fatty dismally. 'It's too maddening to have something like this under our noses, so to speak, and not to be able to get even a bite at it!'

'The only thing that's new was in the paper this morning,' said Larry.

'What?' asked Ern, who hadn't seen a paper.

'Well, the Lorenzos were spotted somewhere up north,' said Larry. 'Near an airfield, in a small hotel. And what is more, they had a crate with them this time, as well as two small suitcases.'

'Coo, the picture!' said Ern. 'Weren't they caught then? Did they get away?'

'Yes – fled in the night – took someone else's car out of the garage and went,' said Fatty. 'Complete with suitcases and crate. I don't somehow think they will try to get out of the country at present. They'll hide somewhere safe and wait.'

'Would they come back to Peterswood?' asked Ern, thrilled. 'I'd better keep a strict watch from my tree house.'

'They might,' said Fatty. 'And, as we said before, they might send someone to fetch Poppet, so keep a watch for any stranger at the Larkins' cottage, Ern, and keep a watch too to see that the poodle is always there.'

'Oh, I will!' said Ern.

He spent a pleasant morning with the others and then, remembering that his dinner was at half past twelve, not one o'clock, he rose to go.

'I'll be along again sometime,' he said. 'Good-bye, all. Thanks for the biscuits. Good-bye, Buster!'

Buster came with him as far as the gate, and saw him off politely, his tail wagging fast. He liked Ern. Ern mounted his bicycle and rode off at top speed. He rang his bell going round the corner just at the same moment as somebody else rang theirs. Ern swung round the corner, pedalling furiously – to meet his uncle, Mr Goon, also pedalling furiously on his bicycle! Mr Goon, unfortunately, had cut the corner and was on his wrong side. The bicycles were about to crash together, when Ern quickly swerved. His pedal caught Mr Goon's, and over they both went.

'Oooh! Oh!' groaned Mr Goon, as he landed very heavily indeed. His bicycle fell on top of him.

'Oooh!' yelled Ern, and he too fell to the

ground. He sent a terrified glance at Mr Goon and got up. Mr Goon groaned again. Then he saw who the other cyclist was, and stared open-mouthed.

'What! *You*, Ern! How dare you ride at sixty miles an hour round a corner! How . . .'

'It wasn't my fault, Uncle,' said poor Ern, scared stiff. 'You were on the wrong side.'

'I was not!' said Mr Goon, most untruthfully. 'Do you mean to say you're accusing me of causing this here accident? You just wait, young Ern! What you doing in Peterswood, anyhow?'

Ern was not prepared to tell him that. He put his foot on the left-hand pedal, and was about to swing his leg over to sit on the saddle, when his uncle gave a really most alarming groan.

'Oh, my back! It's broken! Here, young Ern, you help me up, come on now!' He held out an enormous hand to Ern. 'Come on, give me a pull!'

Ern put out his hand too – but saw the gleam in Goon's eye just in time. He snatched back his hand and jumped on his bicycle, panting hard. Coo, his uncle had *almost* got him!

9. MR HOHO-HA!

Ern cycled back to his aunt's at top speed, turning round every now and again to see if Goon was after him. But, mercifully, there was no sign of his uncle.

It took Goon quite a minute to heave himself to his feet, and examine his bicycle to see if it could be ridden in safety. It appeared to be all right. Goon knew that it was no good trying to chase Ern. Indeed, if he did, Ern would certainly win!

Goon said a lot of things under his breath. 'That Ern! Wait till I get him! Why, he might have killed me. Speed fiend, that's what he is! What's he doing in Peterswood, I'd like to know!'

Goon had no idea that Ern was staying in Peterswood – and certainly none at all that he was living next door to the Lorenzos' house. He got on his bicycle very, very carefully, fearful that something might be broken and give way beneath his weight.

He wondered what Fatty was doing. He hadn't seen or heard of him since the morning that all Five had visited him. He began to scowl.

That boy was too cunning for words. Was he hoping to do something about the Lorenzo mystery? Had he gone to see the Larkins and got out of them more than he, Goon, had managed to get? Was he working out something? Mr Goon began to worry. He pedalled back to his house, still frowning.

I think I'll go up to the cottage at Tally-Ho House and pop in to see the Larkins again, he thought. I'll ask Bob Larkin if that big boy has been snooping round – and if he has, I'll have something to say about it.

But Fatty had not been to see the Larkins because the Superintendent had said that he did not wish him to. Fatty was still rather down in the dumps, though he kept a cheerful face with the others.

He thought about Ern's rough notes, and wondered how little Poppet was getting on. In his notes, Ern had put that she was afraid of Mrs Larkin. She was terrified of Mr Larkin too, so her life couldn't be a very happy one. After seven years of love and fuss and petting, life must seem very grim to little Poppet these days!

I'm sure Mrs Lorenzo will try to get her dog back if she can't get out of the country, said Fatty to himself. Or she will send someone to fetch her, and put her in a home with kindly people. I think it wouldn't be a bad idea if I went to see Ern's tree house this afternoon, and did a bit of snooping round myself.

He sat and thought a little more. Better not go as myself in case I bump into Mr Goon. I'll disguise myself, as Bets suggested!

He looked at himself in the mirror, and twisted a face-towel over his head like a turban. Bets was right – he looked exactly like a foreigner! Fatty grinned and felt much more cheerful.

'It doesn't suit me to sit and do nothing when there's something on,' he said. 'That's not the way to make anything happen! Come on, Fatty – stir yourself. Get out your fancy clothes and dress up!'

Immediately after he had had lunch, Fatty set

to work down in his shed. He found a fine strip of cloth that would do for a turban, and looked up, 'Turbans – how to wear', in a very useful little book called *Dress up Properly*. He practised turban-tying for some time and at last produced a most satisfactory one, wound correctly round his head.

He pencilled a faint black moustache, rather thin, on his upper lip, and darkened his chin to make it seem as if he had a shaved beard. He put cheekpads in to alter the shape of his face, and at once looked older, and fatter in the cheeks. He darkened his eyebrows and made them thicker, then gazed at himself in the glass, putting on a sinister, rather mysterious expression.

That's all right, he thought. Gosh, it's funny looking at myself in the mirror and seeing somebody quite different! Now, what else shall I wear?

He decided that the Eastern clothes he had were a bit too bright for January weather. He didn't want a crowd of kids following him around! He suddenly thought of some Eastern students he had seen in London.

They wore turbans, and rather tightish, but ordinary black trousers, and an overcoat, he remembered. Didn't want to shiver in our cold climate, I suppose! Perhaps it would be best if I just wore a turban, and ordinary clothes. My face is so very sunburnt that just wearing a turban makes me look Eastern!

He found a pair of rather dirty, very tight black trousers, which he couldn't do up at the waist. He had a brain-wave and tied a sash round his middle instead. Then he put on an old overcoat.

A foreign student from somewhere out east! he said to himself. Yes, that's what I am! Come on, Fatty – off to Tally-Ho!

He left Buster behind, much to the little Scottie's dismay, and set off, passing rapidly by the kitchen window, hoping that the maids would not see him. But his mother saw him, and gazed after him in surprise.

Who's that? she wondered. A friend of Frederick's, I suppose. What a peculiar-looking fellow in that turban!

Fatty went off down to the river, and made his way along the river path. He only met an old lady with a dog, and she gazed at him uneasily.

Fatty came to the river gate leading into the grounds of Tally-Ho. It was only a small wicket gate, quite unlike the two imposing drive gates at the front of the big house, through which so many cars had driven in and out that summer.

Nobody was about at all. Fatty went a little way along and climbed over the fence into the grounds. He made his way cautiously to the big house, standing desolate and empty, with no smoke coming from its many chimneys.

He peeped into a window. Inside was a big room, with dust sheets over the chairs. A large, polished table stood in the middle. On it was a great bowl full of dead flowers.

Fatty's gaze slid round the room. Chairs. Little tables. A stool – and lying on the floor beside the stool was a curious little object – grey, solid, and rubbery.

Fatty wondered what it was. And why was it on the floor? He stared at it curiously. Then he suddenly knew what it was. Of course! It was a little rubber bone, the kind given to dogs to play with and chew.

'Must be Poppet's,' said Fatty. 'One of her playthings that she left behind on the floor.'

He left the window and went along a path under a rose pergola – and suddenly, just at the end of it, he came face to face with Mr Larkin, who was trudging round the corner with some firewood.

Mr Larkin jumped violently and dropped all his wood. Fatty stepped forward at once and picked it up. Then he addressed the scared Mr Larkin in a very foreign-sounding voice indeed!

'Excuse, please! I come here to see my old friends, the Lorenzos – ah, such old friends they are! And I find the house shut tight – nowhere is there anybody. Please, good sir, you can tell me of my friends?'

'They've gorn,' said Mr Larkin. 'Ain't you seen the papers? Bad lot, they are.'

'Gorn?' echoed Fatty, in a very puzzled voice. 'I do not understand.'

'Well – they've gorn – just *gorn*,' said Mr Larkin impatiently. Fatty stared at him. He looked just the same miserable fellow as before – plumpish under his untidy old overcoat, a scarf round his chin and throat, and a cap pulled down over his eyes. He peered at Fatty suspiciously through his thick glasses.

'We don't allow no strangers here,' said Mr Larkin, backing away from Fatty's stare. Fatty was taking him all in, suddenly filled with a longing to disguise himself like this old fellow. If he disguised himself as Bob Larkin, he could go all round the house and peep into every window without anyone being surprised. He might even get into the house if he could find the keys. Possibly Larkin had some. Yes, he would do it one night – it would be fun.

'You'll have to give me your name,' said Mr Larkin, suddenly remembering that the police had asked him to take the name of anyone coming to the house. 'Foreigner, aren't you?' He took out a dirty little notebook and sucked a pencil.

'You can write down my name as Mr Hoho-Ha,' said Fatty politely, and spelt it out carefully for Mr Larkin. 'And my address is Bong Castle, India.'

Mr Larkin laboriously wrote it all down, placing his notebook on a window ledge to write legibly. When he looked up again, Mr Hoho-Ha had gone.

Larkin grunted and picked up his firewood. All this silly police business annoyed him. Why couldn't he be left in peace to do his job? But he didn't seem to have much of a job now! All those boilers raked out – nothing to light or keep going. No nice warm boiler house to sit in and read his paper. Nothing to do but look after a silly little poodle!

Fatty was behind a bush, watching Larkin going down the path. He noted every action – the shuffling limp, the stoop, the way the cap was pulled half-sideways over the man's face. Yes, he could disguise himself well enough as Larkin to deceive even his old wife!

Fatty had a good look round while he was about it. He looked into the shed and greenhouses, boiler house and summerhouse, keeping a sharp look out for anyone else. But he saw nobody.

He would, however, have seen somebody if he had been near the Larkins' cottage! He would have seen Mr Goon! Mr Goon had ridden up to have another talk to the Larkins, and he was at that moment trying his hardest to get something out of Mrs Larkin besides coughs, groans and sniffles.

Fatty would also have seen two other people if he had looked up into the tall fir tree that grew beside the hedge which separated Tally-Ho grounds from the grounds of High Chimneys next door. He would have seen Glad and Liz!

They, faithful to their trust, had been on guard in the tree for two hours, while Ern was mending his bike. Ern's brakes had gone wrong, owing to his crash with Mr Goon, and he wanted to put them right.

'Glad and Liz, you sit up there and keep your eyes open,' he said. 'And here's two bull's-eyes each to keep you going.'

Glad spotted the strange foreigner as soon as he climbed over the fence. She was so surprised that she swallowed the bull's-eye she was sucking and choked so violently that she nearly fell out of the tree house.

When at last she recovered, the foreigner had disappeared. She found that Liz had spotted him too, and the twins gazed at each other in excitement.

'He must still be there!' said Glad. 'Come on, Liz – let's climb down and tell Ern. He'll go after him all right. Won't he be pleased with us!'

10. ERN SHADOWS A SUSPECT!

Glad and Liz almost fell down the tree in their hurry. They went into the little shed where Ern was busy with his bicycle.

'Ern! We've seen somebody,' said Glad, in a penetrating whisper that could be heard all over the garden. Ern looked up, startled.

'Where? Who?' he asked, getting up at once.

Glad and Liz told him, and Ern straightway made for the hedge, and disappeared through it. He went cautiously round the Larkins' cottage – and then stopped in horror. Mr Goon was standing at the door talking to Mrs Larkin! The twins had not seen him because he had arrived after they had climbed down the tree.

Mr Goon caught sight of Ern at the same moment that Ern caught sight of him. He couldn't believe his eyes. Ern again! Ern, here in the Larkins' garden!

Mr Goon gave such a roar that Mrs Larkin disappeared indoors immediately and shut the door with a slam. Ern was too petrified to move. Mr Goon advanced on him majestically.

'*You* here!' said Mr Goon. 'Now you just come-alonga me, Ern. I've a few things to say to you, I have.'

Ern fled just in time. He ran blindly down the path and charged full-tilt into Mr Larkin, who was shuffling along still carrying his firewood. He dropped it for the second time as Ern ran straight into him and almost knocked him over. He caught hold of the boy and held on – and was then almost sent flying by the burly form of Mr Goon chasing after Ern.

''Ere! What's all this!' said Mr Larkin, startled and annoyed.

'Hold that boy!' commanded Mr Goon breathlessly. 'Hold him!' Mr Larkin tried to hold the wriggling Ern, but had to let him go – and Mr Goon just pounced in time to stop poor Ern from escaping. He shook him so hard that Ern didn't quite know what was happening.

'What you doing here?' demanded Mr Goon

angrily. 'Is that big boy here too, snooping round?'

'No,' said Ern, feeling certain that Fatty and the others were playing some nice, friendly game far away in Fatty's shed.

'Mr Goon, sir,' said Mr Larkin, 'there's bin a furriner wandering round Tally-Ho grounds just now. Name of Hoho-Ha.'

'Why didn't you tell me?' said Mr Goon unfairly. 'Standing there saying nothing. Where *is* the fellow?'

He hung on to Ern so tightly that the boy groaned. 'Uncle, let me go. I'm after him too. I'll look for him, if you'll let me go.'

'What do you mean, you're after him too?' said Mr Goon, looking all round as if he thought he would be able to see plenty of 'furriners'.

'You let that boy look for him, sir,' suggested Mr Larkin from under his old cap. 'A kid can snoop round quietly and not be seen. You're too big for that. You let this boy loose and tell him to find that furriner – yes, and follow him for you till you can catch up and nab him!'

Goon gave Ern a shake. 'If I let you go, will you do that?' he said.

'You let me find that fellow for you, and I'll shadow him wherever he goes. I promise you, Uncle!' said Ern.

'He wears a turban,' said Mr Larkin. 'Sort of a towel round his head,' he added, as Goon looked mystified. 'Can't mistake him. He can't be far off, so let this kid go now or you'll lose the furriner.'

Goon let go of Ern's arm and the boy darted off thankfully. Oh, what bad luck to run into Goon again – just as he was hoping to get some news for Fatty too! Now he had got to find and shadow someone for his uncle – someone who might have been of great use to old Fatty!

Ern remembered the lessons in shadowing that he had had from Fatty, and went silently from bush to bush, watching and listening – and soon he heard the crack of a twig on a path. Ah, the 'furriner' must be there!

Ern peeped round the bush. It was getting rather dark now but he could see a man – and he was wearing a turban!

Nasty-looking chap, thought Ern. Up to no good. I'd better be careful!

Ern felt very thrilled. Almost as if I was in a

film! he thought, remembering the dramatic moments in some of the films he had seen lately. Coo! What will Fatty and the others say when they hear about this!

The man in the turban moved down the path to the little wicket gate. Ern followed cautiously some way behind. Goon caught sight of both of them and followed cautiously too. Ern was after the man, so if he kept the boy in sight, Ern would lead him to wherever the man was going!

Fatty had absolutely no idea that he was being shadowed by Ern, with Goon some distance behind. He sauntered along, thinking of Larkin, and what fun it would be to disguise himself as the old fellow, and meet him some morning down the street! What *would* Larkin say if he came face to face with himself?

Ern followed carefully, holding his breath. Fatty went along the river path and turned up into Peterswood village. Ern stalked him, keeping in the shadows.

Goon followed, wishing he hadn't left his bicycle behind at the Larkins. Now he would have to walk all the way back to get it that night!

Fatty suddenly felt that he was being followed, and looked round. Was he or wasn't he? Was that a figure hiding beside that bush? Well, never mind, he was nearly home!

Fatty suddenly took to his heels and ran for home, thinking that it wouldn't do to be stopped by Goon, if it *was* Goon. He had no idea it was Ern. He came to his gate and slipped through it, ran to the garden door and into the house. Up the stairs he went, two at a time, and into his bedroom. Buster welcomed him with a volley of delighted barks.

It didn't matter what disguise Fatty put on, Buster was never deceived. Fatty always smelt like Fatty, no matter what he looked like – a 'furriner', an old man, a gypsy woman, a butcher's boy. One sniff and Buster knew him!

'Coo,' said Ern, stepping out of the shadows as Fatty went in at his gate. 'Look at that! He ran off all of a sudden, and I'm blessed if he didn't go in at Fatty's gate. Perhaps he's a friend of Fatty's. Gosh, here's Uncle!'

'Where'd that man go?' demanded Mr Goon, holding Ern's shoulder in a vice-like grip.

'Into Fatty's gate,' said Ern. 'I say, Uncle – perhaps he's a friend of Fatty's. You'd better not go after him.'

'Ho! I'd just like to know who Frederick Trotteville is sending to snoop round Tally-Ho grounds,' said Goon. And in at the gate he went, leaving Ern miserably outside. Had he got Fatty into trouble?

Mr Goon knocked loudly at the door and the maid answered promptly.

'Is Frederick in?' asked Goon, in his most pompous voice. Before the maid could answer, Mrs Trotteville came into the hall.

'What do you want, Mr Goon?' she inquired. 'Was it you who knocked so loudly?'

'Er – well, yes, I suppose it was,' said Goon, forgetting to be pompous. He was rather afraid of Mrs Trotteville. 'I came about a stranger.'

'A stranger?' said Mrs Trotteville. 'But there is no one here. What makes you think there is?'

'Well, he came in at your gate,' said Goon. 'Man in a turban.'

'Oh, dear me, I remember seeing a man in a turban going past the windows this afternoon,' said Mrs Trotteville. 'I'll call Frederick. He may have seen him too.'

'Frederick!' she called up the stairs. 'Are you in?'

'Yes, Mummy,' said Fatty, appearing suddenly at the top of the stairs, dressed in his ordinary clothes, and looking very clean and tidy. 'I was just reading. Do you want me?'

'Mr Goon has come about some man he thinks is here,' said Mrs Trotteville. 'He says he came in at our gate a little while ago.'

'I think Mr Goon must be seeing things,' said Fatty, in a concerned voice. 'Do you feel quite well, Mr Goon? What was this fellow like?'

'He wore a turban,' said Goon, beginning to feel annoyed.

'Well, I really haven't seen anyone walking about just wearing a turban,' said Fatty. 'I think I'd have remembered if I had.'

'Don't be stupid, Frederick,' said his mother. '*I* saw somebody wearing a turban this afternoon, but as far as I could see his other clothes were ordinary ones. Who can this fellow be, Frederick?'

'A new paper-boy perhaps,' suggested Fatty. 'Or some friend of the maids? Or just somebody taking a short cut through our garden? People do, you know.'

'Well, this man is obviously not here, Mr Goon,' said Mrs Trotteville. 'I don't imagine you want to search the house?'

Goon would dearly have liked to, but Mrs Trotteville looked so forbidding that he said a hasty goodnight and went off to the front gate. Fatty ushered him politely all the way and watched him stride away in the twilight.

He was just going in when a low whistle reached his ears. He swung round. Ern's voice came urgently from a bush nearby. 'Fatty! I've some news for you!'

'Ern! What in the world are you doing there?' said Fatty, startled. Out came Ern, very cautiously.

'There was a strange man snooping about in Tally-Ho grounds this afternoon,' he began. 'And I followed him to your house. He wore a turban.'

Fatty groaned. 'Fathead, Ern! That was ME! I disguised myself and went up and had a snoop round and a few words with our friend, Mr Larkin! How on earth did Mr Goon come into this?'

Ern explained sadly, feeling that he had not been at all clever. He had even taken Goon to Fatty's house! Golly, Fatty might have been caught in his disguise! What an upset that would have been. Poor Ern was really very miserable.

'Cheer up, Ern,' said Fatty, patting him on the shoulder. 'It just shows two things – *one,* that my disguise was really very good – and *two,* that you're certainly quick off the mark!'

Ern felt more cheerful. Good old Fatty, he always took things the right way, thought Ern. He determined to be even more on the look out than ever. Next time he would track a *real* suspect – not just Fatty!

Fatty went up into his bedroom again, rather depressed after his interesting afternoon. This wasn't a real mystery – it was just a stupid, idiotic newspaper case!

11. QUITE A LOT OF TALK

Fatty was tremendously surprised to see the papers the next morning. Somehow they had got hold of the fact that a stranger of some kind had been seen wandering about the grounds of Tally-Ho House.

'Mystery of the Lorenzos and Stolen Picture Flares Up Again,' said one headline. 'An Old Friend found in the Grounds.'

'Turbaned Man chased by Brave Constable,' said another paper.

'Stolen Picture Probably hidden in Tally-Ho House,' said a third. 'Foreigner Found Breaking in.'

Fatty stared at these headlines in the utmost dismay. Goodness – what in the world had Mr Goon been saying? Some reporter must have got hold of him last night and had asked if there were any news about the Lorenzos, and Goon hadn't been able to stop himself from enlarging on his encounter with the disguised Fatty.

Fatty's heart sank down into his boots. Why, Mr Goon hadn't set even a finger on him! He had only followed Ern, who had been following him. Suppose Superintendent Jenks got to hear of this?

Fatty went round to see the others as soon as he could. They hadn't known, of course, that he was going to disguise himself, and had been most astonished to see the papers. Larry and Daisy had gone to call for Pip and Bets, on their way down to Fatty's, and they were very pleased to see him.

'Seen the papers?' said Pip, as soon as Fatty came in at the playroom door, with Buster at his heels. Fatty nodded. The others stared at him in surprise.

'What's up? What are you looking like that for?' asked Larry. 'We were really pleased about it – it looks as if something might happen here after all!'

Fatty sat down and groaned in such a desperate manner that Bets ran to him at once. 'What is it? Are you ill, Fatty?'

'I *feel* ill,' said Fatty. '*I* was the turbaned man – didn't you guess? I thought I'd disguise myself as a foreign student, and just go for a little snoop. And, of course, first I bumped into old Larkin and gave him a shock – and then *Ern* discovers me and tells old Mr Goon, who happens to be interviewing Mr Larkin – and then Ern is told to shadow me so that Mr Goon can see where I go.'

The others listened in horror. 'Fatty! And now you're in all the papers!'

'Yes, but mercifully nobody knows *I* was the stranger – except Ern. I told him. Wish I hadn't now. He'll never be able to keep his mouth shut. And oh, I've just thought of something else. Oh, my word!'

'What? What is it?' said Bets, quite overcome with all this. All kinds of dreadful ideas filled her mind.

'Old Larkin met me – and I asked him where my old friends the Lorenzos had gone,' said poor Fatty. 'And when he asked me for my name I told him an idiotic one – and he *wrote it down*! If Mr Goon gets it out of him, and realises the stranger was a spoof – in other words, me – there'll be an awful lot of fat in the fire!'

'What name did you give?' asked Larry.

'Mr Hoho-Ha of Bong Castle, India,' said Fatty with another groan.

There was a moment's silence – and then a squeal of laughter from Daisy. 'Oh, Fatty! Oh Mr Hoho-Ha! Do you mean to say old Larkin *really* wrote that down?'

'Yes,' said Fatty, still unable to raise even a smile. 'It's no laughing matter, Daisy. If Ern splits on me, I'm in the soup – hot soup too. We're sure to get the reporters down here then, interviewing me as the boy who deceived the police. Frightful! Why did I do it?'

'Ern won't give you away,' said Bets.

'I think he *would*,' said Pip. 'He's not very brave and he's so scared of Mr Goon that he'd say anything to get away from him.'

There came a knock at the door. Everyone turned their heads, expecting they hardly knew what. Goon perhaps – except that he wouldn't knock. He'd walk straight in!

The door opened. It was Ern! Ern, looking very flushed and rather fearful.

'Ern! We were just talking about you,' said Bets. 'Have you split on Fatty? You haven't told

Mr Goon that Fatty was the turbaned man, have you?'

'Coo, no,' said Ern, much to everyone's relief. 'Uncle's been at me like anything this morning but I never said a word about Fatty. What do you take me for?'

'I knew you wouldn't, Ern,' said Bets.

'I just came to tell you something,' said Ern. 'My uncle's gone all funny-like this morning. Don't know what to make of him.'

'Exactly what do you mean?' asked Fatty, interested.

'Well, he came up to my Aunt Woosh's place this morning, though goodness knows how he found out I was staying there,' said Ern. 'And he took me into the woodshed and shut the door. I was really puzzled!' said Ern, ' but he was as sweet as sugar. Kept patting me on the shoulder, and telling me I wasn't such a bad kid after all – and then he said he wanted to keep me out of any unpleasantness, so he wanted me to promise I'd not say a word about how I had discovered the stranger yesterday, nor a word about me shadowing him . . .'

Fatty laughed suddenly. 'Gosh! He's so proud of this business that he wants everyone to think *he* discovered him, tackled him, and shadowed him! He doesn't want *you* to figure in this show at all, Ern.'

'Oh – so that's it, is it?' said Ern. 'Well, my Aunt Woosh got a paper this morning, and when I saw all about you in it, Fatty – well, about the foreigner, I mean – I got the shock of my life. I was all of a tremble when my Uncle Goon came in – and I was worse when I saw him. I'm all of a tremble now, even when I think of it.'

'Have a sweet?' said Pip. 'It's good for trembles.'

Ern took one. 'Phew!' he said. 'I wasn't half glad when my uncle let me go. I promised I wouldn't say a word to anyone – and I was never so glad to promise anything in my life! Never!'

Fatty heaved a sigh of relief. 'Good old Ern,' he said, with much feeling. 'You've taken a load off my mind. If Goon goes about saying *he* discovered the man, and tackled him, and then shadowed him, I'm all right. Though he shouldn't really say anything, if he's on a case.'

'Suppose one of the reporters from the papers

finds out from Larkin that the man gave him the name of Mr Hoho-Ha of Bong Castle,' said Pip. 'Won't he smell a rat?'

'No. I don't think so,' said Fatty, considering the matter. 'He'll probably think the man was just spoofing the old fellow. I hope Superintendent Jenks doesn't hear that though – he'll know it's the sort of idiotic name I'd think up myself.'

'You are a one!' said Ern, round-eyed. 'How you dare! Coo, Fatty, *I* never knew it was you! You don't even *walk* like yourself when you're in disguise. You ought to be on the stage!'

'Good gracious, no!' said Fatty. 'Be on the stage when I could be a detective? Not on your life!'

'We'd better lie low for a day or two, hadn't we?' said Daisy. 'Not go anywhere near Tally-Ho House. Once this new excitement has died down, things will be all right – but Fatty oughtn't to risk anything at the moment.'

'You're right, Daisy,' said Fatty. 'But personally I'm beginning to think that the next thing we'll hear is that the Lorenzos have managed to get out of the country – with the picture – and that will be that.'

'Oh, I hope not!' said Pip. 'This is a most *annoying* mystery – there's nothing to get hold of – no clues, no suspects . . .'

'Except the foreigner,' said Larry, with a grin.

'Well, let's drop the whole thing for a couple of days,' said Fatty. 'Then we'll see if anything further has happened. We'll know by the papers.'

'Shan't I keep watch from my tree house?' said Ern, disappointed.

'Oh yes, no harm in that,' said Fatty. 'Do those twin cousins of yours still enjoy themselves up there?'

'Oooh yes, they've got all their dolls up there now,' said Ern, sounding rather disgusted. 'There's nowhere to sit except on dolls – and one squeaks like anything if you tread on it. Gave me a real fright, I can tell you!'

They all laughed. 'Well, you let the twins sit up there as much as they like, and report to you *if* they see anything,' said Fatty. 'I wish I'd known I could be so easily seen from that tree when I wandered in yesterday. I forgot all about it! Those cousins of yours must have been keeping a pretty sharp look out.'

'They're not bad,' said Ern. 'I've got them properly under my thumb now. They think I'm the cat's whiskers and the dog's tail and the kangaroo's jump, and . . .'

'Oh, Ern!' said Bets, and joined in the laughter. Ern beamed. He did so love the Five to laugh at any of his jokes.

'Ern, have you written any more poems?' asked Bets. Ern was very fond of writing what he called 'pomes' but as he rarely got beyond the first three or four lines, they were not very successful.

Ern pulled out a notebook, looking pleased. 'Fancy you remembering my pomes,' he said. 'Well, I began one last week. It might be a good one – but I got stuck again.'

'What is it?' said Fatty, grinning. 'Let me help you.'

Ern read out his 'pome', putting on a very solemn voice.

A pore old woman had a dog,
And it was always barkin,
Its name was . . .

'Well, that's as far as I've got,' said Ern. 'There's all sorts of ideas swarming round in my head, but they just sort of won't come out.'

'My dear Ern, it's a fine poem,' said Fatty earnestly. 'Don't you really know how it goes on? Listen!'

Fatty stood in the middle of the room and recited in a voice exactly like Ern's,

A pore old woman had a dog,
And it was always barkin,
Its name was Poppet, and of course
The woman's name was Larkin.

She sniffed and coughed the whole day long,
And said the wind was cold,
And when the dog got in her way
She handed out a scold.

Her husband shuffled in an out,
He wasn't very supple,
They weren't at all what you might call
A really pleasant couple!

Fatty stopped to take breath. Ern had listened in the greatest awe. The others laughed in delight. Fatty could go on like this for ages, without stopping. It was one of the many extraordinary things he could do.

'Coo!' said Ern. 'How do you do it, Fatty? Why, that's *just* what I wanted to say in my pome but I got stuck. You're a wonder, Fatty!'

'Oh, that was just a lot of nonsense,' said Fatty, feeling much better.

'It wasn't. It was simply marvellous,' said Ern. 'I must write it all down – but it's really *your* pome now, not mine, Fatty.'

'No, it's yours,' said Fatty generously. 'I don't want it. I'd never have thought of it if you hadn't told me the first three lines. You can have it for your very own, Ern.'

Ern was delighted and, for the next twenty minutes, he didn't join in any of the fun. He was most laboriously writing out his new 'pome'.

12. A QUIET TWO DAYS

There was nothing more in the papers about the 'strange foreigner'. In fact, as far as Fatty could see, there was no mention of the Lorenzo case at all. He was rather relieved.

For two days, the Five led perfectly normal lives, with Ern and Buster following them around. The Lorenzo mystery wasn't even mentioned, except that Ern volunteered the information that the twins were getting rather tired of the tree house.

'You see, it's been windy, and their things keep falling out of the tree when the wind shakes it,' explained Ern. 'And they got annoyed because I wouldn't let them blow bubbles over the Larkins' cottage.'

'Blow bubbles over the cottage?' said Fatty, in surprise. 'But why should they want to? The bubbles would burst at once, anyhow.'

'Not the kind they've got,' said Ern. 'They aren't ordinary soap bubbles – you make the mixture, and blow the bubbles – and they come out very big and strong – they can bump into things without breaking, so they go on flying about for ages.'

'I see,' said Fatty, having a sudden vision of Mr and Mrs Larkin being surrounded by big, bouncing bubbles every time they put their noses out of doors. 'Well, it does sound a most tempting thing to do, I must say, but you'd better restrain the twins at present, anyway. The tree house spyhole would certainly be discovered if they start anything like that.'

'I've told them not to do it,' said Ern. 'But they're not all *that* obedient, Fatty. They keep on and on about it. When they first thought of it they almost fell out of the tree with laughing.'

'Yes. Well, it's quite a bright idea,' said Fatty. 'One we might use sometime, but not just now. Come on, we are all going to the cake shop for coffee and hot buttered scones.'

They cycled off to the cake shop. Ern thought that this custom of the Five of popping out to eat and drink in between meals was a very, very good one. His aunt didn't feed him as well as his mother did, and poor Ern was in a constant state of hunger.

The cake shop woman was very pleased to see them. Six children and a hungry dog were better than twelve grown-ups, because they seemed to eat three times as much! She brought out a plate heaped with hot, buttery scones.

'Curranty ones!' said Pip. 'Just what I like. It's decent of you to keep treating us to this kind of thing, Fatty. You always seem to have a lot of money.'

'Well, this is my Christmas money,' said Fatty, who had a good supply of generous aunts and uncles and grandparents. 'Sit, Buster. Well-mannered dogs do NOT put their paws on the table, and count the number of scones.'

'They'd take some counting!' said Ern, eyeing the plate with much approval. Then he jumped violently, as a large burly figure suddenly appeared at the door.

'Oh, good morning, Mr Goon,' said Fatty. 'Do come and join us. Do you like hot, buttery scones?'

Mr Goon stalked in, his lips pursed up as if he was afraid he might say something he didn't mean to. He eyed all the children, and Ern squirmed.

'I've bin looking for you,' he said to Fatty. 'Mr Hoho-Ha! Ho yes, I've read it in Larkin's notebook. Think you've made a fool of me, don't you? Do you want me to tell the Superintendent?'

'What do you mean?' said Fatty. 'I read in the papers that you tackled a strange man very bravely the other day in the grounds of Tally-Ho House. Congratulations, Mr Goon. I wish I'd been there.'

Ern disappeared under the table, and Buster welcomed him heartily, licking his face all over. Goon didn't even see him go.

'What do you mean – you wish you'd been there?' demanded Mr Goon. 'You were there all right, Mr Hoho-Ha! Just let me say this, Frederick Algernon Trotteville, you'd better go back to BONG CASTLE, see? Else you'll get into very serious trouble.'

Having made this extraordinary fierce joke, Mr Goon marched out again. The cake shop woman stared after him in amazement. Whatever was he talking about?

'Poor man. Mad as a hatter,' said Fatty sympathetically, reaching for another scone. 'Come out, Ern. You're safe now. Hurry up, or all the scones will be gone.'

Ern came out from under the table in a hurry, still looking rather pale. He opened his mouth to ask a question.

'We're not talking about certain things just now, Ern,' said Fatty warningly, and Ern's mouth shut, only to open again for a bite at a scone.

'I suppose Mr Goon saw all our bikes outside, and couldn't resist coming in to say a few words to you,' said Daisy in a low voice. 'I thought he was going to burst!'

The rest of the day passed very pleasantly, as Pip's mother had asked all the Find-Outers to tea and games.

'Mummy says she will be out from three o'clock till seven,' said Pip. 'So if we want to make a noise or do anything silly, she says now's our chance!'

'Very thoughtful of her,' said Fatty approvingly.

'Your mother is strict, Pip, but always fair. I hope your cook is in?'

Pip grinned. 'Oh yes – and she says if you go down to the kitchen and do your imitation of the gardener when she's been and picked some parsley without asking him, she'll make you your favourite gingerbread.'

'A very reasonable bargain,' said Fatty. He had once been at Pip's when the hot-tempered gardener had discovered the cook picking his parsley, 'without so much as a by-your-leaf'. Fatty had thoroughly enjoyed his remarks, and the cook had been delighted to hear Fatty acting the whole thing to the others afterwards. She had even lent him her cooking apron for an imitation gardening apron.

Fatty was amused to see the apron waiting on a chair for him. Pip chuckled. 'It must be nice to be you, Fatty,' he said. 'Getting your favourite cake because you can imitate our hot-tempered old gardener – getting the finest oranges at the greengrocer's because you do a bit of ventriloquism there, and make a cow moo at the back of the shop just to please the shop-boy – and getting . . .'

'That's enough,' said Fatty. 'You make it sound like bribery but it's merely good bargaining! Now, let's go down and do the Parsley Act straightaway, so that your cook has got plenty of time to make a smashing plate of gingerbread!'

They all went down, Ern following behind. Ern was like Bets – he thought Fatty was a wonder – there couldn't be anyone else like him. He considered that he was very, very lucky to be made welcome by every one of the Five. For the hundredth time, he made up his mind to serve Fatty faithfully. Or die! thought Ern dramatically, as he watched Fatty doing his ridiculous Parsley Act, croaking in the old gardener's voice, and flapping his apron at the enraptured cook, who was almost dying with laughter.

'Oh, bless us all!' she said, wiping her eyes. 'I never saw such a thing in my life. You're old Herbert to the life. He flapped at me just like that! Stop now, I can't bear any more!'

They had their gingerbread – a magnificent pile – and old Herbert, the gardener, was immensely surprised to see Pip coming out with a very large piece for him. He took it in astonished silence.

'As a mark of gratitude from us all,' said Pip solemnly and Herbert was even more mystified.

The evening paper came just as they were all in the hall, saying good-bye to Pip and Bets. It was pushed through the letter box and fell on to the mat. It lay there, folded in half, with the top half showing clearly. Fatty gave an exclamation as he picked it up.

'Look here! See what it says! "The Lorenzos reported in Maidenhead!" Why, that's quite near here!' He read the paragraph quickly. 'Oh well, apparently it's only just a guess by someone. Anyway, surely the Lorenzos wouldn't be foolish enough to travel about undisguised. I expect we'll keep on getting these reports from all over the country, just to keep interest alive.'

'Coo,' said Ern. 'Maidenhead! If it *was* them, they might visit Tally-Ho House – or the Larkins' cottage to get Poppet.'

'Will Mr Goon be watching the place tonight, do you think?' asked Larry.

'I don't know. Possibly, if there *is* anything in the report,' said Fatty. 'Ern, keep your eyes skinned tonight, will you?'

'Oooh, I will,' promised Ern, thrilled. 'I wouldn't mind scouting round a bit myself – but Uncle may be about, and I wouldn't dare. I'd be sure to bump into him.'

'I'll be along before midnight,' said Fatty, making up his mind. 'Just in case.'

'Right,' said Ern, more and more thrilled. 'I'll be up in the tree house watching, Fatty. I'll hoot like an owl to let you know I'm there.'

He put his shut hands to his mouth, with the thumbs on his lips and blew softly. Immediately, the hall was filled with the sound of quavering owl hoots.

'Very good,' said Larry admiringly. 'It's all right, cook, we haven't got an owl in the hall!'

The cook, who had run out in surprise, went back into her kitchen. 'Frederick again, I expect,' she said to her friend sitting there. 'What a one!'

But it was Ern this time, and he hooted again, pleased to have such an admiring audience.

'Right,' said Fatty. 'You be up in the tree house, and I'll be scouting around till midnight. I don't really expect anything to happen, but I won't leave anything to chance. I'll look out for Mr Goon, of course.'

'Good-bye!' said Larry, hearing seven o'clock strike. 'Thank you for a lovely time. Hurry up, Daisy!'

They all went off, and Pip shut the door. Ern left the others at the corner and rode back to his aunt's, full of excitement over his night's plan. The tree house at night! He'd take a rug and some cushions, and make himself comfortable. And a bag of bull's-eyes to suck.

So, at nine o'clock, when his aunt and uncle had gone early to bed, and the twins were sound asleep in their small room, Ern sat bolt upright and listened to hear if his uncle and aunt were asleep. Yes – as usual they were both snoring – his uncle with great big, long-drawn-out snores and his aunt with little polite ones.

Ern dressed warmly, because the night was cold. He decided to take both the blanket *and* the rug off his bed. He had already put a couple of old cushions up in the tree house, and in his coat pocket he had the bag of bull's-eyes and a torch. Now for it!

He crept out of bed, and down the little stairway, carrying the blanket and rug. He opened the kitchen door and went out into the garden. In a minute, he was at the foot of the tree. He climbed up carefully, the rugs round his neck.

He was soon in the little tree house, peering through the peephole in the branches. The moon was coming up and the night was quite light. Ern popped a bull's-eye in his mouth and prepared to keep watch. He had never in his life felt so happy!

13. AN EXCITING TIME

Fatty did not arrive at Tally-Ho grounds till much later. His parents did not go to bed until ten past eleven that night, and Fatty waited and waited, fully-dressed. He was not in disguise, because he did not intend to meet anyone if he could help it!

He had on his very thickest overcoat and a cap pulled over his thick hair. He whispered to Buster to keep quiet. The little Scottie watched him sorrowfully. He knew that Fatty meant to go out without him, and he was grieved. He wouldn't even wag his tail when Fatty gave him one last pat.

The night was light and dark alternately. When the moon sailed out from behind a big cloud, the road was as bright as day. When it sailed behind a cloud, it was difficult to see without a torch. Fatty kept in the shadow of the trees, and walked softly, listening for any footsteps.

He met no one at all. Peterswood had certainly gone to bed early that night!

He went down to the river and walked along the river path to the wicket gate leading into Tally-Ho grounds. He felt that to go in at the front gates would certainly attract attention – and, indeed, it was possible that Goon might be there, keeping watch also. Though I don't really believe that Maidenhead report, thought Fatty. For one thing, it would be silly of the Lorenzos to try and come back so soon – and for another, if they *were* going to, they would disguise themselves too thoroughly to be easily recognised!

He let himself in at the gate. The Larkins' cottage was in darkness, and there was not a sound. Fatty remembered that Ern would be watching from the tree house, and he stopped under a bush to send out a hoot.

'Hoo!' called Fatty, on exactly the right note. 'Hoo-hoo-hoo-HOO!'

And back came the answer from Ern in the tree, 'Hoo! Hoo-hoo-hoo-HOO!' It was so exactly like an owl that Fatty nodded his head approvingly. Ern was good!

He began to make his way to the big house. It was in utter darkness. Fatty wished he could suddenly see a flicker or flash there, to tell him that somebody was about – that would be exciting. But everything was silence and darkness in the deserted house.

Ern hooted again. Then, before Fatty could answer, there came another hoot, and then another.

Whatever was Ern doing? Then Fatty laughed. Of course! It was real owls this time. They liked hunting on a moonlit night like this.

He thought he would send back a hoot, however, in case it *was* Ern. So he put his thumbs to his mouth and sent out a long and quavering hoot.

Immediately an answering hoot came, one that sounded quite urgent! *Was* it Ern? It was impossible to sense exactly the right direction of the hoot. Could Ern be trying to give him a message – was he warning him?

Fatty decided to stand under a thick dark bush for a while and wait quietly. The night was so silent that he might be able to pick up any noise if someone was about.

So Fatty stood absolutely still and listened. He heard nothing at all for about five minutes. Not even a hoot!

Then he was sure he heard a soft crunch as if someone was walking carefully on frosty grass. Oh, very carefully!

Fatty held his breath. Could it be one of the Lorenzos? Had he – or she – come back to get something from the house? They would be sure to have keys. He stood still again. The moon swung out from behind a cloud and everything was suddenly lit up. Fatty crouched back into the bush, looking round to see if he could spy anyone.

Not a sound! Not a sign of anything at all suspicious. The moon went behind a cloud again – a big cloud, this time, likely to last for some minutes.

The sound came again – a little crunch of frosted grass. Fatty stiffened. Yes, it came from round the corner of the house, he was sure of it. Someone was there – standing there – or moving very cautiously bit by bit.

A loud hoot sounded so near Fatty's head that he jumped violently. This time it really *was* an owl, for he saw the dark shadow of its wings, though he could not hear the slightest sound of the bird's flight.

The tiny crunch came again. Fatty decided that it was someone waiting there, standing on the frosty grass, and occasionally moving his feet. Who was it?

I really must see, thought Fatty. If it *is* Lorenzo, I'd better scoot off and telephone Superintendent Jenks. It can't be Mr Goon – I would hear his heavy breathing. This fellow doesn't make any sound at all, except the tiny crunching noise.

As the moon was still behind the cloud, Fatty decided he had better try and have a look at the man, whoever he was, straightaway. He made his way very, very carefully from the bush, glad that the grass was not so frosty on his side of the house.

He trod unexpectedly on some dead leaves and they rustled. Fatty stopped. Had the noise been heard? He was nearly at the corner of the house now. He went forward again, and then nerved himself to peer round.

He slid his head carefully round the corner

and, very dimly, he saw a figure standing by the windows of Tally-Ho House. The figure was absolutely still. Fatty could not see any details at all, except that it seemed to be a fairly tall man. It was certainly not the short, burly Goon.

Fatty's heart began to beat fast. Who was this? He fumbled for his torch, meaning to flash it suddenly on the man's face, and then run off at top speed to telephone a warning.

He forgot about the moon! Just as he was about to switch on his torch, the moon shot out from behind the cloud, and immediately the place was flooded with light!

Fatty found himself gazing at a tall policeman in a helmet – and the policeman was also gazing at Fatty, looking most astonished! He put a whistle to his mouth and whistled shrilly, taking a step towards Fatty at the same time.

'It's all right,' began Fatty, 'I . . .' And then, up galloped Goon from his hiding-place behind the nearby summerhouse. His mouth fell open when he saw Fatty.

Then he advanced on him in rage. 'You! You again! Don't I ever get rid of you, Toad of a Boy!

You were all them owls, I suppose, hooting like mad! What you doing here? I'll tell the Chief of this. Obstructing the course of duty – interfering with the law – messing up things when we're on watch!'

'I didn't know you were watching, Mr Goon,' said Fatty. 'I'm sorry to have disturbed you. This is honestly a mistake.'

The other policeman stood gaping in surprise. Who was this boy?

'What's your name?' he said, taking out a notebook.

'I know his name!' said Goon angrily. 'I've heard it too often, I can tell you that! This is Frederick Trotteville, and this time he's going to get into trouble. Arrest him as an intruder on private property, Constable!'

'Wait a minute – is this really Frederick Trotteville?' said the other policeman. 'He's a friend of the Chief's, isn't he? I'm not arresting *him*, Goon. You can do that if you want to!'

'You do as I tell you,' said Goon, losing his temper. 'Who do you think you are, giving me my orders? You're under *my* orders tonight,

PC Johns, as well you know.'

The moon went most conveniently behind a thick cloud at this point, and Fatty thought it would be just as well if he slipped away. He really didn't want to be arrested – and he was sorry that he had barged into Goon's little spot of night-duty. No wonder Ern had done such a lot of urgent hooting – he must have seen Goon and the other policeman wandering about in the bright moonlight!

Fatty slipped out of the wicket gate and trotted swiftly home, pondering over what was the best thing to do. Should he ring up the Superintendent and tell him of his unfortunate meeting with Goon and his companion? Surely the Chief would know that Fatty was only trying to help?

Perhaps on the whole it would be best to leave it till the morning, and then telephone. Goon would have simmered down by then. Fatty would go and see him and apologise for barging in. Goon loved an apology!

So Fatty did not telephone, but went soberly to bed, hushing Buster's ecstatic but silent welcome. He heard an owl hooting nearby and grinned as he pulled the sheet up to his chin. Poor Goon!

He must have been quite bewildered by all the owl hoots sent out by the terrified Ern!

Ern was still up in the tree. He had an extremely good view of the grounds when the moon was out, for everything was then as distinct as in the daytime, though the shadows were very black.

Ern was shivering, not so much with cold as with excitement and panic. He had spotted Goon and his companion about eleven o'clock, before Fatty had appeared, when the moonlight had suddenly glittered on their helmets. There was no mistaking his uncle, of course – plump and stocky. The other policeman Ern didn't know.

Ern watched them walking round the big house peeping into all the windows and trying the doors. Then they disappeared. Were they expecting the Lorenzos after all? Were they hiding and lying in wait?

Old Fatty wouldn't know that! He might walk straight into them. Ern fell into a panic and shivered so much that he shook the little tree house from end to end.

He wondered what to do. Should he slip down

the tree and go and see if he could meet Fatty and warn him? No, he didn't know which way Fatty would be coming – by the river gate or the front gates. He might miss him!

Well, should he stay in the tree and wait for Fatty to come, and then try to warn him by hooting and hooting? But would he *see* Fatty? The moon might be in behind a cloud, and then he couldn't possibly see anyone!

Ern decided, shivering, that the best thing to do would be to wait and hope to see Fatty – and then hoot for all he was worth.

He spotted Fatty easily as the boy trod stealthily up the garden. Ern's spyhole was indeed a good one! He hooted – and Fatty answered him. And then poor Ern spied Goon and the other policeman, standing behind the corner of the house – and now, where had Goon gone? Oh, yes, behind the summerhouse! Ern hooted urgently and to his utter disgust, an owl flew over in surprise, hooting too. Ern shook his fist at it for spoiling all his plans! Now Fatty wouldn't know one hoot from another!

Ern then saw the encounter between Fatty and

Goon and the other policeman, though he could hear nothing except a murmur of voices. His eyes nearly fell out of his head with trying to see what was happening. Oh, Fatty, Fatty, make a run for it! Ern found himself saying the words over and over again.

Then the moon went behind a cloud – and when it came out again, oh joy! Ern saw a running figure on the river path – and the two policemen hunting here and there for the vanished Fatty!

Ern heaved an enormous sigh of relief. He slumped back into the tree house, feeling quite tired after all the suspense.

Stir yourself, Ern! The night isn't finished yet!

14. ERN IS MOST ASTONISHED

Ern gave a few more sighs, each one less enormous than the last. By now, Fatty would be well on the way home. Had Goon recognised him? Ern was afraid that he had. He sat up again and peered out.

Ah – there were Goon and the other constable walking side by side, arguing. Then Goon stood and began to swing his great arms to and fro across his chest.

He's cold, said Ern to himself. Serve him right! I hope he freezes! I hope he's got to stay and watch Tally-Ho House all night long. Grrrrr!

It was a most blood-curdling growl that Ern gave, and he even scared himself. He realised that his hands and feet were remarkably cold, and he thought longingly of his warm bed.

I can't do anything more tonight, he thought, beginning to climb down the tree, with the rug and blanket draped round his neck. I'll go back to the house.

He climbed right down and went to the cottage. To his horror, the kitchen door was now locked! He shook it quietly, filled with dismay. Who had locked it? He supposed that his uncle must have awakened at some noise – and had got up to investigate, and found the door unlocked. Blow, blow, blow!

Well, I'm not going to knock at the door and give everybody a fright, thought Ern. I'll just go back to the tree now and explain tomorrow morning that I thought I'd like a night out up there, and that's where I was. They'll think I'm potty, but I can't help that!

Ern debated with himself. He would have liked another blanket. He remembered that there were piles of old newspapers in his Uncle Woosh's shed. He had heard that newspaper was a very, very warm covering, so he decided to take a few dozen papers up the tree with him.

Armed with these, he went back to the tree house. It really seemed very cosy and comfortable after the cold air down in the yard. Ern spread out the newspaper and made himself a kind of bed. Then he wrapped a few papers round him, pulled the blanket and the rug over him, and put his head on the cushion. He had to lie curled up, because the tree house was really very small. On the other hand, Ern was not really very big!

He began to get warm. He felt quite comfortable. He yawned a huge yawn. At the same moment, an owl passed by the tree and hooted.

'Hoo! Hoo-hoo-hoo-HOO!'

Ern was up like a shot. Was that old Fatty back again? He peered out of the tree but could see nothing – not even a sign of Goon and his companion. The gardens lay bathed in the brilliant moonlight, undisturbed and peaceful. The owl flew by again, and this time Ern saw it.

'Hoo!' began the owl, 'hoo, hoo . . .'

Ern put his hands to his mouth in the proper position for hooting, and joined in loudly. 'Hoo-HOO-HOO-HOO-HOO!'

The owl gave a frightened 'tvit' and swerved off at once. Ern watched it go. 'Now don't you come hooting round me again!' he said. 'I've had enough of you tonight!'

And once more, Ern cuddled down in his newspapers and blankets and shut his eyes! This time he fell fast asleep, and slept for about two hours.

Then a noise awakened him. At first he couldn't think where he was. He sat up in a fright. Then he saw the moonlight outside the tree and remembered. What had awakened him?

He heard a noise. It was a quiet, humming kind of noise, some way away. Was it an aeroplane? Perhaps. Was it a car far away on a road? Yes, it sounded more like that.

Ern lay down again. He shut his eyes. Then he heard another noise and sat up.

Splash! Splash-splash! Ern looked out of the tree again. Was somebody swimming in the river at this time of night? No, not on a frosty night in January! Still, there was that soft splash-splash again! Ern strained his eyes over towards the river.

He saw something white sailing on it – two white things – and one or two shadowy ones behind. He laughed.

'It's the swans, and their babies! I'm daft!

Imagining all kinds of things when it's only a couple of swans and their family. Well, fancy them keeping awake all night! I thought they put their heads under their wings and slept.'

Ern lay down again, determined that he wouldn't be disturbed by any more noises. There was no sign of Goon now, or of his companion. The owl had stopped hooting. The swans had stopped splashing. He didn't mean to let himself be disturbed by ANYTHING else!

He was soon half-asleep. Small noises came to him on the night wind, and once he thought he heard voices, but was sure he was dreaming. He imagined he heard a dog barking and half-opened his eyes. Yes, it was. Probably Poppet – it sounded exactly like her high little bark.

Ern fell into such a sound sleep that not even the owl awoke him when it came and sat on his very tree, and gave a sudden mournful hoot. Ern slept on. Dawn came slowly, and the sun sent golden fingers into the sky. Soon it would be light.

Ern awoke. He sat up, bewildered, but then remembered everything. He'd better get up and climb down the tree. His aunt would wonder where he was – she must be up and about.

Ern was just about to climb down the tree when he heard shouting. Loud, angry shouts – and then he heard bangs – bang-bang-bang! BANG, BANG, BANG! Goodness gracious, what was all that? Ern slithered down the tree and went to the hedge and listened. The noise came from somewhere in the grounds of Tally-Ho House. Ern wondered what it was. It couldn't be Fatty back again, and in trouble, surely!

He slipped through the hedge and went by the Larkins' cottage. The door opened and the old man came out, plump in his old overcoat, his scarf and cap on as usual. He limped over to Ern.

'What's that noise?' he said, in his hoarse voice. 'You go and see. My wife's ill today and I don't want to leave her.'

Ern nodded at the dirty old man and went cautiously in the direction of the noise. It grew louder. BANG-BANG! HELP! LET US OUT! BANG-BANG!

Ern was mystified. Who was locked in and where – and why? It wasn't Fatty's voice, thank goodness.

Ern went in the direction of the noise. It sounded round the further corner of the house, where the boiler house was. Ern turned the corner and saw the small boiler house not far off.

Yes, the noise was coming from there. Ern looked at the little place fearfully. He wasn't letting anyone out till he knew who they were!

He went cautiously up to the boiler house and stood on a box outside to look in at the small window. He was so astounded at what he saw that he fell off the box.

Inside the boiler house, furiously angry, were Mr Goon and the other policeman! Their helmets were hanging on a nail. Ern saw two hot, furious faces upturned to him as he appeared at the window, and heard more loud shouts.

'Open the door! ERN! What you doing here? OPEN THE DOOR AND LET US OUT!'

Goon had been most astonished to see Ern's scared face at the tiny little window, but very thankful. Now perhaps they could get out of this stifling boiler house and get something to eat and drink.

'Why did we ever come in here?' groaned

Goon, as he heard Ern struggling with the large, stiff key in the outer side of the door. 'It was so cold, and it seemed such a good idea to light up the boiler and shut the door and have a little warm!'

'Must have been the fumes that sent us off to sleep so sudden-like,' said his companion dolefully. 'I feel as if my head's bursting. Drat that boy, why can't he unlock the door?'

'Hurry up, Ern, you dolt!' roared Mr Goon. 'We're cooking-hot in here.'

'Who locked us in?' said the other man. 'That's what *I* want to know. It wouldn't be the Lorenzos, would it now? They couldn't have come after all, could they?'

'No! I've told you, it was that boy Frederick Trotteville – the one we found here last night,' said Goon crossly. 'One of his funny tricks – ho, he'll laugh on the other side of his face this time. I'm going straight to the Chief about this, dead straight! Locking us into a boiler house – why, we might have been dead with the fumes this morning! ERN, what you doing out there? You've only got to turn the key. Are you asleep, boy?'

'No, Uncle. And don't you talk to me like that

when I'm doing my best to help you,' panted Ern. 'It's a whopping big key and very rusty. I've a good mind to leave you here if you don't talk proper to me when I'm trying hard.'

Mr Goon was amazed to hear this cheek from Ern. But he had to swallow his wrath and speak in honey-like tones, afraid that Ern really would go off and leave them.

'Now Ern, it's only because we're almost cooked,' he said. 'I know you're doing your best. Ah, there's a good lad – the key's turned!'

Ern fled as his uncle and the second policeman walked out of the boiler house. One look at their beetroot-like faces and protruding eyes was enough for him. Goon and his companion walked with as much dignity as they could muster past the Larkins' cottage on their way to the river.

The old fellow came out of his door, shuffling as usual. 'What was the matter?' he said, in his hoarse voice.

'Tell you later,' said Goon, who was not particularly anxious that the tale of the boiler house should go all round Peterswood. 'Nothing much. We just kept watch last night, that's all.

You didn't hear anything, did you? We never heard a sound, so we're going off-duty now.'

Mr Goon went back to his house and took up the telephone, a grim look on his face. He made a brief report, which caused quite a stir at the other end. It even made the Chief himself come to the telephone.

'Goon? What's this story about Frederick Trotteville? I don't believe it.'

'Sir, I wouldn't tell you such a story if it wasn't true,' said Goon earnestly. 'And PC Johns, who was with me, will tell you that this boy was in the grounds last night, snooping round after us – one of his little jokes, sir, this was. He thought it would be funny to lock us in.'

'But what were you doing in the boiler house, Goon, when you should have been outside on duty?' said the Chief's sharp voice.

'Just looking round, sir,' said Goon, and then let his imagination get the better of him. 'We heard footsteps outside, sir, then the door banged and the key turned in the lock, and we heard Frederick's laugh, sir – a most horrible laugh, sir, and . . .

'That's enough, Goon,' said the Chief's voice.

'All right. I'll see to this. Did you hear or see anything at all last night?'

'Nothing at all, sir,' said Goon, and then the telephone was clicked off at the Chief's end. Goon stood quite still, his face red with delight.

'Ho, you toad of a boy,' he said. 'Now you've gone too far at last. You're finished!'

15. FATTY IS PLEASED

Fatty was just going down to breakfast when a big black police car swept up the drive to the front door, and out got Superintendent Jenks, looking rather grim. Fatty was thrilled.

He's got some news! And he wants me to help in some way! thought Fatty joyfully. He went to open the door himself.

'I want a word with you, Frederick,' said the Chief, and Fatty led him into the study, struck with the Superintendent's sharp voice.

Once the door was shut, the Chief looked straight at Fatty.

'What possessed you to lock Goon and the other fellow up last night?' he demanded grimly.

Fatty stared in surprise. 'I don't know what you mean, sir,' he said at last. 'I really don't. Where am I supposed to have locked them up? In the cells?'

'Don't play the fool,' said the Chief, his eyes like gimlets, boring into poor Fatty. 'Don't you realise that you can go a bit too far with your jokes on Goon?'

'Sir,' said Fatty earnestly, 'do believe me when I say I haven't the remotest idea what you are talking about. I saw Mr Goon last night, in the grounds of Tally-Ho House, where I was keeping watch in case the Lorenzos turned up – I had seen a report that they had been spotted at Maidenhead. Mr Goon had another policeman with him. I left the grounds a few minutes after I had seen them and said a few words to them, and went straight home to bed. They were not locked up when I left them. I must ask you to believe me, sir. I never tell lies.'

The Chief relaxed, and sat down. 'Right, I believe you, of course, Frederick,' he said. 'But I must say it's odd how you always turn up in the middle of things. Goon and Johns were locked up all night in the boiler house at Tally-Ho, and Ern let them out this morning.'

'Ern!' said Fatty, startled.

'Yes, *he* seemed to be about too,' said the Chief.

'Goon and Johns were apparently half-cooked, the boiler house was so hot.'

'The boiler wasn't going when I left them, sir,' said Fatty. 'I'd have noticed if it was – I'd have seen the glow when I went near it.'

'Oh. Then who lit it?' said the Chief.

'Goon and Johns, I suppose,' said Fatty. 'It was a cold night, and they might have thought it a good idea to light up the boiler and have a warm, sir. And possibly they – er – well, quite possibly they fell asleep.'

'Yes. That thought also occurred to me,' said the Chief.

'It might have been the fumes that sent them off, of course,' said Fatty generously. 'They might not have meant to sleep there – only get warm.'

'Yes. Quite so,' said the Superintendent. 'Still, the fact remains that SOMEBODY locked them in.'

'Yes. WHO?' said Fatty. 'Do you think the Lorenzos *could* have slipped back, sir – for some reason or other – perhaps to fetch the little poodle Mrs Lorenzo is so fond of – or even to get something from the house?'

'It's possible,' said the Chief. 'Yes, quite

possible. They've a reputation for being dare-devils. We'll find out if the dog is gone or if the house has been entered and anything personal taken – something that they had left behind and wanted. What a fathead that fellow Goon is, isn't he? Still, I'm glad I came over here. I'd like you to take a hand now, in this mystery, Frederick.'

'Oh, thank you very much, sir,' said Fatty, thrilled.

'I'm not telling Goon this, because he's such a blunderer,' said the Chief, 'but I have a distinct feeling that the Lorenzos are back in Peterswood for some reason or other – perhaps, as you say, to get back the dog. Mrs Lorenzo is quite mad about it – idolises it – and I think it possible that they will try to get it. Or again, it's just possible that they didn't take the picture with them, but have left it behind in case they were caught – for some accomplice to fetch.'

'But what about the crate they were said to have been seen with up north?' asked Fatty.

'That might have been a blind to put us off,' said the Chief. 'They're clever, these Lorenzos. You wouldn't believe the things they've done

– and got away with too. They are about the cleverest tricksters I've had to deal with.'

'Well, I'll be proud to help,' said Fatty, as the Chief got up to go. 'Is there any particular thing you'd like me to do?'

'No. Go your own way. Do what you like,' said the Chief. 'Short of locking Goon up in a boiler house, of course! Though I feel very like doing that myself this morning!'

Fatty saw him off and went into the breakfast room feeling most elated. So Goon had told the Chief a thumping big lie about him, had he? Well, it hadn't done him any good. He, Fatty, was now more or less in charge of something that was turning out to be jolly interesting – in fact, a very promising mystery!

Ern came to see Fatty immediately after his breakfast. He had had to do a lot of explaining to his aunt about his night in the tree house, but it was over at last. Now all he wanted to do was to tell Fatty about Goon and his companion in the boiler house – and how they had said that it was Fatty who locked them in.

'*Did* you, Fatty?' said Ern, looking at him in awe. He was half-disappointed when Fatty shook his head.

'No, Ern. Much as I wish I could have done it, I didn't. Ern, you were up in that tree all night you say. Did you hear or see anything at all?'

'Well, owls, of course,' said Ern. 'What with you and me and the owls *all* hooting . . .'

'I don't mean owls,' said Fatty. 'Think hard, Ern – did you hear any out-of-the-way sounds at all?'

Ern thought back to his night in the tree. 'Well, I heard a kind of humming noise,' he said. 'I thought at first it was an aeroplane. But it might have been a car.'

'Ah,' said Fatty. 'Go on. Anything else?'

'I heard splashing, and saw the swans swimming in the moonlight,' said Ern. 'They looked as white as snow. And I *thought* I heard voices once, and a dog barking.'

Fatty was alert at once. 'Voices? A dog barking? Would that be Poppet?'

'Yes. I think it was,' said Ern. 'Her bark is sort of high, isn't it? – more like a yelp.'

'You're *sure* about the voices?' said Fatty. 'And the barking? You see, *some*body besides me and Goon and Johns must have been there last night – and locked them up!'

'Coo, yes,' said Ern. 'Lot of people about last night, it seems! Well, these voices and barking were some time after you'd left. I tell you, I was half-asleep by then.'

'You couldn't have heard voices unless they had been fairly *near,*' said Fatty, frowning and thinking hard. 'Would they have been in or near the Larkins' cottage, do you think?'

'Well, I don't reckon I'd have heard them if they'd been *inside* the cottage,' said Ern. 'I'd have heard them *outside* all right.'

'Did Poppet's bark sound pleased or frightened?' asked Fatty.

'Pleased,' said Ern, at once.

'Oh. That's interesting,' said Fatty. '*Very* interesting. Ern, I think the Lorenzos came to get their dog from the Larkins last night – and perhaps to get a few things from the big house as well. They saw Goon and Johns asleep as they passed the boiler house and neatly locked them in.'

'You're right, Fatty,' said Ern, in great admiration. 'It's wonderful to see how you work these things out. Well, if the dog's gone, we'll *know* it was the Lorenzos who were there last night.'

'Yes. But it doesn't *really* get us any further forward,' said Fatty. 'I mean, we still won't know where the Lorenzos are – or where the picture is either.'

'You'll find all that out too, Fatty, I'm sure you will,' said Ern solemnly. 'You and your brains!'

'You go and tell the others to meet down in my shed at half past nine,' said Fatty. 'We'll all have a talk together.'

So, at half past nine, the whole company was gathered together in the little shed, and heard the grand tale of the night in the grounds of Tally-Ho, and all that had happened there. Pip was so tickled to hear about Goon and Johns being locked in the boiler house that he laughed till he ached.

'Now the first thing we must do is to go up to the Larkins and find out about Poppet,' said Fatty. 'If she's gone, it proves that the Lorenzos were there last night. We'll then put the Larkins through a lot of questions, and try to get out of them what really did happen last night.'

'Right,' said Larry. 'Let's go now.'

'We shan't be able to see *Mrs* Larkin,' said Ern. 'She's ill. I saw old Bob Larkin this morning when I went to set Mr Goon free. He heard the shouting and banging too.'

'Well, we can perhaps get something out of Larkin,' said Fatty. 'Everyone got their bikes?'

Everyone had. Buster was put into Fatty's basket, and off they all went. They chose the river path again because the Larkins' cottage was so near it.

They leaned their bikes against the railings, and marched up the path to the cottage. Fatty knocked on the door.

It opened and out came Mr Larkin, still with his cap and scarf on, though he had discarded his overcoat and now wore a shapeless, baggy old tweed jacket.

'Oh, what do you want?' he said in his hoarse voice, peering through the thick lenses of his glasses at the six silent children. When he saw

Buster, he shut the door behind him, and stood just outside it.

'Er, Mr Larkin, could we have a word with you?' asked Fatty.

'I don't charge nuffin' for that,' said the man. 'What's up?'

'Er – could we come inside? It's a bit cold out here,' said Fatty, feeling certain that Mr Larkin had carefully shut the door behind him so that they couldn't see that the little dog was no longer running about inside.

'You can come in if you leave your dog outside,' said the man. 'I don't want the little poodle upset. She's over-excited today.'

Fatty stared. It sounded as if the poodle was still there! 'She's in her basket, beside my wife,' said Larkin hoarsely. He coughed.

Oho! thought Fatty, so *that's* going to be the tale! His wife's not well – keeps to her bed – and the poodle keeps her company – though really it has been taken away in the night. Very clever. The Lorenzos must have thought that out!

'I'd like to see the poodle,' said Bets suddenly, seeing that Fatty was now in a difficulty. 'Can

I go into your wife's room and stroke her?'

'No,' said the man. The children looked at one another. Very, very suspicious!

And then something surprising happened. A loud excited barking came from the little cottage – then a patter of feet could be heard – and then the little white poodle appeared at the kitchen window, her nose pressed against the pane as if she was looking for Buster! *How* all the children stared!

16. A RECAP!

All the six stared at Poppet as if they couldn't believe their eyes! As for Buster, he nearly went mad with excitement to see the dear little poodle with her nose at the window, looking down at him.

Poppet wagged her tail hard and barked loudly. She seemed full of life and happiness – quite different from when they had seen her before.

I suppose she's so pleased because she saw her beloved mistress last night – but did she, after all? We just thought it must be the *Lorenzos* who had come and gone – and fetched Poppet. But it might have been anyone, now, because Poppet is still here! Gosh – I've got to work things out all over again! Fatty frowned as he stood looking at the dog.

Mr Larkin stood blinking at the children through his thick glasses. He wiped his sleeve across his nose and began to shuffle away, half limping as he went.

'Mr Larkin!' called Fatty. 'Just half a minute – did you hear much disturbance last night? Did you see anyone – or do you know who locked up the two policemen?'

Larkin shook his head. 'I heard noises,' he said. 'But I didn't stir from out my bed.'

He shuffled off towards the boiler house, and the children watched him go.

Fatty looked back at the little cottage. Somebody *had* come there last night – Ern had heard voices and that meant that people were talking outside the cottage. Larkin was not telling the truth when he said he had not stirred from his bed. He *had* left his bed to open his door and talk to someone. Had he taken a message? Had he – ah yes – had he perhaps taken in a parcel – a *crate*? It would surely be an ingenious idea to bring the picture back and store it in the little cottage!

He went to the window where Poppet was still barking, pawing at the pane excitedly. He looked in cautiously, trying to see what was in the small room. It was a poor, dirty place, with makeshift furniture. There was certainly no crate there, or large, wrapped-up parcel.

There was no sign of Mrs Larkin. Larkin had told Ern she was ill, so presumably she was in bed in the back room.

A thought suddenly struck him. Could the Larkins *possibly* be hiding the Lorenzos? The couple were apparently unable to get out of the country, and must be on the run, hiding here and there, running the risk of being spotted. It would be a clever thing to do to come and hide in the very place where no one would think they would dare to be!

There didn't seem anything else to do now but walk away. Now that Poppet *was* still there, after all, new plans would have to be made, and new ideas thought of. Especially some plan that would bring in the possibility of searching the cottage in case the Lorenzos *were* hiding there!

'Larry! Pip! Let's go!' called Fatty. 'Hey, Buster, stop trying to paw down the wall under Poppet's window. Come on, Bets and Daisy – you coming too, Ern? Let's go back to my shed and talk.'

They left Poppet still barking happily at the

window, her stiff tail wagging hard. There was no sign of Larkin. He was presumably raking out the boiler fire, still warm from the night before.

They all rode off together, Fatty thinking hard. They piled their bicycles against Fatty's shed, and went in. Fatty lit the little oil-stove.

'Biscuits on that shelf, Larry,' he said. 'Lemonade below – or shall we have cocoa? I feel cold.'

Everyone voted for cocoa, and Pip was sent up to the kitchen to ask for milk.

'We can boil it on the oil-stove as usual,' said Fatty. 'Daisy, will you see to it?'

It was soon cosy and warm in the shed, and the milk boiled quickly on the top of the stove. Everyone sat down on boxes or rugs, Ern too. He loved times like this. He gazed round the shed in awe – coo, the things that old Fatty had there!

Fatty's shed was indeed a medley of all kinds of things – old clothes of every kind for disguises – a few wigs hanging on nails – boxes of make-up, with many kinds of moustaches inside, as well as grease paint and powder. There was no end to the fascinating array. There was even a postman's hat and uniform! Now, how in the world did Fatty get that? Ern wondered.

Once they were all supplied with biscuits and hot cocoa, Fatty began to talk.

'I think the time has come for a recap,' he said. 'We . . .'

'What's a recap?' said Bets, much to Ern's relief. He too had no idea what Fatty meant by a 'recap' but did not dare to ask.

'Oh, recap is short for recapitulation,' said Fatty. 'I . . .'

'Yes, but I don't know what recapit – pit – whatever you said, is either,' said Bets.

'Dunce!' said Pip, in his brotherly way.

'All right, you tell her what it is, Pip,' said Fatty, at once.

'Well, it's – it's – well, I don't exactly know how to explain it, but I know what it means,' said Pip.

'Dunce!' said Fatty, and turned to Bets. 'A recap just means I'll go quickly over all that has happened, so as to give us a clear picture, and then it makes future planning easier. Got it, Bets?'

'Oh yes,' said Bets gratefully. 'Go ahead, Fatty.'

Fatty began. 'Well, the tale begins when we all

saw the Lorenzos that day at the station, being seen off by their friends. Poppet was with them – but was given to old Larkin who had apparently been told to fetch her and take her home when the Lorenzos had departed in the train. He went off with her under his coat. Correct?'

'Correct,' said everyone.

'Right. The next thing we heard was that the police were after the Lorenzos because they had apparently been clever enough to steal a very valuable picture from some picture gallery. They probably meant to leave this country with it and sell it abroad somewhere. Correct?'

'Correct,' chorused everyone.

'They were then spotted here and there, and apparently gave up the idea of trying to get out of the country for the time being. A crate was seen in a car which they stole to get away from one of their hiding-places – presumably containing the picture.'

'But, Fatty, they only had two little suitcases with them when *we* saw them,' said Daisy. 'No crate at all.'

'Well, they wouldn't go off on a journey with

an enormous crate!' said Fatty. 'I imagine that after they had stolen the picture, frame and all, they got some friend of theirs, someone as dishonest as themselves, to hide the picture for them – and have it crated and put ready for them at some place where they could call for it.'

'So wherever they go, they've got to take the picture with them now, I suppose?' said Pip. 'A bit of a nuisance, I should think!'

'A *great* nuisance!' said Fatty. 'But unless they can undo the crate, destroy it, take out the picture and hide it somewhere really safe, they've *got* to carry it around!'

'And that's what they've been doing,' said Larry. 'And I bet they've brought it here and hidden it somewhere! I bet they came last night with it!'

'I was coming to that,' said Fatty. 'It does seem to me that if they *were* seen at Maidenhead they would not have come so near their home if they were not making for it for some reason. And the only reasons that are possible are – to hide the picture, and to take Poppet.'

'And they *didn't* take Poppet,' said Bets.

'No they didn't, so we were wrong there,' said Fatty. 'Well, I think perhaps we were silly to think they'd take that little poodle. Once it had disappeared from the Larkins, the police would have been told to keep a watch-out for a couple with a beautiful little poodle – you can't hide a dog if it's with you all the time!'

'They could have dyed it black,' said Bets.

'Oh yes, they would certainly have done that,' said Fatty. 'But it would still be a poodle and would arouse suspicion, black, white or red, if the police were looking for one accompanying a couple of people in a hotel, or boarding-house, or wherever the Lorenzos went.'

'I suppose we come now to last night,' said Pip. 'Ern's the only one who really knows about that.'

'Yes. Ern, relate what you know,' said Fatty. 'We already know it, but it might clear things a bit, and make us think of something new.'

Ern cleared his throat and stood up as if he were going to recite in class.

'Well, I was asleep in the tree house and a noise woke me up – a sort of humming noise, like an aeroplane or car. Then after a bit, I heard splashing and I looked out and saw the swans on the river, sailing on the water. Fine they looked, too. Then I went to sleep and I woke up again thinking I heard voices not far off – maybe outside the Larkins' cottage – and I heard Poppet barking madly, sort of happy-like. That's all.'

Ern sat down abruptly, blushing red. Everyone felt as if they really ought to clap, but nobody did. Bets gave him an admiring smile and Ern felt proud of himself.

'Now we come to this morning, when we all go off expectantly to the Larkins' cottage, feeling sure that Poppet will be gone – and, lo and behold, she is there, as happy as a sand-boy!' said Fatty.

'Which is a bit funny,' said Larry, 'because the Larkins haven't been nice to her, as *we* know!'

'Yes,' said Fatty. 'Well, there's our recap, Bets. Now, has anyone any remarks to make, or any good suggestions?'

'I'm sure the Lorenzos were there last night, because Poppet is so happy this morning,' said Pip.

'I thought that too,' said Bets. 'But now I'm

wondering! If they had come *and gone* last night, wouldn't Poppet be down in the dumps again?'

'You've got a point there, Bets,' said Fatty.

'I say! Perhaps they're still there!' said Pip. 'Hiding in the cottage!'

'Yes. Or perhaps in the house,' said Daisy, 'the *big* house, I mean. They would have keys, wouldn't they?'

'Oh yes,' said Fatty. 'Actually it did cross my mind that the Larkins might be hiding the Lorenzos. It would make the cottage very crowded though – and the Larkins would be scared in case the police came to search. But Poppet is so very happy that I can't help thinking they are still somewhere about. *Mrs* Lorenzo anyhow!'

'Fatty! Can't we somehow manage to look in the cottage?' said Bets. 'Oh, do think of some way. It would be too marvellous if *we* discovered the Lorenzos, after the police have been looking for them for ages!'

'Right. That's a good plan,' said Fatty. 'Does anyone happen to know if the cottage has got electric light? I didn't notice. Very remiss of me!'

'Yes. It has,' said Larry, surprised. 'Fatty! What are you going to do? I *know* you've got a plan. What is it?'

17. OFF TO TALLY-HO HOUSE

Fatty certainly had a plan. That was quite clear. His eyes shone and he looked excited.

'Yes! I'll tell you what I'll do! I'll dress up as an electricity man, and go to the Larkins' cottage to read the meter!' He looked round at the others with a broad grin.

Larry slapped him on the back. 'Wizard! You can get right in then and it wouldn't take you a minute to see if there was any place for people to hide in that tiny cottage. There can only be three rooms at the most – all downstairs. There's no second storey.'

'It's a pity Mrs Larkin is ill, or you could have gone today,' said Bets.

'Blow!' said Fatty. 'I forgot that for the moment. I can't very well go blundering into the cottage if she's sick in bed.'

'I'll watch from the tree house,' said Ern,

excited. 'If I see her about, I'll nip along and tell you, Fatty. I'll sit up there all the afternoon.'

'Right,' said Fatty. 'Well, anyone else got any suggestions or brainwaves?'

'I was wondering how the Lorenzos arrived last night,' said Daisy. 'If they came by car – which would be rather a silly thing to do, I should think – wouldn't the car be hidden somewhere in the grounds? That's if the Lorenzos themselves are still in hiding there, I mean. Unless, of course, someone drove them there and dropped them off. It might have been the car that Ern heard.'

'That's a point too,' said Fatty. 'We could go up to the grounds this afternoon, and have a look at the drive entrances. If we see recent tracks, we'll know a car came last night – and we'll look for it!'

'Another thing,' said Pip, 'can we find out if the big house has been entered by the Lorenzos? They might even have been daring enough to go into it and hide the picture there. The house has been already searched for that – so it might be a very good hiding-place.'

'Yes. We can find that out too,' said Fatty. 'I

could ring up the Superintendent to ask him if he's had any report about it.'

'Well, we're getting on!' said Pip. 'My mind is certainly a lot clearer since our recap!'

'I don't see that there's anything more we can suggest,' said Larry. 'At the moment, we are going on the hope that the Lorenzos came by car last night, hid it in the grounds, got into the big house, hid the picture there, went to the Larkins and woke them up, and persuaded them to let them into the cottage to hide till all the hoo-ha has blown over.'

'Right!' said Fatty. 'You put that very well, Larry. This has been a very good conference – *real* detectives couldn't have had a better one! Now, let me see – my first job is to ring up the Superintendent and ask if he knows whether the house was entered last night or not. Next, we must go up this afternoon and examine the drive entrances. Third, I must disguise myself as a meter reader, and see if I can examine the cottage.'

'Meter readers carry a kind of card backed by a board with elastic round, don't they?' said Daisy. 'I know ours does. And a peaked cap – and a torch to read the meter. That's all. Ours doesn't have a uniform.'

'I'll find out from our cook,' said Fatty. 'But I don't think it much matters what I wear really, so long as I produce a card and flourish a torch, and announce "Come to read your meter, Mam!" in a loud voice.'

They all laughed. 'You'll get into the cottage all right if you say it like that!' said Bets.

'I say! What about you dressing up in whatever you're going to wear, and coming with us to examine the drive entrances,' said Larry. 'You can put your torch and cap and card into your pocket to use if we find out that Mrs Larkin is out and about again. Otherwise, you'd be sitting at home waiting for Ern to nip down and fetch you as soon as he saw any sign of Mrs Larkin. And if he *doesn't* see anything of her, you'll be moping at home all alone!'

'Yes. That's an idea,' said Fatty. 'Ern, listen – you can do what you suggested this afternoon, and sit up in the tree house, with a whistle – and if you see anything of Mrs Larkin, just whistle three times, because we shall be somewhere snooping around the grounds.'

'Whistle *twice* if you want to warn us about anything – Goon or strangers and so on,' said Larry. 'Three times for Mrs Larkin.'

'And I'll then come up to the cottage and do my meter reading act,' said Fatty. 'Well, is that all understood?'

'Yes,' said everybody.

'Be here at two thirty,' said Fatty. 'We'll all go together – except you, of course, Ern. You'll be up in the tree as soon after your dinner as you can, won't you?'

'Yes, Fatty,' said Ern importantly. Then he leapt to his feet with a yell that startled everyone considerably and set Buster barking madly.

'Coo, look at the time! Twenty to one and my Aunt Woosh said I was to be back by half past twelve. I won't get no dinner at all! So long, everybody!'

Ern disappeared up the garden path at top speed, Buster running excitedly beside him. Everyone laughed. Good old Ern!

That afternoon at half past two, everyone but Ern was outside Fatty's house with their bicycles.

Fatty, looking rather peculiar, came out with his, Buster with him.

'Are you going to take Buster?' said Bets, pleased. 'I didn't think you would.'

'Well, I can leave him with you if Ern gives the signal for me to go and do some meter reading!' said Fatty. 'He does so badly want to come – don't you, Buster?'

'Wuff!' said Buster joyfully. He couldn't bear it when the children went off without him. He ran beside the bicycles as they all rode off. Fatty said the run would take off some of his fat, and it wasn't too far for him to run all the way to the river.

'Wait, we're not *going* to the river path this time!' said Larry, as they all turned down the river road. 'We've forgotten, we're going to the drive gates that open on to the lane that leads out of the main road.'

'So we are!' said Pip, and they all swerved the other way. Bets looked at Fatty and giggled.

'You don't really look respectable enough to come riding with us,' she said. 'Did you *have* to make yourself so untidy, Fatty?'

'Not really,' said Fatty, with one of his grins. 'I just let myself go, rather!'

He wore an old suit, too big for him, no collar but a scarf instead, and had brushed his hair over his forehead instead of back. In his pocket was a cap with a black shiny peak, a card with figures scribbled on it, backed by a small board, a pencil tied to it with string, and a torch.

'No Electricity Board would employ *you* as a meter reader,' said Bets. 'For one thing, you're not only untidy but you don't look *old* enough.'

'Oh, I'll soon remedy *that*!' said Fatty, and put his hand into his pocket. He pulled out a silly little moustache and stuck it on his upper lip. At once he looked older. Bets laughed.

'You look really *dreadful*! I'm sure no one would ever let you into their house!'

They turned off the main road and came into the little lane that led to the entrance gates of Tally-Ho. They got off when they came to the big gateposts.

The big double gates were shut. There were two at each entrance to the long, curving drive. Fatty looked at them.

'Well! Whoever drove in there with a car would have quite a business opening those big gates – they're so heavy. I wonder why they're shut?'

'So that people can't drive in, I suppose,' said Larry. 'Fatty, did you ring up the Chief about the house, to know if by any chance anyone had got into it last night?'

'Yes, I did. And, apparently, even if the Lorenzos had keys to the back, front and side doors, it wouldn't be any good,' said Fatty. 'All the doors have been bolted inside, except a side door. The police bolted them all – and got out by the side door in which they have had a special lock fitted. So nobody can get in except the police – and they only by the side door! Apparently there are a lot of valuable things in Tally-Ho belonging to its real owner – the ones who let the house furnished to the Lorenzos.

'Oh. Well then we needn't bother about the house,' said Larry. 'We'll just concentrate on trying to find out if a car came here last night, and is hidden away somewhere.'

Fatty was looking at the ground, which was very frosty that day. 'There are wheel marks,' he said, 'but I can't tell if they are old or new. Anyway, of course, they might be the marks of any police car that has been here.'

Pip had gone up to the gates to look through them. He gave a sudden exclamation. 'Look here – no car could come through these gates – they have a wooden bar nailed across them!'

The others went to see. Pip was right. A bar was nailed right across each of the double gates. Obviously the police did not mean anyone to go to the house at the moment!

'Well, that rather rules out the Lorenzos coming by car, and leaving it in the grounds,' said Fatty. 'Let's go to the river path entrance, and see if Mr Larkin is anywhere about. He might have something to say for once. You never know!'

They went back, and took the road down to the river path. They were soon standing outside the wicket gate.

'Look!' said Bets. 'The swans again. What a pity we haven't any bread for them!'

They stood and watched them, the big swans leading the little cygnets to the bank. A boat came by, the oars splashing in the water with a pleasant noise. The swans swam off out of the boat's way.

'Splash-splash!' said Bets, remembering something. 'Ern said he remembered hearing splashes in the night. I wonder now – could he have heard a *boat*?'

'Gosh! I never thought of that!' said Fatty. 'A boat! Yes, they could have come by boat, of course! Let's look and see if there's one in the boathouse – that's the boathouse belonging to Tally-Ho over there, isn't it?'

It was. It was not locked. The children pushed the little door open and looked inside. A small boat lay there, bobbing gently on the little ripples that ran into the boathouse.

Fatty looked at it. Its name was Tally-Ho, so there was no doubt that it belonged there. He was about to step into it when he stopped. A shrill sound had come to his ears.

'Ern's whistle!' he said. 'My goodness, he must have got hold of a *police* whistle! What a row! He's whistled three times – that is to say he's seen Mrs Larkin. I'll go and do my meter reading. Have a look round the boathouse while I'm gone, you others. I'll join you later!'

18. SOME VERY GOOD IDEAS

Fatty pulled on his cap with the black peak, and smoothed his ridiculous little moustache. He tightened the scarf round his neck, and off he went. The others grinned at one another.

'He'll be reading that meter in two minutes!' said Pip. 'I wish I was with him to see what happens.'

Fatty strode off to the wicket gate and went through it, whistling loudly. He marched straight up to the door – and then saw Mrs Larkin outside, with Poppet dancing about.

She looked round at him, startled. She really was a peculiar-looking person with her extraordinary wig, her dead-white face, and dark glasses. She sniffed loudly.

'What is it?' she said hoarsely, and coughed. She took out a dirty handkerchief from behind her dull red shawl, and wiped her nose vigorously. She coughed again and kept her handkerchief over her mouth, as if the cold air was too much for her.

'You've got a bad cold, Mam,' said Fatty politely. 'Sorry to bother you, but I've come to read the meter, if it's convenient.'

The woman nodded. She went to the little clothesline and began to take down some washing. Fatty took his chance and went into the house at once, hoping that Mr Larkin was not there.

There was no one in the front room. Fatty took a hurried look round, and could see nowhere at all for anyone to hide. He went into a back room – a small bedroom in which the bed took up most of the room. Nobody was there either. Fatty looked under the bed to see if anyone was hiding there. No, there were only cardboard boxes and rubbish of all kinds.

The little dog suddenly ran in and put her tiny paws on his leg. Fatty petted her and she wagged her tail. The woman called her, 'Poppet!', and the poodle rushed out again. Fatty went into the third room, an untidy kitchen, with a miserable little larder. There was not much in it, and it was very dirty.

What a place! thought Fatty. Certainly the Lorenzos are not being hidden by the Larkins – and, anyway, they'd never be able to endure hiding in a filthy little hole like this. Pooh, it smells!

He looked at the ceilings of the three rooms, wondering if there might be an attic or boxroom up above. There was no trapdoor, no opening of any kind. The Lorenzos were definitely not there – so that was that, thought Fatty!

The woman appeared at the little front door. 'Ain't you finished yet?' she said, her harsh voice grating unpleasantly on Fatty's ears. She sniffed and pulled her old shawl tightly round her.

'Yes. Just going,' said Fatty briskly, snapping the elastic round the card and the board he carried. 'Bit of a job to find the meter. Well, so long!'

He stepped out into the little garden. Then he looked back suddenly. 'Can I get into Tally-Ho House to read the meters?' he asked. 'I did hear as the folk had done a bunk. Did you know them?'

'It's none of your business,' said the woman sullenly. She sniffed again and shut the door. Poppet had gone in with her.

Well, I've learnt something definite – and that

is that the Lorenzos are certainly not being hidden in that cottage! he thought, as he made his way to the wicket gate.

He found Ern just outside, waiting for him. Ern had done his job of watching and whistling and now wanted to join up with the others again. He stared hard at Fatty.

'Lovaduck! You don't half look peculiar with that moustache, Fatty,' he said. 'Did you find out anything?'

'Only that the Lorenzos are definitely not there,' said Fatty. 'And we also decided that no car had been to the house last night, Ern, because the gates are nailed together with wooden bars.'

'Oh,' said Ern. 'It couldn't have been a car I heard then.'

'Ern, do you think the splashing noise you heard could have been *oars*?' asked Fatty, as they walked along to the boathouse.

'Oars? Well, yes, they might have been,' said Ern. He watched a boat coming up the river and nodded his head. 'Yes, of course! The noise those oars make is exactly like the splish-splash noise I heard.'

'Good! I didn't think it could be the swans,' said Fatty. 'They swim so silently. Well, we think now that perhaps last night's visitors came by *boat*!'

'By boat! Where from?' said Ern, startled.

'We don't know – we haven't thought yet,' said Fatty. He hailed the others as they came up to the boathouse. 'Here's Ern, and he thinks those splashes he heard *were* made by the oars of a boat!'

'Oh, it's you, Fatty!' said Bets, looking out of the boathouse door. 'Any news? You don't look very excited!'

'I'm not,' said Fatty, and went into the boathouse, where the others were waiting with Buster. 'I went to read the meter – which I couldn't find, by the way; and there are only three rooms in the place. There was absolutely no sign of the Lorenzos there. I only saw that awful woman with the wig and the sniffs. I must say she looks really ill.'

'Oh. Then we're all wrong again,' said Larry, in disappointment. 'The Lorenzos *aren't* hiding here! Now we've got to think of something else. Do you suppose they just came and went away again – without even taking Poppet?'

'Let's get into the boat and talk,' said Fatty. 'We're nice and private in this boathouse.'

They all got into the little boat and let it bob under them up and down, up and down, as the waves ran in and out.

'What I can't understand now is why the Lorenzos *came* last night – if it was them – talked to the Larkins, and then went away again,' said Fatty. 'And where did they come from, in the boat? They must have taken a boat from the opposite bank – or from somewhere further up or down the river . . .'

'Maidenhead!' said Bets, at once.

'Why yes, of course – *Maidenhead*!' said Fatty, at once. 'What an idiot I am! Of *course*, that's why they *went* to Maidenhead, so that they could come here by river.'

'Very long way to row,' said Larry. 'Miles!'

'Did they come by motorboat?' wondered Fatty – and immediately got a clap on the back from Ern.

'You've got it, Fatty! You've got it! *That* was the noise I heard last night! Not a car – nor an aeroplane – but a motorboat!'

The boat rocked with Ern's excitement! Fatty sat up straight. 'Yes, Ern! That's what you heard! And the oars you heard splashing were the oars of *this* boat going out in mid-stream to the motor-launch! She couldn't come close in here because the water's much too shallow!'

'WHO took this boat out to the launch?' said Larry at once. There was a pause as all the children sorted out these new ideas.

'There must be somebody here who took out the rowing-boat and brought one or both of the Lorenzos back in it,' said Pip. 'And then probably took them back to the motor-launch again, as they're not hiding here after all.'

'Then, if that's so, the only thing they could have come for would be to bring the picture here to hide!' said Fatty.

'Yes! And if it was Mrs Lorenzo, she came to see her little poodle too,' said Bets.

'I think you're right, Bets,' said Fatty. 'Certainly the poodle seems much happier now – and her little tail was wagging like anything. Just as if she had seen her mistress – and her master too, probably – and felt that they hadn't really deserted her.'

'I'm sure we're right,' said Daisy, in excitement. 'We've reasoned it all out really well! The Lorenzos went to Maidenhead in order to get here by boat. They came by motorboat – and old Larkin met them in this rowing-boat. He rowed them back here to the bank – helped them to carry the crated picture to shore – took Mrs Lorenzo to see her precious dog . . .'

'Yes! That's when I heard the talking and the barking!' said Ern, almost upsetting the boat in his excitement.

'And then, when the picture was put in some safe hiding-place, old Larkin rowed them out to the motorboat again, rowed himself back here and put the boat in this boathouse – and went to bed,' finished Fatty triumphantly.

'We've solved the mystery!' said Ern, thrilled. The others laughed.

'Indeed we haven't, Ern,' said Fatty. 'We still don't know the two important things – where the Lorenzos are – and where the picture is!'

'Sright!' said Ern, his excitement fading.

'We really ought to have a VERY GOOD LOOK for that hidden picture,' said Pip. 'We *know* it was brought here last night – at least, we're pretty sure – so it must be somewhere in the grounds. A big crate wouldn't easily be hidden. It's in some outhouse or somewhere like that. It might even be buried.'

'It's too late to look for it now,' said Fatty, looking at his watch.

'Oh, Fatty, just let's have a *quick* look round,' begged Bets. 'We could easily pop our heads into the greenhouses and outhouses.'

'All right,' said Fatty. 'Let's get out of this boat then. Be CAREFUL, Ern – you nearly upset us all, leaping out like that!'

'Hey, here's something at the bottom of the boat,' said Bets, 'something bright.' She bent down to get it. 'Oh – it's only a nice new drawing-pin, look!'

Fatty took it and stared at it. 'I bet I know where *that* came from!' he said, in excitement. 'From the crate the picture was in! I bet this was one of the pins that pinned the label to the crate – big crates usually have labels fastened on with drawing-pins. This is a good find, Bets – it's certain now that the picture and its crate were in this boat last night.'

'Come on, quickly! Let's find it!' cried Pip, and he too almost upset the boat as he leapt out. Everyone felt suddenly excited again.

'It's a clue!' said Bets, taking the pin from Fatty. 'Isn't it, Fatty? Our first real clue!'

Fatty laughed. 'I hope so. Come on, Buster – keep to heel.'

They all left the boathouse and went back to the wicket gate. They looked to see if the Larkins were anywhere about. There was a light already in the little cottage and the six felt sure that the old man and his wife were safely indoors.

They slipped silently into the grounds. Pip stopped and pointed over to a distant corner. 'What's that?' he said. 'It's a bonfire, isn't it? Let's go and see it. I could do with a bit of warmth!'

They were soon standing round the bonfire, which was roaring up as if it had had paraffin put on it. Bets gave a sudden exclamation, and bent down to pick something up. 'Fatty! Look, another drawing-pin, just like the other one. The crate must be somewhere here!'

19. A LITTLE BIT OF FUN

Fatty looked at the pin and compared it with the first one. Yes, they were exactly the same. Then he looked closely at the roaring flames. He picked up a fallen branch of dead wood and poked the fire, raking out what was in it.

'Look!' he said. 'Here's the crate! It's burning in the fire! It's been chopped up well, and thrown here – and then set alight so that no sign may be left of it!'

The children stared as Fatty pointed out bits of wood that had obviously come from a cheap crate. 'Here's a fragment of a label,' said Larry, pouncing on a burning piece of thick paper. He blew out the flames. Only three letters still showed on the paper.

'n-h-e,' said Larry. 'That's all that's left, I'm afraid.'

'It's enough,' said Fatty, at once. 'It tells us

where the crate comes from – where it was last sent to be picked up by the Lorenzos! "n-h-e" are the sixth, seventh and eighth letters of the word "Maidenhead"! Count and see!'

'Gosh, yes!' said Pip. 'You're very sharp, Fatty. Well, I suppose the picture's gone now – burnt with the crate, so that no one can discover it.'

'Don't be an idiot,' said Fatty. 'The picture has been *unpacked and hidden* – and the crate has been burnt to destroy all signs of it. It would be easy to hide just a painting. I expect it was cut neatly out of its frame – and then the frame and crate burnt together. There's some funny golden-looking stuff here and there in the fire – I bet that's all that is left of the lovely frame.'

The fire was still blazing, for the crate had been quite big. The children left it, certain that there was nothing more to be learnt there.

'We're getting warm!' said Fatty, as they walked away. 'We know now that the picture we have to look for is no longer in a big crate, nor even in a frame. It's probably just a rolled-up bit of canvas!'

'Yes. That would be *much* easier to hide!' said

Daisy. 'It's probably in the Larkins' house.'

'I don't think so,' said Fatty. 'The Lorenzos wouldn't give the picture itself into the care of those dirty old Larkins! They might easily ruin it. No, it's put in a very safe place – but not in that cottage!'

They went out of the wicket gate and took their bicycles. They were just about to walk them down the path to the river road when Fatty pulled them back.

'Look out! There's Mr Goon!' he said. And, sure enough, skulking in the shadows not very far in front of them was the familiar figure of Mr Goon!

'What's he doing?' whispered Fatty. 'He's following someone, isn't he?'

'Yes, there's a man some way ahead of him, carrying a bag of some kind,' whispered back Larry. 'Who is it?'

'I don't know. But we'll soon find out,' said Fatty briskly. 'As soon as we get to the road, and can ride our bikes, get on them and ride right up to Mr Goon, ringing your bells madly, just to tell him we're here – and then ride on as fast as you can to see who he's following. I've no idea who it can be – but we ought to find out if Mr Goon has got some kind of a suspect he's trailing!'

They leapt on their bicycles as soon as they reached the road and raced after Mr Goon, who was still hugging the shadows. It was getting dark now and the children had switched on their lamps. They made quite a bright light on the road. As they overtook Mr Goon, he crouched back into the shadows, not wanting to be seen.

Jingle-jingle-rrrrrr-ing, tinga-linga-long! went the bells as they raced past him.

'Night, Mr Goon!' yelled Fatty. 'Pleasant walk to you!'

'Goodnight, goodnight, Mr Goon,' shouted everyone, and Ern boldly yelled, 'Night, Uncle!' as he raced past, almost deafening Goon with his very loud bell.

'Gah!' said Mr Goon in angry disgust. Now they had warned the man he was trailing – yes, he had shot off into a nearby wood. He'd never find him again! Gah!

The six bicyclists saw the man quite clearly. It was Mr Larkin, with a shopping bag over his arm, shuffling along, his back bent and his head poked forward. His old cap was down over his nose as usual. He went into a little thicket of trees and disappeared.

'He must have been going shopping,' said Bets. 'Why is Mr Goon trailing him? Perhaps he thinks he may lead him to some clue!'

'Probably,' said Fatty. 'Well, he'll find it difficult to trail old Larkin now. How I'd love to lead Mr Goon a good old dance if he followed *me*!'

'Yes! You'd have him panting and puffing!' said Pip. 'You'd better disguise yourself as Larkin, and have some fun with Mr Goon!'

Fatty laughed. 'I've a jolly good mind to! I really have! It would serve Mr Goon right for telling that frightful fib about me to the Superintendent – saying I'd locked him up in the boiler house – and Johns too. I don't suppose either of them even *heard* the door being locked. I bet they were snoring too loudly.'

'Oh, Fatty – will you *really* dress up as Larkin? When?' asked Bets. 'Please, please show us yourself if you do.'

'All right,' said Fatty, feeling very drawn to the

idea of giving Goon a slight punishment for his untruthful tale to the Chief. 'I'll have my tea and then I'll have a shot at it. I only hope Mr Goon won't retire to bed for the evening, seeing that he had a late night last night! I'd dearly love to lead him round the town!'

'Don't forget to come and see us first!' called Bets, as they parted at the crossroads. Fatty grinned to himself as he rode on. Yes, he'd certainly like to have a bit of fun with Goon!

Fatty had a very good tea indeed. He had it by himself because his mother was out, and the cook, who completely spoilt him, piled his tray with all the things he liked best. By the time he had finished, Fatty didn't feel very like having a bit of fun with anyone!

Well, at any rate, I'm big enough to masquerade as the plump Mr Larkin! he thought, looking at himself in the long mirror down in his shed. Now then – let's sort out a few Larkin-like clothes.

He went rapidly through his enormous collection of clothes, pulling out drawer after drawer of the big old chest. Ah, baggy trousers, stained and messy. Good. Old boots. Frightful old overcoat – my very worst one!

He pulled out a coat that had long since been discarded by the last-but-one gardener the Trottevilles had had. Just right!

Scarf – dirty grey and raggedy. This will do. He shut his eyes for a moment and pictured old Bob Larkin clearly in his mind. Fatty had a wonderful gift for clear observation, and he could see the old fellow almost as if he were there before him.

Nasty little unkempt beard – straggly moustache – shaggy eyebrows – glasses with thick lenses – and a horrible cap with a peak pulled sideways over his face. Yes, I can do all that!

Fatty worked quickly and happily. First of all, he made up his face and changed it utterly. Wrinkles appeared, and shaggy eyebrows over eyes almost hidden under thick glasses. A straggly moustache, a tooth gone in front (Fatty blacked one out!), and a beard that he trimmed to resemble Mr Larkin's – thin and untidy. He glued it to his chin and looked at himself in the glass.

'You horrid old fellow!' said Fatty to his reflection. 'You nasty bit of work! Ugh! I don't like you a bit! Put on your scarf and cap!'

On went the scarf, and then the cap at exactly the right angle. Fatty grinned at himself. He was old Larkin to the life!

'I hope to goodness I don't meet Mummy coming in or she'll scream the place down!' said Fatty. 'Now, Buster, I regret to say I can't take you with me tonight – and, in any case, a self-respecting, well-brought-up dog like you wouldn't want to be seen out with an old rogue like me!'

Buster didn't agree. He didn't mind *how* Fatty looked – he was always his dearly-beloved master!

Fatty shut Buster up and made his way cautiously to the road. It was dark now and no one was about. Fatty took his bicycle and rode to Pip's. He gave their special whistle and Pip came flying down to the garden.

'Is it you, Fatty? I'm longing to see you. Larry and Daisy are here – and Ern's come along too. I can't see you here, it's too dark – it's quite safe to come up because Mummy's got a bridge party on. Don't make a noise, that's all.'

Fatty went up to the playroom. Pip flung the

door open and Fatty went in, bent and stooping, shuffling along with a half-limp just like old Larkin.

Bets gave a little scream. 'Oh no – it's not Fatty. It's Mr Larkin himself. Fatty's sent him in to trick us!'

'Lovaduck!' said Ern, startled.

'Marvellous, Fatty, marvellous!' cried Larry, and clapped him on the back.

Fatty gave a horrible hollow cough, and then cleared his throat as he had heard Larkin do. He spoke in a cracked old voice.

''Ere! Don't you slap the stuffing out of me like that, young feller! I'll have the police on you, straight I will. Yus – I'll call in me old pal, Mr Goon!'

They all roared with laughter. 'It's the best you've ever done, Fatty, quite the best. Oh, can't we come with you?'

'No,' said Fatty, straightening up and speaking in his own voice. 'For all we know, I won't find Mr Goon wandering about on the watch for me, thinking I'm Larkin – he'll probably be in his armchair, snoozing over a pipe.'

'You'd better go now,' said Pip urgently. 'I

can hear Mummy bustling about. She's probably coming up here to fetch something. Go, Fatty – and really good luck. You look simply FRIGHTFUL!'

Fatty went downstairs cautiously, and crept to the garden door just as Mrs Hilton came along to go up the stairs. He found the big black cat outside the garden door, waiting to come in, and gave her such a shock that she leapt into the night with a howl!

Fatty mounted his bicycle and rode off to Goon's. He saw a light in Goon's front window and looked in. Yes – Mr Goon was there, looking through some letters. Fatty decided to give him a fright.

He went up to the window, and pressed his face against it. Then he coughed his hollow cough. Mr Goon looked up at once, and gaped when he saw what he thought to be the face of old Larkin at his window.

'Hey, you!' cried Mr Goon. 'I want to speak to you! Hey!' He grabbed his helmet, put it on and rushed out.

Fatty hurried away, and then began to walk like old Larkin, shuffle-limp, shuffle-limp. Goon saw him in the distance and paused. Oho, so old Larkin had been spying on him through the window, had he? Well, he, Goon, would have another try at stalking him. Where was he going to at this time of night? Goon felt very, very suspicious of Mr Larkin!

Peering in at me like that! Must be mad! He knows more than he's said he does, thought Goon to himself, and set off after the supposed Mr Larkin, keeping well to the shadows.

Fatty chuckled. 'Come on, Mr Goon! I'll take you for a lovely walk! Do you good to take off some of your weight. Come along!'

20. A GOOD DEAL HAPPENS

Goon followed Fatty as closely as he dared. Fatty, looking back every now and again, decided to lead Goon to an allotment, where there were a few sheds. He could look into each one and make Goon wonder what he was doing.

He went as quickly as he could, shuffle-limp, shuffle-limp, and Goon marvelled that old Larkin could get along so quickly with his bad leg. Fatty, having a quick look round, also marvelled that big, burly Goon managed to hide himself so well in the dark shadows. Goon was really quite clever sometimes!

He came to the allotments, and Goon took a loud hissing breath! Oho! He was after tools or something, was he? That Larkin! He had never liked him, and now that he was mixed up in this Lorenzo case, Goon was even more suspicious of him. He even began to wonder if Larkin knew where the stolen picture was!

Fatty enjoyed himself. He examined sheds and even bent down to pick some grass, which Goon immediately noted. 'Ah – what's he picking now? Brussels sprouts, I'll be bound! The rascal!'

Fatty left the allotments and went into the children's playground not far off. Goon, standing behind a tree, watched him suspiciously. Now what was old Larkin going into the playground for? Something strange, anyway!

To his great astonishment, Fatty went to one of the swings and sat down. He began to swing to and fro watching the amazed Goon out of the corner of his eye.

Look at that! said the mystified Goon to himself. He must be daft – quite daft. Coming here at night to have a swing! Ah, he's off again. I wouldn't be surprised if he's not on the look out for a little burglary!

Fatty slipped out of the playground chuckling. He went into the well-lit main street. There someone stopped him.

'Well, Bob Larkin! Haven't seen you for

some time! Come and have a bite with me and my missus!'

Fatty looked at the speaker – a tall, thin man with a drooping moustache. He answered in Larkin's quavering old voice.

'I'm not too bad! Can't stop just now though. Got some business to do!' And off he went, shuffle-limp, shuffle-limp. Goon loomed up out of the shadows. Who was that that Larkin had spoken to? Had he come out to meet anyone – someone sent by the Lorenzos perhaps? Dark suspicions began to form in Mr Goon's mind. What was old Bob Larkin up to?

Fatty took him back to the playground again and had another swing. By this time, Goon didn't know whether to think that Larkin was completely mad, or was waiting about to meet somebody – and filling in his time with a few odd things such as having a swing.

He decided to tackle old Larkin. This wasn't funny any more – hanging about under bushes and trees on a cold January night, watching somebody rush up and down through the town, peep into sheds, swing to and fro . . . he'd have to find out what he was doing. So he hailed the shuffling fellow in front of him.

'Hey, you! Bob Larkin! I want to speak to you!' But the figure in front only hurried on more quickly, trying to keep under the dark trees. Goon became much more suspicious.

'Why doesn't he stop when he's told to! He knows my voice all right! HEY! BOB LARKIN!'

On went Fatty, grinning to himself. Come on, Mr Goon – a nice long walk will do you all the good in the world. Where shall we go now?

Fatty thought that a really good finish would be to take Goon right back to Larkin's cottage! He could easily disappear somewhere there, and Goon would think that old Larkin had gone into his little house. Fatty chuckled.

Goon soon realised that Larkin was off home, and he began to run. To his enormous surprise, the figure in front began to run too! Gone was the limp, gone was the shuffle! Goon couldn't believe his eyes.

Down to the river – along the river path – through the little wicket gate – up the path to Larkin's cottage which stood under the shadow of the tall tree that held Ern's tree house.

Goon panted after Fatty. Slam, went the gate and up the path came Goon, full of rage. He'd teach old Larkin to lead him a dance like this, and not answer when he was shouted at!

Fatty hid in a bush, and watched Mr Goon stride up to the little cottage. He knocked so fiercely on it with his knuckles that he almost scraped the skin off. The door opened cautiously, and Bob Larkin's head appeared in the crack, gazing at Goon's angry face in amazement.

'Now then, you!' said Goon angrily, 'what's the meaning of all this?'

'All what?' said Larkin.

Goon snorted. It was one of his very best snorts. 'Gah! Don't try and put it across me that you don't know what you've just been doing. Leading me such a dance – swinging in the playground . . .'

Larkin looked more and more amazed. He called back over his shoulder to Mrs Larkin. 'I haven't set foot out of doors tonight, have I?'

'No,' came back the answer, followed by a sniff and a cough.

'There you are!' said Larkin. 'You've made a silly mistake.' He tried to shut the door but Mr Goon put his big foot in to prevent him.

'You mean to tell me you haven't been trotting in front of me this last hour?' he panted in rage. 'You mean to tell me you didn't snoop in them allotment sheds to see what you could take – and . . .'

'You're mad!' said Mr Larkin, really alarmed now.

'What were you out for tonight?' asked Mr Goon. 'That's what I want to know. You'll be sorry for this, Larkin. Obstructing the law, that's what you're doing. And you can be put in prison for that, and well you know it. Where's me notebook?'

He took his foot out of the door for half a moment and, quick as lightning, Mr Larkin crashed it shut. There was the sound of a key turning in the lock.

Fatty began to laugh. He had been bottling it up, but now he couldn't hold it in any longer. Afraid that Mr Goon would hear him, he made his way to the back of the cottage, his handkerchief over his mouth. He stood there, shaking with mirth, thinking of old Larkin's amazement, and Goon's fury. Oh, what a night!

After a while, he quietened down. Where was Goon? There wasn't a sound of him now. He must have gone home in rage, to write out a report of the night's doings. How funny it would sound!

Fatty decided to wait a minute or two, in case Goon hadn't gone. He sat down on an old box, looking exactly like a poor, tired old man!

Then things began to happen again. The back door suddenly opened, and a beam of light shone right on the surprised Fatty. Mrs Larkin stood there with some rubbish in her hand to put into the dustbin, and she saw Fatty clearly. She put her hand up to her mouth, and a look of real terror came over her white face. She rushed screaming indoors.

Fatty got up at once, suddenly sobered. He hadn't meant to frighten anyone – but, of course, Mrs Larkin must have been completely amazed to see him sitting there.

She leaves her husband sitting indoors – opens the back door and apparently sees him sitting outside too! thought Fatty. No wonder she screamed. A husband behind her, and a husband in front of her – not too good!

Fatty crept away to the Woosh's garden, which was very near the back of the Larkins' cottage. He didn't want to risk being seen by Mrs Larkin again – she would probably faint with fright, poor thing!

He was just squeezing through the hedge into the Woosh's garden, when he heard someone coming out of the Larkins' back door, someone speaking in an urgent whisper, though Fatty could not hear what was said.

He wished he hadn't chosen such a thick piece of the hedge – blow it, he couldn't get through! Then somebody came right up to the hedge, and caught hold of him. Fatty caught the glint of glasses, and saw that it was old Larkin himself. Now what was he to do!

He shook off the man's hand and, with one great heave, fell into the garden next door. The voice came urgently again. 'How did you get back? What have you come for?'

But Fatty did not wait to answer. He fled.

He ran to the Woosh's gate and slipped out of it, only to hear a familiar voice say, 'Ah! I *thought* you'd be out and about again, Bob Larkin! You *are* up to some mischief tonight, aren't you! You come-alonga me!'

Goon was standing in the shelter of some bushes, and he made a grab at Fatty's arm as he passed. Fatty had a terrible shock! He pulled away, and heard his coat ripping. But he was off like a hare, with Goon after him. Where now?

The wicket gate of the Larkins' had been left open – and Fatty dashed back through it. He could easily hide somewhere in the grounds. Goon panted after him – and just then, round the corner of the cottage, attracted by the noise, came Bob Larkin himself, having found it impossible to get through the hedge after Fatty.

Fatty ran full-tilt into him, and they both fell over. Goon came up, and shone his lamp downwards in glee. Ah, now he'd got that fellow all right!

To his enormous astonishment he saw *two* Mr Larkins on the ground. Two faces with straggly beards and shaggy eyebrows and thick glasses looked up at him, blinking in the light of the lantern.

'Ow!' said Goon, his hand beginning to shake. ''Ere – what's all this? I don't like it! I . . . I . . . d-d-don't li . . .'

Poor Goon couldn't bear it any longer. He turned and ran down the path as if a dozen Mr Larkins were after him. He made a peculiar moaning sound as he went, and if Fatty hadn't had all the wind knocked out of him by the collision with Larkin, he would have laughed loudly.

'Now,' said Mr Larkin, in a peculiarly unpleasant voice, 'now, just you . . .'

But Fatty was off again, and away into the darkness. He made for Tally-Ho House. There were many corners there to hide in if Larkin came after him.

But he heard no more sound from Larkin. He stood for a while near the boiler house, listening, but could hear nothing at all. Fatty gave a little sigh. What an evening! He thought it would be just as well to go home again now – he really felt astonishingly tired!

He cautiously left his hiding-place and made his way round the house. It was very dark there, with high trees all round, overshadowing the house. Fatty didn't dare to put on his torch, for fear of being spotted, so he stepped forward slowly and carefully.

He bumped his head into something hard, and stopped. What was this? He put out his hand and took hold of something. It felt like a long pole of wood, slanting upwards – and wait, there was more – gosh, of coursc, it was a laddcr! A laddcr leading up to the balcony. Wheeeew! What was this now?

Fatty went up the ladder! It led to the balcony rails. Fatty cautiously climbed over the rails and felt about for the door. Was someone inside the house?

But the door wouldn't open. It was locked. Fatty remembered what the Superintendent had told him – all doors were bolted on the inside except the garden door, which had had a special lock put on it so that only the police could get in and out.

Who put the ladder there then? An ordinary burglar? Was he still waiting about in the shadows, furious with Fatty for discovering his ladder?

Fatty was suddenly overcome with panic, and slid down the ladder at top speed. He tore off to the wicket gate, seeing Goons and Larkins and burglars in every shadow! It wasn't till he was safely in the very middle of a well-lit road that he calmed down, and felt ashamed of himself – gosh, he didn't often feel scared! Whatever had come over him?

21. MORE PUZZLES

About half an hour later, Fatty sat in a hot bath and thought over the extraordinary evening. It needed a little sorting out!

First of all, should he ring up the Chief and tell him about the ladder? No, he might have to explain his mad idea of disguising himself as Larkin and leading Goon such a dance. Fatty felt that the Chief might not see the funny side of that. He wondered if Goon would make a report on the evening. How would he explain two Larkins?

Then that ladder. Fatty was inclined to think that the thief had been up it, tried the door and given up the idea of getting in when he found it was both locked *and* bolted. In any case, it would take a bold burglar to come back again after he had heard all the shouting and scrimmaging that had been going on. Fatty felt sure that if the burglar *had* been anywhere about, he would certainly have gone while the going was good!

He was sorry he had frightened Mrs Larkin. Then he remembered Goon's face of horror when he shone his lantern down and saw *two* Mr Larkins on the ground looking up at him. *Two!* He must have thought he was seeing double! Fatty grinned, and began to soap himself thoroughly.

He thought about Mr Larkin. What was it that he had said to Fatty when he first saw him? Fatty frowned and tried to remember. It was something like, 'How did you get back? What have you come for?'

It seemed a funny thing to say – unless Larkin imagined he was Lorenzo. He probably couldn't see him properly in the dark. Or, more likely, Fatty hadn't heard him correctly. Fatty dismissed the incident from his mind and began to worry once more about whether he ought to telephone Superintendent Jenks or not.

No, I'll leave well alone, thought Fatty, soaping himself all over again. Of course, if Mr Goon telephones him with his tale of chasing two Bob Larkins, and the Chief puts two and two together, and jumps to the fact that one of them was me, then I shall quite likely be all set for trouble – I'll chance it. I don't think Mr Goon *will* send in that report!

Goon didn't. When at last he got home, in a state of fury, fright and utter bewilderment, he sat down heavily in his armchair, and stared at nothing. He forgot that he had asked his housekeeper to come in and cook his dinner for him that night, and when she knocked at his door, he almost leapt from his chair in fright. He gazed at the door, half-afraid that another Mr Larkin would appear round it.

'Who – who is it?' he said, in husky tones.

The woman put her untidy head round the door, surprised at Goon's unusual voice. 'Only me, sir. About your dinner.'

'Ah,' said Goon, in a more ordinary voice. 'Yes. Yes, bring it in.'

The evening's mishaps had not spoilt Goon's appetite. He thought hard as he ate his stew, and gradually recovered from his fright. He jabbed at a bit of meat.

'*Two* Larkins. Sure as I'm here, there were two. But what will the Chief say if I send in a report and say I saw *two*? "My dear Goon," he'll say, "you must have been seeing double. Hadn't you better buy yourself some glasses?"'

Goon mimicked the Chief's voice, and felt very pleased with his imitation. 'Ho, Chief!' he said. 'Ho! Glasses I need, do I? Let me tell you this – I don't need glasses, and I don't need advice from you – all I want is a spot of promotion, which is more than due to me . . .'

He jumped at another knock at the door, but it was only the woman again. 'Oooh, I thought you must have someone here,' she said. 'I heard talking.'

'Bring in the pudding,' said Goon loftily. Ha, *he'd* tell the Chief a few things if he had him here this very minute! But no, not about the two Larkins. On the whole, it would be better to keep that to himself. Goon began to doubt whether he *had* seen two? Had he? Yes, he had. No, he hadn't. Yes – ah, here was the pudding, steaming hot too!

Next morning, Fatty sent for the others early. He had such a lot to tell them. He had got up very early himself because he had suddenly remembered that he had left his bicycle somewhere near Goon's house, and he didn't want Goon to spot it there. So, before eight o'clock, Fatty had shot off to get it, and was very thankful to see that it was still there!

'Fatty! What happened last night? Did Mr Goon see you?' asked Bets, as soon as she saw him.

Fatty nodded. He felt rather pleased with himself now. What a tale he had to tell! He began to tell it, and the others roared with laughter. As for Ern, he rolled over and over on the floor, unable to stop – the thought of his fearsome uncle chasing Fatty all over the place, and even watching him on the swings, was too much for him.

'Stop, Fatty! Stop a bit, and let me get over this,' begged poor Ern. 'Oooh, my sides! Fatty, stop!'

The story went on to its thrilling end. Everyone listened with the utmost attention, even Buster. When Fatty came to the bit where he had bumped into the ladder, everyone exclaimed. 'Here's the bump I got on my forehead – see?' said Fatty, displaying quite a satisfactory bump.

'Oh! I *wish* I'd been there to see all this!' said Bets. 'What did you do after you had come down the ladder, Fatty?'

'Oh, I just went home and had a bath,' said Fatty, deciding that he needn't spoil this thrilling tale by relating how he had scuttled back home at top speed!

'A very interesting evening!' said Pip. 'But it doesn't seem to get us much further, Fatty, does it? Do you plan for us to do anything this morning?'

'Well, I thought we'd go and see if the ladder is still there,' said Fatty. 'We might find footprints or something at the bottom – you never know.'

'I can't think why old Larkin asked you why you had come back, when he saw you,' said Larry. 'He must have thought you were Lorenzo.'

'Yes. That's what *I* thought,' said Fatty. 'If he'd seen me *properly* – looking exactly like himself, of course – he wouldn't have asked such an idiotic question. Mrs Larkin saw me all right though – that's what gave her such a shock, I expect, leaving old Larkin behind her in the house and seeing another Larkin outside!'

'Let's go,' said Pip, getting up. 'That was a marvellous tale, Fatty. I wish I dared do the things you do, but I daren't. And if I did, they wouldn't have such fine endings as yours. I wonder what old Mr Goon is thinking this morning?'

They all went off on their bicycles, Buster in Fatty's basket. They decided not to go in at the wicket gate in case old Bob Larkin was in a temper because of the happenings of the night before.

They went past the gate and came to a place where they could easily get into the grounds. They left their bicycles there and made their way to the big house.

'The ladder was the other side,' said Fatty, and led the way. But as soon as they turned the corner of the house, he saw that the ladder was gone.

'It's not there!' he said. 'Well, I wonder if the burglar got in after I left then – he must have been about, because he's removed the ladder! Gosh, I wish I'd reported seeing it now – I might have prevented a burglary! I wonder if he managed to get in. Look – there are the marks made by the foot of the ladder in the ground.'

'Let's walk round the house and peep in at the windows to see if any rooms have been ransacked,' said Daisy. So they walked all round, peeping into every window. Nothing was disturbed at all, as far as they could see.

They came to the last window and peered through it. 'Ah, this is the one with the big bowl of dead flowers' said Fatty, remembering. 'There they are still – deader than ever! And the chairs are still all in their dustsheets.'

His eyes slid round, remembering everything – and then he frowned. Something was missing. He was sure it was. Something that had puzzled him. Yes, there had been a little rubber bone on the floor, beside that stool. But it was gone now!

Fatty peered and peered, trying to see the bone. But it had definitely gone! How puzzling!

'There's one thing missing,' said Fatty. 'A little rubber bone – a dog's plaything. It probably used to belong to Poppet the poodle. I saw it down by that stool.'

'You must be mistaken, Fatty,' said Larry. 'Nobody would steal a dog's rubber bone! Nothing seems to be disturbed at all. I don't think that burglar could have managed to get in.'

'I *did* see a rubber bone,' said Fatty. 'I don't make mistakes about a thing like that. I call that very curious. Very curious indeed.'

They left the house and wandered around a

little more. Buster left them and went off by himself, having suddenly had a very good idea. He'd go and play with that nice little poodle!

So he trotted off to the cottage and barked a small and polite bark. Poppet at once leapt up to the window ledge and looked out.

Bets heard Buster barking and ran to get him. She saw the little poodle at the window – and how Bets stared! Not at Poppet, but at something she held in her mouth! She raced back to Fatty, her face scarlet with excitement.

'Fatty! Listen! Poppet's up at the window, and she's got a rubber bone in her mouth!'

Fatty whistled. They all went cautiously down the path and, sure enough, there was Poppet trying vainly to bark with the little rubber bone between her teeth.

'Yes, that's the one,' said Fatty. 'Buster, come here. Look, let's all go quietly back to our bikes and have a talk. This is important.'

They all went to their bikes, feeling suddenly excited. Fatty's eyes shone. 'It must have been the *Larkins* who went into the house last night! Nobody else would have bothered about a rubber bone. *They* had a dog, so it was an ordinary thing to do to pick it up and take it back to Poppet, and . . .'

'*I* don't think it was an ordinary thing for them to do,' said Bets. 'We know they're unkind to Poppet – we've even heard about them punishing her. I don't think they'd even *bother* to take her bone back to her!'

'Yet she's got it,' said Fatty. 'Well then – who else could have taken it to her?'

'Mrs Lorenzo might,' said Bets. 'Perhaps it was the Lorenzos who got in last night. Perhaps they were here again.'

'Yes, they might have been,' said Fatty. 'If so, that looks as if Larkin did mistake me for Lorenzo when he saw me last night and asked me why I had come back.'

'Oh – here's Poppet! She must have escaped out of the house to look for Buster!' said Bets. 'Listen – Mrs Larkin is calling her.'

'Take her back, Bets,' said Fatty, 'and see if you can have a chat with Mrs Larkin. Go on – *you* might be able to get something out of her!'

'All right,' said Bets, half-scared, and took little

Poppet into her arms. She went up the river path to the wicket gate, Buster at her heels, trying his hardest to jump up and lick the little poodle's nose.

Bets went right up to the cottage. She could hear Mrs Larkin calling 'Poppet! Poppet!' and knew she was looking for her over by the big house. Perhaps Bets would have time just to have a look at that rubber bone so that she could tell Fatty exactly what it was like.

So Bets slipped into the small cottage and looked round for the bone. She couldn't see it, but she saw a few things that made her stare!

The kitchen table was piled with tins of food – big, expensive tins! How strange! Bets tiptoed into the bedroom. On the bed, neatly folded, were spotlessly clean blankets and an eiderdown! So it *was* the Larkins then who had put that ladder up – and they *had* got in, and *had* stolen things – food – and warm coverings – and they had picked up Poppet's rubber bone and taken it back to her.

WELL! Fatty must be told this at once!

22. A BELL RINGS FOR FATTY

Before Bets could put Poppet down and run to Fatty, there came the sound of footsteps hurrying to the door. Bets turned. It was Mrs Larkin, in the same old red shawl, hideous wig and dark glasses.

'Oh, you've got Poppet!' she said. 'I thought she'd fallen into the river.'

She took the little poodle from Bets, and the girl watched Poppet licking the woman's face. 'You're kind to her now,' said Bets. 'You weren't at first.'

The woman put Poppet down at once. 'Now you go,' she said harshly. 'You shouldn't have walked in without permission.'

'I'm going,' said Bets. 'Is that Poppet's basket? Oh, there's her rubber bone!'

She took it out of the basket, but the woman snatched it out of her hand and gave her a rough push. Bets ran out. She was puzzled. She waited till the door was shut then she tiptoed back and peeped in at the window. The woman was putting a mat down under the dog's basket, with Poppet fussing round.

Bets made her way back to the others, still puzzled. Why did Mrs Larkin treat Poppet differently? Perhaps the little dog was so sweet that nobody could be unkind for long. No, it would need something more than that to make the Larkins kind. Well, perhaps the Lorenzos had promised them a lot of money if Poppet was kept happy. That must be it.

Bets told her tale to the others. 'Big, expensive tins! Nice blankets and rugs! They must have helped themselves well,' she said. 'I didn't get anything much out of the woman though. She was cross and pushed me out.'

'Look, there's somebody going in at the wicket gate,' said Pip. 'Oh, it's old Larkin. Been shopping, I suppose. No, he's got no basket and, anyway, they're plentifully supplied with tins now. All he's got are some papers.'

Fatty looked to see. 'Quite a few papers!' he said, surprised. 'I suppose he looks through them all each day to see if there is any news of the Lorenzos. He might read at any moment that they had been caught.'

'What do we do now?' asked Pip. 'Go and telephone the Chief? Nobody but us knows that things have been taken from the house. It beats me how the Larkins got in, because the police said they hadn't keys. I suppose they *must* have some and knew that possibly the only door that might not be bolted would be the balcony door. And they were right.'

'Come on,' said Fatty, taking his bicycle. 'We'll telephone.'

'I'm glad that horrid Mrs Larkin is so much nicer to dear little Poppet,' said Bets. 'Honestly, she might be Mrs Lorenzo the way she fusses about her now. Why, she was even putting a rug down under Poppet's basket when I peeped in at the window!'

Fatty suddenly gave such a terrific wobble on his bicycle that he almost fell off. Bets looked at him in surprise.

'What's up, Fatty?' she said.

'Don't speak to me for a minute,' said Fatty in

a peculiar voice. 'I'm going to get off. You ride on, all of you.'

Bets looked at him in alarm. 'Are you ill?'

'No. I've just got an idea, that's all. Something you said rang a bell in my mind. Leave me alone for a minute,' said Fatty urgently. The others, quite mystified, rode on a little way and then got off to wait for Fatty. He was standing frowning by the side of the road, still holding his bicycle, and so lost in thought that he didn't even notice Mr Goon cycling by.

'Ho! What's the matter with *you*!' said Mr Goon, surprised.

'Be quiet,' said Fatty. 'I'm working something out.'

Mr Goon went purple. Telling him to be quiet indeed! 'What you working out?' he said. 'Still worrying about them Lorenzos! They're in America or somewhere by now – so's the picture. You'll see! You just work out how to behave yourself and learn a few manners!'

Buster suddenly appeared out of the nearby hedge and flew at Mr Goon's ankles, barking delightedly. The big policeman hurriedly mounted his bicycle, and rode off, kicking out at Buster as he went.

Not even that disturbed Fatty. Goodness, what *could* he be thinking of?

'The great brain's working overtime,' said Pip. 'What *can* have struck him so suddenly?'

'He'll come along and say he's solved everything in a minute,' said Ern. 'You see if he doesn't. He's a wonder, he is!'

Fatty mounted his bicycle again, and came sailing up, looking extremely happy.

'I've got it,' he said. 'I've solved the whole thing! All tied up neatly, ready to lay at the Superintendent's feet! My word, I've been an idiot. So have we all!'

'I told you so!' said Ern triumphantly, looking round at the others. 'I said he was solving everything, didn't I, Bets?'

'But – what have you solved?' said Pip. 'Not *every*thing, surely!'

'I think so. I'm just not quite certain about one thing,' said Fatty. 'However, we'll soon know!'

'Tell us,' begged Larry. 'It's horrible not knowing what you're talking about! Do tell us.'

'No time,' said Fatty, riding fast. 'I must get to a telephone immediately. Hury up, all of you!'

Everyone rode behind Fatty in a terrific state of excitement. Fatty pedalled furiously, as if he was in a race. Poor old Buster was left far behind, and Bets felt very sorry for him, but not even she felt that she could slow down and pick him up. Buster was most surprised at everyone's hard-heartedness!

Fatty leapt off his bicycle at the nearest telephone box. He dashed in, shut the door, and rang a number. The others congregated outside in wonder.

An answer came at once. 'Police here.'

'I want to speak to the Superintendent, please,' said Fatty. 'Tell him it's Frederick Trotteville here, and I've something urgent to say.'

'Right,' said the voice. In a second or two, the Superintendent's crisp voice came over the line.

'Yes? What is it, Frederick?'

'Sir, can you possibly come over here at once?' said Fatty. 'I've got everything tied up nicely for you!'

'What do you mean?' said the Chief. 'You don't

mean the Lorenzo case, surely?'

'Yes, sir. I know everything!' said Fatty exultantly. 'I suddenly tumbled on to it this morning. It's too long to tell you over the phone, sir. Can you come over at once – before things go wrong?'

'You're talking in riddles, Frederick,' said the Chief. 'But I'd better trust you, I suppose. I'll get the car and come at once. Where shall I find you?'

'Up by the Larkins' cottage, sir,' said Fatty. 'Do you know where it is?'

'Yes,' said the Chief. 'I'll be there.' He rang off, and Fatty put back the receiver, his face glowing. He rubbed his hands in glee before he stepped out of the kiosk.

'Fatty! You *might* tell us what's up,' said Pip. 'It's too bad – seeing you shouting into that phone and not hearing a word you were saying – and then you rub your hands in glee when you've finished. Whatever has happened so suddenly?'

'Tell you as soon as I can,' said Fatty, wheeling his bicycle into the road. 'Come on, we've got to go back to the wicket gate leading to the Larkins' cottage. The Chief will be there as soon as possible.'

'Gosh, so that's who you've been ringing!' said Larry, cycling madly after Fatty. 'Is he really coming over?'

'Yes, at once,' said Fatty. 'Hello – where's Buster?'

'We've left him all behind again,' panted Bets. 'He's so miserable. Oh Fatty, do stop and pick him up.'

Fatty stopped. Buster came up at a valiant trot, his tongue hanging out almost to the ground. Fatty picked him up. 'My Poppet!' he said ridiculously, and put him into his bicycle basket. Buster heaved a great sigh of relief.

They set off again, and came to the river path, where they had to get off and wheel their bicycles. Ern called to Fatty. 'Can't you tell us now, Fatty?'

'Too many people about,' said Fatty aggravatingly. 'Hello, who are these?'

Two small girls had just rushed out of a nearby gate and flung themselves on Ern.

'Ern! Come and play with us! Mum's given us a picnic dinner to eat up in the tree house.'

'Sorry,' said Ern, shaking them off. 'I've got important business to do, Liz and Glad. Er – these are my two cousins, Fatty – Liz, or Elizabeth. And

Glad. Glad, what's *your* name short for? I never did know.'

'Gladys!' said Glad, with a giggle. 'Ern, we kept watch up in the tree house as usual this morning, but we only saw Mr Larkin once – he's just come in – and Mrs Larkin once. She hung an old rug out on the line, and she's beating it.'

'All right, all right,' said Ern, while all the others looked on, amused. 'They sit up in the tree house for me and keep their eyes open,' he explained to Fatty. He turned back to Liz and Glad.

'You go back,' he said. 'I *might* come and have dinner with you in the tree house. Buzz off, now! I'm busy.'

They buzzed off, two skinny little things, delighted that Ern was going to have dinner with them.

'Better not gather round the wicket gate all in a bunch,' said Fatty, in a low voice, when they got there. 'Let's go up the river path a little way. Hello, who's this coming?'

It was Mr Goon, on his way to tell Mr Larkin what he thought of him for leading him such a dance the night before. Goon had decided that he hadn't really seen two Mr Larkins – he was so tired he must have seen double – that was what it was – and Mr Larkin was going to hear what he thought of old men who went on the swings in the playground at dark of night. Ho!

Goon saw the children further up the path and scowled. 'You clear orf!' he called to them. 'And keep hold of that there dog! What you doing here, crowding up the pathway?'

'We're waiting for someone,' said Fatty calmly.

'Ho yes!' said Mr Goon rudely. 'And who may you be waiting for, I'd like to know? Your friend the Superintendent perhaps? You just clear orf!'

'Actually, yes, we *are* waiting for him,' said Fatty. 'That was a clever guess of yours, Mr Goon.'

'Now don't you try to trick me with your Superintendent Jenks!' said Goon, most sarcastically. 'He's miles from here. That I do know, for he telephoned me himself this morning.'

'Well, *you* don't need to wait and see him,' said Fatty. 'He's coming to see *us*, actually!'

Mr Goon went slowly purple. 'Telling me fairy tales like that!' he said. 'You clear orf, I say.'

There came the sound of a car in the distance.

It stopped. A car door slammed.

'Here he is,' said Fatty to Goon, as quick footsteps came up the river path. Goon swung round – and his mouth fell open.

It *was* Superintendent Jenks, tall and broad-shouldered as ever, followed by another man. He grinned at Fatty. 'Well,' he said, 'here I am!'

23. A TRULY REMARKABLE TALE!

'Good morning, sir,' said Fatty. Goon was quite tongue-tied, and couldn't say a word. The Chief nodded to Fatty and then to Goon.

'Good morning, Frederick. Well, Goon – you here too? I didn't expect to see you as well.'

'He came along by accident,' said Fatty. 'All the others are here too, sir.'

The Chief saluted all of them solemnly and they saluted back.

'Well, now, let's get down to business,' said the Chief. 'You telephoned to say you'd got this Lorenzo business nicely tied up. Do you mean you know where the Lorenzos are?'

'Yes, sir,' said Fatty at once, and Goon's eyes nearly fell out of his head. He stared at Fatty and swallowed hard. That boy! That toad of a boy. How could *he* know where the Lorenzos were?

The Chief laughed. 'Don't tell me you know

where the *picture* is as well!' he said.

'I *think* I do,' said Fatty, 'but if I don't, you can easily make the Lorenzos tell you.'

The Chief turned to Goon. 'I suppose you're in on this too?' he said.

Goon shook his head. He didn't dare to trust himself to speak.

The Chief turned back to Fatty. 'Well, where *are* the Lorenzos?' he said. 'As you've brought me over here, I imagine they're hiding in this district.'

'Yes, sir,' said Fatty. 'They're hiding in the Larkins' cottage.'

'That they're not!' burst out Goon. 'Begging your pardon, sir, but I've gone through that cottage three times – there's no one there but the two Larkins. I'm ready to swear to that.'

'Well, the Lorenzos *are* there,' said Fatty. 'Come along, Chief – I'll show you.'

He led the way, the others following in wonder. What kind of hiding-place were the Lorenzos in? It must be a very small one! Goon went along too, angry and disbelieving.

Fatty rapped at the Larkins' door. It was opened by old Larkin himself, cap on head as usual, and dirty old scarf round his throat. He peered through his thick glasses at Fatty.

'What you want?' he said. Then he saw the rest of the children and the tall Superintendent of police, and made as if to shut the door quickly. But Fatty put his foot in at once.

'We're coming in,' he said. The man that the Chief had brought with him held open the door and everyone filed in, even Buster. Mrs Larkin was not in the room. They could hear her out in the little kitchen, rattling pans and crockery.

'What's all this?' said Larkin gruffly, in his old man's voice. 'I ain't done nuffin'.'

The little room was very crowded with so many people in it. Larkin shrank back.

'Here's *one* of the Lorenzos,' said Fatty and suddenly snatched off old Larkin's cap. Then, with a quick twist, he stripped off the man's beard, and grabbed off his shaggy eyebrows! Off came the thick glasses too! At once Larkin became a much younger man, an angry man, and a frightened one.

'Wheeeew!' whistled the Superintendent astounded. '*Bill Lorenzo*! Well, you may be a fourth-rate film actor, but you're a first class fraud! Masquerading as old Larkin! I saw you myself at the beginning of this case – and I could have sworn you were old Bob Larkin.'

'He wasn't Bob Larkin at *first,*' said Fatty. 'Not for some time. The real Mr and Mrs Larkin were here at first. Oh, here comes the other one!'

Mrs Larkin, hearing voices, had opened the kitchen door, and stood there, staring in fright, with little Poppet in her arms. Before she could shut the door, Fatty had stepped behind her.

'And here's *Mrs* Lorenzo!' he said, and twitched off the extraordinary wig. Underneath was pale golden hair, wavy and thick. She took off her dark glasses and looked defiantly at the surprised Chief.

'All right! I'm Gloria Lorenzo – and glad to get out of that filthy old wig of Mrs Larkin's.' She turned to her husband. 'Bill, the game's up.'

The man nodded. It was surprising how the years fell off both of them once they had their glasses off, their own hair exposed, and stood up straight, instead of stooping. How could anyone have thought they were old and ugly?

'A marvellous disguise!' said Fatty in great

admiration. 'And you both got away with it too. Nobody had any suspicions at all that *you* were here instead of the Larkins.'

'Where *are* the Larkins?' inquired the Chief, looking all round as if they were there too.

'Bob Larkin was about last night,' said Goon. 'I saw him – *and* this fellow too.'

'What – *both together*?' said the Chief, in astonishment. 'Why didn't you do something about it? Surely it must have struck you as rather odd that there should be *two* Bob Larkins?'

'One of them was *me*,' said Fatty smoothly. '*I* disguised myself like old Larkin too. Sorry I led you such a dance last night, Mr Goon – still, I had a nice swing!'

Goon almost passed out. He staggered back against the wall and put his hand in front of his eyes. So he'd been chasing *Fatty* last night, not Bob Larkin – and even the other Larkin he had seen wasn't the real one. Goon began to feel extremely muddled.

'What happened to the *real* Larkins?' said the Chief. 'I really do want to know. Are they all right?'

'Well, sir, the real Larkins were left here in

charge of Poppet, as you know,' said Fatty, 'and they were not kind to her at all. Then, one night, the Lorenzos hired a motor-launch at Maidenhead, and took it down the river. It stopped in mid-stream opposite the boathouse here . . .'

'How do you know all this?' asked Bill Lorenzo angrily. 'Has anyone split on us?'

'No,' said Fatty. He turned to the Chief. 'Ern heard noises in the night, sir, and we put two and two together, you see – about the motor-launch, I mean. Well, the *real* Bob Larkin had been warned somehow – I don't know how – to be ready that night with the rowing-boat from the boathouse. So out he went to the launch, and came back with the two Lorenzos.'

'Go on,' said the Superintendent, listening intently.

'Well, my guess is that the Lorenzos and the Larkins changed clothes,' said Fatty. 'The Lorenzos stayed behind in the cottage, and the Larkins went back to the launch, and were whisked off somewhere safe – probably paid quite a bit of money too!'

'I see, I see it all,' said the Chief, glancing at the

two sullen Lorenzos. A very astute idea – to come back into the heart of things, where nobody would possibly be looking for them.'

'Yes, very smart, sir,' said Fatty. 'And as they are both actors, and used to making themselves up and acting all kinds of characters, it was easy to imitate the old Larkins. Er – as I have already told you, I myself imitated Larkin so successfully last night that Mr Goon chased me all over the place!'

'It was *you* I saw here yesterday evening then!' said Bill Lorenzo. 'I thought it was old Bob Larkin himself come back again, and I couldn't understand it!'

'I know – and it was your words to me that partly helped me to understand everything,' said Fatty. 'You said, *"How did you get back? What have you come for?"* And that seemed a pretty strange thing to say to someone masquerading as *yourself*! It could only mean one thing – that you were not Bob Larkin – and therefore thought the other fellow *was*. But he was me.'

The listening Goon gave a groan. He simply couldn't follow all this. But the others could. Bets gave a little scream. 'Oh, Fatty, of course! That's why he asked you such peculiar questions – I never thought of that!'

'What made you *really* stumble on the whole thing?' asked the Chief. 'You'd have telephoned me last night if you had guessed then.'

'Yes, I would,' said Fatty. 'Well, lots of things gave me hints, sir. For instance, someone broke into the big house last night – and the only thing that appeared to be taken was that rubber bone on the floor there. And why should anyone take *that*? Only because they had a dog they wanted to give it to! And Bets saw tins of food on the table, and rugs and blankets on the bed – things that the Larkins wouldn't have thought of.'

'I *told* you not to take that bone!' said Bill Lorenzo angrily to his wife.

'And then we noticed that whereas, at first, Mrs Larkin was very unkind to the poodle, after a bit she wasn't – and the dog ran about happily all the time. That seemed peculiar too. And then Bets said something that rang a bell in my mind – and everything was as plain as daylight!'

'Whatever *did* I say?' said Bets, in wonder.

'You said, *"I'm glad that horrid Mrs Larkin is*

so much nicer to dear little Poppet. She might be Mrs Lorenzo, the way she fusses her now!" And immediately I saw it all – of course, the supposed Mrs Larkin *was* Mrs Lorenzo – hence the fuss she made of Poppet, the taking of the tins, and the blankets for warmth – and, of course, the curious taking of such a thing as a rubber bone. It was all easy after that,' said Fatty modestly.

'Well, I'm blessed!' said the Chief. 'You've solved some things in your time, Frederick, but this beats the lot – it really does! What do you say, Goon?'

Goon said absolutely nothing at all. He was in a complete fog. He wished he was the rubber bone on the floor. He wished he was anywhere but where he was!

'You've done a remarkably fine piece of detection, Frederick,' said the Chief warmly. 'I congratulate you. What about the stolen picture? Any idea where it is? You said you weren't sure.'

The Lorenzos both stiffened, and looked quickly at Fatty.

'The Lorenzos hope I *don't* know,' said Fatty. 'They don't mind going to prison if they can hope to sell the hidden picture and get plenty of money for it when they come out! I'm not certain about the picture, sir – it's not in the crate any longer, I can tell you that. It was brought here in the boat that night, when the Lorenzos changed over with the Larkins. It was still in the crate then.'

'What happened to it?' asked the Chief.

'The picture was taken out, and the crate and frame were burnt,' said Fatty.

Bill Lorenzo gave a loud exclamation. 'How do you know all this, boy?'

'Brains, just brains,' said Fatty. He turned to the Chief. 'Now sir, Bets happened to look in at the window here this morning, and saw Mrs Larkin putting a rug under the poodle's basket – putting it down very carefully too. Quite a nice rug it was, too good to put under a dog's basket – and I think probably the picture has been sewn inside that rug. It's probably backed with hessian, or something – and you'll find the picture between rug and lining.'

'There's no rug under the dog's basket now!' said Bets, looking.

'Lovaduck! *I* know where it is!' said Ern. 'Liz

and Glad told us, don't you remember?'

The Chief looked puzzled. So did everyone else. 'They're my twin cousins, sir,' said Ern. 'They've been keeping an eye on the Larkins for me. Well, they came rushing out to us this morning and said that they'd seen Mrs Lorenzo hang a rug on the line, sir. I bet that's it! Nobody would ever bother to examine a rug on the line, sir! It would be a fine hiding-place – right out in the open too! Nobody would think anything of a rug on the washing-line!'

Fatty glanced at the Lorenzos. A look of utter dismay had come over their faces. The Chief turned to his man. 'Get that rug,' he said.

They all went out of the cottage, and watched the sergeant take a rug from the washing-line. Goon stood near to Mrs Lorenzo, and the Chief was beside Bill Lorenzo – just in case!

The rug was slit open and inside, just as Fatty had said, was the picture, packed flat in greaseproof paper, quite unharmed.

'Phew! Five hundred thousand pounds' worth of picture sewn inside a rug!' said the Chief. 'It makes me feel quite ill. Take it to the car, Sergeant.'

The Lorenzos were also taken to the car too, carefully escorted by a rather green-faced and very silent Goon, and the big Sergeant. Poppet barked a good-bye to Buster, who had been held tightly in Bets' arms all the time.

'Dear little Poppet,' said Bets, almost in tears. 'She oughtn't to belong to horrible people like that.'

'Cheer up,' said the Chief, swinging her up into the air. 'You haven't grown much, Bets! Frederick, I think this last remarkable – yes, truly remarkable – feat of yours deserves a celebration! You've surpassed yourself, my boy. My word, how I shall enjoy myself when you come to work for *me*!'

'Thank you, sir,' said Fatty modestly. 'May I suggest, sir, that as it's rather cold, we all go to my shed and celebrate there? I know our cook's making mince-pies today, sir, and I've got a few things I'd like to show you – a new set of false teeth, sir, and a gadget to make large ears, and . . .'

The Chief roared. 'Large ears! Why don't you invent something in the way of large brains, Frederick – and hand a few out to poor old Goon?'

'That's an idea, sir!' said Fatty grinning, and off

they all went, Ern too. What a morning!

We can't follow them, alas! The shed door is shut and there is a fine smell of mince-pies in the air.

Hey, Fatty, don't wait too long for another mystery, will you!

Egmont Press is committed to Ethical Publishing

EGMONT PRESS: ETHICAL PUBLISHING

Egmont Press is about turning writers into successful authors and children into passionate readers – producing books that enrich and entertain. As a responsible children's publisher, we go even further, considering the world in which our consumers are growing up.

Safety First
Naturally, all of our books meet legal safety requirements. But we go further than this; every book with play value is tested to the highest standards – if it fails, it's back to the drawing-board.

Made Fairly
We are working to ensure that the workers involved in our supply chain – the people that make our books – are treated with fairness and respect.

Responsible Forestry
We are committed to ensuring all our papers come from environmentally and socially responsible forest sources.

For more information, please visit our website at www.egmont.co.uk/ethical

FSC MIX Paper FSC® C018306

Egmont is passionate about helping to preserve the world's remaining ancient forests. We only use paper from legal and sustainable forest sources, so we know where every single tree comes from that goes into every paper that makes up every book.

This book is made from paper certified by the Forestry Stewardship Council (FSC®), an organisation dedicated to promoting responsible management of forest resources. For more information on the FSC, please visit **www.fsc.org**. To learn more about Egmont's sustainable paper policy, please visit **www.egmont.co.uk/ethical**.